"IS OUR PACKAGE BACK THERE?"

"Unknown," Jack Grimaldi replied. "But these guys put down a cop."

Lyons cursed under his breath. An instant later Blancanales fell in step with him. At the same time the Able Team leader caught the sound of sirens closing in from the distance, the wails eliciting another oath.

The ex-LAPD cop keyed his throat mike and spoke. "Get the bird into the air. And call the Farm for a cleanup crew on this. Tell Hal or Barb to start greasing the wheels. Otherwise we'll be stuck here."

"Roger that, Ironman," Grimaldi said.

Blancanales had stepped in close to a nearby building, raising his weapon to cover Lyons while the man edged along the line of the store until he reached the mouth of an alley. Halting, he craned his neck to peer around the corner. Another shot rang out, followed by a strangled cry.

Gabe Fox was nowhere in sight.

DON PENDLETON'S

STONY
AMERICA'S ULTRA-COVERT INTELLIGENCE AGENCY
MAN®

HELL DAWN

A GOLD EAGLE BOOK FROM
WORLDWIDE®

TORONTO • NEW YORK • LONDON
AMSTERDAM • PARIS • SYDNEY • HAMBURG
STOCKHOLM • ATHENS • TOKYO • MILAN
MADRID • WARSAW • BUDAPEST • AUCKLAND

First edition October 2006

ISBN-13: 978-0-373-61969-6
ISBN-10:   0-373-61969-3

HELL DAWN

Special thanks and acknowledgment to
Tim Tresslar for his contribution to this work.

PROLOGUE

Frisco, Colorado

Rolling his chair back from the desk, Gabriel Fox stared once more at his latest creation, shivered, then cursed himself under his breath. He'd created a monster, one he damn sure intended to slay. But first, he'd have a cigarette and maybe another drink.

Getting to his feet, he crossed the luxuriously appointed bedroom, moved to a window and, turning a small hand crank, opened it. He was supposed to leave them shut. That'd been the first thing the craggy-faced CIA agent had warned him against.

We have the whole place wired, every entrance, every door, the guy had said. *You want to open a window, you come find me and we'll bypass the alarm for you. I'll have a couple of guys sit in here and baby-sit you. Otherwise, leave the windows alone. Don't fuck with me on this, Gabe.*

Which, of course, had been all the challenge Fox needed. It had taken him all of five minutes to bypass the alarm system, allowing him to open the window—

a heavy pane of bulletproof glass—undetected and at will. With the grounds outside the mountain chalet crawling with armed guards, he assumed it'd only be a matter of time before he got busted by the dour security chief, a tight ass named Oliver Stephens, and suffered a severe tongue-lashing for it.

But hell, getting caught was half the fun.

Grinding out his cigarette, he tossed the butt out the window and watched as it fell three stories before hitting the sidewalk, joining two others he'd dropped earlier that night. He figured the guards would eventually see them there, put two and two together, and figure out that he was opening his window and having a smoke. Let them, he decided. He already was a dead man. Why delay the inevitable?

Leaving the window open, he walked to the bed, perched himself on the edge of the mattress and considered whether to light another cigarette. Or maybe dive into that glass of whiskey he'd promised himself. Dive in and drown.

That seemed to sum up how he felt. His life to this point had been anything but seamless. But, within the last couple of weeks, it had turned into a damned horror show. The cold mountain wind blew through the window, raising gooseflesh on his tattooed arms. He rubbed them, trying to generate some heat. At six feet, six inches, head shaved bald, body covered in tattoos— a multicolored montage of eagles, Sanskrit symbols, big-busted women and alcohol logos—Fox usually turned heads. Not admiring glances, but the surreptitious kind people cast after you've already passed, a sort of morbid fascination, like watching paramedics drag a bloodied corpse from a mangled car. He didn't care.

His rule in life had been that negative attention was better than no attention, so he took what he could get.

And lately he'd been getting plenty of attention, all of it negative.

He headed for the dresser, stopping only long enough to close the window, and poured himself three fingers of whiskey. He downed it in a loud gulp, poured another and returned to his desk. Seating himself, he enjoyed the whiskey's warmth as it enveloped the inside of his stomach. A glance at the laptop's screen doused the pleasant burn and brought him back to reality.

Lord help him, what had he done? Fox stared at the lines of code he had written and felt an avalanche of guilt fall over him, smothering him. When the lines had sprung from his fingertips, he hadn't fully considered their implications. He'd been in the zone, unaware of reality. He'd felt more like a pianist, like Ray Charles or Ahmad Jamal, a maestro unleashing his creative juices, making something beautiful, an extension of himself.

Only after he'd completed the worm, the product of three days' straight work, his weary body fueled by caffeine and alcohol, had he realized just what he'd created. And it was horrible.

His handlers at the CIA had dubbed his latest work Project: Cold Earth. It was a benign name for a malignant computer worm capable of shutting down the cooling systems for nuclear reactors. It was, for all intents and purposes, a digital gateway into hell. It was his, and he couldn't wait to be free of it.

Unfortunately he wasn't sure when that moment might come. Once he created one of these little beauties, he then had the unenviable task of reverse engineering them, tearing them apart and creating defenses for them. He had created the disease and it was up to him to find the cure. And until then, he'd stay locked away in this mountain chalet with Agent Tight Ass and his posse of paramilitary robots, having them try to control his every move and him having to score little victories, like figuring out how to bypass the alarm and open a window.

It was just like reform school, where he'd first shown an aptitude for computers, not only as a programmer and repairman, but also as a practitioner of the dark arts, particularly hacking and authoring malignant code. Except now the government gave him a security clearance, a paycheck and at least feigned respect for him.

Scanning his surroundings again, taking in the stone fireplace, the mahogany furniture and fully stocked bar, he grinned tightly. At least now when they jailed him, they did it in style.

He set to work at the computer once again, his thoughts and fingers greased by the whiskey, and began to analyze the code for Cold Earth. In theory, anyway, it should have been easy for him to backtrack and write security patches capable of stopping the malignant program from harming anything. In theory. The reality was that without Maria, who'd helped him write the program, he was having to learn its every nuance before he could create a good defense.

An image of her—strawberry-blond hair, golden eyes, cheeks colored by a perpetual blush—flitted across his mind. Grief squeezed his heart followed by a dull ache in his throat. He doused both with another swallow of whiskey, replacing the sensations first with rage, followed by the gray numbness he'd blanketed himself with for the past few days, ever since his world had been turned upside down back in Langley, Virginia.

Forget about it, he told himself. So, after a third

drink, he did. Enjoying the light-headedness, he immersed himself into his work, his fingers gliding over the keyboard as he worked on the code. The technicians back at Langley had yanked the modem card from the computer, which also lacked wireless capability. They wanted to keep him incommunicado, in part to protect his location but also to make sure he didn't ship Cold Earth—either accidentally or on purpose—out into the world over the Internet.

Rage seared his insides as he considered the notion. His creation had already cost him the only thing in life that he'd ever valued. Selling it for a few bucks or to save his own miserable skin was unfathomable to him. Given a choice, he'd just as soon walk away from all of it. Forget about the Company, about Cold Earth, about Maria. Say to hell with it and drink himself into an early grave.

In spite of the whiskey, a chill passed through him, causing him to shudder. He stood and moved to the fireplace. With the flip of a switch, gas burners ignited to life and the warmth began to cut through the chill. He returned to his desk and resumed his work, another twenty minutes racing by before something from below caught his attention.

Quiet. Or, more precisely, less noise. Just a few moments ago the chatter of sportscasters, the occasional cheer of excited fans, wafted through the floor, accompanied by talking or laughter from the off-duty guards. Two more guards had stood at the bottom of the stairwell, discussing how they'd rather be hunting or trout fishing than be stuck inside, as one of them put it, "playing Babysit the Geek." He'd smiled at that one. The feeling's mutual, buddy.

All that had changed. The television continued to

pump out what amounted to little more than white noise. But all human noises had ceased. The realization caused a chill to race down his spine even as he rocketed out of his chair and headed for the door.

Grasping the knob, he twisted it, pulled open the door. Glancing through the space between the door and the jamb, he saw one of the guards, a blond woman in a black, pin-striped pantsuit, climbing the stairs. She clutched a submachine gun, a sound suppressor threaded into the muzzle in her right hand. He opened his mouth to speak.

Placing a finger to her lips, she motioned for him to be quiet. When he noticed the shiny smears on her blouse and jacket, her pretty features flecked with crimson, the words died in his throat. His heart began to slam in his chest as he recognized the small splotches for what they were—blood. Putting a hand to his chest, she shoved him back through the doorway. The alcohol coursing through his system had left him unsteady and her strong shove sent him hurtling backward. Shooting him a disgusted look, she closed the door behind her and locked it.

Even as he tried to right himself, she glided past him and took up a position next to the window.

"What the hell is going on?" he asked.

"Someone bypassed the alarms, cut through the exterior fence," she said without looking at him. "We're getting hit from all sides."

When he spoke, it came out louder than he'd expected. "Hit? By whom? Tell me what's going on."

She glared at him over her shoulder. "Shut up."

"The hell I will."

She whipped around and centered the SMG's muzzle on his torso.

"Look, I'm taking you and that computer out of here. Now shut the hell up. Or else."

He ground his teeth as he stared at the woman's back and tried to determine his next move. A fireball of anger engulfed his insides as he realized he had been set up again. He was once again a pawn, a prize to be grabbed and handed over to the highest bidder. It was that sort of mind-set, that single-minded greed that had cost his wife her life. And now it was happening all over again.

With speed that belied his bulk, Fox grabbed the laptop and crossed the distance between himself and the woman. When he got to within a few feet of her, she sensed his approach, turned to him. He grabbed her shooting hand, squeezed so hard he swore he could feel bones grinding together. Breath exploded from between the woman's clenched teeth. Her other hand darted out in a knife-hand strike that caught Fox in his soft middle. He gasped, and she pulled her hand back for another blow.

Raising the laptop, he swung it around in a punishing arc. A corner of the machine caught her in the chin, knocking her head violently to one side. Her fingers went limp and her weapon fell to the floor. She turned to him, wild-eyed, blood streaming from her mouth. She tried to kick him, but was too off balance to put any steam behind it. Fox reached down and struck her in the head with his own forehead. The woman groaned and fell unconscious.

Moving quickly, he packed his laptop into its carrying case, grabbed the woman's weapon and moved to the window. Forcing his big frame through the opening, he shoved himself away from the window. He hit the ground, bent at the knees and rolled onto his back.

He rose and trotted around the side of the house, heading for the driveway. He saw a pair of black SUVs parked there, a man standing between them, watching the road. Overloaded with terror and adrenaline, Fox found himself struggling for breath. He held the gun in close to his leg, keeping it out of sight. The guy, hearing him approach, spun to meet him.

"I'm going with you guys," Fox said.

"Damn straight you are. Hands up."

Fox extended his arm carrying the laptop. "Here. Quit fucking around and take this. It's what you guys are here for. Right?"

"What the hell?" the guy asked. "What's going on here?"

Autofire continued to rage within the house at their back.

"Damn it, I'm getting cut in. Take this thing."

Still eyeing Fox suspiciously, the guy reached out for the bag's shoulder strap. The instant he took it, Fox raised the pistol and fired several rounds point-blank into the guy's gut, wincing with each shot. The gunner staggered back a few steps, dropped the case and his gun. Bloody wounds glistened in the light cast by outdoor halogen lamps. The gunner's legs gave out from underneath him and he fell to the earth.

Fox grabbed his laptop and darted for the nearest SUV. He opened the door, tossed the case inside. From the house, he heard yelling and saw several men disgorging through the front door. Aiming the handgun at the tire of the second vehicle, he fired off several rounds, flattening its front tire.

Climbing inside the Jeep Cherokee, he found the keys inside. The engine turned over smoothly and he gunned it, heading for the road. A couple of the raiders ran up behind him, trying to grab hold of the vehicle before he got away.

Moments later he was heading down the curvy mountain roads. The images of the thug, his midsection rent by bullets, and the CIA agent, her face bloodied and battered by him, continued to play in his mind. After another mile, he pulled the car off to the side of the road, got out and threw up. When he was back on the road, his mind raced through the details of his situation. He needed help. He needed it fast.

He needed to contact Aaron Kurtzman.

CHAPTER ONE

Stony Man Farm, Virginia

Sitting in front of his computer, Aaron Kurtzman's fingers flew over the keyboard as he monitored a half dozen or so secure communication channels, searching for news of his friend. Gabriel Fox's disappearance had set off alarm bells throughout the nation's intelligence networks—the FBI, CIA, Homeland Security and at least half a dozen other federal agencies were looking for the young hacker. When his search yielded no new information, Kurtzman's brow puckered. Worried but undaunted, he used a series of lightning-fast keystrokes to prompt two other programs. One scanned the various news Web sites for stories referring to Fox by name; a second gathered four-paragraph synopses with any story detailing the discovery of John Does. Neither program yielded results.

Leaning back in his wheelchair, he raked his fingers through his hair, scowled at the screen. Fox had disappeared seventy-two hours earlier. Kurtzman had been seated at his computer for nearly fifty-four of those hours, leaving only long enough for an occasional shower or to grab a cup of coffee. His eyes ached and he noticed his thoughts had slowed, his mind occasionally becoming a blank slate exactly when he needed to be sharp.

"C'mon, Aaron," he muttered. "Keep going."

"You need sleep," said Barbara Price, Stony Man Farm's mission controller. A moment later a hand settled gently on his shoulder and he smelled traces of the woman's perfume. Glancing over a shoulder, he flashed her a tight smile before returning his attention to his work.

"I'll sleep in a couple of hours," he said.

"I don't think you have a couple of hours left in you," she replied. "I understand that you're concerned. But right now we're in a lull. It's a good time for you to grab a couple hours' sleep. I want you fresh if they find him."

"When they find him," Kurtzman corrected.

"When," she said, patting gently on the shoulder.

Kurtzman placed his hands on his chair's wheels. Price moved back, giving him room to maneuver. He backed the chair away from his computer and turned it in a tight 180-degree turn until they faced each other.

"You look bad," she said without a trace of derision. "Tired and worried. You want to talk about it?"

"You know everything," he said, shrugging.

"I know that you have some sort of relationship with Gabriel Fox, and that somehow you've convinced yourself that going without sleep, food or exercise is the best way to make him reappear. Otherwise, I'm a little sparse on the details. You've hardly said three words during the past two days, other than to bark out an order to one of your crew. I'm worried about you."

Price, her honey-blond hair held back in a ponytail, her arms crossed over her chest, leaned against a nearby cabinet and stared at him. "So talk."

For what seemed like the millionth time, Kurtzman noticed that even without makeup and clad in blue jeans and an oversize flannel shirt, his old friend was a beautiful woman. The concern in her eyes only made her doubly so. The two had a close but purely platonic relationship, one in which they shared the emotional burdens that came with working for the country's ultrasecret counterterrorism operation.

"It's the kid," he said. "When I was in the think-tank business, before coming to work at this little Taj Mahal, Gabe was just a screwed-up kid from the Bronx. Not a drug-addicted, street-gang kind of kid, mind you. But he was definitely headed down the wrong path."

"How so?"

"He was hacking into everything—Justice Department, Pentagon, Fortune 500 companies and banks. You name it and he was busting into it, making the security gurus in the business look like a bunch of damned monkeys. Occasionally he stole money when he could get it. But mostly he just seemed to enjoy the challenge. He'd break in, leave his signature and disappear."

"Signature?"

"Called himself, X. Razor," Kurtzman said, gesturing quote marks around the name. "The moniker was stupid as hell, in retrospect, just what you'd expect from a kid. But damned if he didn't have everyone in the IT community scrambling."

"And you met him how?"

"The Pentagon asked me to join a task force tracking him and I agreed. Frankly, I was intrigued. At least at first. After a while, I just got obsessed. You know, missing meals, sleep, all so I could work on finding this bastard."

"Imagine that."

"Funny, lady. Very funny. Anyway, the more I looked into it, the more I followed his patterns, studied his language, the more I realized he was just a kid. A talented hacker, hell, yeah. But just a kid nonetheless."

"And you found him?"

Kurtzman nodded, smiled. "Yeah, our great hacker was a kid in a reform school in Cleveland. And he was breaking into all these systems using the principal's computer. After hours, of course."

Price grinned. "You're kidding."

He shook his head. "I kid you not. Little bastard had brass clangers. Anyway, once I'd located him, I decided to wait before turning him over to the Feds. The last thing I wanted was a couple of G-men busting into the place, flashing guns and badges. I hopped a plane for Cleveland, went to the school and caught him in the act. This big gangly kid with a green Mohawk haircut, earrings and tattoos turning all of us adults on our ears. And you know what the hell of it was?"

Price shook her head.

"He said, 'I wondered when you dumb bastards would find me.' Most kids would have been soiling their drawers and professing innocence. Or being quiet and defiant. But he seemed more disgusted than anything else. That it had taken us so long to track him down, I mean."

Kurtzman sipped his coffee and smiled at the memory. "That was when I got it," he said. "Gabe just wanted attention. He was a genius, smarter than most of the adults he encountered, angry and bored with us all. The money he stole? He put most of it into accounts he'd set up at the banks. And it wasn't because he had a moral problem with stealing. He just knew better than to go on a wild spending spree when you steal money." Kurtzman tapped a thick forefinger against his temple. "Like I said, smart as hell. He was fourteen years old. How many fourteen-year-olds are that smart?"

"A handful, maybe."

"Exactly."

"So what did you do with him?"

He shrugged again. "What could I do? I couldn't pretend like it didn't happen or let him escape the consequences. But I also wasn't going to let this kid rot in a detention center somewhere. I got him moved as close as I could to Virginia, a juvenile lockup in Alexandria. On my days off, I'd visit with him. I took him books and we'd talk computers for as long as they'd let us."

"You were like a surrogate parent."

"Maybe. The real articles weren't exactly a national treasure. But I stayed in contact with him over the years, helped pay for his college, that sort of thing. He got married a year ago. In August."

"I remember you took the time off."

Kurtzman nodded. "Bastards took his wife," he said. "Maria was a good woman, but whoever wanted to get the Cold Earth worm decided to kill her in the process. She was home when they broke in. Gabe wasn't. So they killed her."

Kurtzman's throat ached and he swallowed hard to dispel the feeling. This was one of the rare times when he wished he were an operative rather than some wheelchair-bound geek locked away in the Blue Ridge Mountains. Fox needed muscle, firepower. These were the only things Kurtzman couldn't provide and it pained him to admit it, even to himself.

"You're doing all you can," Price said, as though she

could read his mind. "Trust me, Aaron, if I was in trouble, you're one of the people I'd want in my corner."

Kurtzman gave her a grateful smile and a wink.

"Frankly, if everything was going to hell, I'd rather have Mack the Bastard on my side," Kurtzman said. He was referring to Mack Bolan, aka. the Executioner, the soldier who kept an arm's-length relationship with Stony Man Farm, but often conducted missions on the ultrasecret organization's behalf. Bolan, like most all of Stony Man's paramilitary fighters, had been forged in the hellfire of combat.

The corner of Price's mouth wrinkled in a perturbed expression that told Kurtzman she was having none of it. "Go get some rest, Aaron. Or go work on your project. What's it called?"

"You mean, Predator?"

"Right. The offensive firewall stuff you developed. We could sure use that around here."

He waved her off. "Sure. Yeah. I'll be out of here in a few minutes. Besides, I finished that project a couple of days ago. I just have to test it."

"Whatever. Go. Sleep. Now. Don't make me order you off the floor."

He threw a mock salute and a smile. "Ma'am, yes, ma'am." He gestured over his shoulder at his computer with his thumb. "Let me just make sure I'm at a stopping point, and I'll disappear for a couple of hours."

"Bear…" Price said, using his nickname.

"Promise."

Price nodded and moved away. Wheeling back around, Kurtzman checked his encrypted e-mail account and saw a new message. His heart skipped a beat when he read the address: foxhound362. Gabe! He popped open the message and scanned through it.

AK,
Leadville.
You won't see me, but I'll see you.
GF

Pumping a fist into the air, Kurtzman yelled, "Yes! Sleep can wait. We have contact."

AN HOUR LATER, Kurtzman was seated inside a Stony Man Farm's Lear jet specifically designed to accommodate his wheelchair. Accompanying him were four of the finest warriors he knew. Pilot Jack Grimaldi was seated in front, finishing last-minute preparations for takeoff, and seated around the cabin was the trio known as Able Team—Carl "Ironman" Lyons, Rosario "Politician" Blancanales and Hermann "Gadgets" Schwarz.

Whatever fatigue Kurtzman had felt previously had vanished with the arrival of Fox's message. Though his eyes still ached from lack of sleep and his trademark bad coffee was causing his stomach to roil, his mind was more alert than it had been for at least twenty-four hours, and for that he was grateful.

It was heading into late evening and Blancanales let loose with a big yawn.

Kurtzman held up a stainless-steel thermos. "Coffee?" he offered.

Blancanales waved him off. "Save it, amigo," he said. "Just in case the plane runs out of fuel."

"I didn't make it," Kurtzman lied.

"Well, in that case."

Kurtzman poured the coffee into three foam cups and handed them out. "You girls are going to be needing this," he said.

"Sounds ominous," Blancanales said. Swigging down some of his coffee, he made a face. He looked at Kurtzman, flashing a knowing smile.

"It's always ominous," Lyons said, an edge in his voice. "Why you dragging me—us—out in the middle of the night like this?"

"Simple snatch-and-grab mission," Kurtzman replied. Reaching into a pocket on the side of his wheelchair, he extracted three mission packets, handed them to Schwarz who was seated across from him, who, in turn, distributed them to the others. The plane had been configured for briefings, with four of the cabin seats facing one another.

"Before we leave the plane," Kurtzman said, "I need to take back these dossiers and put them in a burn bag. None of this stuff is supposed to leave the airplane, so commit the photo to memory."

Schwarz held out the photo so that it was visible to the others. "Kind of hard to forget a mug like this," he said. "He's a hard-looking kid. He the target?"

Kurtzman nodded. "In a manner of speaking, though he's on our side, all appearances aside. Name's Gabe Fox and he's a computer genius." Kurtzman brought the others up to date on the recent kidnapping attempts on Fox, the murder of his wife, how he'd gone underground and contacted Kurtzman less than two hours ago.

Blancanales was leafing through the file on his lap. "He's what, twenty-three years old? What makes him so special that everyone and their brother's trying to hunt him down?"

"It's not Gabe, per se, they're after," Kurtzman said. "It's what he's created. A little bit of background. He works for the CIA's counterterrorism unit. He's not a field operative. He's strictly a lab guy. Like I said, he's a maestro at the computer, and we're lucky to have him on our side. He's created some downright scary computer viruses and worms. Stuff capable of shutting down electrical grids or air-traffic-control systems. Remember all the Y2K doomsday scenarios with airplanes falling from the sky and all that crap? Forget it. This kid can program that stuff in his sleep."

"So someone wants him for his brain power?" Schwarz offered.

"Sort of," Kurtzman replied. "He's created a computer worm called Cold Earth. The thing's capable of shutting down the cooling systems in nuclear reactors, then frying the computers so that they'll do nothing but crash repeatedly. If you're working at a nuclear power plant and the computers go blooey, what would you do?"

"Soil myself," Schwarz said.

"After that," Kurtzman said, smiling.

"Try to restart the system," he replied. "See if I could get the cooling system to kick back on."

"Right. Thing is, though, every time you do that, the worm changes the computer's password. So you just sit there restarting the damn thing while the reactor core overheats."

"Wow," Schwarz said.

"Yeah, wow. Pretty soon, you have a meltdown like nothing the world's ever seen. You multiply that by every nuclear reactor around the country, hell, around the world, and you've got Armageddon a hundred or so times over."

"Okay, fine," Lyons said, "so this little lab rat comes up with this thing. Surely he came up with a way to counteract it."

"He's working on it," Kurtzman said.

Lyons's face reddened, and Kurtzman knew the

former Los Angeles cop was having a meltdown of his own. "Working on it? What the hell? If he's 'working on it,' then he ought to be sitting on his rusty can in a basement at Langley. Not skulking around the damn Rocky Mountains."

"That's why we're going after him, Carl," Kurtzman said.

"That's not what I meant. What I meant was, why wasn't this guy under heavier lock and key? Shit, if it was me, I'd stick him in the Situation Room in the White House's basement, cordon the place off with Delta Force troopers and not let him out until he came up with a way to counteract this thing."

Kurtzman nodded. "Agreed. Unfortunately someone at Langley was more focused on playing 'cover your ass,' rather than doing his or her job. According to the background information Barb and I were able to piece together, someone in Virginia didn't want the White House to know there was trouble."

"So they handled it 'in-house,' so to speak," Blancanales said.

"Yeah, they handled it, all right," Lyons said. "Let the toilet overflow, and guess who has to handle the mop-up."

"Eloquent," Schwarz said.

"He's right, though," Kurtzman interjected. "Apparently someone, or several people within the Agency, for that matter, knew about Gabe's problem. They also knew that someone was acting as a mole, handing out information about his latest creation. But they kept trying to handle it themselves, rather than go to the President or someone else for help."

"The big questions are, who sold him out and who's

trying to kidnap him?" Blancanales said. "We have any-one covering that angle?"

Kurtzman nodded. "Hal's working on it. As soon as word went out about the whole situation, he hopped a plane to Wonderland. I guess the National Security Council's still getting up to speed and debating whether to yank this from the Agency."

Blancanales scowled. "Doesn't seem like there ought to be a hell of a lot to debate here."

"More politics," Kurtzman said, sighing. "In the meantime, we're heading to Leadville, Colorado, to hunt for Gabe. Or more precisely, we're going there so he can find us. There's a municipal airport in Dillon. From there, it's about an hour or so's drive to find him. He knows me and will be looking for me. That's the rea-son I'm going along on this mission. Plus, Barb and Hal figured my computer expertise might help. I may draft Gadgets, too, before it's all over."

Schwarz nodded. "What then?" he asked.

"Carl, you and Pol need to form a human cordon around him. Gadgets and I will work with him on try-ing to counteract this thing."

"If we're that worried about losing him," Blancanales countered, "why not haul him back to Stony Man Farm? No one would find him here."

Kurtzman shook his head. "Unfortunately, the word from upper management was pretty clear. Someone al-ready has traced Gabe to one safehouse. It's pretty safe bet that someone inside the government's selling him out. Hal and the Man agree that they don't want to risk Stony Man's security by making it a target. That's also why he's not cooling his heels at Langley, or any other facility at the moment."

"Fasten your seat belts, ladies," Grimaldi called over his shoulder. "We're about to go airborne."

The assembled warriors strapped themselves in, and the engine's whine intensified, audible through the craft's hull. Kurtzman felt his bulky torso press against his harness as the force pushed him forward. He shuffled through some papers, looking for a copy of the two-page memo Price had supplied for the briefing. While the Lear taxied down the runway, he handed copies of the memo to the members of Able Team, each man scanning his copy when he received it.

"So they don't want to put Stony Man Farm on the bull's-eye," Blancanales said without looking up from his briefing packet. "What do we know about the kidnapping attempt?"

"We found one of the agents in Gabe's room. She'd been shot dead. According to the forensics report, she'd taken one in the stomach at close range. The bullet punched through her spine and—" Kurtzman snapped his fingers "—the lights went out instantly for her. We think Gabe's the one who shot her. And we think he did it with her weapon."

"Why?" Blancanales asked.

"She had scratch marks on her face and hands, bruising on her midsection, all consistent with a struggle, like she'd been tackled. Now her gun's missing. We recovered the bullet, but it was so mangled from tearing through bone and colliding with the floor that a good ballistics match is damn near impossible."

"Okay," Blancanales persisted, "but why kill her?"

A cold sensation settled into Kurtzman's gut as he spoke. "We have a couple of theories at this point. One, Gabe actually went rogue himself and used the chaos created by the raid to kill her and escape. The more likely scenario, though, is that she was actually working in concert with the kidnappers."

"Explain," Blancanales said.

"These guys were pros. They did what they could to haul their dead away. But they missed a couple. One of the raiders got knocked into a crevice and the bad guys had to leave him. We ran his prints and came up with some interesting results. Name was Ricardo Montoya. Apparently he worked for the Mexican government, along with about two dozen other men and women, forming an elite counter-terrorism team called Project Justice.

"Project Justice?" Blancanales said.

"Yeah. Unfortunately, Montoya and his group disappeared about six months ago, along with enough guns, ammo and explosives to supply a small army."

"Which is precisely what they are," Schwarz said.

"According to Mexican intelligence sources, there have been rumors that the group decided to sell its collective skills on the open market," Kurtzman said.

"Mercs?" Lyons asked.

Kurtzman shook his head. "A couple of the group's foot soldiers have been spotted in the Tri-Border in South America, meeting with a multitude of bad actors, everyone from Chinese triads to al Qaeda. Some of our best people—Delta Force, Navy SEALs—trained these folks in counterterrorism tactics."

"And now they're sharing what they know with terrorists and criminals," Lyons said. "Beautiful. And this fits with your buddy Gabe how exactly?"

"Two weeks ago, the lady Gabe killed apparently traveled to Mexico. Puerto Vallarta to be exact. She used her own passport, so she wasn't necessarily trying to hide her travels. A day or so later, a Mexican intelligence agent shoots a picture of a man named Pedro Vasquez meeting with an American woman in a small beachfront café. Vasquez is sort of their bagman, or business manager, depending on how you want to look at it. Mexican intelligence has been shadowing him for a couple of months, hoping to catch up with the group, but to no avail. He rarely makes direct contact, but instead relies on cloned cell phones that they constantly churn through and hand-delivered messages left at drop-off points."

"Old school tradecraft," Schwarz said. "Smart group."

"No e-mails, no single home base. Frankly, they've stolen a page from guys like Osama bin Laden and Saddam Hussein, using primitive communications whenever possible and constantly staying on the run."

"What happened to Vasquez?" Schwarz asked.

Kurtzman shrugged. "Not sure. He's an attorney in Puerto Vallarta, but he recently came up missing."

"Dead?"

"Possibly. More likely, though, he found a hole to crawl into until things settle down a little bit. The Mexicans had a stroke of luck and found the guy supplying the disposable phones, and he had a list of phone numbers for the phones. They passed this stuff along to the National Security Agency, which is hoping to catch a stray phone call, one they can trace back to the group. Once they do, the Mexican authorities have promised to drop the hammer on these bastards."

"What are we?" Lyons said, his face flushing. "Chopped liver? I'd like to be there for that, not babysitting some damn egghead and cleaning up the Agency's messes."

Kurtzman nodded. "Understood, Carl. But we need

to look at the bigger picture here. Someone wants to get hold of Gabe for a reason. And, if they do, they'd have something horrible in their grasp. They don't call this worm Cold Earth for nothing. Imagine multiple meltdowns occurring at once."

Lyons held up his hands defensively. "I get it. I get it. I just don't like sitting on my rump when something needs done, is all." He displayed one of his snakeskin cowboy boots. "These boots were made for kicking tail, baby."

"Nancy Sinatra you're not, amigo," Blancanales said, grinning. "Aaron, do we have any of our own people following up on the Mexican lead, just in case things start happening?"

"We've got Phoenix Force on standby. Until we get a little more hard intel, Hal's decided to leave them in Virginia. We have no idea where these guys might surface, or whether a second crisis might pop up. So he's trying to conserve resources, as they say in the business world."

"That's a euphemism for cooling your heels," Lyons said with a smirk. "Good. No sense in us having all the fun. Let's just hope your boy's got an eye out for us."

CHAPTER TWO

Where the hell were they?

Fox peered through the coffee-shop window again for the fourth time in twenty minutes, eyes scouring the streets for some sign of Kurtzman. This was his third day on the run, and he found himself jumping at shadows. He'd arrived in Leadville two days earlier, after hitching a ride from a trucker. He'd been able to get some clothes from a church, and public rest rooms had given him a place to wash, making him look like just another hiker stopping in town for a shave and warm meal. A dull ache in his back and neck reminded him that he'd spent the last couple of nights sleeping on the ground in a meadow behind the local elementary school.

Setting down his coffee, he reached for the nylon satchel he normally used for carrying his laptop. Unzipping it, he stared at the weapon inside, an Uzi submachine gun. Computer nerds weren't supposed to know how to use such weapons. But he did, thanks largely to a couple of gang bangers he'd known in his hometown who were given to driving to the country, dropping hits of acid and shredding rabbits and squirrels with well-placed bursts from the Israeli-made subgun. He'd never had the stomach to shoot an animal, but he'd wasted more than one discarded beer can during those trips. So he could shoot straight, if necessary.

Besides, you didn't need to be Annie Oakley to shoot yourself in the head. Just the proper motivation. He figured losing a wife, being betrayed by his own government and having every creep in the world chasing him gave a guy all the motivation he needed. A crashing realization of what he was about to do struck him, causing his hands and knees to tremor. He shoved the bag aside, leaving it closed, but not zipped, and lit up a cigarette.

"Might as well smoke 'em," he muttered. "You'll likely be dead in an hour."

"Sir?"

The voice caused him to start. Yanking the cigarette from his mouth, he whipped his head around and found the waitress standing next to his table. Brushing aside her kinky brown hair, she gave him a confused smile.

"Sir, did you say something?"

He waved dismissively. "Just yapping to myself," he said.

She nodded. "Can I get you something else?"

He looked at her face, oval-shaped with pale blue eyes, and felt that heavy sensation settle into his chest again. His wife also had had blue eyes. "Just the check." The uncertainty still in her eyes, she nodded and headed back toward the counter to tally the bill.

With his left hand, he rubbed his cheeks, now bare because he'd shaved his goatee in an attempt to alter his appearance. Good luck. A man mountain covered in tattoos trying to hide himself by removing a little facial hair, it seemed a vain effort. Like trying to dress up hell with a flower garden.

Kurtzman's reply to his e-mail had been brief, but comforting. *We're coming,* he'd written. *Stay cool.* So he'd been doing just that for the last several hours, but he'd yet to see any sign of his old friend.

Fox had been operating as a computer nomad of sorts over the past few days, using the machines at the local libraries to check his e-mail account and to scan media Web sites for any word of his appearance or of the shootings at the safehouse. As expected, he'd found nothing. He'd checked his e-mail account about an hour ago, looking for any further communications from Kurtzman, but had found nothing.

The sound of car doors slamming outside pulled him from his thoughts. Maybe it was Aaron, he thought. Glancing through the window, he spotted three men climbing from a black Cadillac Escalade. A fourth already stood by the driver's-side door, scanning his surroundings. A matching SUV had parked a few spots back and three more men were disgorging. Blood thundered in Fox's ears and sweat immediately broke out on his forehead. How the hell? When the realization struck, his stomach plummeted. The credit card. He'd used a credit card to pay for the Internet access, and apparently someone had been waiting for him to do just that.

He rocketed to his feet, grabbing his satchel. Turning on a heel to bolt, he nearly collided with the waitress. Her eyes wide, she crossed her arms over her chest protectively and inhaled sharply as she came to a halt. Reaching into his pocket, Gabe grabbed a crumpled ten-dollar bill and held it out to her.

She took it. "It's going to be a minute on the change."

"Keep it," he said, his voice sharp and loud. "A back door. You got one?"

The volume of his voice, his size and his erratic behavior seemed to take her aback. Eyes wide, her lips parted but no sound came out.

"A door!" Without taking her eyes from him, she turned and gestured toward a pair of swing doors at the other end of the counter.

"There. Through there."

"Thanks," he said, his voice dropping in volume. He darted for the back of the restaurant. Pushing through the swing doors, he wound his way between a series of tables covered with chopped food and kitchen appliances. A twenty-something man, his hair dyed green and three earrings on his left ear, his skinny torso covered in a stained apron, stepped into Fox's path, a butcher's knife clutched in his right hand, but not upraised to strike.

"What's the—" he said.

Fox's stiff-armed the cook, planting the open palm of his left hand into the man's sternum, sending him spinning backward into a wall. The cook yelled, but it only vaguely registered with Fox. He pushed through a wood-framed screen door, which emptied into an alley that ran the length of a row of commercial buildings, most of them stout and more than a century old. Cutting right, he began to move along the alley, his lungs already feeling the exertion from years of smoking combined with the thin mountain air.

Even as he moved, he heard the screen door slam behind him, prompting him to glance over his shoulder. He spotted the cook from the restaurant, knife still in his hand, yelling and cursing at him.

A corridor, little more than the space between two

buildings, opened up to his right and Fox darted into it. Footsteps pounded the pavement and he heard a faint thumping in the distance. Flattening himself against the wall, he reached inside the satchel and fisted the Uzi, but kept the bag over it for the moment. Chances were the irate cook or the waitress was already calling 911, summoning the local police. If they showed up, he'd lose the weapon, give himself up and hope to stay alive in custody until Kurtzman arrived. Fox wasn't in love with the police, and the memory of his betrayal by the CIA was fresh in his mind, but he wasn't about to draw down on some local cop trying to do his or her job. He'd die before doing that.

The whupping of chopper blades rent the air and the craft passed overhead, the whine of the engine reverberating from the alley walls. Biting off a curse, Fox headed for the mouth of the alley, which led back onto the main street. Chancing a look around the corner, he spotted two of the guys from the SUV moving up the street toward him. Jerking back, he spun on a heel, retraced his steps toward the other end of the alley. The helicopter's engine grew louder as it returned for another pass. Had they spotted him during their previous pass? He had no reason to think otherwise.

A stout man clad in a black leather bomber jacket and jeans stepped into view, bringing a gun to bear on Fox. With less than ten yards separating them, Fox started to raise his own weapon when he suddenly heard tires screech in the alley, snagging the guy's attention and causing him to snap his head toward the source of the noise.

Already committed, Fox continued running until he came right up on the man and threw himself into the guy, tackling him, both men crashing to the ground in a pile. Breath whooshed from between the man's lips as he struck the ground. Fox pressed his advantage, lifting the Uzi, ready to crack the other man in the jaw with the submachine gun.

"Freeze!"

Fox complied, holding both hands aloft. He glanced briefly to his right and saw a police cruiser, a female officer crouched behind it. She gripped her weapon in both hands and laid her arms over the car's hood, using it to steady her hands.

"Drop the guns!" she yelled. "Now! Both of you."

Fox set the Uzi on the asphalt and, with a hard shove, sent it sliding toward the cruiser. The other man tossed aside his pistol. She ordered both men to their feet and Fox did as he was told. He hated taking orders, especially from a cop, but he didn't mind grabbing some distance from the stocky bastard who a few moments earlier had been gunning for him. The woman rose, the weapon still held in front of her, and gestured toward a wall.

"Up against it," she said.

"Look, Officer—" Fox began.

Her face reddened and her voice gained volume. "The wall. Now!"

He started for the wall, still keeping his distance from the other man. As he moved, he noticed the guy fumbling in his pocket for something while he used Fox's body to shield his movements from the cop. Before Fox could say anything, the man's hand came free and Fox caught the glint of something metallic, followed by a gunshot.

EMILIO CORTEZ WATCHED as his men fanned out over the small mountain town's main drag, looking for Gabriel

Fox. Two men disappeared inside the coffee shop across the street, while another slipped into a nearby bookstore. Three more began moving down his side of the street, peering through store windows. With a gesture, he sent the two SUVs inching down the street, the drivers ready to return should he summon them with a call through the throat microphone.

Despite the chill, he opened his knee-length black leather coat, putting his Ithaca 37 stakeout model shotgun within reach. The shotgun hung from his rangy frame in a custom-made rig, and he carried extra shells in his right coat pocket. A Browning Hi-Power handgun, a custom sound suppressor affixed to its barrel, rode in snap-out leather on his hip, opposite the shotgun. Laminated FBI credentials hung from his neck, and he carried a snap-out wallet containing a forged Bureau ID and badge in his coat pocket, in case he encountered the police.

Cortez scanned the street, listening to the radio traffic buzzing in his ear.

The helicopter zoomed by, the rotor wash tousling his black hair. His black eyes squinted even as he followed the craft as it passed him by.

A moment later one of the van drivers spoke. "Picking up a 911 dispatch. A guy matching our rabbit just bolted from inside the coffee shop using the back door. Apparently he got a visual on us."

"We've got two in the coffee shop," Cortez said.

A moment later the helicopter copilot spoke. "Clear. I've got a visual on our guy. He's running down the alley behind the coffee shop. Ben, you and Alex got that?"

"Right," said Ben Waters, one of the men searching the coffee shop, "we're coming out the back now."

"Clear," the pilot responded.

Cortez adopted a grim smile as he listened to the chase unfold. He was ready to put this guy under wraps, forever and for good. They'd spent the past couple of days scouring Frisco, Breckenridge, Dillon, Leadville, and any other Rocky Mountain town within a fifty-mile radius, looking for some sign of him. They'd come up empty. Cortez had to admit that, for a computer geek, Fox had done a pretty fair job of covering his tracks. Fortunately for them, he'd gotten sloppy, overconfident and had made a rank amateur mistake, using his own credit card to access a public Internet terminal. The cyberteams in Mexico and Denver had caught the transaction and alerted Cortez. The contents of the e-mail had been encrypted so Cortez couldn't be certain who the programmer had contacted. The uncertainty just added a measure of urgency to their chase, which the young Mexican didn't mind at all.

A voice buzzed in his earpiece. "Cortez?"

"Go."

"Got him in the alley," Juan Vasconez said. "Tell the chopper to scoot. We don't need the damn thing hovering overhead and drawing attention."

"Clear. Warbird, you heard the man. Go!"

"Right." An instant later the thrumming of helicopter rotors intensified and the craft headed west, likely circling outside the city limits, but staying within earshot of the fighting.

"He just cut between buildings," Vasconez said. "The boot shop and the antique mall. Can we get a vehicle there to cut him off?"

"You heard the man," Cortez said.

From a couple of blocks away, one of the SUVs screeched into a U-turn and made its way to the position. Cortez was in motion, closing in on Fox with long, quick strides, his hand inside his coat and yanking the Browning from its holster. Pressing the gun against his side, he let the folds of his coat swallow it.

"Shit, he's turning back on me," Vasconez said.

"Let him," Cortez replied. "Don't shoot. I repeat, do not shoot."

"Right." A pause. "He's got a gun!"

The sounds of a scuffle filled his earpiece and he cursed under his breath as he crossed the street and came within twenty yards of the SUV, which had rolled to a stop. The driver's-side door popped open and the guy stepped out. A siren blared from somewhere beyond view. Someone shouted something, and, though he couldn't make out its content, Cortez knew it was a command of some sort.

"Shit," Vasconez breathed. "Cop."

Cortez's heart pounded as he closed in on the scene. "Do not engage," he said. "I repeat—"

The crack of a gunshot stopped him in midsentence. Damn, damn, damn.

Even as he continued toward his quarry, the beating of helicopter blades sounded from behind, growing louder, reverberating from the walls of the nearby storefronts, the noise drowning out all else. Rotor wash caught the tails of his coat, whipping them around his legs.

Whipping around, expecting to see his team's helicopter, he caught sight of another craft, a black helicopter, touching down in the middle of the street. He stopped dead, and a moment later a side door slid open and a big, blond-haired guy stepped onto the pavement. A gray-haired man with the thick chest and shoulders of a bull and a smallish guy with brown hair and a mustache followed. The maelstrom whipped up by the helicopter parted their jackets and Cortez was sure he spotted at least one holstered weapon among the three of them. Apparently they'd missed the gunshot and had no idea they'd just touched down in a hot zone. Good, he thought. He knew how to play this one to his benefit.

He surveyed the craft and felt an unsettled feeling move into his gut. Other than a tail number, the craft carried no identifying markings, and the men wore no uniforms. His weapon still hidden, he spun on a heel and started for the group. Cortez fastened a single button on his coat to keep from revealing the Ithaca, and fumbled for the FBI credentials looped around his neck. Another of his men, the driver of the second SUV, a Chicago killer named Johnny Hung, fell into step behind him.

Cortez knew all his players, of course, meaning he had three interlopers stepping onto his territory. His mind working overtime, he decided on a plan. Take out these bastards, take their helicopter and go home with the big prize.

CARL LYONS HAD a bad feeling about the black-clad guy from the get-go. Forget the credentials hanging around his neck or the smile creasing his thin lips. It was the hand that remained at his side, lost in the folds of a black leather duster that spoke volumes to Lyons, telling him everything he needed to know. Instinct honed first as an L.A. detective and later as a covert commando screamed that the guy was looking for blood, even before Lyons's eyes confirmed this.

The guy's eyes narrowed, a harbinger of something bad, and Lyons felt himself tense. A glance left told him that Blancanales, though smiling, was also eyeing the guy warily. With the helicopter's rotors thumping overhead, the two men couldn't easily converse, and Lyons had made the mistake of not yet putting on his earpiece and throat microphone.

Three other men had fallen in with the approaching man, their presence only heightening Lyons's cautiousness.

Schwarz was just behind the other two men, working to set down the wheelchair ramp for Kurtzman. Turning, Lyons motioned for Schwarz to stop and pay attention. Before he could turn back, he saw Kurtzman's eyes widen and he raised his hand to point. Lyons whipped around, his hand already stabbing under his jacket for the Colt Python.

Things began to happen quickly.

The lead guy's hand was coming up in a blur. He snapped off two shots in Lyons's direction, immediately putting him on the move. The rounds burned through the air, missing the big commando by inches before smacking into the Chinook's hull.

Lyons cleared leather. He brought the Python to bear on the guy, ready to line up a shot. He halted. A young man stood on the curb, frozen by the gunfire. The black-coated shooter squeezed off two more rounds at Lyons. The commando thrust himself to the asphalt. His elbow absorbed the impact, white-hot bolts of pain emanating from the joint. He ground his teeth and rode out the pain. He tried to line up another shot at the guy, but he'd stepped onto the curb. Turning to Lyons, he smiled, then grabbed a handful of the bystander's jacket and shoved him into the street just as Lyons was trying to get in a shot.

The man disappeared through the front door of a nearby building.

Holstering the Colt, Lyons fisted the .357 Desert

Eagle he carried on his right hip in a cross-draw position. He paused long enough to put his earpiece in place before crossing the street with long strides.

A voice buzzed in his ear. "Ace to Ironman." It was Grimaldi.

"Go."

"According to the scanner traffic, we've got shooters behind the line of buildings ahead of you."

"Is our package back there?"

"Unknown. But these guys put down a cop."

Lyons cursed under his breath, but kept moving. An instant later Blancanales fell into step with the Able Team leader and the two men moved onto the sidewalk. At the same time Lyons caught the sound of sirens closing in from the distance, the wail eliciting another oath. Adding more guns, even those wielded by good guys, introduced new variables into this volatile equation. And he knew, again from experience, that these officers would hit the scene with blood in their eyes, wanting to put down the shooters.

And since Able Team had the guns…

Lyons keyed his throat microphone and spoke. "Get the bird in the air. And call the Farm for a cleanup crew on this. Tell Hal, or Barb, or whomever, to start greasing the wheels. Otherwise we'll be stuck here."

"Roger that, Ironman," Grimaldi replied.

From behind, Blancanales had stepped in close to a nearby building, raising his weapon to cover Lyons while he edged along the line of stores, occasionally ducking below the length of a window. Covering another building length, Lyons found an alley opening to his left. Halting, he craned his neck to peer around the corner. Even as he did, another shot rang out, followed by a strangled cry.

CHAPTER THREE

Kneeling behind the front bumper of a maroon Ford Taurus, Schwarz ground his teeth and rode out a blistering fusillade of gunfire as two hardmen emptied automatic weapons into his cover. Bullets pounded through the vehicle, flattening tires, rending upholstery, shattering glass. An occasional round pierced the car's sloped hood, exiting within inches of Schwarz's crouched form. Lead pounded the engine block, pinging like metallic rain as the block stopped the rounds from ripping Schwarz apart.

Only moments earlier, the Able Team commando had started around the edge of the sedan, his micro-Uzi carving a path for him while he looked for the black-clad killer. When a flash of motion had registered in his peripheral vision, he had dived behind the Ford, his combat-honed reflexes taking him off the firing line a heartbeat before death found him.

A momentary break in the gunfire provided Schwarz a chance to raise his head slightly over the hood to scan the scene, but he saw no one. His opponents apparently had gone undercover while reloading their weapons.

Moving in a crouch, Schwarz rounded the car's front end, now with his M-4 assault rifle leading the way. Climbing onto the sidewalk, he moved along the edge of the line of vehicles, his senses alert for any sign of trouble.

The sudden slap of feet against concrete drew his attention. He wheeled toward the sound, scanning for a target, his finger tightening ever so slightly on the trigger. A heavyset woman, apparently considering the silence a chance for escape, darted out from inside a drugstore, her worn leather purse clutched tightly to her chest. Seeing the commando, his weapon pointed at her, the woman froze and screamed.

Shit!

Schwarz pointed the rifle barrel skyward and waved her on with his free hand. Eyes bulging, the woman stood there rooted to the spot, her lips working wordlessly as her overloaded mind tried to process the events unfolding around her. Realizing the numbers were falling too fast for such a distraction, Schwarz felt his own anxiety creep up a notch.

"Move!" he yelled, hoping that the sound, if not the word, might jar her into action.

His command startled her, but she stood still.

Damn it! Left with no other choice, Schwarz surged forward and grabbed the woman by the arm. The instant his hand gripped her bicep, the fingers sinking into the cushy flesh, the woman screamed and threw a haymaker at Schwarz's jaw.

The punch connected, jarring his teeth. He'd experienced a lot worse, of course, but the sudden sensation of pain emanating from his jaw diverted his attention for an instant. Almost long enough for him to miss the furtive figure rising from behind a nearby parked car.

Almost.

With a shove he bulled the woman out of the way and brought up his assault rifle. The weapon spit a line of 5.56 mm rounds that pounded into his opponent's head, reducing it to a fine red mist. His attacker's smoking weapon slipped from dead fingers as the partially decapitated corpse folded into a boneless heap, disappearing between two parked cars. Seeing the violence, the bystander screamed again and darted back toward the drugstore. Schwarz felt a rush of relief when the electric door slid closed behind her.

Moving with slow, deliberate steps, he crossed the space between himself and the felled shooter, figuring he ought do a visual check to make sure he'd cleared the nest. He found the man's crumpled form where it had fallen. He made a mental note to search the guy later, even as he acknowledged that such an effort likely wouldn't yield much. These guys obviously were pros and if they carried any identification at all, it likely would be fake. But they'd run the traps nonetheless.

The crackle of gunfire died down for a few moments. Schwarz heard a terse exchange between Lyons and Grimaldi. Moments later the helicopter's engine grew louder and the craft rose from the street, cresting the rooftops as the pilot executed a starboard turn.

Almost as soon as the thought crossed his mind, Schwarz noticed his combat senses kicking into overdrive, the small hairs at his nape brushing against his shirt collar, a cold sensation rushing down his spine.

Turn! his mind screamed.

He spun. Even before his mind registered the threat, Schwarz knew he was going to take a bullet. The guy with the black coat was poised on a second-floor balcony, his weapon aimed dead-center on Schwarz's chest.

Move!

The Able Team warrior shot up.

Flames lanced from the other man's weapon. Almost the same instant Schwarz felt something smack hard into him, the force robbing him of his footing, sending him tumbling to the ground. The shot, sounding oddly far away, registered with him even as his mind struggled to grasp the sudden trauma seizing his body.

Fire tore through his shoulder. Through blurred vision, he saw the other man adjust his aim, saw more flames leap from the gun's barrel. White-hot pain lanced through his abdomen and he cried out in spite of himself.

He tried to raise his own gun hand but found it unresponsive.

I'm going to die.

He'd imagined it a thousand times, and here it was. If he was going to go, he'd make some damn noise.

Cocking his knee, his working hand stabbed down to his ankle, groping for the Colt Detective's Special holstered there. Fire ripped through his bent calf, causing him to grunt in surprise and pain, making him forget about the weapon. His leg went limp. When he dropped to the ground, he glimpsed the shooter, poised and grinning, surveying his shattered form with satisfaction.

Schwarz struggled to remain conscious but found himself slipping away. The popping of gunfire, the wail of sirens, grew faint, distant....

A TAUT VOICE EXPLODED in Blancanales's earpiece.

"Man down!" Kurtzman said. "Gadgets is injured and taking fire."

The commando keyed his headset. "Location?"

Kurtzman told him. Blancanales turned and began retracing his steps, moving at a dead run to reach his fallen comrade.

"Ironman?" he said into his throat microphone.

"Go."

"You're on your own."

"Right. Take the bastards down."

"Clear."

Blancanales surged into the street, his eyes scouring the area for the shooter. He spotted the black-coated man, his lips twisted in an ugly grin, drawing down on an unseen target. Blancanales assumed his friend was on the ground somewhere beyond the string of parked cars lining the street.

From behind him, he heard the police cars closing in, a cacophony of blaring sirens and squealing tires. He did his best to ignore their approach, knowing he had less than a second to save his friend.

Twin Berettas chugged 3-round bursts, the bullets cleaving through the air to reach the shooter. His aim thrown off by the jarring impact of his footsteps smacking against concrete, the first volley cleaved through the air and collided with a brick wall several feet to the shooter's right. Shards of brick exploded from the wall, nicking the man's face, causing him to screw up the right side of his face and bunch up his shoulder in a protective gesture.

Whipping around, the guy spotted Blancanales and his pistol flared to life. The Able Team commando surged left, his weapons spitting another blistering fusillade. As before, most of the shots drilled into nearby brickwork or tore through the man's long coat, driving him back, but not biting into flesh.

Blancanales darted right, purposely moving away from what he believed to be Schwarz's position. Stuck in the middle of a four-lane street with no protection, Blancanales knew he made too tempting a target to pass up and he wanted to draw fire away from his comrade.

As he ran, bullets kicked into the asphalt, snapping at his heels. Turning at the waist as he moved, he squeezed off matching tribursts from the Berettas. This time a 9 mm Parabellum round cleaved into the side of the man's neck, apparently just nicking the skin. He slapped a hand over the wound as though striking a bug. The realization that he'd been wounded seemed to unnerve the guy a bit, prompting him to unleash a final barrage from his weapon, the flurry of lead forcing Blancanales to sprint for cover behind a parked car. Even as he did, his opponent backed away, disappearing through the balcony door.

Springing to his feet, Blancanales crossed the street, his eyes taking in the carnage as he did. He counted at least three fallen hardmen, though there could be more sandwiched between cars or slumped in recessed doorways. Dozens of pockmarks scarred the historic buildings, pierced car bodies and caused spiderweb cracks to form on the car windows.

Even as he closed in on his friend, the commando kept an eye trained on the front door of the building that only scant heartbeats ago had provided a perch for a killer, knowing the guy might burst through the front door, gunning for a rematch. However, Blancanales considered the chances remote. The shooter more likely would find a rear exit, get the hell out of there while he still could.

He knelt next to Gadgets and checked to see whether his old friend was breathing.

CARL LYONS SPED through the diner, winding his way between patrons sprawled facedown on the hardwood floors scuffed and scarred from more than a century of use.

Thrusting his full body weight against the swing doors, he surged into the kitchen, intent on reaching the rear exit. He found himself facing a young man, hair dyed green, standing there, his face etched in terror. The kid clutched a butcher knife in a white-knuckled grip. Lyons halted, eyeing him warily, unsure whether he planned to attack. The young man held the knife to his heaving chest, as though it were a shield.

The young man's face was pale, making his green locks seem all the more garish.

"We got a problem here, kid?" Lyons asked.

The young man shook his head, squeezing the knife against his chest.

"How about you put down the knife?"

"Can't."

"Kid, I'm losing time here. Drop the damn knife."

"My fingers. They won't move."

Impatience flared within him, but Lyons squashed it with a deep exhale. He needed to get through that door, but he didn't want to charge a panicked kid with a knife. Under normal circumstances, the kid likely wouldn't pose a threat. But he had the look of a cornered animal and Lyons didn't want to push him.

He adopted what he called his "jumper" voice, a soothing, patient tone he'd learned to use as a cop.

"It's okay," he said. "I'm a federal agent. I need to get through that door. What say you drop the knife?"

"They shot her. I saw it."

"Who?"

"The lady cop."

"Kid, we're burning daylight. I gotta go through that door. You're in my way."

Hesitating another heartbeat, the young man finally shuddered and dropped the knife.

"Good," Lyons said. He gestured the kid away from the door, and this time he complied. "Hide somewhere until the cops come to get you," Lyons said as he brushed past the young man.

Lyons stepped into the alley and immediately found the pungent smell of rotting food assailing his nostrils. A garbage Dumpster stood to his right. Police cars barreled into the alley from both ends, their sirens screaming.

The Python extended, Lyons skirted the garbage bin, his eyes searching either for Gabe Fox or for another killer. Footsteps slapped against concrete and a moment later Lyons caught sight of a stocky man with coffee-colored skin bearing down on him. He remembered the guy as one of the gunners who'd been with the black-coated shooter a few minutes earlier.

The guy spotted Lyons and began to raise his gun.

The gesture came a microsecond too slow. The Colt Python bucked twice in Lyons's hand. The slugs hammered into the hardman's stomach and he collapsed to the ground. Even though he was sure the guy was dead, Lyons kicked away the man's gun as he moved past him.

"Ironman to Ace."

"Go, Ironman," Grimaldi replied.

"You have any contact with our runaway?"

"Negative."

"Politician?"

"With me. We're watching the paramedics treat Gadgets."

"Give me a sitrep."

"Give us five and I'll let you know."

"Make it three."

"Roger that."

Before he could make another move, a police car skidded to a halt twenty yards to his left. Doors popped open on either side and a pair of county deputies surged from the vehicle, guns drawn. Anticipating this, Lyons had already holstered the Colt, exchanging it for his fake Justice Department credentials. He raised his hands, flipping open his badge case as he did, and played it cool. Experience told him that a downed officer put everyone on edge, igniting a volatile combination of fury and fear. He felt it burning in his own gut and wanted to chase down the bastards who'd shot Gadgets and the other fallen officer. He also didn't want to waste precious seconds tangling with the locals. One of the officers, his gun drawn, approached him. From the corner of his eye, Lyons could see another deputy, a sergeant, closing in from the opposite direction.

The officer snagged Lyons's ID from his hand, stepped back and inspected it. Holstering his weapon, the guy returned Lyons's credentials and other officers emerged from cover.

"The other guys told us to look for you, Agent Irons," the cop said. "We lost your shooter."

Lyons nodded. "I'm going. I hope everything turns out okay for the lady." Without waiting for the man's reply, he turned and walked away.

CHAPTER FOUR

Fox thrust himself inside a doorway as a pair of police cars whizzed by, sirens blaring. The move was more of a reflex than a rational action. He'd spent too many years in the juvenile justice system to regard the police as friends, even under the current circumstances. The CIA—or at least someone within the Agency—already had sold him out. Who was to say the police around here weren't also bought and paid for?

Moving quickly, he covered two blocks on foot, his gaze cast downward, though he continued taking in his surroundings with surreptitious glances.

Pain seared through his ribs, causing him to wince with each step. The knife thrust had been a glancing one, striking bone, skittering off it, without biting into the vital organs beneath his rib cage. But Fox knew he was losing lots of blood. He could feel his warm life fluids grow cool as the breeze whipped inside his long coat. Each step caused bolts of pain to emanate from the wound, and he clenched his jaw to keep the pain in check. Gunshots continued to ring in his ears, reminding him of the rare occasions when as a teen he'd attended concerts and his ears would buzz for twenty-four hours as they recovered from the audio assault.

Taking his hand away from the wound, he found it covered with blood. In fact, blood had soaked his wrist and then his sleeve, turning the fabric black almost up to his elbow. Unbidden, the face of the thug he'd just killed flickered across his mind and he felt his stomach roll. He saw the man's gaze transform from one of controlled rage, a predatory confidence, to shock and finally helplessness as he realized he was dying. Fox had shoved the man away and exploded from the alley, passing the fallen police officer, leaving her also to die as he'd tried to save his own skin.

Tears stung his eyes as he chastised himself for his cowardice. How many more people were going to have to die because of him? Because of what he'd wrought with his own hands? His vision began to blur and his footsteps grew heavier. Shit! He'd lost so much blood that his body was ready to give out, to shut down, if not forever, at least for a time to heal.

Move!

He passed a couple of slab houses covered in peeling paint and fronted by small rock gardens and spotty grass. In the backyard of one, laundry hung from a line, blowing in the breeze. In the other, a black Labrador retriever stood on his hindquarters, his front paws hooked over the fence, barking at him and wagging its tail in welcome. He kept moving and hoped its noise didn't prompt the home's occupants to peer through their window where they'd see a blood-soaked man lumbering down the street.

He was beginning to feel shaky, and knew he couldn't keep walking forever. Ahead, he saw a refuge, a wooden shed painted an odd green color that he guessed matched his skin tone at this particular moment. It sat inside a fenced yard, its door seized by the strong winds whipping through town, fanning open and closed.

The structure lay forty or so yards away. It might as well have been a mile for the way he felt. Eyes locked on the building, he stumbled to the corner and felt his legs grow rubbery. His hand lashed out and he caught hold of a street sign's metal post. Leaning his body against it, his eyes slammed shut and a seductive blackness began to envelop his mind, summoning him to surrender to it.

The cell phone in his pocket trilled, pulling him back out. Dipping a hand into his pocket, he retrieved the phone and answered the call. "Hello."

"Gabe?" Even in his shaky condition, Fox recognized Kurtzman's voice immediately.

"Yeah."

"Where the hell are you?"

"Good to hear your voice."

"Yeah. C'mon. Where the hell are you?"

"Not sure. Some street."

"You sound like hell. You injured."

"Guy stabbed me, Aaron. Cut my side open. Hurts. Like. Hell."

"Understood, brother. Where are you at? We'll come get you."

Fox peered up at the street sign, trying to bring the words into focus. "Peak Street," Fox said. "I'm on Peak Street."

"Okay, we're on our way."

"Man, I killed two people."

"Right. You did what you had to. No worries, huh?"

"I didn't want to. I feel like shit."

"Like I said, no worries. We'll work stuff out. Just hang on for a minute. I've got guys coming for you. Plainclothes. A mouthy blond guy and a gray-haired Hispanic fellow. They'll take good care of you."

His eyes slammed shut again until Fox heard a car engine growl to his left, prompting him to turn and look. He watched as a van rolled up to the curb. In his delirium, he'd lost his feel for time.

"That was fast," he said.

"What was fast?" Kurtzman replied.

"Your guys are here."

He heard Kurtzman mutter an oath. "Those aren't my people, guy. Can you move?"

"Don't. Think. So." His tongue felt fat and clumsy, his mouth dry.

"Roger that. We're on our way."

Fox sank to his knees, his head whirling. He heard the dull *thunk* of an automatic transmission slipping into park, followed by a door opening. The idling engine buzzed in his ear like an insistent insect, but he kept his eyes shut as he felt himself slip closer to unconsciousness.

Boots thudded, and he cracked an eye. A pair of snakeskin cowboy boots came into view, the leather creaking as the wearer bent to kneel next to him. An instant later he saw a face, Latino, he thought, and he felt relief wash over himself. *A mouthy blond guy and a gray-haired Hispanic fellow,* Kurtzman had said. Did the guy have gray hair? Fox thought so, hoped so.

He fell unconscious as Cortez grabbed him under the arms and dragged him roughly toward a stolen Hyundai.

BLANCANALES SPRINTED toward the spot where Fox had claimed to have fallen. He was in good shape by almost anyone's standards. Still, he felt his lungs burn for air as he exerted himself at the mountain town's altitude.

From two blocks away, he heard a car door slam. Looking up, he saw two men dragging Fox toward a small red sedan. He poured on the speed, snatching one of the Beretta's from beneath his coat as he did.

He also recognized the man who'd shot Schwarz. Blancanales's heart drummed harder as rage flared inside him, causing him to run that much harder. The men hadn't seen him yet and he stepped into the grass median between the sidewalk and the street, hoping the softer terrain would eliminate the sound of his pounding feet.

Lyons was across the street, surging forward at a similar pace, his form hidden behind parked cars. Unsure of what they'd find, the two men had decided to leave some distance between them, rather than bunching into a knot, forming an easy target.

"That's our shooter," Blancanales said.

"Right," Lyons replied.

"You got the shot?"

"Negative. Too far away. Too clustered."

"Let me fix that."

Lyons darted out from between a pair of parked cars and uttered a war whoop. The sudden flurry of sound and motion caused the three men to look up from their captive. The guy in the black coat, the one who'd shot Schwarz, went on the defensive immediately. Crouching, he spotted Lyons heading his way and capped off two shots that whizzed well past the approaching figure. Lyons held his own fire, in part because of the proximity of houses and because the men remained too tightly wound around Fox. There was a good chance that Fox would take a hit.

Lyons ran in a zigzag pattern as the air around grew heavy with gunfire. Bullets perforated car windows, tail- and headlights, or glanced off steel. He watched as the third man dragged Fox's body toward the car, opening up more precious space between him and the shooters with each passing second.

One of the hardmen got brave. He separated from the others and unleashed a volley of gunfire at Lyons. The former cop dived forward, rolled, before coming up in a prone position. The Python thundered twice more, spitting jagged columns of flame from the barrel. A moment later the shooter flew backward, as though hit dead-center by a wrecking ball. The guy in the black duster reacted, wheeling toward Lyons and unloading another deadly barrage of fire. The bullets chewed into the ground, showering Lyons with dirt and grass. Without aiming, he emptied the Python at his attacker, hoping the slugs at least would throw the guy off his stride.

The guy's weapon went dry at the same time, forcing him to break off the attack. Lyons watched as the shooter let the submachine gun fall on its strap, spin and head for the vehicle's driver's side. The other man already had succeeded in stuffing Fox into the back seat of the car, and was scrambling to grab a weapon from under his jacket.

Popping the Python's cylinder, Lyons was emptying spent brass even as he came to his feet. Stuffing a hand inside his jacket pocket, his fingers encircled a speedloader and he charged the weapon on the run, completing the task in the same microsecond that the other guy freed a pistol from its holster and began to raise it.

Before Lyons could fire, the man suddenly stiffened, his expression morphing from one of shock to terror. Wounds sprang open across his torso. His knees suddenly gave out beneath him, and he crashed forward to the ground.

In the same instant, Lyons caught a glimpse of Blancanales heading for the car. However, the driver gunned the engine and sent the vehicle hurtling straight toward the commando, forcing him to leap out of its path.

Even as the car gathered speed, Lyons already was rocketing forward, trying to catch up with it. Legs pumping like pistons, the Able Team leader surged after the car, trying to get to it before it hit at full cruising speed. It was a wasted effort. In the seconds it took him to reach its starting point, the vehicle already had put another two blocks between itself and him.

He watched as it blew through a stop sign, nearly colliding with an oncoming car before disappearing over a hill. Stopping next to Blancanales, he radioed the information to Kurtzman.

"Shit," the computer expert said. "Gabe's as good as dead."

"Scratch that, mister," Lyons replied. "We're not done here. Not by a long shot. Pass along the description to the police while Pol and I try to round up a vehicle. We're going to keep looking for him."

"Roger that," Kurtzman said, his voice telegraphing the same doubt that Lyons's felt roiling in his own gut.

"And tell Jack we need to get that bird up in the air. I want a visual on this SOB, like five minutes ago. Got it?"

"But Jack needs to airlift Gadgets—"

"Jack needs to pick up the pursuit."

"Carl—"

"Don't even go there, Bear. It's one life against the potential loss of thousands. You read?"

"Understood."

CHAPTER FIVE

Cortez navigated the car out of the city limits, heading north, higher into the Rocky Mountains. Checking his watch, he smiled. He still had three minutes to reach the rendezvous point. The mission had come about as close to going to hell as one could imagine, with this crazy group of federal agents busting up his play. But he still had time to salvage the whole thing, if he kept his head about him.

A groan sounded from behind him, and he glanced over the backrest to scan his prisoner. The guy's skin was pale, and he was shuddering, most likely slipping into shock. Cortez sent a mental prayer heavenward that the guy would make it. If the guy died, if Cortez failed to produce the goods, he knew the consequences of that failure. Miguel Mendoza wasn't a man you wanted to disappoint under any circumstances, but particularly not when a big payday was involved. Cortez didn't know all the details, but he definitely knew that the guy in the back seat was worth lots of money to someone. But not if he died.

Driving with one hand, Cortez torched a cigarette

and puffed away, squinting through the blue-gray smoke at the road ahead. As it was, the guy was going to be pissed off at him. After all, the simple snatch-and-grab had turned into a bloodbath with at least two downed cops, a handful of his own guys dead or missing and perhaps even some wounded civilians. So Cortez had no delusions about the warmth of the welcome he'd receive when he returned to Mexico.

Glancing into the back seat, he eyed the guy again and shook his head.

"Easy, gringo," he called over his shoulder. His English was nearly flawless from years of studying criminal justice at UCLA before returning to his homeland. "We'll fix you up real good. You're our little cash cow."

Two minutes later he pulled onto the side of the road, parked it and exited. Taking out his cellular telephone, he hit the redial button. When the verbal prompt came, he hit three more buttons and terminated the call, tossing the phone back inside the car.

Grabbing the big man under the shoulders, he dragged him from the back of the vehicle, pulled him about thirty yards from it and laid him out flat on the dirt and sparse grass. Moments later a pair of helicopters crested a nearby mountain peak and knifed toward him. The crew worked quickly, strapping the prisoner onto a stretcher and loading him onto the helicopter. Two more guys, both heavily armed, sprinted for the car.

Mendoza's son, Bernardo, appeared in the door of one of the choppers and gave Cortez a questioning look. He replied with a nod and the younger man hopped from the craft, an olive drab duffel bag in his hand, and strode up to Cortez.

Taking the bag, Cortez ran after the two gunners.

Sliding down a small incline next to the car, he ran to the two men, both of whom gave him a questioning look.

Pulling open the rear passenger's-side door, he stuffed the bag into the space on the floor between the front and back seats.

"More ammunition," he said. "In case you need it. Now go, get out of here."

The driver nodded. Cortez slammed the door and dismissed the two men by banging a fist on the roof of the car, watching as the vehicle backed up, then drove back onto the road and roared away. Grinning, he sprinted for the helicopters and boarded the nearer one.

Moments later, both craft were aloft.

Cortez pulled out a black box that featured several switches.

The Mexican stared at the box for a moment. He realized it was only a matter of time before the police caught up with the Hyundai. Most likely, the pigs would force the vehicle from the road and take the men into custody. He'd like to think his people were dead-enders, that they'd sooner take a bullet than sell him out. Sure, he'd like to think that. But he was a realist. If the police applied the right amount of pressure, his men would give him up in a heartbeat. He knew this because he'd do the same to them, in even less time.

Casually, he flicked a switch and snuffed out both men's lives. Just the first of many to die this day, he thought.

MIGUEL MENDOZA FINISHED his morning swim in his Olympic-size pool. He climbed the ladder out of the deep end, water sluicing off his body. A young maid was on hand, a towel in her hand. He snapped his fingers and she unfurled it and wrapped it around his shoulders.

He strode up from the pool to his terrace. His wife, Rosa, looked up from her newspaper and smiled at him, exposing perfect white teeth. Her wavy hair was pulled back into a ponytail. She wore a long T-shirt over her bikini-clad body as per his instructions, and he was pleased.

"How was your swim?" she asked, still smiling.

"It was fine, my love. Thank you."

He walked past and admired her, like another man might admire a fast car. She was thirty years his junior, and he considered her his most prized possession, something to be trotted out, shown off and appreciated by others. He guessed that that was how others felt about great art, something he'd never developed a taste for. But like other treasures, he knew others wanted her. And he made sure he tucked her safely away, particularly when he wasn't around to watch her.

She chewed on a small piece of grapefruit while he seated himself. He scanned the smooth concrete walls that surrounded the estate and congratulated himself once again on the stronghold he'd created for himself and his family. The maid handed him a short-sleeved cotton shirt and helped him shrug into it. He snatched the newspaper from a second maid's hands and whisked them both away with a wave of his hand.

"Darling," Rosa said, "I want to take the children to town today. We are going shopping. After that I promised them that we'd eat shrimp at the old man's restaurant on the beach."

He nodded. "That's fine. You'll take Carlos and his people with you."

Carlos was his personal security chief and one of the

few men Mendoza trusted to guard his wife. The man was exceedingly loyal to Mendoza, almost as though he were one of his own children. As he spoke, he saw something flicker in the woman's eyes.

She looked down at her plate. "Of course," she said. She speared a grape with her fork, popped it into her mouth and chewed. He felt her unhappiness from across the table. His hands clenched into fists and he slammed one of them down on the table. Dishes jumped from the table and silverware clattered against the china. "What?" he yelled. "What's your problem, woman?"

She looked up at him, her eyes wide with shock, terror. "I have no problem, darling. I swear."

"Is it Carlos?"

She looked down at her plate and shook her head. "No, no."

"What did he do?"

"He did nothing.

"Really, it's not him."

"Then what is it?"

"Please, please. Let's forget I said anything."

His voice dropped into little more than a whisper. When he spoke, he did so through clenched teeth. "Tell. Me. Now."

"I just wanted some time alone. With the children," she said. "Everywhere we go, we have guards. It just makes me self-conscious."

"It keeps you alive, you ungrateful bitch."

She nodded. He saw tears beginning to brim over. He considered letting it go at that. But obviously he needed to teach this little bitch a lesson. She'd either taken leave of her senses or she just didn't appreciate all he did for her. Regardless, the woman needed to be taught a lesson.

He noticed her hand had slipped off the table and she clutched her stomach. "So you never complained before, but now you are. Now, it's a big deal, yes? Suddenly you must complain."

When she spoke again, her voice was barely audible. "Forgive me. I have no right to complain."

"But here you are, feeding me this bullshit. You think this is a bad life? You think I'm giving my children, my babies, a shitty deal, right? I'm a bad Papa to my babies. Is that it?"

He turned and found one of his guards standing in the door leading from their bedroom onto the terrace. "Go get your boss. We'll settle this bullshit once and for all."

Rosa gave him a panicked look. "Miguel?"

He silenced her with a wave of his hand. They waited in tense silence for a couple of minutes. The security chief, dressed in khakis and a starched white shirt, sauntered through the Mendoza's bedroom and onto the terrace. He winked at one of the guards, pointed a finger and smiled at the other one. When Carlos approached the table, he nodded politely at Rosa, but didn't look at her too long. Rather, he turned to face Mendoza.

"You wanted something, sir?" he asked.

Mendoza leaned back in his chair. He laced his fingers together and rested the back of his head in the palms. "Carlos," he said. "I have news."

"News?"

"Yeah, news. I gotta let you go."

Carlos smiled and began to shift on his feet. "Let me go? You're firing me?"

Rosa interjected, "Miguel, no."

His face whipped toward her. "You shut up!" he said. He underscored each word with a jab from his finger. "This is between him and me. Understand?"

"Is there a problem, boss?"

"You've offended my wife. Let's just leave it at that."

Carlos's face tightened with anger. "Ma'am, is this true? I offended you somehow?"

Mendoza came out of his chair and punched Carlos in the stomach. The younger man staggered back, but almost immediately got his footing. He started to bring up his fists in a fighting stance, thought better of it and let them drop to his sides.

Mendoza glanced over his shoulder. He wanted to make sure the others were watching, particularly his wife, who now sat sobbing at the table. He knew they weren't just questioning him, they were questioning his authority, his competency. They wanted to take him down. His wife, this pack of overpaid killers. They were all a bunch of damn savages. They all wanted what he had, and he needed to take them down before they took him.

He turned to the guards at his back. He nodded at Carlos. "Take him out." The guards, both of them armed with Uzis, stared at him for a moment. "What, are you deaf? I said—"

One of the guards suddenly reached out, shoved him out of the way. He hit the ground, his outstretched hands breaking his fall. He heard autofire erupt overhead from the guards' SMGs. Shell casings struck the ground and rolled underneath him. Somewhere in all the noise he heard his wife's screams of terror. A moment later, the shooting had ended. He rolled over onto his rear. Carlos lay facedown on the ground, his back ravaged by bullet exit wounds. His handgun lay on the ground next to him, inches from his outstretched fingers.

Roberto Cardenas, the guard who'd shoved Mendoza to the ground, held out a hand to help him up. Mendoza slapped it away and came to his feet.

"You're the new chief of security," Mendoza said. "Think you can handle it?"

"Sure I do."

"Good, clean up this mess. Then come with me. We've got a special delivery coming from America

"THE OLD MAN'S GONE crazy," Cardenas whispered.

"Crazy?" Emilio Cortez replied, his confusion evident.

"Crazy, man. He just had Carlos killed for no fucking reason."

"What the hell are you saying? Killed him why? When?"

Cardenas lightly gripped Cortez's upper arm to steer him away from the others. He cast a last glance over his shoulder and watched as his team from Colorado unloaded Fox from the small jet they'd used to flee from the States. The big programmer's body was limp thanks to drugs injected into him before they'd loaded him on the plane and returned to Mexico. The guys carrying Fox hauled him over to a black Mercedes, shoved him inside and shut the doors. Each took up a position next to the vehicle, apparently awaiting further orders.

Satisfied, Cortez turned his attention back to Cardenas.

"So, what happened? Why'd the old man have him taken out?"

Cardenas recounted the whole story. When he finished, Cortez slowly shook his head, feeling his stomach knot. He ran a hand over his mouth and swore. "He has lost it. And over some whore."

"It's not her fault," Cardenas said.

Cortez shot him a look and the guy shrank a little bit. "So now you're sticking up for her."

"All I'm saying is, it's not her fault. Mendoza did it, not her. She just asked to go into town without the guards. She wasn't trying to start trouble. She sure as hell didn't want Mendoza to flip out or Carlos to die."

Cortez started to argue the point, thought better of it and clamped his jaw shut. The other man was right. Mendoza's wife wasn't the problem; he was the problem. He'd been losing his grip on reality for months now, becoming increasingly paranoid and irrational with each passing day.

"When's the guy coming?" Cortez asked.

Cardenas checked his watch. "Twenty-five minutes."

Cortez nodded. "Good."

"Yeah, good unless Mendoza loses his cool and blows the deal. Then Jack Mace will turn tail and leave. And he'll take his money with him."

"The hell he will! Mace wanted this Fox guy in the worst way. You think that once he stands within grabbing distance of Fox he's suddenly going to change his mind, turn tail and head back to Africa? All just because Mendoza's a flake? C'mon, man, keep your damn head on straight. This is bigger than a couple of personalities."

"I don't know…"

"You're right. You don't know. So quit worrying about it and leave stuff to me. Now, get the hell out of here and get to work."

When Cortez was alone, he stared skyward. He squinted against the sun's glare but enjoyed the warm rays bathing his skin. He sighed deeply and thought about what had to be done next. Though he still considered himself loyal to Mendoza, his first loyalty lay with himself. In the past several months the old man had become more and more out of touch with reality. Maybe it was the drugs he used. Maybe he was intoxicated with the beauty of the caramel-skinned woman who shared his bed. Cortez didn't know and he didn't care. All he knew was that he'd sacrificed his career, his honor, to serve Mendoza.

Cortez would have to see for himself how far gone Mendoza had become. If he didn't like what he saw, he would take out the bastard. As far as he was concerned, Mendoza had already served his purpose. He'd paid for their trip to the United States, their weapons and equipment and the bribes necessary to snatch Gabriel Fox. And, whatever Cortez's boss failed to supply, Jack Mace had happily filled the gap.

Frankly, Cortez neither liked nor trusted either man. But he dismissed his misgivings with a shrug. He was in it for the massive payday it promised. Other than that, everyone could go to hell.

Cortez slipped inside the house. The air-conditioned atmosphere cooled the sweat that had beaded on his forehead, his neck and the small of his back. He slid off his sunglasses, slipped them into his breast pocket and wound his way through the corridors of the massive house. Occasionally he passed one of Mendoza's gunners and acknowledged the guy with a nod. All the security people knew him and let him pass without incident.

The Mexican knew that Mendoza took his lunch on the terrace, and he likely still would be there. Or he would be about ready to take a siesta. Either way, Cortez wanted to see him, look into his eyes, look into his soul, to see if he was still up to the challenge that lay ahead.

If not, Cortez would have no problem using the Glock 19 that rode at his waist. A couple of well-placed shots and he'd send the guy straight to hell.

Cortez had grown up in Puerto Vallarta, Mexico, one of eight children raised in poverty. His father worked at the docks. Though he broke his back fourteen hours a day unloading ships, he barely made enough to feed his family or to keep the bank from snatching away the hovel they'd called home. His mother was given to long bouts of depression that caused her to stay in bed for days and sometimes weeks, shutters drawn despite the sweltering heat, and weep for hours on end. It was this sort of misery Cortez associated with poverty, and he wanted no part of it.

When he had become old enough, he'd lied about his age and joined the Mexican army. After that, he had become a police officer, and eventually joined an antidrug squad. The endless hours of paramilitary drills and urban combat training had helped hone his killing skills to a keening edge. The work had meant a steady paycheck. But he still supplemented it with bribes offered up by drug lords willing to exchange their money for their lives. In short, he knew how to survive. He'd proved that much when he'd chopped down that damn American in Colorado. And he would do it again as many times as was necessary to get where and what he wanted, which was money and security. Get that, he reasoned, and anything else he could want would follow.

He took the elevator to the second floor, made his way down the corridor until he reached Mendoza's room. He rapped sharply on the door but waited for an invitation to enter. He heard footsteps and moment later, the door opened and he saw one of his men, Garcia, peering at him through the space between the door and the jamb.

"Hey," Garcia said.

Cortez nodded. The door swung open.

Stepping inside, Cortez glanced around the room and found Mendoza seated in a corner. The old man nursed a cigar and a bluish haze hung heavily in the room. Mendoza gave Cortez a wide grin and gestured for the younger man to sit in a chair opposite him. Cortez strode to the chair, dropped into it.

"Welcome back, my friend," Mendoza said. "I trust your mission to Colorado went well? You did a good job for me?"

Cortez seated himself across from the drug lord. He smiled and nodded at the older man. "It went well. The proof's downstairs. You hear anything from Mace?"

"He's coming. It won't be long now."

"Has he transferred the rest of the money yet?"

Mendoza shook his head. "We got a third up front. We get the rest when we hand over the American. You already knew that. What's the problem? You don't trust me now?"

Cortez feigned a surprised look. "Hey, you know better than that. I trust you with my life. It's Mace I've got the issues with. I want to make sure we get what's coming to us."

Mendoza gave him a hard look. "You heard something?"

"No," Cortez replied, shaking his head. "Just my gut talking. Something tells me this SOB will stick us. I'll feel better when we're rid of him, that's all I'm saying. I don't want him to put one over on you."

"You let me deal with Mace."

"Sure. I was just giving you something to think about."

Mendoza cut him off with a gesture. "I don't need it. This is all under control. My control."

"Sure. I'm just saying this scientist is the most important thing. If I were you, I'd focus on getting the money."

The drug lord smacked an open palm against the table and it caused a thunderous noise. "I got it, damn it! I got it! You understand me?"

Feigning surprise, Cortez held up his hands, palms facing outward in a calming gesture. "Sure. I got it."

"Any problem with the snatch?"

"We took out at least one police officer and left two others for dead. We killed some bystanders, too. What can I say? They were in the wrong place at the wrong time."

"It will put them on our trail."

"You think they weren't going to follow us otherwise? What, we were going to kidnap a guy in broad daylight and the police wouldn't investigate?"

Mendoza's eyes narrowed and he leaned forward in his chair. "You should've paid some people off. That's what I'm saying."

"With all due respect, that was risky, too. The more folks we bribe, the more there are to sell us out. This was supposed to be a quick strike. In and out. It went bad."

Mendoza's nostrils flared and his fists clenched until the knuckles whitened. Cortez felt adrenaline spike through his system. The muscles in his neck, shoulders and legs tensed as he prepared to launch himself at Mendoza.

Before either man could act, the door opened and a small man dressed in a well-tailored blue suit stepped inside. "Mace is here," he said.

Mendoza stood and two men helped him shrug into his jacket. He stared down at Cortez who waited for him to speak his piece.

"I want you to stay here," he said.

"What?"

"You don't trust this guy? Fine. But I don't want you out there asking questions and pissing him off. You stay here."

"Damn it—"

"Stay!"

Cortez threw up his hands and looked away from Mendoza. The drug lord smiled and, flanked by his security entourage, left the room.

Reaching into his pocket, Cortez touched a business-card-size CD that lay inside and smiled. The CD contained a copy of the Cold Earth worm that he had found hidden within the seams of the American's coat. Cortez had known for months that his partnership with Mendoza was fragile, primarily because of the fragility of Mendoza's mind. When he'd found the small CD during the return trip to Mexico, Cortez had known instantly that he had found a way to profitably end the partnership.

CHAPTER SIX

Denver, Colorado

The wait seemed to last forever.

Lyons and Blancanales sat in the hospital waiting room. Lyons, his face scarlet with anger, tapped his foot to some unheard manic beat and stared at the double doors leading into the critical care unit. Blancanales drummed his fingers on the arm of his chair as both men waited for information regarding their wounded comrade.

"That black-coated son of a bitch is mine," Lyons said.

"Stand in line," Blancanales replied. Lyons gave him a look that told him he was willing to do anything but that.

"Did the Farm get anything on him yet?"

"Negative," Blancanales said. "They're running all the usual traps. They found the abandoned car, or what was left of it, anyway, on the outskirts of town. Got a forensics team checking it out. And we do have some satellite photos that the cyberteam is running through its databases. Aaron said they look to have some positive ID within the hour."

"Good. He doing okay? About Gabe, I mean?"

Blancanales shrugged. "As well as can be expected. He's kicking the shit out of himself because he couldn't do anything to help."

"That isn't right. I ought to kick his ass for even thinking that way. No one expected him to do any ground fighting. He was just there to make the contact."

"Sure, but that isn't how he sees it. He feels responsible for this kid and seems to think he should've done more. And I guess if I was in his situation, I'd feel the same damn way."

Lyons grunted. "Maybe. But that doesn't make it right."

Blancanales smiled at his friend, who continued staring at the doors. "Anyway, maybe Jack can give Aaron a pep talk. You know, snap him out of it," Blancanales said.

Lyons grunted once more and the two men fell silent.

Blancanales had just downed a Coke and some peanuts when a doctor stepped through the doors. She was petite, with blond hair and the golden tan of someone who spent a lot of time outdoors. A white lab coat covered her surgical scrubs and she clutched a clipboard to her chest. Letting the door swing shut behind her, she swept her eyes over the room and searched for the Stony Man commandos.

Blancanales uncoiled from his chair and met her halfway across the room, Lyons right behind him. The three exchanged brief introductions and handshakes. Using a right forefinger, the woman pushed her wire-rimmed glasses off the bridge of her nose and studied the chart in her left hand.

"Your friend's been through a lot," she said. "One slug penetrated his abdomen, but fortunately missed his vital organs. Another bullet cracked two ribs. One of the ribs struck a lung and bruised it. If you hadn't gotten him in here when you did, he could have died within hours."

Blancanales's hands bunched into fists. He squeezed them tight as rage coursed through his body, a malignant force that seemed to overtake him. He hoped that Kurtzman and the cyberteam had been able to track down information on the shooter. He'd known Schwarz nearly his entire adult life. The two guys, along with Lyons, were fellow warriors, brothers in blood. And Blancanales vowed at that moment to extract some payback from the guy responsible for nearly killing his oldest friend. A glance at the man standing next to him told Blancanales that his friend was likewise ready to unleash a torrent of hell on the man responsible for this.

"Can we see him?" Blancanales asked.

"I can take you back there for a couple of minutes. But no longer. Like I said, he's been through a lot, and he needs his rest."

"Understood," Lyons said. Blancanales nodded in agreement.

When they reached the unit, Lyons bulled his way through a pair of curtains that led into Schwarz's room. Blancanales saw his friend stiffen, his jaw clench. An instant later he saw why. Schwarz lay on the bed, pale, unconscious. A ventilator tube wound from his mouth, held in place by medical tape. IV tubes snaked down from liquid-filled plastic bags before biting into the flesh of his arms. A heart monitor was clamped over his index finger and an occasional beep sounded as the monitor did its work. Blancanales swallowed hard.

"He unconscious?" the warrior asked.

The doctor nodded. "We had to sedate him heavily to keep him from rejecting the ventilator tube."

"He looks like hell," Lyons said.

"He'll be okay," the doctor replied. "Now that we've found the problem, he just needs time to recuperate."

The doctor excused herself. Lyons and Blancanales stood at their friend's bedside. Both men remained quiet, their eyes focused on Schwarz, for a full two minutes.

Lyons, his face a mask of rage, turned to Blancanales. "The guy who did this." A cold rage, barely restrained, was audible in his voice. He paused as he searched for the right words. "When we find him, it isn't going to be pretty."

Blancanales nodded. "No, it won't."

"This is going to cost the bastard. We're talking serious payback."

"In spades, amigo."

"We watch out for each other, right?"

"Damn straight."

CHAPTER SEVEN

"Just think. Within days, we could have it. And it would give us the power necessary to get revenge on the United States for daring to desecrate our lands with its troops. It's a like a gift from almighty God Himself."

"Perhaps," Ahmed Quissad said, unimpressed.

The former Iraqi soldier stood and crossed the room with long strides until he reached a pane of one-way glass. Stretching the length of one wall, the glass looked down upon a crowded nightclub located in one of Prague's busier tourist districts. Quissad watched as men and women danced, drank and caroused. He found himself alternately fascinated and disgusted by their behavior, grinding against one another, sweating like animals, succumbing to decadent abandon. Though muffled by layers of soundproofing, Quissad still heard the thumping of industrial dance music as it reverberated through the nightclub below.

Animals and nothing more, he thought. Reflected in the glass, he saw his lieutenant—Tariq Khan—standing behind him, staring at his back. Apparently the little man wanted a reply. Quissad waited, knowing that the heavy silence, and the man's sickening need for praise, would cause him to become restless.

"It is good news, yes?"

Quissad took a drag from his cigarette, shrugged. "Perhaps. What does our friend want for this piece of technology?"

"It's a disk, one containing a virulent program—"

"Yes, yes. We've been over that before," Quissad said. "Answer my question. What does our newfound friend want for his discovery?"

"One hundred million—U.S. dollars."

Quissad turned and pinned the other man under his gaze. "One hundred million? For a diskette the size of a business card? Surely you must be joking."

Khan shook his head. "Not at all. And, with all due respect, I think it's a bargain."

"And I think you're very generous with my money."

"It will sell for five times that much. Perhaps more."

Quissad shrugged again, turned back to the one-way window. He watched the club patrons as they continued their rapturous gyrations on the dance floor. "You have a buyer?"

"Yes. And I can get us more, if you'd like."

"I'd like."

Khan straightened his posture, smiled. "Consider it done." He backed away to the door.

Quissad watched his reflection in the glass, but didn't turn and directly acknowledge his departure. He'd learned a long time ago that ignoring others only made them want to please you more. Khan, a former intelligence officer with Saddam Hussein's government, was no exception. Though he boasted an impressive array of underworld contacts and provided invaluable information almost daily, his need to please drained Quissad.

Quissad made sure those working for him got very little in the way of acknowledgment. If he'd learned anything from the deposed dictator, it was to control others through fear and uncertainty. A man who found himself on uncertain ground had little time to plot against you, not when he was worried about his own fate.

The small man exited, shutting the door softly behind him. Quissad watched the dance floor a few minutes longer. He fixed his gaze on a leggy brunette, her eyes closed, pelvis gyrating in tandem with the pounding rhythms. For a moment his mind toyed with the notion of those same hips grinding hard against his own, accompanied by sweetly satisfied groans filling his ears. He'd seen her in the club twice during the past two weeks and found himself struck by her beauty. She'd made eye contact with him both times, rousing his suspicions. He was, after all, a man on the run. He didn't want to betray himself by involving himself with a strange woman who might also be an undercover agent. No, he'd come much too far to take such chances. Still, she intrigued him in a way he found almost intoxicating. He loved the hunt a great deal, but it was the kill that he lived for.

He made his way to a brown leather sofa and fell heavily into it. His jacket popped open, revealing the SIG-Sauer P-226 holstered in a shoulder rig. He liked the gun, and it made him feel safe. A glance at a bank of monitors on a nearby wall told him that his guards were posted outside his door, ready to stop any interlopers dead in their tracks.

He was secure and alone, and it gave him time to think about how he'd gotten to this point. He'd been a commander with Fedayeen Saddam, the former dictator's elite army, before America had invaded his homeland. During the initial days of the invasion, he'd welcomed the challenge, been all too happy to ply his bloody skills against American soldiers. He'd even taken it a step further, occasionally killing Iraqi citizens and making it appear that they'd died at the hands of Americans. Yes, he'd fought like a man possessed. It wasn't so much a loyalty to Iraq's ruler, or to his homeland. Quissad had just needed the release. He'd spent a good deal of his time feeling like a fighter jet that flew unarmed and in slow, small circles. Lots of deadly capacity, but no chance to unleash it. For him it had been a mind-blowing pleasure as he'd never experienced.

When Baghdad fell, he, like other Iraqi soldiers, had shed his uniform and melted into the background. For months he performed double duty. He supplied his tactical expertise and muscle to the insurgency, while also commanding a small group of kidnappers that stole children from Iraq's upper crust: doctors, lawyers, even his former comrades from the regime.

It had been with great reluctance that Quissad had left the country. Again, his reluctance had had nothing to do with patriotism; he'd simply wanted to spill blood. He'd been born with an unquenchable bloodlust. He knew he could kill. He'd burned, stabbed, shot and otherwise savaged Iraqis and Kurds dozens of times. Each time he'd expected the repetition to rob the experience of its joy. It never did. Rather, his bloodlust continued to return, each time with greater regularity, an unquenchable thirst that cried out with greater volume to be satisfied.

Before the war, he'd always reasoned that all-out combat would provide him with ample bloodshed to slake his thirst. Instead it had only intensified his need until it drove his every action. Now, with the Cold Earth worm and its potential to kill hundreds of thousands, perhaps even millions, he could finally satiate and silence the voices that drove him, prompted his every action and decision.

The very notion of such wholesale destruction caused his mouth to feel dry and hot, his nerves to tingle, and he knew better. Whether the worm was used once or a dozen times to snuff out life, it'd never be enough for him. And the best part was that he'd sell it to someone else and let them take the fall while he took their money.

He swallowed two amphetamine capsules, washed them down with a glass of water, and thought longingly of the joint in the glove compartment of his BMW parked in a garage under the club. Later, he decided. He slipped another cigarette into his mouth. Torching it with an ornate gold lighter, he settled back into the couch and stared up at the ceiling. Things definitely were falling into place for him. Within a few days, he'd be a hell of a lot richer and the world much bloodier. It was almost too good to be true.

CHAPTER EIGHT

The Black Hawk helicopter carrying Able Team skimmed over the trees. The rotor wash beat down on branches below, flattening them or causing them to whip about wildly as the craft closed in on a predetermined landing spot.

Blancanales checked over his weapons and other equipment. A glance around told him that Lyons and Grimaldi were doing likewise. A Drug Enforcement Administration pilot was navigating the craft to their destination. Another DEA agent, James Larkin, rode with the commandos.

A second chopper carrying another team of DEA agents buzzed just behind Able Team's craft. An insertion into Mendoza's home was on the agenda, and Grimaldi's fighting skills were needed with the team being down one person. The DEA had been able to provide the pilot, a former Army soldier who'd flown missions in Iraq, for this particular mission.

Blancanales inventoried his equipment. His lead weapon on the raid was the Colt Commando fitted with an M-203 grenade launcher. He'd kept the Beretta

93-Rs from the Colorado conflict. Like the other men, he was togged in a black combat suit, and carried knives, garrotes and other equipment in the pockets of the suit. A satchel containing smoke, high explosive and CS grenades for the launcher, hung on his hip.

Lyons had just finished loading his Smith & Wesson A-10 automatic shotgun. The weapon was capable of firing 12-gauge shells in single, semiautomatic and automatic modes and was one of the former cop's favorite tools of war. He'd also elected to carry a pair of Israeli Arms Desert Eagle handguns chambered in .357 as well as his ever-present .357 Colt Python. The Desert Eagles hung in thigh holsters while the Colt was holstered at his left armpit. His web gear bristled with grenades and a combat knife was sheathed on his right pectoral, hilt pointing downward.

Grimaldi, who'd also selected the Desert Eagles, had chosen a Heckler & Koch MP-5 with a sound suppressor. The ace pilot slammed a magazine home into the short weapon, set it aside and eyed his comrades.

"Judging by all this firepower we're carrying, I assume we just came to talk," he said.

"Talk all you want," Lyons said. "Right after we put some holes in them."

Grimaldi laughed. "Tact, Carl. You ooze tact."

Minutes later the helicopter landed in a clearing situated about a quarter mile from Mendoza's estate. The doors slid back and Grimaldi and the members of Able Team disembarked from the craft. A second team of DEA agents, all togged in black SWAT uniforms disgorged from the second chopper. Two of the DEA agents busied themselves setting up a satellite dish that would allow Able Team, the DEA team and the Farm to speak to one another via headsets. A pair of female agents slipped into the nearby woods to check the perimeter for any unwanted surveillance by Mendoza's heavies.

The Stony Man warriors silently completed final checks on their weapons and equipment. They and the federal agents carried D-DACT handheld computers outfitted with wireless modems and GPS capabilities. In addition, Lyons, as team leader, carried a shock-resistant laptop encased in magnesium alloy and capable of stopping a bullet. Though he hated to add the extra eight pounds of weight, he wanted the Farm to be able to send him the latest satellite photos of the compound. The laptop also allowed him to send encrypted e-mails directly to the Farm.

And if it took a bullet on his behalf, who the hell was he to complain?

SOMETHING WAS WRONG.

Lyons couldn't shake the feeling as he pushed his way through the foliage that surrounded the estate's south quadrant. He'd gotten within three hundred yards of the security wall ringing the massive compound. Yet he hadn't encountered a single guard. It just made no damn sense. Like his comrades, Lyons always planned for the worst. He didn't do it just because he was a dyed-in-the-wool cynic, but also because it was a law of combat. Always expect the unexpected.

But here he was, standing within spitting distance of a well-heeled drug lord's walled compound, and no one had tried to stop him. He readjusted his grip on the Smith & Wesson shotgun and continued moving through the foliage, covering another twenty or so yards. Suddenly he felt the hairs on the back of his neck stand up and his breathing became shallow. Something or someone was out there, he thought. He couldn't see it, but he could feel it. Dropping into a crouch, his body partially hidden by the trunk of a large palm tree, he swept his eyes over his surroundings, searching for possible threats. He listened for snapping branches, the brush of tall grass against a boot or a pant leg, or other telltale sounds of a sneak attack. A heartbeat later a pungent, cloying odor registered with him, one he instantly recognized as the smell of death. More specifically, a corpse exposed to the heat and humidity of coastal Mexico's climate.

Rising slowly from the ground, he took a few more steps toward the other stand of trees. A creaking, like a porch swing suspended by rusted chains swaying in the wind, reached his ears. He halted and dropped into a crouch, listening for several more heartbeats until he confirmed that the steady sound was emanating from the thick stand of trees located to his left. As he moved closer, the creaking continued, almost, but not quite drowning out a chorus of squeaking and scratching noises that originated from the same spot. The smell also grew stronger and he felt his stomach roll.

Swallowing hard, Lyons moved into the trees, the A-10 shotgun held at waist level and set for full automatic fire. He spotted an M-16 lying on the ground several yards ahead at the base of a tree. Taking another step or two forward, he spotted what he was sure was a hand, fingers curled, knuckles pointed toward the ground. He guessed that the hand was positioned ten feet or so above the ground.

With his shotgun leading the way, Lyons crept up to the tree, rounded its trunk and looked upward. When he saw it, he swallowed hard and stared at the horror in front of him.

A man, or at least what had once been a man, hung suspended from a tree limb, eyes and mouth hanging wide open, flies gathering in both places. One end of a rope was looped around his ankles, the other end hooked over the top of the tree. A pack of rats covered his torso, their gathered bodies undulating like a single gray mass while dozens of sharp teeth rent flesh from bone. The fabric of the man's white shirt, the tail of which had gapped around his armpits, was soaked in blood. More blood had soaked the dirt beneath the man, transforming it into a black mud.

"Shit," Lyons muttered under his breath. Next to the M-16 lay a pistol belt, also smeared with the man's life fluids. Lyons guessed that the guy was one of Mendoza's guards. If he'd been an intruder, it was more likely that Mendoza's people would have taken him inside for interrogation before killing him and disposing of the body miles away from the drug dealer's estate. Even though Mendoza probably had friends in high places, he likely wouldn't want to antagonize the local police by decorating his trees with corpses.

Lyons keyed his headset. "We've got problems," he said. "Big fucking problems."

"What's wrong?" Blancanales asked.

"I've got a dead guy here," Lyons replied. "I think he's a guard, but I don't know that for sure."

"Someone got here before us?"

"I'd damn near bet on it. That means someone else knew that Fox and the Cold Earth worm were being brought here. And that same third party might have gotten their grimy mitts on both those things before we could."

"I'm no strategic genius," Grimaldi said, "but I think that means we're screwed."

"Nice analysis," Lyons replied.

SEVERAL MINUTES LATER Lyons had made it to the sheer concrete wall that surrounded the compound. From inside his gear bag, he extracted a length of rope tipped with a grappling hook. With a toss, he hooked the rope over the wall's edge, tested it with a quick yank and began to climb the barrier.

Blancanales, Grimaldi and he had spent the past several minutes scouring the perimeter for more guards, either living or dead, and had found seven. Lyons had called back to the DEA crew and put them on standby. He'd also contacted the Farm and asked for any more up-to-date intelligence to be fed to them via satellite. The cyberteam had downloaded fresh satellite images to the laptop. Lyons had looked at them, but had found nothing, no moving people or vehicles.

Price was working her contacts at the NSA and other intelligence agencies to get more satellite photos. Lyons had waited as long as he could. But impatience had seized him. So he'd given the order to hit the compound.

When he reached the top of the wall, he levered himself up until he could see into the compound. The estate, filled with curving driveways and walking paths made of ornate brickwork, remained empty.

At least what he could see from his limited vantage point, it was empty. He brought himself onto the ledge, lying flat to create as small of a silhouette as possible while he gathered the rope from the ground. Sliding off the wall, he suspended himself for a moment by his fingertips, let himself fall to the earth. As his feet struck the ground, he coiled his knees to absorb the impact. He fisted the Desert Eagle and scanned his surroundings. Three cars—two Toyota sport utility vehicles and a white Lexus—stood in the driveway outside the home.

Lyons trotted award a windowless brick building. He

cautiously circled the perimeter until he finally found an opening. The heavy steel door that led into the building was ajar. An appraising look told Lyons that it had been blown inward by a carefully placed explosive charge of some sort. A dozen or so spent shell casings littered the ground in front of the building.

In spite of himself, he felt his heart begin to hammer in his chest and he tightened his grip on the Desert Eagle. Bulling his way through the doorway, the pistol extended in front of him, Lyons surged into the building, ready to put up one hell of a fight.

Instead he found only more carnage.

Two hardmen lay dead. One lay facedown in the middle of the concrete slab floor, a pool of blood spreading from beneath the body. His weapon lay several inches from his dead fingers. A second gunman lay balled up in a corner. The wall behind the corpse was pocked by a dozen or so bullet holes and stained by splattered blood. More spent brass was spread over the floor. Lyons stepped carefully to avoid it, not wanting to kick a shell casing and announce his presence in the building. He guessed the place was empty of any living humans, but he didn't want to chance it.

Blancanales's voice buzzed in his ear. "You got anything?"

"Yeah," Lyons whispered. He briefly told Blancanales about finding what appeared to be an empty prison as well as the dead guards.

"What about you?" Lyons asked.

"Two more bodies, both stuffed in the back seat of an SUV. The smell damn near knocked me over, and it's only going to get worse in this heat. Gonna play hell on the leather interior. But they definitely aren't fresh kills. Looks like they were waxed execution-style with one shot each to the head. I found the spot on the ground where I think someone did them both. I guess they were put in here as an afterthought."

"Roger that. Give me five minutes and we'll hit the house. See what we can turn up in there."

"Clear."

Lyons finished checking the small building. In the rear, he found three cells, all of them empty. If Fox ever did make it here, he was gone now, the warrior realized.

Exiting the building, Lyons hugged every shadow cast by a tree, automobile or decorative wall that he could find until he reached the main house. He caught no movement in the windows. He considered calling back to the member of the DEA team, asking them to bring forward their thermal-image scanning equipment to see if anyone or anything living was moving through the structure. Suddenly his combat senses tingled, alerting him to danger. Lyons began to turn. Immediately he saw a black blur hurtling toward him, colliding with his midsection with the force of an eighteen-wheeler careering down a steep mountain grade.

The impact knocked him from his feet. An iron hand closed around his wrist. Lyons made a grab for his second weapon even as he hit the ground. His fingers curled around the handgun's butt, and he yanked it free.

His attacker landed hard on his chest, and the Able Team leader's breath exploded through clenched teeth. Though reeling, Lyons planned to end this battle decisively. His hand blurred as he brought around the Desert Eagle. The other man batted the weapon away and drove a fist toward Lyons's face. Jerking his head to one side, the big blond commando felt the fist graze his cheek, though he avoided the punch's full impact.

Lyons brought his free hand around and jabbed the

Desert Eagle's muzzle into the folds of the other man's gut. Understanding dawned almost immediately in the other guy's eyes. He halted and raised his hands. "Get off me," Lyons said through clenched teeth.

The guy got to his feet and backed away from Lyons. It was the first time the former L.A. cop got a good look at his attacker. Lyons guessed that the man stood eye to eye with him. The man had broad shoulders and arms, but a belly that protruded as if he'd swallowed a VW Beetle.

"The wall," Lyons said through clenched teeth. "Up against it."

The guy complied and Lyons patted him down. He found a shoulder holster and spare magazines for a submachine gun, but no weapon. He tossed the magazines aside and continued searching the man. His fingers found something moist and sticky under the man's jacket and along his ribs. The commando pulled back his hand and saw his fingertips stained with blood.

"You took a round?"

"A couple, and I'm bleeding like a damn stuck pig," he replied in heavily accented English. "Otherwise I would have killed your gringo ass. You'd already be dead."

"I'll try to contain my terror," Lyons said. "On your knees, tough guy."

The man went to his knees, and Lyons cuffed him with dual-ring plastic restraints. By now the Able Team leader's breathing had returned to normal and he noticed a small buzzing noise. Reflexively he touched his ear and realized his headpiece had fallen off during the struggle. Retrieving it, he slipped it back in time to catch Blancanales whispering his name.

"What?" Lyons replied.

"Jeez, where the hell you been? I've been trying to raise you."

"I ran into somebody."

Relief crept into Blancanales's voice. "Friend or foe?"

"Let's just say he's seeing things my way."

"I'm coming around the house," Blancanales said. "I started over here when I lost contact with you."

A few seconds later Blancanales came around the corner of the imposing home, the stock of his Colt Commando held snug against his shoulder. If Lyons hadn't known he was coming, he'd never have heard his friend's stealthy approach. Blancanales sized up Lyons prisoner and asked, "Who's your friend?"

Lyons gave the guy a sharp jab to the shoulder. "He asked you a question."

"Ernesto," the man replied. "Ernesto Chavez."

"You one of the guards here, Ernesto?" Blancanales asked.

The guy nodded. "Only one left."

"The others?"

The man shrugged. "Dead. Hell, I should be dead. If my Uzi hadn't taken a bullet for me, I *would* be dead."

"You still look pretty bloody," Blancanales said.

"Bullet grazed my skull. I took another through the ribs. Speaking of which, you guys going to get me to a doctor or what? I'm bleeding here."

"Maybe," Lyons replied. "If you give us a reason to. Otherwise I'm inclined to save the doctor a trip. I'm not feeling too charitable today."

The guy gave Lyons a hard look, though it seemed somehow pitiful with his face covered in blood and his big torso wavering. Lyons attributed the man's unsteadiness to weakness brought on by blood loss.

"Shit," the guy said, "ask your damn questions. I got nothing to lose at this point."

"How many more of your buddies are still alive and kicking?"

The guy shook his head. "None as far as I know. I've been through this place once and haven't found anyone who's still alive. Every man, woman and child slaughtered like cattle, as far as I can tell."

"Who's responsible?" Blancanales asked.

"Guy named Jack Mace. You ever heard of him?"

"No," Blancanales said.

"From what some of the guys told me, he's an arms buyer. He usually operates off the continent, but we had such good merchandise, he decided to drag his ass here, pay us a visit."

"Merchandise being the American," Lyons said.

"Yeah, that big goofy gringo. He looks like a dumbass, if you ask me. But Cortez swore he was smart as hell. He must be for Mace to be willing to come in here and start slaughtering everybody."

"What happened?" Blancanales asked. "How'd it go down?"

"Went down like fucking clockwork is how it went down," the guy replied, a grim smile playing over his lips. "Mace and his people landed their helicopter here, just like they said they would. What we didn't know was, his heavies shortly before that began nailing our perimeter guards. When it all hit the fan, we were missing about a dozen of our best people."

"We found them," Blancanales said.

Chavez's eyes narrowed and the right corner of his mouth curled up in a sneer. "Sure it warmed your hearts, too, you pigs. Who you with anyway? DEA? FBI? CIA?"

"Let us ask the questions," Blancanales said. "No sense in you wasting what little energy you have asking us questions that we won't answer. What happened after that?"

"You're a smug bastard, aren't you? Ah, fuck it. What have I got to lose? Mendoza was making nice to our visitor. You know, introducing him to the wife and kids, showing him the estate. We're sitting around with Mace's people and it's real tense, like nobody's talking or nothing. Suddenly one of the guy's cellular phone rings, he whips out a gun and opens fire. Suddenly we're in the fight of our lives and we don't even know for sure what the hell's happening. All I know is that son of a bitch Mace set the old man up. Set him up so he could knock him down."

"I'm overwrought with pity," Blancanales said.

Chavez whipped his head toward him. His face was a mask of rage. "Look, the old man had a wife, two kids. They all took a bullet. I saw the whole thing happen. I've killed a few folks in my time, but never a bitch and her kids. You know what I'm saying? And I couldn't do jack. I'd just taken one to the head and couldn't even focus very well."

Lyons cut the man off. "What about Cortez? What happened to him?"

"Hell if I know. One minute he's getting his ass chewed by the boss. Next minute we're taking fire and that son of a bitch is nowhere to be seen."

"That's awful," Lyons said. "Who can you trust these days?"

"Fuck you, pig."

"Where do you think he went?" Blancanales asked.

"Hard to tell. Hey, look man, I'm starting to feel shaky. How about you do something for this bleeding, and I'll tell you everything I know?"

"No deal," Lyons said. "Talk."

"Son of a whore. Fine. My boss is dead and that little bastard ran out on us, so screw him, right? Here's what I know. Cortez has a contact here in Puerto Vallarta, an American just like you two. 'Cept he's not as big an asshole. Name's Tony Drake. He showed up in town about five years ago, opened a little seafood grill on the beach. Spends most of his time drinking bar, screwing the local women and jabbering on his cell phone."

"Sounds pretty harmless," Blancanales said.

"Looks it, too," Chavez said. "But don't you believe it. That bastard would cut you open just as soon as look at you."

"What's the book on him? I mean, what's his background?"

"That's just it. Guy has no background. His background started five years ago. He just appeared with a bunch of cash and started asking a lot of strange questions. You know, like who's got the juice in around here? Who are the players? Mendoza immediately figures him for DEA or something."

"But he wasn't," Blancanales said.

"Hell, no. He was just some guy, you know? Some guy dropping cash like it was nothing. He treats Mendoza like a damn king, dropping the bucks on him, kissing his ass. And Mendoza, the old sucker, he loved it. Anything he wanted, Drake could make appear. You want shoulder-fired missiles? Bam, he'd get them by the crate. Assault weapons? We got three boxes of CAR-15s straight from the U.S. military. One time, he said he could get us enriched uranium if we wanted it. I thought he was bullshitting. Mendoza swore he wasn't."

"Did Mendoza take him up on it?"

Chavez uttered a bitter laugh that quickly degener-ated into coughing. "You kidding, man? Mendoza, he was scared to death of the stuff. Thought it'd make his pecker fall off or some such crap. I don't know. Hell, he was a drug dealer, that's all."

"Which is why he wanted the weapons," Blanca-nales said, his tone doubtful.

"Look, he bought weapons, sure, but he did it for de-fense. And occasionally he'd give something to a cli-ent, you know, as a gift. Or give it to the local cops. But he didn't mean nothing by it. He wasn't a damn gun-runner, not on a big scale, anyway. He knew if he started poking his nose in there, he'd have everyone down on his neck."

"So he stuck to his core competencies," Blancanales said.

"I don't even know what that means."

"So if he just deals in drugs, how did he get mixed up with Mace and the Cold Earth worm?"

"It was just more money than he could walk away from," Chavez replied. "Those guys came around here, started slinging their crap about making hundreds of millions of dollars, maybe a billion dollars. You know, shit like that. Mendoza couldn't say no. Who could? So he agrees to be the go-between. Cortez steals the thing for Mendoza who then sells it to Mace. Everybody walks away with some money in their pocket."

"I don't suppose it occurred to him that thousands of people could die because this thing ended up in the wrong hands," Lyons said, his face flushed with anger. "Or occurred to you for that matter."

"Spare me your morality speeches, man. I don't

make the damn decisions around here. I just take orders."

"Right," Lyons replied.

Blancanales reached into one of the pockets of his blacksuit and extracted a pair of wound dressings. He knelt next to Chavez, applied the dressings to the man's wounds and secured them with tape. Grabbing him by the collar, he dragged the guy out of the sunlight and let him sit. "Rest up," Blancanales said. "I'm sure the DEA folks are going to want to have a nice, long heart-to-heart with you."

Chavez said nothing, but instead rested his head against a downspout and shut his eyes.

Lyons and the others continued to search the grounds for clues. Inside the house, Lyons found one of Mendoza's children, a boy no older than four years old, lying dead on the floor in a pool of his own blood, his eyes frozen open. Lyons knelt next to the child, and with his thumb and forefinger shut his unseeing eyes.

CHAPTER NINE

Akira Tokaido drummed his fingers on his desk in time with the fuzzed-up heavy metal tune blaring through the earbuds of his MP3 player. A red light on his telephone flashed, alerting him that a call was coming through. He peeled away the earbuds and looped them around his neck. Slipping on a telephone headset, he picked up the receiver and set it on his desk next to the telephone.

"Hello?"

"It's Ironman. I need you to run a name," Lyons said.

"Shoot, and here I thought you were calling 'cause you missed me," the young Japanese-American said.

"Thanks, kid, but I already have a metric ton of wiseasses here. I don't need to start importing them."

Tokaido chuckled. "What's the name?"

"Tony Drake. According to our source, Drake appeared out of nowhere. Chances are it's an alias."

"Probably. It sounds pretty common, too. I'll probably find a thousand of them at least. You got anything else on him?"

"He owns a beachfront grill down here in Puerto Vallarta. He's been living here for about five years."

"You got a physical?" Tokaido asked.

Lyons shared the physical description they'd gotten from Chavez before he'd passed out. "Here's a tip. Check to see if the guy is former or current CIA."

"You think he might have gone rogue?"

"I don't know what to think. Just check it out."

"Give me twenty."

"Make it fifteen. We're on our way to see him, and I want to know everything I can about him."

"No promises, but I'll do my best. What else?"

"Get us something on a gunrunner and mercenary named Jack Mace. I have even less information about him than I do our other guy."

"I'll work my magic."

"The big guy there?"

"Hal? Yeah. Hang on."

Tokaido turned to his boss, Hal Brognola, director of the Justice Department's Sensitive Operations Group, who was at the coffeemaker, filling his foam cup with steaming coffee. "Boss," Tokaido said, "Ironman wants to speak to you."

"Switch it to the speakers," Brognola said.

The big Fed returned the coffee carafe to the burner and legged it over to his chair. Seating himself, he plucked a chewed stogie from his mouth, stuck it in the breast pocket of his dress shirt and took a swig of the coffee.

"Hal?" Lyons asked.

"Go," Brognola said.

"What's the word on Gadgets?"

"He's okay. Resting comfortably. We sent a team of blacksuits to guard his room just in case. Doctor says he's out of danger."

"That's good news, anyway," Lyons said, sounding relieved.

"Agreed. Hopefully he'll be back in fighting form sooner rather than later. Now what did you folks find down there?"

Lyons brought him up to date on the massacre at the estate and that someone had taken off with Gabriel Fox.

Brognola heaved a sigh. "The Man's going to use my rear for a chew toy when he hears this," he said. "Ah, to hell with it. What do you make of it?"

"Seems like a typical double cross. This Mace guy let Cortez and Mendoza do all the heavy lifting, shoulder all the risk. Then he swoops in afterward, kills everyone and takes off with the prize."

"And we're sure Cortez went with him?"

"No," Lyons said. "But we're pretty damn sure he's still up and kicking. We didn't find his body anywhere. And our informant here swears he walked away from all this. So we need to find him. That's why I asked Akira to track down this Drake guy. He seems like our best lead, at least until we can find out more about our mysterious buyer, Jack Mace."

"Understood," Brognola said. "What do you need on our end? We can activate Phoenix Force."

"I don't think we need them in the field," Lyons said. "But you might want to put them on standby. We have no idea where these guys went. So we might need to dispatch teams to more than one location."

"I'll get them rolling. If you need them, let me know."

"Roger that," Lyons said.

"I don't mind telling you we're getting some pressure from the Man," Brognola said. "He's worried about this, worried about the pace and our direction."

"How so?"

"While you guys were in transit, I gave him an impromptu update via telephone, just something to let him know we're on the case. Since there were others on the line, I didn't identify Stony Man or any of you guys by name. But his advisers are second-guessing the hell out of us, questioning whether pursuing Cortez is the right move."

"They have a Plan B?"

"Hell, no. Otherwise you'd already be implementing it, if I thought it was any damn good."

"So tell the suits to piss in someone else's pool then."

"Don't worry, I already did, in a manner of speaking, anyway. But the President was clear. If we don't produce some results, he's going to throw more bodies at it. He might let the Company and the FBI move out of a supportive role and into something more aggressive."

"That's all we need," Lyons said, his voice rising in volume. "Look, don't get me wrong, those guys are good. But the last thing we need is an army of federal agents crowding the front lines on this thing. If everyone starts busting down doors and does it without coordinating, we're either going to drive these bastards underground or someone's accidentally going to get killed because they can't tell friend from foe."

"Understood," Brognola said." I told the Man the same thing. He agrees, and he's always played it straight with me. But he's worried as hell and rightfully so. After all, if Cold Earth goes live, then we could have multiple meltdowns of nuclear power plants all over the world. It'd be a damned nightmare.

"And he'd consider himself responsible. So would a lot of other people. After all, our government created this little nightmare, and we let it get out of hand. We'd be culpable for the outcome. He just wants to make sure that rescuing Gabe Fox and recovering Cold Earth remain our top priority. But his private army of bureaucrats is worried that we'll get so hot to take down Cortez that we'll lose sight of the bigger picture."

"I still think it's crap, Hal. You know where our priorities are, even if this bastard shot our guy."

"Sure, and so does the President. You're in the clear with him and me. But we have no margin for error on this thing. And here's one more thing to chew on."

"Can't wait," Lyons said.

"We're starting to get some murmurings from within the intelligence community about the Cold Earth worm being in play."

"What?"

"Somehow the safehouse attack in Colorado has been leaked to a couple of foreign intelligence services. I'm guessing that a double agent in the Company sold the info, but it's hard to know for sure. The only thing I do know is that it didn't come from here."

"Almost goes without saying."

"Almost, though I'm sure someone in Wonderland is going to start pointing fingers at the first possible opportunity. But that's not the point. What I'm saying is, now you can expect to encounter some competition as you wade into this thing. I know for a fact that Mossad and Britain both have word of this."

"They going to play it cool?"

Brognola sighed loudly. His temples were starting to pound as he considered just how complicated things were getting.

"That's the party line," he replied. "But whether that actually happens, we'll just have to wait and see. Frankly, I'm not confident. I mean if the roles were reversed, I can guarantee we wouldn't sit here on our thumbs waiting for Mossad or British intelligence to solve the problem."

"True enough. So I guess we just need to keep our eyes peeled. I assume that if these people try to engage us, we have the authority to ram it back down their throats."

"If it comes to that," Brognola said.

A heavy silence hung between the two men. Brognola fished in his pants' pocket for a roll of antacids. Peeling away the foil wrapper with his thumbnail, he dropped a couple into his palm, then popped them into his mouth. He washed down the chalky tablets with some coffee.

Tokaido, who'd been typing furiously at his computer, let out a war whoop and pumped his fist in the air.

"What the hell was that?" Lyons asked.

"I got your information, Ironman," Tokaido said. "And I did it in five minutes. Who's your daddy now?"

Lyons's voice boomed from the speaker. "Good Lord, kid, what do you want, a hug? Give it up."

Tokaido winked at Brognola, who grinned in spite of himself at the young man's exuberance.

"Your friend Drake's former CIA. He worked with the Directorate of Operations. According to his file, he was trained in paramilitary stuff, but spent most of his time as a spy recruiter. He did a lot of work in Mexico and Central America. First, he was a cold warrior. When that came to an end, he participated in the CIA's drug-interdiction work. That's where he first met our boy Cortez."

"So Drake knew Cortez long before he mysteriously appeared in Puerto Vallarta," Lyons said.

"I'm still piecing it together," Tokaido stated. "But

from what I can tell, he and Cortez go back longer than five years. They worked together on drug-interdiction projects during the 1990s. Maybe he turned Cortez into a double agent. Regardless, according to what I found, whenever someone in the Mexican government was working at cross purposes with our goals in the drug wars, Cortez would pass the info along to Drake. Drake would then turn around and wax whoever it was who was taking money off the dealers. He killed at least a dozen crooked cops during a two-year period."

"So far," Lyons said, "I kind of like the guy."

His fingers flying across the keyboard, Tokaido smiled. "Figures. But I don't think he's a good drinking buddy for you. From what I gather he's been selling weapons to anyone who'll buy them. He's got contacts with al Qaeda, Hamas and Hezbollah, and he's been selling these people weapons either for cash or drugs. I guess that was his connection with Mendoza. Drake would get drugs for guns and munitions, and Mendoza then would turn the drugs into cash for him."

"You're right. I don't like the guy."

"I figured as much. From what I've gathered so far, he still kept in contact with his old cronies at the Agency. I'm still compiling a list of names, but my guess is that that's how he knew about Gabe Fox and the Cold Earth worm. It was just something he couldn't pass by. Here's the kicker, though. The guy has no real money to speak of. The CIA's been watching him for a while, and it lists several accounts under his name. But none of them has more than a few thousand dollars in it. He does own other places besides the grill, by the way. I'll e-mail a list to your laptop."

"Maybe he's stuffing the money away somewhere else," Lyons said. "You figure that, if he starts having

CHAPTER TEN

Drake's seaside grill consisted of a flat-roofed brick building, a bar and a few tables and chairs situated on a patch of concrete. The Stony Man commandos, clad in civilian clothes they'd stored in the DEA helicopter, reached the grill about an hour after their call to Stony Man Farm. They'd left their submachine guns hidden in the rear of an SUV they'd stolen from Mendoza's estate. Instead, they came armed with handguns and fake credentials identifying them as Justice Department agents.

Lyons and Grimaldi arrived first. They set up camp at a table on the patio and ordered beers. About fifteen minutes later, Blancanales came on the scene. Grinning and humming, he walked to the bar and summoned the bartender, a shapely Hispanic woman dressed in cut-off shorts and a white tank top that accentuated her light brown complexion.

His eyes hidden behind mirrored shades, Blancanales surreptitiously took in his surroundings. Aside from his fellow warriors, he saw a pair of Mexicans, one built like a grizzly bear, the other slim but formidable-looking. The pair sat at a table nursing drinks. They scrutinized the new arrivals like hungry lions eyeing a lame zebra. Politician noticed the bigger man giving him a pointed look. Smiling, the warrior made a gun out of his right hand and shot at the guy. The right corner of the man's lip curled up in a snarl, but he turned back to his drink.

As the woman made her way to him, Blancanales leaned sideways against the bar and stared off toward the ocean. The bartender wiped clean the stretch of bar in front of Blancanales with a towel and gave him a smile, friendly but not flirtatious. She placed a paper cocktail napkin in front of him. "What can I get you?" she asked.

"Tecate. No glass. And some limes."

A couple of minutes later she returned with the beer and limes.

"Anything else?"

Turning to face her, Blancanales pinned her under his gaze. "Tony Drake," he said.

Apprehension flickered in her eyes, but didn't stay. She gave him another smile, her lips parting slightly to reveal perfect white teeth. "It's Tony's day off. You might want to try back tomorrow, Mr.... I'm sorry, I didn't catch your name."

Blancanales stripped away the sunglasses and offered his hand. "My name's Rosario Garcia. Mr. Mendoza assured me that Mr. Drake would be here today. He wanted me to speak with him as soon as possible. We have, um, business to discuss."

"Perhaps Mr. Mendoza was mistaken," the woman offered. "When did he give you this information?"

Blancanales gave a nonchalant shrug. "Hour ago. Maybe two hours. I'm very bad with time, you understand. Mr. Mendoza's even worse. Damn guy acts like he has all the time in the world. You know what I'm say-ing?"

He gave her an easy smile. She licked her lips and returned the smile. "He's a great customer. We love him here. But, really, Mr. Drake isn't here and he won't be for the rest of the day."

"That's too bad," Blancanales said. He sampled the beer and set it back on the counter. "Mr. Mendoza said he had some issues to discuss with your boss. In private, if you know what I mean. He sent me here personally to pick Tony up. Something about settling accounts over this afternoon. He said Tony would understand ex-actly what that meant."

He noticed that the woman was holding her towel next to her stomach, her fingers kneading the fabric. "Honestly," she said, "I can't say it more clearly. He won't be here today."

"He be back tomorrow?"

"I believe so."

Blancanales smiled. "Great, that means he's home to-day."

She bit softly into her lower lip and shook her head. "I don't know what Mr. Drake does during his private hours. But I can check his schedule, if you'd like, and make sure he'll be back in tomorrow."

"Fine."

The woman pivoted and disappeared into the brick building behind the bar, the area that Blancanales pre-sumed housed the kitchen and the manager's office. Once he was sure she was inside, he turned toward the other Able Team warriors and gave them a nod.

Blancanales rounded the bar and headed inside the building. A short hallway opened to his right and light spilled through two open doors. Ahead, he heard the sizzle of meat on a griddle and smelled fish cooking with onions and garlic.

Reaching under his coat, he whipped the Beretta 93-R from the shoulder holster and held it at hip level. A quick check of the offices showed them empty. He turned and headed for the kitchen. He'd barely stepped inside when motion to his right caught his attention. He whirled and caught a man swinging a meat cleaver at his head. The Beretta sighed as it pumped out a 3-round burst that punched into the soft bridge of his attacker's nose. The man stumbled, crashing into a wall. His knees went rubbery and he collapsed to the floor.

The crack of a bullet caused Blancanales to whirl left, the Beretta's snout leading the way. He caught a Caucasian man framed in the door, lining up another shot. Blancanales fired off another triburst, the Parabellum slugs missing the man by several inches and chewing into the wooden molding that framed the door. The gunner squeezed off another quick shot that sizzled a couple of inches over Blancanales's head. Before he could respond, the guy spun and slipped out the door.

Blancanales sprinted after him, but waited a couple of heartbeats before plunging through the door. He went around it low, his weapon held at the ready. The door emptied onto a street lined with small two- and three-story buildings occupied by restaurants and shops. He heard the fast pounding of footsteps. Jerking his head right, he spotted the shooter sprinting toward a black BMW parked alongside the building.

Blancanales sprinted after the gunner as he tried to line up a decent shot at the man's back. "Freeze," he yelled.

The hardman turned toward Blancanales and tensed, leaving the commando to wonder for a moment whether the guy would bolt. Instead he swore, dropped his keys and held up both hands. In the same instant, two rounds lanced through the German luxury car's back windshield and burned a path toward Blancanales.

ONCE BLANCANALES disappeared into the kitchen, the two thugs exchanged looks and rocketed up from their chairs. When they made their move, Lyons shot up from his own chair, his hand slipping under his shirttails and scrambling for his .357 Desert Eagle.

While the Puerto Rican had chatted up the bartender, Lyons and Grimaldi had done their best to occupy the hardmen. He figured the more they focused their pea-size brains on Grimaldi and him, the better it was for Blancanales who likely would have his hands full, too.

The bigger of the two moved faster than Lyons had expected. In a second he was in Lyons's space, digging his fingers into Lyons. The move pinned the warrior's hand and made it impossible for him to free his Desert Eagle. The man leaned into Lyons, and his weight sent them both tumbling backward into the table, which collapsed under their combined weight.

As they fell, Lyons's right foot slammed upward into the man's gut. The steely muscles of the Able Team leader's lower body, combined with the man's own momentum, allowed Lyons to send the guy hurtling over him. Lyons rolled off his back and made a second try for the Desert Eagle, this time freeing it from the holster. The grizzly-size hardman had used his head to break his fall. But if it hurt, he gave no outward signs. Instead he shot to his feet, his hand already gripping a handgun.

Before the guy could acquire Lyons as a target, though, the Stony Man commando bracketed him in the Desert Eagle's sights and triggered the weapon. The handgun cracked twice, a foot-long tongue of flame licking out from the barrel. The bullets pierced flesh and broke the man's collarbone before drilling into his torso. His limbs went slack and he pitched forward, his lifeless form sprawling on the patio.

The warrior rose from the ground. He saw that Grimaldi was locked in hand-to-hand combat with the second fighter. From what Lyons could see, he was holding his own.

The pilot balled his right hand into a fist and fired an uppercut that connected with his opponent's chin, staggering him. Sensing an opening, the pilot stepped in to press his advantage. The thug fired off a kick that struck Grimaldi's leg. The blow missed his knee by inches, instead striking his thigh. The miss spared him a debilitating injury. But the sudden eruption of pain emanating from his leg still forced him to split his attention between the point of impact and his opponent.

The ace pilot clumsily took a step back, trying to gain time for his leg to recover. Apparently sensing weakness, the small Mexican tried to press his advantage. He reached under his shirt, produced a knife and lunged for Grimaldi's gut.

The Stony Man fighter's right arm lashed out, cut an arc through the air. His wrist collided with the other man's, knocking away the man's knife hand. Grimaldi's foot blurred upward and he snapped out a sidekick that hammered against the other man's stomach. Eyes bulging, the man loosened his fingers and the knife clattered to the ground. He wrapped both arms protectively around his gut and tried to regain his breath. With the outer edge of his hand as a striking surface, Grimaldi delivered a blow to the man's neck that dropped him to the ground. The man hit his head against the concrete patio and fell unconscious.

"You call that fighting?" Lyons asked. "You're just lucky I gave you the easy one."

"Least I won with my hands," Grimaldi replied, grinning.

"So did I," Lyons replied. "We both know this gun doesn't fire itself."

Gunfire crackled from the front of the building. Acting on instinct, the two men broke into a run and headed for the source. Grimaldi, his Desert Eagle clutched in his hand, headed through the building. Lyons skirted the exterior, heading for the street that fronted the building, wishing he'd been able to wear his headset to this strike so he could check in with Blancanales, make sure he was safe.

Instead he had to race to the front line to see firsthand. And hope his teammate didn't get taken down.

A TRIO OF SPIDERWEB CRACKS formed in the BMW's rear window as bullets punched through the glass and flew toward Blancanales.

Left with no time to move or to strategize, the Able Team commando did the only thing he could do. He bent slightly at the knees and triggered the Beretta, unleashing a punishing fusillade of Parabellum slugs at the vehicle. The rounds punched through the disintegrating wall of glass as he squeezed off 3-round bursts. The shots from within the car stopped and Blancanales ran in a crouch toward the vehicle.

As he passed, Blancanales glanced inside and saw the female bartender crumpled in the front seat. Her blood slicked the dashboard. A SIG-Sauer autoloader lay just a few inches from her hand.

Drake popped up from behind the car and tried to line up a shot with his handgun. Arms stretched across the BMW's hood, the former CIA agent laid down a barrage of gunfire that streaked just past Blancanales, lancing through the space between his arms and his torso. The onslaught drove the warrior to ground. He crouched behind the vehicle's front end, hoping the engine block would protect him from bullets. In the meantime, he reloaded his Beretta and fisted the second. Bullets sizzled the air above him and pounded into the brick structure at his back.

Jabbing one of the guns underneath the car, he squeezed off four rounds. The car sloped to the left as a bullet punctured the front tire. He heard Drake cry out as at least one slug rent flesh.

The Able Team commando vaulted onto the BMW's hood. Driven by pain and survival instincts, Drake surged up from behind the vehicle and found himself faced with Blancanales's twin Berettas. The slide on Drake's weapon had locked back, empty.

He dropped the pistol and raised his hands.

CHAPTER ELEVEN

"You guys can blow me," Drake said. "I know how this works. You guys are with the Justice Department, right? Justice guys have to do the right thing and take me back to the United States so I can sit on my rear in a cell, eating three squares a day and lifting weights to my heart's content. It won't be as nice as all this. But I can hack it."

Blancanales, who'd been pacing the room as Drake spoke, stopped and nodded. "Damn, you're a smart guy," he said. "Way smarter than any of us are. Which is why your girlfriend's dead and you're handcuffed to a chair. Nice tradecraft, man. I genuflect in awe."

"Kiss off," Drake replied. "I don't know who you guys are, but you are so screwed, coming in my place and shooting it up like that. I'll sue you and the U.S. government, you bastards."

While Blancanales paced, Lyons leaned against a wall, his lips compressed, his face cherry-red. He started to open his mouth to speak, but Blancanales silenced him with a wave of his hand. Grimaldi, a lit cigarette dangling from his lips, leaned against the wall opposite Lyons.

After Drake had surrendered, Blancanales and the others had stuffed him into the back of the SUV and hauled him back to his house situated in the hills around Puerto Vallarta. Using a pair of double-looped plastic cuffs, they'd secured him to a wooden chair in a two-car garage situated next to his house.

Blancanales was already tired of the smart-mouthed SOB and was ready to use creative means to get the information he wanted. He spotted an old burlap bag, one soaked with oil and dust, lying on the floor underneath a rusted toolbox. He retrieved it and slipped it over the former agent's head. Laughter emanated from underneath the bag.

"Oh, guys, this is lame. You think sensory deprivation's going to work on me. What next? Soak me in cold water and lock me in a dark room for three days? Make me drink my urine? Go for it. I already did all this crap when I trained with the Agency."

Blancanales laughed. "Well, damn, Drake, you've got us all figured out then. Maybe we ought to just untie you and slink back to America because we'll never get you to talk, will we? You're just too tough for us."

"That's what I'm saying. Cut the crap. It don't move me."

Blancanales turned his head toward Lyons and winked. "Get the SUV."

"On it," Lyons stated.

"See, here's the tough thing," Blancanales said. "You have information that we need badly. I'm talking like national security information that could help prevent a catastrophic event. Something with massive casualties. But you want to screw with us, swing your little tiny bit of manhood around and demonstrate just how tough you are."

Blancanales hefted a jerrican filled with gasoline, took it to Drake and set it down with a thud. Gasoline sloshed around inside the can and it gave off a telltale odor. He noticed Drake beginning to squirm a bit. "My problem is that I don't have time to figure out which of us is the bigger man here," Blancanales said. "So I'm just going to have to do what I do best. Cheat."

Upending the fuel can, he doused the floor around Drake with gasoline.

"Aw, c'mon," Drake said, "you can do better than this. You aren't going to set fire to me."

Blancanales heard an engine roar. He gestured with a nod to Grimaldi to move farther into the rear of the garage. The engine noise grew louder until a loud thump signaled that the truck had slammed into the door. The door caved inward, splintering into dozens of pieces, sending boards and metal fasteners bounding throughout the garage. The truck came within a foot or so of Drake before it halted, rubber squealing against concrete.

"What the hell?" Drake shouted. "What're you trying to do? Kill me?"

"Try, hell," Blancanales said. "I'd say it's only a matter of time."

The front driver's-side window slid down and Lyons's head and elbow protruded through it. "Should I roll him or do you still want to burn him?"

Blancanales shrugged. "Gotta get rid of the wheels. Might as well wax this mouthy jerk at the same time. Hell, maybe we could set fire to him and drag him around a little bit."

Rivulets of sweat rolled down Drake's face, but he tried to keep his voice confident. "You guys are full of crap. You're not going to kill me. You told me you were with the Justice Department on our way here. You folks don't kill people."

"Tell that to your lovely assistant back at the grill," Blancanales said. "The one going stiff in the BMW."

"That was different."

"This'll be different, too. I promise," Blancanales said. "Variety is the spice of life. Our SUV here has a full tank of gas in it. I've got a bag of C-4 and a detonator inside it. I figure we blow up the wheels, which, by the way are stolen, and take you out in the process." Blancanales clapped his hands twice. "Bang, bang. The world's a better place. If the explosion doesn't get you—and I don't see why it wouldn't—the flames will immolate you. Frankly, I don't care how you go, just so long as you do. I get paid either way. So good riddance."

Drake bit his lower lip. "What do you want?"

"Nothing you got."

"Bull. Otherwise you wouldn't be here. Everyone's got a price. What's yours? Name it."

Blancanales pretended to consider it. His brow furrowed, he looked to Lyons, drew his forefinger across his throat. "Damn it! Shut that thing off. I need some quiet so I can think."

Lyons complied and the garage fell silent.

"Look," Blancanales said, "the reality is, you're just a small player in all this. The guy we really want to find is Cortez. He's the one with the target on his back, not you."

"I can't give you Cortez."

Blancanales shot a hand in the air. "Start her up," he said. "It's time to play rolling pin with this guy."

"No, no, that's not what I mean. Good God, man, are you guys screwed in the head? What I mean is, I can't just hand him over to you, but I can point you in the right direction. Shit, I'm not his mama. I don't watch every move he makes."

Blancanales gestured to Lyons. "All right. Let's hear this creep out. You said you could point him out. So, point. Where the hell is he?"

"Prague. He's in Prague."

"Why? What's in Prague?"

"Connections, man. He's got the goods and he wants to sell them. Prague's just the place to do it."

"What goods? The computer guy?"

"Nah, he lost him. That bastard from South Africa took him. I always told Cortez that damn guy was trouble, but he never listened. Well, it almost got him killed."

Blancanales held up a hand. "Already heard that story. So, if Cortez doesn't have the kid, and he doesn't have the kid's laptop, just what the hell does he have?"

"The kid had something sewn into his clothes, one of those little CD-ROMs, about the size of a business card. Cortez pocketed it, checked it and found out it has a copy of the worm on it. He's on his way now to sell it."

"Bull."

"No, really. I saw it. He figures he can unload it for a sweet price."

"Sell it? Sell it to whom? Who's his contact?"

"Guy named Ahmed Quissad."

"Who is…?"

"Weapons dealer. He does a lot of work with Cortez. Cortez finds the stuff and gives it to Quissad to sell overseas. Then they split the profits."

"And you fit in where?"

"Shit, I'm just a businessman. I got caught up in the

wrong crowd is all. Hell, I came down here wanting to live off my pension, soak up some rays, screw a few women. You know. Have a little fun before I punch out. Now I'm up to my neck in this stuff and I can't figure out how it happened."

The right corner of Blancanales's mouth quirked up in amusement. "You're just a victim. You poor bastard."

"Not a victim, but not a participant, either."

"Not how we hear it."

"Who cares what you heard? I'm telling you straight up."

"Good. You can tell it again to the DEA. And the FBI. I'm sure they'll be happy to make your acquaintance."

CHAPTER TWELVE

Hal Brognola, his face locked in a grim-as-hell expression, watched Phoenix Force file into the War Room.

David McCarter, commander of Stony Man Farm's international counterterrorism team, dropped into the seat next to Brognola. The fox-faced Briton took a swig from a cold can of Coke, belched and set it on a table next to him. "That's good medicine," he said.

Three other commandos—Gary Manning, Rafael Encizo and Calvin James—seated themselves around the table. T. J. Hawkins walked to the coffeemaker and filled his cup with the hot beverage.

Staring down into the cup, he studied its contents for a moment. He looked up and raised the cup in a mock toast toward Aaron Kurtzman, purveyor of the world's worst coffee. Hawkins, a former U.S. Army Ranger, took a sip and let it drain down his throat. His smile melted away and his face began to contort as though he'd just swallowed a live lizard.

"Damn, Bear, this stuff's thick as molasses and as rancid as aged horse piss."

"I made some adjustments to the brew," Kurtzman said, grinning. "Hope you like it."

"Son, I like it like a cat likes a bath."

"So quit whining and don't drink it," Kurtzman said. He held out a hand. "Here, give it to me."

Hawkins clutched the coffee to his chest. "Get your own," he said. "You'll pry mine from my cold, dead hands. Even this cyanide-laced rat piss."

Hawkins strode toward his seat while Kurtzman chuckled after him. Others assembled in the room grinned or rolled their eyes in amusement.

As Hawkins sat, Barbara Price entered the room, her arms loaded with mission packets. She handed them out to the assembled warriors.

"Want some coffee, Barb?" Kurtzman asked.

"Maybe next month, Bear," she replied.

Brognola uncoiled from his chair, a sheaf of papers clutched in his hand. He cleared his throat to get everyone's attention. "Okay, I'd like to start the briefing," he said. He looked at Hawkins, then Kurtzman. "That is, *if* you jokers can drop the curtain on your vaudeville show."

Without waiting for a response, the big Fed strode to the front of the room. "Let me spare you folks the preamble," he said. "We're about to experience the equivalent of an openmouthed swim through a sewer with this mission. 'Huge' doesn't begin to describe the stakes. The Man's breathing down my neck on this one. Considering the situation, I can't say as I blame him. We have a handful of leads, but nowhere near as much solid intel to pass along as I'd like. You guys will need to do most of the legwork yourself, too."

"Sounds like another day at the office," McCarter said. "Is this connected to Able Team's mission?"

The big Fed nodded. "Inextricably so. Within the past several hours, Able Team's brief rescue job has morphed into a nasty two-front war." He explained about Gabe Fox and the Cold Earth virus.

"And guess who's shipping out to the second front?" McCarter stated.

"Exactly. Carl checked in with us a little while ago. According to him, a third party showed up in Mexico, grabbed our computer guy and hightailed it for parts unknown. At the same time, from what we've ascertained, a second copy of Cold Earth is floating around, ready to hit the open market."

"Which means exactly what for us?" McCarter asked.

"It means you folks are bound for Sudan. We're prepping a plane to transport you and your equipment there right now. From what Able Team has pieced together, so far, a gunrunner named Jack Mace is responsible for setting this whole thing in motion. He hired the men responsible for kidnapping Gabriel Fox. And, by extension, he helped put Gadgets into the damn hospital."

"That alone qualifies him for a bullet in the head," Hawkins said.

"Amen," Brognola said. "And I'm sure one of you gentlemen will deliver the goods on that."

The big Fed went on to update Phoenix Force on the mass killings at Mendoza's estate and the information provided by the injured guard Able Team found on the premises.

"Able Team's primary target in Prague is a man named Ahmed Quissad, a real piece of garbage," Brognola continued. "The military and the CIA are all too familiar with this guy. According to the intelligence we dug up, he hails from a family of loyal Baathists. His father was a member of parliament and his mother taught at a university. They had a big house in Tikrit and an impressive bank account. In 2003, they saw the writing on the wall and fled the country for Damascus, Syria, two months before we invaded Iraq."

"What about junior?" Calvin James asked. "Did he make a run for the border or stay in the old neighborhood?"

"He stayed. He was an officer in Fedayeen Saddam, Saddam Hussein's squad of thugs. His list of 'honors' included beheading the regime's enemies in public and procuring victims for the government's torture chambers and rape rooms. After the invasion, Quissad remained in Iraq and participated in the insurgency for about nine months before he abandoned it."

"Not, I'd imagine, because he had a sudden attack of conscience," McCarter interjected.

"Not even close," Brognola stated. "Apparently the only force more powerful than his bloodlust is his greed. When he realized that all the bloodshed wasn't going to get him what he wanted, he got the hell out. At this point, facts get a little sketchy and the CIA and military intelligence analysts had to make some educated guesses. The current theory is he escaped through Syria, Iran or one of the other border countries and kept on running until he reached Prague."

"Why Prague?" James asked.

Brognola shrugged. "Truth is, Cal, we aren't sure why he chose Prague. In fact, we don't even know with one hundred percent certainty that he's still there. But, according to Able Team's source, that's where he operates. I'm sure he uses an alias. A team at the Treasury Department is searching like hell to see whether we can locate and freeze this guy's money. Our own folks are turning over their share of rocks, too. The Israelis also have been sharing intelligence with us. I guess his name's come up a couple of times in relation to big arms deals to Palestinian terrorists. Fortunately, they don't know *why* we want him. They just know we do want him."

"So Able Team can expect to run into Mossad," Hawkins said.

"Good chance of that. Frankly, the chance of interference from friendly or unfriendly intelligence agencies is pretty big. Once it becomes common knowledge just what the Cold Earth worm is and that it and its creator are up for grabs, all hell could break loose."

Brognola fished a half-chewed cigar from his breast pocket and stuck it between his lips.

"As for you guys," he said, "I need you in Sudan to find our wayward computer geek. The Man's as worried as hell that Fox will reproduce Cold Earth. So am I. We're still working up a profile on his alleged captor, Jack Mace. But we do know a little about him. He spent about ten years with South Africa's Apartheid-era secret police. He was known for his unrestrained brutality. Once things changed there, he fled the country and became an arms runner."

"He have any CIA contacts?" Encizo asked.

Brognola flipped through his notes. "Negative. Not that we can see, anyway."

"Which begs the question, how'd he learn about Fox or Cold Earth in the first place? I assume the CIA didn't issue a press release touting its latest development in cyberwarfare."

"You think he had inside help," Brognola said.

"Unless he's clairvoyant," Encizo said.

Brognola allowed himself a smile. "I thought the

same thing," he said. "In fact, that seems to be the general consensus among everyone involved with this situation, a list that includes everyone from the National Security Council to select Cabinet members and department heads. The CIA's internal inspectors are turning the Agency upside down, looking for leaks. Obviously they're also investigating the rogue elements at the Colorado safehouse. If they turn up anything of use, I'll pass it to you folks in the field."

"Right," McCarter said.

"As for Mace himself, he used to hang his hat in Sudan's Darfour region. According to our local CIA station chief, Mace hires the Janjaweed to act as his heavies, and surrounds himself with a cadre of hand-picked killers."

"We have a lock on his place?"

Brognola shook his head. "Mace has a home in Khartoum. But, according to the CIA's Sudan station chief, it's sitting empty. He's your contact in Sudan, by the way. He'll be familiar to you, David. Does the name Dane Whitley ring any bells?"

McCarter grinned. "That daft bloke's the station chief? So much for standards, that's all I can say."

"You've met this guy?" Encizo asked.

"Sure. We served together in the SAS. He's a hard-drinking, skirt-chasing lunatic. And, besides those attributes, he's a good man to have with you in a firefight."

Brognola smiled. "He'll help nail down specifics on Mace's location. Right now, the plan is simple. Find Gabriel Fox and pull him out of there. Burn down his kidnappers in the process. But getting hold of Fox and debriefing him are your most important tasks."

McCarter gave his boss a wry smile. "And I'm sure it'll proceed exactly as you say. Hell, those blokes will take one look at us, throw down their weapons and run like scalded goats."

"Look," Brognola said, "I won't lie to you guys. Jack Mace, without a doubt, is a bad actor. And in all reality, I'm not sure I'm ready to believe the bastard's working alone. He definitely has resources and clout, but not enough to pull the crap he has within the last twenty-four hours."

"My only complaint," Hawkins interjected, "is that I won't get to wax the bastard that put Gadgets into the hospital. Otherwise I'm always up for a trip to the desert."

McCarter crushed an empty Coke can in his hand and tossed it into a nearby trashcan. "Well, start packing your sunscreen, mate," he said. "You're about to get all the sun, sand and fun your little heart can stand."

THE PHOENIX FORCE commandos prepared for war. David McCarter watched his men as they toiled, each preparing to face death without hesitation, and he marveled at their bravery and dedication.

He'd seen his comrades get hurt in the line of duty. Seen two of them—most recently Yakov Katzenelbogen and several years before that Keio Ohara—pay the ultimate price. Not that he tried to forget his fallen friends; an impossibility even if he wanted to attempt it, which he didn't. Rather, he willed his mind to recall the best about those brave men who'd made the ultimate sacrifice to preserve freedom and protect innocents. He acknowledged and honored their deaths, but didn't dwell on them. Or dwell on the possibility that another of his crew might someday fall in the line of duty. Their work was too important for that, for him to let trepidation factor into his decision making.

Still, in unguarded moments, he couldn't help but wonder who might fall next. And, if they did, would it happen because they were following orders?

"Hey, David."

A gruff voice behind McCarter snapped him from his thoughts. He turned and spotted Aaron Kurtzman wheeling into the room. The cybergenius had black nylon briefcases attached to both sides of his wheelchair, like saddlebags. McCarter guessed they contained a laptop, personal-digital assistant and other equipment. A SPAS-12 shotgun hung at a forty-five-degree angle from the backrest of his wheelchair. A shoulder rig was strapped across his chest.

"What brings you down here, Bear? If you're bringing us more computers, I think T.J. already packed a laptop," McCarter said.

Kurtzman shook his head. "This is my stuff. I'm going with you."

McCarter leaned back in his chair, a surprised look on his face. "Come again?"

"I'm going with you," Kurtzman said. "I convinced Hal that it was a good idea for me to go."

"I don't agree."

"Why?"

McCarter considered the "why" so obvious, he had to struggle not to shout it out. Heaving a deep sigh, he leaned forward, rested his elbows on his thighs and stared his old friend square in the eye.

"This is a combat mission," the Briton said. "You're not a soldier. It's too damn dangerous. Hal makes the decisions here at the Farm. Carl and I make them in the field. We operate with as much independence as possible."

"I have firearms training. And I have more upper-body strength than probably anyone this side of Ironman."

McCarter nodded. "Sure. And you're good. Don't get me wrong. I'm sure you could handle yourself better than ninety-nine percent of the population if you got yourself into a scrape. But you are not a soldier. This is a combat mission. We have to be nimble. Nimble and mobile."

"You think I'll slow you down."

McCarter paused, picking his words carefully. "In a manner of speaking, yes."

"Because of the wheelchair."

The Briton's face and neck flushed with blood and began radiating heat. He felt as though all the eyes in the room were on him, and a sidelong glance confirmed it. He caught the commandos stealing glances from the corners of their eyes, even as they feigned involvement in other tasks. He felt put on the spot, which fueled his temper like wood into a stove.

"The wheelchair's part of it," the Briton said, absently fishing in his shirt pockets for a lighter. "I'd be lying if I said otherwise. But there's also a matter of training and experience. I know this lad's a friend of yours, and I hope we find him, but I can't risk having you in the field."

McCarter shut up and let his words sink in.

A few seconds later Kurtzman nodded. "Look, I know that when it comes to combat, I'm washout. But I want to do something, be involved, even if it means sitting on the damn plane and providing cybersupport from the air. I want to be there when you guys bring Gabe home. We're going to need to debrief him, and he's more likely to trust me than he is any of you guys."

"You need to know the score. I can't promise we'll

get him. We'll try our damnedest. You know that. But sometimes fate doesn't give a tinker's damn about my best or your best. I think you know that in your head, but I want you to get it in your gut." McCarter pushed his fist into his own stomach for emphasis. "We may come away empty-handed. Or we may have to carry your friend away in a body bag. Can you handle that?"

Kurtzman nodded. "I've had friends die in action before. Back when Stony Man Farm was attacked. When April was killed." He was referring to the Farm's former mission controller, April Rose.

"I just want to make sure we're clear," McCarter said. "I don't want you harboring false hopes."

"I get it."

McCarter nodded. "Good. Glad to have you along. It's always possible that we might need your computer expertise out there. Especially if Mace gets his mitts on Cold Earth itself and not just its creator."

"That was my thinking, too. Besides, Gabe's got a hell of a memory. My guess is, given the right motivation, he could recreate this thing in no time."

"Sounds like we're burning daylight then, even on a gloomy day like this. Let's get the hell out of here."

CHAPTER THIRTEEN

"We could use this to bring the American oppressor to its knees, pay it back for the humiliation and chaos it has heaped upon our homeland," Ibrahim Libbi said into his mobile phone. "We could once again make things right for our country. You understand this, don't you, my friend? You are an Iraqi and a patriot."

"I understand this, yes," said Tariq Khan, the man on the other end of the call. "My employer, however, sees things differently. He believes you want to play upon his patriotism in order to cheat him out of something valuable. He said, and I quote, 'I'm not so patriotic that I will run my business as a charity.'"

Libbi snorted disgustedly. "He speaks of patriotism as though it were a vice rather than a virtue."

"Unfortunately, he doesn't have your skills and grace when it comes to negotiating, old friend," Khan replied. "He worries only about the money."

"So he can pursue women and drugs."

"He believes the price is reasonable."

Libbi leaned back in his chair. He was seated in the passenger area of a jet chartered for him by his leader,

Kamal Ramadan. According to his itinerary, he was to be in Prague in a matter of hours. However, the longer he talked to Khan, the more he wondered whether he was about to embark on a fool's errand. He said as much to Khan, whom he had known since the two were members of the Baath party in Iraq.

"That we differ on price is an unfortunate but not insurmountable issue," Libbi said.

"Believe me, I want nothing more than to work with you and to help you," Khan stated.

Libbi rolled his eyes at the other man's fawning statement. Harsh experience told him that whenever someone asked you to believe them, you should do anything but.

"I believe in your cause," Khan continued, "but there's no way to make Mr. Q do something once he's made up his mind." Libbi knew from previous phone calls that Khan refused to say Quissad's name unless the man was standing right there. He operated with a level of paranoia that would have made Saddam proud, Libbi thought.

But in his most soothing tone he said, "I see your point, of course."

This was why he needed to get this weapon. This was a perfect example of how far he and his associates had fallen since the Iraq war began in 2003. In the old days, "negotiating" for Libbi had meant his telling the other party what he wanted and when, and knowing with unshakable faith that it'd be delivered to him even sooner.

He knew that in Saddam Hussein's Iraq, the *real* Iraq, treating him or his colleagues with such disdain— an act from which Quissad seemed to derive great pleasure—would have been unthinkable.

But that was back when Libbi had been a high-ranking officer in the intelligence services, back when he enjoyed privilege and power. Now he had money, but only a finite amount. And, even among a cadre of terrorists, gunrunners, criminals and other unsavory characters, he had little status. Certainly not the status he'd boasted in the Baath Party. He had no army, no secret police or intelligence agents to back him up. So here he was, taking guff from Quissad and his sniveling lieutenant.

Still, all the headaches could prove worthwhile. If this devastating technology truly existed, and it fell into their hands, he and his associates had a chance to hobble America, to force it to remove its vast armies from his homeland.

With the soldiers gone, he and his associates—a group of former Iraqi government officials who called themselves the Seven—could use the billions skimmed from Saddam to buy the guns, soldiers and loyalty necessary to overthrow Iraq's fledgling government. The way he saw it, this was the best possible chance for him and the others to return the world to its rightful order.

"The price you ask, Libbi said, "is too much."

"Respectfully, I assure you it's not. I think you and your associates could shoulder the cost easily. It really depends on how committed you are to your cause."

Libbi's voice turned wintry. "We're quite committed," he said. "Of that you need not worry. You want a quarter billion dollars for this thing. We don't have that kind of cash."

He heard Khan heave a sigh on the other end of the line. "Respectfully, my employer believes otherwise. He thinks you have more money than perhaps you want to acknowledge. From what we understand, you skimmed money from Saddam just before the war and put it into a series of black accounts."

Derisive laughter exploded from Libbi's mouth. "So this is where you're coming from? This is how you work? You listen to petty gossip and baseless rumors and then base critical business decisions on it. This is certainly good information for me to have. Perhaps your little computer virus—"

"It's a worm."

"Whatever, perhaps that also is based on rumors and gossip. Maybe it's little more than a figment of your employer's overactive imagination. Should I assume that he dreamed the whole thing up?"

"No."

"Let me tell you something," Libbi interjected, his voice gaining volume. "Saddam had little money toward the end. Certainly not the fortune that you and others seem to want to believe. He lived an opulent lifestyle that sucked away most of the cash. And he kept a strict accounting of every dime. Had I been stealing his money, as you allege, I'd have been buried in an anonymous grave somewhere on the outskirts of Baghdad before the Americans dropped their first bomb."

"Mr. Q seems to believe otherwise. You'll find he's quite stubborn when he wants to be."

"Of that I have no doubt."

"We want a quarter billion dollars for this device, period. He's made it quite clear that there's no room for negotiation on this."

"How do we know this thing even works?"

"It works. Trust us, it works."

"You know this how?"

"Do you want it or not?" Khan asked, his voice hard.

"I'll believe it, when I see it."

"Get the money or you won't see it. We will pick you up at the appointed time."

The phone went dead.

Libbi slipped his encrypted phone back into a leather valise propped against his seat. Leaning again into his backrest, he ran his palm over the few salt-and-pepper strands of hair that lay across his bald scalp, smoothing them down. Five men entered the passenger area. The four younger men, all Arabs, fanned out and began a final search of the cabin, checking under seats and in baggage compartments for explosives or surveillance devices.

The fifth man, slender and in his fifties, moved to Libbi and they greeted each other. Walid Salih, another member of the Seven, also had once been a high-ranking official in Saddam's intelligence network.

"You spoke with Khan?"

"I did."

"We can get it?"

"For a price. Always for a price. But yes, we can have it."

"Excellent."

"We shall see."

"You have concerns?"

Libbi shook his head and smiled thinly. "Not concerns. Only regrets. At one time, we could get whatever we wanted. Now we must beg like street urchins. We no longer get the respect we are due."

Salih nodded. "A temporary circumstance, my friend. At least it will be if this weapon performs as they say."

"If it doesn't, I will hunt down Quissad and kill him myself."

"Even if it does work, we must eliminate Quissad. Once we unleash the fire, the world need not know how we did it. Once we get what we want, there will be no reason for him to continue drawing breath."

A smile tugged at the corners of Libbi's lips. "You are right, my friend."

"But until then we have more pressing concerns. Before we can take back what is rightfully ours, we must make sure that the United States cannot strike back at us. It must be too tattered and torn itself to even worry about us. We must devastate it."

Libbi broke into a full smile. "That will be the most gratifying moment of all."

"THEY WILL ARRIVE in Prague tomorrow," Khan said.

"You told them the price?" Quissad asked.

"Yes, I told them the price." Khan was pacing his office, his mobile phone pressed to his ear. "Yes, it's a price they're willing to pay."

"Make sure they pay us on the spot."

"Of course. I will have them transfer the money electronically. It should be in your accounts before midnight."

"And I want them gone shortly after that."

Khan halted. "Gone? You mean, out of Prague?"

"I mean in the damn ground. Deal with them. Make them go away."

"But Cold Earth…"

"Will be fine. I plan on selling this at least a couple more times before all's said and done. The last thing I need is a washed-up Iraqi bureaucrat shooting his mouth off to the wrong people and derailing our plans. But I'll be happy to take the damn fool's money."

Khan felt his stomach roll and sweat break out on his palms. "You're sure of this?" he asked.

"Khan?"

"Yes?"

"Don't ever ask me that again. Or you'll end up in the same hole as them. Are we clear?"

Khan felt his throat tighten. He swallowed hard to loosen it. "Of course we're clear," he said.

"Good."

CHAPTER FOURTEEN

Khartoum, Sudan

"I don't know how I let you talk me into this," David McCarter muttered as he parked the van in a vacant lot between two weathered brick buildings. He turned to look at his back seat passenger.

"What?" Kurtzman said. "I'm just trying to help."

"Help land me in the stockade or on the damn dole," McCarter replied. "Hal's going to flip his lid when he learns I've taken you into the field with us."

"Hal doesn't have to know," Kurtzman said, flashing a conspiratorial smile. "Does he?"

McCarter's scowl stay rooted in place. "Sneaky bastard."

"Where's the love, David?" Kurtzman said. "That's what I want to know."

"Look, I bent on this. But if you try to push me any further, we're going to go through life together—my foot in your ass. Get me?"

"I'll be good."

"Good."

Manning, who sat in the front passenger seat, snickered. McCarter pinned him under his gaze. "What're you laughing at, Gary?"

The big Canadian jerked a thumb toward the van's exterior. "C'mon, tough guy. Save it for the bad people."

McCarter continued muttering under his breath as he stepped from the car. Slamming the van door, he saw something reflected back at him in the window that caught his attention. Four hard-looking Caucasians crossed the street and disappeared inside a three-story brick building. A sign on the side read Global Sudanese Airlines. The one below it stated Global Sudanese Import/Export Co.

It was the same destination as the three Stony Man operatives.

The Briton unzipped his windbreaker to give himself easier access to the Browning Hi-Power he carried at his waist. He and the others had come here to meet with Dane Whitley, the CIA station chief for Sudan. McCarter returned to the van and came around its rear bumper. He saw Manning pulling Kurtzman's wheelchair from inside the vehicle. The vehicle didn't have the lifts found in many handicapped accessible vans, but most all but one of the rear bucket seats had been removed, making it easier to carry the wheelchair.

"We've got problems, gents," McCarter said.

"What?" Manning asked.

"Four very bad-looking men just walked into Global Sudanese Airlines."

Manning swore. "I'm betting they're not here to buy a trip ticket."

Kurtzman spoke up. "You guys go ahead and handle it. I'll take care of myself here."

The Phoenix Force commandos looked at each other

for a stretched second, then nodded in silent agreement. Their trepidation didn't come just from Kurtzman's physical disability, but also that he wasn't a combat veteran like them. Brave as hell, no doubt. But Stony Man Farm could scarcely afford to lose his brain power and institutional knowledge.

"Go, damn it," he said, his voice taking on an edge.

Reaching for their side arms, the four men sprinted into action. Before they'd reached the building, McCarter had formulated a plan of attack. Using hand signals, he indicated for Manning to take the front door, while he headed for the fire escape.

The fox-faced Briton drew his pistol and sprinted for the fire escape. The ladder was locked into place. McCarter jumped onto the hood of what he guessed was Whitley's car, grabbed the ladder's bottom rung and pulled himself up. He kept the Browning in his hand as he ascended. When he reached the first platform, he tried the window and found it locked. Stripping away his light jacket, he wrapped it around his hand and drove a fist through the glass. He used the Browning to clear away any remaining glass lodged in the frame and climbed through the window.

As silent as a whisper, he crossed the room and slipped into the hallway. He found it empty, and two other office doors stood closed with the lights off. He moved to the stairwell. Before he took his first step down, autofire rattled from the ground floor.

Manning!

He reached inside his jacket for the handheld radio clipped to his belt. In his haste, he'd left his earpiece and throat microphone in the car. Raising the radio to his mouth, he pressed the transmit button.

And froze.

Two of the office doors on his level were kicked open and hardmen brandishing automatic weapons came into view.

A third appeared on the landing and was lining up a shot with his pistol.

Bloody hell.

MANNING EDGED along the exterior of the building. He ducked under windows to avoid detection until he reached a concrete porch that lay in front of the front door. He wasn't worried that the locals would call the police or the military. If confronted by a Sudanese soldier, though, he wasn't too worried about taking them out. Considering the Sudanese government's record of harboring terrorists and its tacit consent of the rape, torture, genocide and dislocation of thousands of its citizens, he figured he could spill their blood with a clear conscience.

He reached the door, worked the knob and it swung inward. He crossed the threshold, his .40-caliber Glock clutched in his hand. A stairway stood to his left. To his right was a large waiting room with a rear door that led into a corridor. The big Canadian moved through the waiting room. As he approached the corridor, a door inside it slipped open and a shadowy figure came into view.

Before Manning could guess at the figure's intent, gunfire exploded from inside the hallway. Instinctively, the Phoenix Force commando dropped into a Weaver's stance and ripped off three shots from the Glock. All three slugs punched into the target's center mass and knocked him back until he hit a wall and sagged to the ground.

An instant later glass broke to his right. Manning

whirled and spotted the barrel of an assault rifle jutting through the window. The warrior lunged sideways, the Glock thundering twice more. The shots flew wide and tunneled into the wall next to the window frame. In the same instant, jagged tongues of orange flame exploded from the assault rifle's muzzle and a hail of bullets whizzed through the room.

Hitting the ground on his backside, Manning raised the Glock and squeezed off another pair of shots.

KURTZMAN KNEW he had to do something.

The pair of thugs had appeared at the van, seemingly out of nowhere. They'd started by trying to interrogate Kurtzman, but had barely uttered a sentence before shooting erupted from within the structure. One of the strangers, a reed-slim man with a face like a horse, sprinted for the window. Shoving his 5.45 mm AKR through the opening, the man began firing the weapon at an unseen target.

The other man stood next to Kurtzman. He held the cold barrel of a 5.45 mm PSM semiautomatic pistol against the cybergenius's temple. Fear and rage clashed inside Kurtzman as he tried to figure out a way to help his friends and save his own life.

When the gunfire at the house intensified, the man at Kurtzman's side let his gaze drift toward his comrade.

And away from his mark. The pistol's muzzle inched away from Kurtzman's temple. The man's eyes were riveted on the fight unfolding at the house.

Sure, Kurtzman thought, ignore the guy in the wheelchair. What harm could he pose?

He leaned hard against his seatback, and of harm's way. His motion registered with his captor, and the man's head whirled back toward Kurtzman. It took him a moment to realize he'd let the pistol's muzzle stray too far from his target, and he moved the weapon to try to compensate for his mistake.

Kurtzman's hand fired up and his fingers wrapped around the other man's wrist. The Stony Man computer wizard tightened his grip so hard he swore he could feel the man's wrist bones grinding against one another. At the same time, he pushed his opponent's gun hand well away from his own head. Finally the man's fingers opened and the gun plummeted to the ground. With a violent yank, Kurtzman pulled the guy down to him and delivered an uppercut to his jaw. The guy threw a wild punch that breezed past Kurtzman's face. He again buried his knuckles into the man's nose and felt bone collide with bone. With a hard shove, he sent the man stumbling back. Kurtzman reached inside his jacket for his handgun.

Just as Kurtzman's fingers wrapped around the pistol butt, the hardman caught his footing and lunged back at Kurtzman, who freed his own pistol and lined up his shot. The weapon barked out a single round that caught the man in midstride. It tore through his face, taking half his head with it as it exited.

Kurtzman turned toward the house and found the second hardman still firing his gun through the window, presumably at Manning or McCarter. Kurtzman drew a bead on the guy and fired. The bullet tore a hole through the man's jacket, but missed his body.

He whirled toward his attacker, trying to acquire a target. Kurtzman squeezed off three shots in rapid succession, all of which drilled into the building beside him. Though the shots missed their target, they forced the man to dart away from the window. Kurtzman adjusted his aim and ripped off two more rounds.

The second triburst broke the man's sternum and tunneled into his chest. Blood splattered against the building's exterior when the bullets exploded out of the thug's back. Kurtzman swallowed hard and sucked in a big breath. His heart slammed in his chest, hard enough that he thought it might explode.

He was thankful for the range training he'd received from John "Cowboy" Kissinger, Stony Man's armorer. Ever since the raid on the Farm years ago, Kurtzman had made it a point to train with weapons, just in case. The training had just paid off big time.

He maneuvered the chair toward the house. Along the way, he grabbed one of the corpses by a jacket lapel and dragged him along. Whether the Sudanese authorities planned to ignore the fireworks remained to be seen. But he wanted to move the bodies out of plain sight, just in case people grew curious.

He laid the thug's corpse alongside the house in a spot where shadows covered it. Within a couple of minutes, he'd similarly positioned the second shooter.

He heard more gunfire thunder inside the building. He wheeled the chair to the front of the building where he found a makeshift wheelchair ramp—a rectangular sheet of wood supported by stacked cinder blocks—led up to the porch. He rolled up the ramp. It bowed when he reached the middle and he felt his heart lurch. If he was knocked from his chair, he had the strength to turn it upright and pull himself back in. But the effort would cost time and he had none to spare.

Thankfully, the ramp held the rest of the way. He rolled onto the concrete porch and sighed with relief. He rolled for the door. Before he reached it, though, the doorknob turned and it began to swing inward.

He raised his pistol.

CHAPTER FIFTEEN

McCarter had no time to think, only react.

The Briton jerked up the Browning and loosed several rounds. The shots caused his two opponents to scramble for cover. Steel-jacketed slugs sizzled through the air, punching holes in drywall or shattering pebbled windows built into the doors.

He used the break to race up the stairs. The man at the top of the stairs fired at the charging warrior, the bullet whistling just past McCarter's left ear. The Browning Hi-Power cranked out two shots that caught the man in the abdomen. The guy screamed with pain and rage, but remained rooted to his spot. He fired, this time wildly, and the bullets lanced through the air around McCarter, but came nowhere near hitting him.

The man swayed on his feet. The Browning spit out two more slugs, both of which stabbed into the man's head. He crumpled in a boneless heap. Driven by his combat senses, McCarter spun on a heel and caught another shooter coming into view. The gunner laid down a blistering barrage of autofire that tore through the space between the safety railing and the steps.

Drawing a bead on the man, the Briton dealt out a double dose of death from the Browning. The slugs tunneled through his target's skull at a downward angle, seemingly nailing the guy to the floor for a moment before rubbery knees gave out from under him and he went down.

More gunfire chattered on the floor below. McCarter crouched, ready for another attack. However, the third gunner stumbled past his view and dropped to the floor, his torso riddled with bullets.

McCarter wondered whether it was Manning.

A moment later he got his answer. "This is Whitley. Who the devil's up there?"

McCarter allowed relief to come over him. "No devil," McCarter replied. "Just an angel with dirty wings."

Whitley stepped into view. He stood about six feet tall and, judging by his slim build, McCarter guessed he weighed about 150 pounds. He wore his gray hair shaved down to about one-quarter inch above the skin, and gnawed on a cigar butt. He held an MP-5 in his right hand. Smoke still curled from the muzzle.

"'Bout time you ladies showed," he said. "Thought I was going to have to handle this all myself."

"Shame it'd be," McCarter replied, "if you had to do something akin to work."

"Still the same damn McCarter," Whitley stated. He smiled around the cigar. "Not that the old you is a bleeding treat or anything, mind you. But I guess it beats hanging with this bunch of bastards. Especially since they seem to be in an extreme case of dead."

"Especially," McCarter replied.

THE DOOR SWUNG OPEN. Kurtzman's breath halted as he waited to see what waited on the other side. A stocky man, his hand hanging at his side, stood in the doorway. Gary Manning flashed his old friend a smile.

"Nice shooting," he said. "You saved my rump back there."

"Is everything okay?" Kurtzman asked.

Manning nodded. "For the moment," he said. "I just spoke with David on the handheld. He said the top floors are clear. And he found Whitley. My guess is we can expect more company. We probably ought to get out of here as soon as possible."

"Agreed."

AN HOUR LATER, outside Khartoum, David McCarter wheeled the van off the gravel road they'd been traveling and guided it down a long drive. He braked the vehicle a few yards from a gate, put it into park and let it idle. Whitley stepped up to the gate and began working with what appeared to be an elaborate locking system. When the gate opened, McCarter drove the van inside the fence. After he secured the gate behind them, Whitley climbed back into the vehicle.

Three minutes later they pulled up to a ramshackle house topped with sheets of tin. A dozen or so chickens milled around the yard, pecking at the ground. Twenty-five yards distant, two asphalt-covered strips ran parallel to each other. A dozen or so yards farther on stood two more buildings, both outfitted with various antennas and satellite dishes.

McCarter forced twin tendrils of smoke through his nose. "Lap of damn luxury," he complained. He stepped from the van, discarded his cigarette and eyed the house warily. While Manning helped Kurtzman exit the van, Whitley walked up to the Phoenix Force leader and stood beside him.

"What's wrong?" he asked.

"Just a little jumpy after our last encounter at your office."

"Don't let the looks fool you," Whitley said. "This place is locked up tighter than a drum. We have sensors, biometric locks, the whole nine yards, as the Yanks say." He patted a pager clipped to his belt. "If someone trips an alarm here, our satellites pick up the signal and I get the page."

"Lots of security for this dump," McCarter said.

Whitley grinned. "Pardon the cliché, but looks can be deceiving. Just because the government booted Osama bin Laden from the country doesn't mean all his foot soldiers went, too. Same goes for the Iranians and a few other choice groups."

McCarter lit another cigarette and passed the pack to Whitley, who studied it for a minute.

"Player's cigarettes, eh? Still the same old McCarter. Anyway, this 'dump,' as you so indelicately referred to it, is an airport." He pointed to the wide lanes on either side of the building. "These long lanes, obviously, are landing strips. And this—" he spread his arms wide to take in the entire facility "—is the world headquarters of Global Sudanese Airlines."

McCarter slid his sunglasses down the bridge of his nose and stared over them at the other man. "You're yanking my chain. The CIA owns and operates an airline in Sudan? Right under their government's damn noses?"

"With their permission, as a matter of fact," Whitley said. "And if that isn't sweet enough, we own three other tracts of land at other locations around Khartoum. The runways are little more than gravel strips, but good enough to land military airplanes en masse, if we needed to. If we ever decided to give the Sudanese government the bitch slapping it so richly deserves, we could fly planes and helicopters in and out of here at will."

"Lord, but you're sneaky bastards," McCarter replied. He unclipped his mobile phone from his belt, punched in a number and waited for the call to go through. Calvin James answered on the second ring.

"Go," he said.

"We're here."

"Right. We've got your GPS signal. We'll be along soon enough."

"I'll have our host make sure the gate's open."

McCarter ended the call and returned the phone to his belt. Whitley had walked to the door and was working to open it.

After another ten minutes, McCarter and Manning had lugged their equipment bags into the house. McCarter cast his gaze around the place and decided it'd do for the moment. A pair of generators insured that the building had adequate power, and an air conditioner kept it cool.

"We can't leave the windows open," Whitley explained with a shrug when McCarter asked about it. "And it gets too damn hot here to go without ventilation. This primarily is where my staff and I hang our hats. The radars and high-tech communication equipment all are stored in the other buildings. You lads go ahead and make yourselves at home."

McCarter figured it was only a matter of minutes before his teammates showed up. In the meantime, he hunted down the refrigerator and found it stocked with Coke and bottled water. He grabbed a soft drink, dropped into a chair and waited for the others to arrive.

At a discreet cough McCarter turned to see Kurtzman rolling toward him. The former SAS paratrooper noticed his friend's cheeks were a deep scarlet. Kurtzman navigated the chair to within a couple of feet of McCarter and brought it to a halt.

"David," he began.

McCarter held up a hand to silence him. "You did good back at the house, lad. Saved Gary's hide, from what he says."

The computer whiz nodded.

"Bloody good show that. And we appreciate the assist. But you'll understand if I don't take you with us on any infiltration missions."

Kurtzman nodded again. "Understood. And sorry I blew up in the van."

"Forget about it. Someone needed to swat us on the nose."

"I'm just concerned about the kid. He can be a royal pain in the ass, but he's a good kid."

"Sure. We'll do what we can to find him."

James, Hawkins and Encizo arrived several minutes later. With the commandos seated or leaning against walls, Whitley began his briefing.

"Over the past several hours," he said, "I've been running the traps on your man, Jack Mace. As you know, he spends a good deal of his time here in Sudan. He's very generous when it comes to providing weapons to the government and the Janjaweed, the country's Arab militia. He's tied in quite tightly with the latter group."

"Imagine that," James said, scowling. "A guy who used to kill blacks in South Africa now is helping a bunch of creeps do the same thing here. Knock me over with a feather."

"Right," Whitley replied. "He's an unsavory character, to be sure. If I'd had my druthers, he'd already be buzzard food."

"So what stopped you?" James asked.

"Something about the man bothers me," Whitley said.

"Which brings us back to my question…"

"No, no, my friend. What I mean is, he always seemed to have a great deal of resources—money, connections, all that—at his disposal. Even by an arms dealer's standards, he seemed to have these things in abundance."

"Like he had a benefactor?"

"Yes, that's it. Over the past couple of years, I've placed at least three assets within his organization. One turned out to be a double agent. The other two were discovered and, um, dealt with quite severely."

McCarter watched as Whitley paused and stared at the floor for a second. "Rumor has it that Mace had them killed. Unfortunately we never found the remains for one of the men. He just disappeared. The second man, though, well, he was a friend, a pilot from the British army. He wanted some excitement. I tapped him to infiltrate Mace's organization. You know, fly some missions for him and see what turned up. After a couple of months, though, I lost contact with him. Eventually, he showed up at my office. Or what was left of him. In three boxes."

"Wow," Manning said.

"Yes, quite. But my assets all agreed on one thing. Mace seemed to have an inexhaustible supply of cash. When he got an order for something, no matter how large, he always paid his suppliers cash. We're talking high-dollar items, like Soviet tanks and missiles, obscene numbers of shoulder-fired missiles, all sorts of things. He owns, or at least has access, to several airplanes. It's all a theory, of course, but a solid one."

"So where in his network should we start?" McCarter asked.

"A month or so ago, one of my assets told me that Mace was on the market for slave labor. Seemed he had a project of some sort he was working on. I heard that tidbit from one of my mates who frequents the same watering hole as me. He knows a lot of the players and is happy to share his information for a few pints."

"Your tax dollars at work," Hawkins said, grinning.

Whitley cleared his throat. "Yes, well, anyway, he said Jean-Claude Morisi, a Frenchman in Khartoum, had been tapped to act as a go-between for Mace and a man named Yahya, a slave trader. Yahya's a slippery bastard. He has two or three camps and moves between them at random. Morisi, on the other hand, is a typical pencil pusher. You'll find him easily enough. That seems the best place to start."

CHAPTER SIXTEEN

Gabe Fox awakened and cracked open an eye.

He found himself blanketed in complete blackness. With no visual reference points to depend on, he felt as though he were floating. When he tried to raise his head and move his arms, lancets of pain ripped through his limbs, torso and head. He winced against the pain and remained still.

The floor felt cool and rough against his skin. He guessed it was concrete. He flattened his palms against the floor and brought himself up onto all fours. Pain seared every nerve ending. He bit his lower lip to hold in a groan. Waves of dizziness and nausea crashed over him. Before he could stop himself, he was heaving the contents of his stomach onto the floor. Even the act of vomiting sent excruciating waves of pain through his battered body.

His arms collapsed under him and he lay on his side, grateful to not have fallen into his own vomit. He tried to recall what had happened to him, but he found it too hard to focus, as though he'd been drugged. Maybe he had. He had such a hard time remembering. He closed his eyes and ceased to think about such things.

THE NEXT TIME he woke up, Fox was shivering. The stench of vomit filled his nostrils, causing his stomach to heave. Rolling onto his back, he sucked in deep breaths and waited for the sensation to pass. When it did, he noticed he was wet from head to toe. The bastards had doused him with cold water and left him shivering in his cell, which felt as frigid as a meat locker.

Images from his last go-around with his captors flashed through his mind. The bastard called Mace had beaten him like a dog. Multiple blows across the back, arms, legs and head with a nightstick. When he fell unconscious, the man roused him and beat him some more.

Mace had gotten just a few inches from his face. "Boy, it's only going to get worse for you," he'd said.

Fox had spit blood in the man's face. Mace had rewarded him for his efforts with another blow to the head that had plunged him into blackness.

Though the effort pained him, Fox forced himself into a sitting position. He pushed himself backward with his arms and legs until he came in contact with what he assumed was a wall. He leaned against it. Bruised flesh protested the sudden pressure, but he ignored it. It hurt like hell, sure. But the pain also was clearing his brain.

The protracted series of beatings played over and over in his mind and the memories caused a shiver to race through him. He looped his arms around his knees and brought his thighs closer to his chest to help generate some heat. It did only a little good, and he decided to instead focus on his predicament.

God damn him and this Cold Earth computer worm. What the hell had he been thinking? He'd created a world killer, and had thought as little of it as he did playing a video game. Even less, perhaps. Was it because he thought so little of life in general and his own life in particular? Maybe.

He shook his head, tipped it back until it rested against the wall behind him. Give it a rest, he thought. Pity isn't going to do you a damn bit of good. Truth be told, he didn't give two shits about the world. But he had loved his wife and he cared about his old friend, Aaron Kurtzman. For that reason alone, he couldn't let these SOBs win. He wasn't in love with life. He'd happily surrender it if it meant sticking it to them.

Now he just needed to pull the whole thing off.

THE DOOR OPENED. A sliver of yellow light cut through the darkness. An instant later Fox found himself bathed in light. He squinted against it. If he could wait a few moments until his eyes adjusted, he might be able to rush his attackers. It might turn into a suicide run. But, frankly, he didn't much care.

A soft object struck his face. He reached up to grab it. His fingertips immediately recognized the feel of fabric.

"Suit up," a man's voice said. "It's time for you to meet the boss."

Fox cracked his eyes just a hair's width. He caught the shadowy outlines of two men crowded in the doorway, watching over him. To hell with it, he thought. He tensed his muscles to lunge for them. Before he could move, though, the men stepped back and the door slammed shut. Once the cell was sealed, an overhead light clicked on.

Damn!

His eyes had adjusted enough for him to open them a little. He looked at the bundle in his arms. It was an orange jumpsuit, like those worn by jailed felons. A pair of flip-flop sandals lay nearby. Eyeing the cell, he found it was nothing more than a square brick room lit by two fluorescent bulbs. The room stank of ammonia and he realized that, while he'd been unconscious, someone had cleaned up his vomit. He considered yanking the bulb from its moorings, shattering it, using it for a weapon. A metal grate and the lack of something to stand on killed that idea.

Exhaling loud and long, he took what he saw as his only option. He got dressed and waited for his captors to return.

He guessed that another ten minutes passed before they returned for him.

The guard standing in the doorway pulled a pistol from a hip holster and handed it to one of the other guards. He nodded at Fox and made a semicircular motion with his index finger. "Turn around. Put your hands behind your back."

Fox complied, figuring it was his best option for the moment.

The guy looped plastic handcuffs around Fox's wrists, cinched them tight.

"Let's go," the guy said. "Someone here wants to meet you in the worst way."

FOX KNEW HE FACED a killer. The guy standing in front of him was thin, but not weak-looking. His skin seemed to cling to every curve and crevice on his skull. Wireless sunglasses perched on his nose covered his eyes. He looked like a walking skeleton, and from what Fox could tell it was a desired effect. The large handgun holstered on the man's right hip also caught Fox's attention.

The man gestured at a chair. Two guards led Fox to

it and shoved him into it. One of the men reached behind Fox's back and slashed his restraints. Fox brought his hands around and rubbed at his wrists, one of which leaked blood.

The man paced the room, but his movements were silent, as though his feet never touched the ground.

"I'm Dale Farnsworth," the man said.

Fox remained silent but watched the man's every move.

"I'm quite excited to have you here as my guest, Mr. Fox. You do incredible work. I'm a great admirer of your computer skills."

"Piss up a rope," Fox replied.

A hearty laugh exploded from inside the man. He continued pacing, only occasionally looking at his prisoner. Earlier, Fox had felt exhausted, his body racked with pain. Now his heart once again slammed inside his chest and adrenaline seemed to surge through him. His fight or flight instincts kicking into overdrive, he considered exploding from the chair and lunging for the SOB.

He had no illusions. Faced with three armed opponents, he likely would get taken down before he bridged the ten feet separating him from his captor. He realized that all he'd get for his trouble would be another beating and more time in solitary. Chances were that no one would drop a hammer on him unless he got hold of a gun himself. He rolled the option over in his mind, even as the skeleton continued to talk.

"—hoping that you'd cooperate a little more easily," the man was saying. "If you don't, we can, of course, resort to torture. Electrodes to the balls. Cutting off fingers. The whole thing. I'd be happy to do it myself."

"You can kill me for all I care," Fox said.

The man stopped and studied the programmer over the rim of his glasses. His lips parted in a nasty gash that Fox assumed was a weak attempt at a smile. "Kill you? Oh, no. I won't kill you. Not at all. I can keep you alive for weeks, months. Alive in a world of pain without end. You'll have plenty of time to wish you were dead. But you'll be a long time getting there. I'll make damn sure of that."

Fox shifted uncomfortably in his chair. He felt sweat break out on his upper lip and his palms.

"See, I know a lot about you, boy. I know about your time in the orphanages. I know about your scrapes with the law. I read in your file about all your daredevil stunts when you were a teenager. I'm not a psychologist, but I can tell you want to die. You'd love to fall asleep right now and never wake up again. Isn't that right?"

Apparently, Fox's surprise showed in his face. Farnsworth let loose with another laugh. "People like you aren't that complicated, really. You think you are, of course. You think your pain and suffering is as fascinating to the rest of the world as it is to you. It's not. I'd imagine it's rather tiresome. I'd venture to say that I did your lovely wife a favor by having her killed. If you had parents, I'd have done them the same damn favor."

Fox's muscles coiled and rage caused his breath to come in ragged gasps. He had to force himself not to lunge at the bastard. The man stopped in midstride, whipped around toward Fox and grinned at him. "I see you're angry. Did I upset you? Bringing up your wife, I mean? It was my decision to kill her. You realize that, don't you? I ordered her killed. And do you know how much I had to think about it?"

He paused and looked at Fox. The programmer remained silent, but he gripped the arms of his chair so hard that his knuckles turned white.

Farnsworth continued. "I didn't think about it. It was like pulling a dollar out of petty cash. Nothing at all. Just business. I'd kill her five more times if I thought it'd get me what I wanted."

Before he could think about it, Fox sprang from the chair, his arms and fingers outstretched. He moved until he came within grabbing distance of Farnsworth, but halted when a fiery pain registered in his midsection. He wheeled away, his legs giving out beneath him. He ended up on all fours, his body seized by the dry heaves.

As his coughing subsided, Farnsworth spoke again. "Feels horrible, doesn't it? I plunged two fingers under your rib cage. Jabbed your liver. I can do that every day, make life even more unlivable than you think it is. Of course, I wouldn't stop there. I can do a hell of a lot worse than that. Just wait and see."

Silence hung heavily in the room as Fox tried to pull himself together. He came to his feet, slow and unsteady. A guard grabbed him on either side and pushed him back into the chair.

Farnsworth stared at the programmer. Fox considered spitting on the man as a last show of defiance, but decided against it. He wasn't sure he had the strength to withstand any more punishment. At least not today. It was several minutes before he could speak. Farnsworth stood by and watched him, seemingly enjoying the younger man's predicament.

"What do you want?" Fox asked.

"I want the Cold Earth worm. The same damn thing everyone else wants. And I've paid a small goddamn fortune to get it."

"You don't have it. It was on my laptop. Last I

checked, my laptop's gone. I had a second copy on a minidisk. I assume that's gone, too. Am I right?"

Farnsworth gave a curt nod. "Cortez, the man who kidnapped you, didn't give us that. But cut the bullshit." He tapped his finger against his temple. "You've got the whole thing. You could reconstitute it in—what?— twenty-four hours."

Fox shrugged. "Maybe. Maybe sooner. What's in it for me?"

"Your life."

"We already agreed that my life isn't much of a prize."

"The absence of pain."

"You must think I'm a damn chump. You killed my wife. You've kidnapped me, dragged me to God knows where, beat and humiliated me. And now you want me to do your dirty work? For nothing? Fuck you. Obviously, you think there's a hell of a payday coming down. Otherwise, we wouldn't be having this discussion. You want me to help you? Fine, make it worth my while. Because my life ain't much of a bargaining chip."

"You're much shrewder than I thought."

"Yippee."

"What do you want?"

Fox licked his lips. His mouth tasted awful. His body ached in every conceivable place. Dehydration and fatigue made it hard to concentrate. "First of all, I want a shower and some real clothes." He pinched the fabric of his shirt between a thumb and index finger, tugged at it. "I don't want to dress like I'm on some damn work detail. I want a couple hours' sleep."

The other man smirked. "That's it? That's all you want?"

"Hell, no. That's just for starters. I want a $100 million, and a change of identity. And I need the laptop from my apartment. It's got some of the information I need." He tapped his temple with his index finger. "Despite what you think, genius, I can't recall everything I need from memory. But you get me that and we're golden. Think you can swing that?"

"Done." Farnsworth smiled.

The small man gestured for the guards to take Fox away. Fox avoided the other man's gaze as he left the room. He was afraid something in his eyes might betray his uncertainty. Fox knew he'd just made a pact with the devil. It made him sick. But he knew there was no other choice. The less willing he acted, the more scrutiny he'd come under. And, for what he had planned, the last thing he needed was Farnsworth and Mace breathing down his neck.

So, yeah, he'd made a deal with the devil. He hoped he wouldn't get burned in the process.

CHAPTER SEVENTEEN

Something hard struck the door to Jean-Claude Morisi's office, cracked it in two and caused it to surge inward. The pieces bounced across the floor with a clatter.

The sudden violence caused Morisi's heart to skip a beat. He made a play for his lap drawer, the one containing his Walther pistol. Before he could complete the move, a figure appeared in his doorway. Firing one-handed, the man strafed Morisi's office with lead.

The Frenchman froze and held up his hands. The guy let off the trigger and silence suddenly filled the room. When Morisi realized the man wasn't going to kill him, at least not immediately, he squinted at him, sized him up. The gunner was lanky with a face like a fox. In his free hand, the guy clutched the shirt collar of one of Morisi's soldiers. He was using it like a handle and dragging the limp man along like a suitcase.

He grinned at Morisi, uncurled his fingers and let the dead guy plummet to the floor.

"Easy lad," the man said. "You get too rambunctious, and I'd be happy to give you a two-for-one deal."

"He's dead?"

"As King Tut."

"Who the hell are you people?"

"Why don't you let us ask the questions? Seems only proper, seeing as how we're the guests and all."

MCCARTER STEPPED into the office, but kept his weapon trained on the Frenchman. Morisi remained motionless behind his desk. The Briton scrutinized the man, but saw no challenge in his eyes or body language.

"I asked you a question." Morisi's voice thundered. "Who are you? What's the meaning of this?"

"Some folks might call it retribution," McCarter said. "Or perhaps justice."

"Justice? For what? I've done nothing."

By now, Encizo and James had entered the room.

"How 'bout justice for all the flesh you've peddled over the last decade," James suggested. "We already know your record. You're a middleman for slavers. You know, the freaks who snatch the people, and the ones who buy them. That's what we want to discuss with you."

"You're crazy. I run an import-export business here. Coffee, grains, that sort of thing."

"You also import and export people. And when you're not doing that, you're converting diamonds and other minerals to cash, isn't that right? Your client list includes terrorists, drug dealers and syndicate bosses."

"You are insane. And you're trespassing. Get the hell out of here before I call the police."

With quick steps, McCarter bridged the distance between himself and the other man. The Briton reached out to grab hold of Morisi's shirt. The Frenchman smacked his hands aside and his fist rocketed for McCarter's face. He jerked his head back to avoid the blow. It glanced off his cheek and he felt the sting of metal opening skin. Grunting, the Phoenix Force leader lunged forward and caught Morisi with an uppercut to the jaw, followed by a second blow to the solar plexus. Morisi backpedaled and fell into his chair.

The Briton stepped in, grabbed Morisi by the shirt and buried his fist into the other man's face. Dropping him back in the chair, McCarter took a step back.

"Had enough or do you want another go?" the Phoenix Force leader asked. "I can do this all damn day."

The man held up a hand to signal that he'd had enough.

"You hooked a slave trader up with a man named Jack Mace."

"So?"

"So where's Mace?"

"I don't know."

McCarter sighed and ripped his Browning Hi-Power from his holster. He pointed the weapon at the man's face. The gray-haired slave trader backed up in his seat and held out both hands in a gesture of surrender.

"I'm serious," he said. "I don't know."

James spoke up. "You do business with him. How could you not know where he is? You ever talk to him?"

"Of course."

"In person?"

"Yes, of course."

"So where's he keeping himself these days?"

"I've never been to his place. If he wants something, he looks me up."

"What about a phone number?"

Morisi shook his head. "He no longer contacts me by phone. He's too paranoid. He worries that American intelligence will intercept his phone calls with the satellite."

"So how does he contact you?"

"Courier."

"And that'd be who?"

"Ali Hassab."

"I want him. How do you contact him?"

"Satellite telephone."

Encizo stepped up and set a satellite phone on the desktop. All three Phoenix Force members stared silently at Morisi and waited. The European picked up the phone and in less than a minute was connected to Hassab.

"I have something," he said. He paused and McCarter heard murmuring from the earpiece. "Yes, we must speak of this soon. It's unavoidable, I'm afraid." Another pause. "Yes, the usual place will be fine. I will be bringing some paperwork. You must handle it before we can go any further."

Morisi said goodbye and ended the call. The Frenchman stared at the phone for a minute, seemingly lost in thought.

"Let's go," McCarter said.

"He's going to kill me," Morisi said.

"Who, your chum on the phone?" the Briton asked. "Screw him. He'll be lucky to see another sunset."

Morisi shook his head. "I mean Mace. When he learns I've betrayed him, he'll have me killed."

"Sucks to be on the other end of a gun, doesn't it? Get off your rosy red arse or Mace'll be the least of your worries. Cross me and I'll be using your head for a football."

MCCARTER WALKED through the double doors. Scanning the tearoom, he selected a corner booth. Several men sat at small tables, drinking tea and speaking to one another in Arabic. Most fell silent when he entered the room. A dozen sets of eyes locked on him.

The Briton scowled, but tried to ignore their looks. He crossed the room and seated himself. He ordered a chicken and rice dish and some tea from a young woman, her head wrapped in a headscarf. From inside his jacket, he pulled out his mobile phone and placed it on the table. The woman returned with his tea, handed it to him and disappeared through a pair of doors and into what McCarter assumed was the kitchen.

Five minutes later Morisi stepped inside and seated himself at the table to the Briton's right and against the opposite wall. A couple of the men gave the Frenchman a courteous nod, but didn't approach his table. Morisi ignored McCarter, choosing instead to stare out the window. It didn't escape McCarter's notice that the man had selected a table next to the kitchen, ostensibly offering him an exit from the facility if things fell apart.

Distant motion from the corner of his eye and a blast of heat through an open door caught McCarter's attention. He casually turned his head and saw a big man filling the doorway. The Briton guessed the guy stood a few inches over six feet tall. Thick bands of muscle corded his neck and strained against the fabric of his T-shirt. Dark eyes swept over the room and locked on McCarter. He walked to a corner diagonal from the Stony Man warrior, stood and crossed his arms over his chest. His eyes never strayed from the Briton. Under other circumstances, the former SAS commando would gladly take up the challenge. In this case, though, he averted the hardman's gaze and stared into his tea.

At the same time, the soldier let his left hand drift under the table. He unzipped his jacket, grateful for the Browning Hi-Power it concealed. He'd loaded the clip with alternating rounds of hollowpoint and hardball ammunition. A .44 Charter Arms Bulldog was snug in a holster at the small of his back.

A sideways glance revealed that the big man continued to stare at him. Before he could give it another thought, however, another guy walked into the room. This man was whipcord-thin and decked out in desert camouflage pants, a brown T-shirt and combat boots. A second man, heavyset, dressed in worn khakis and a green sport shirt, followed close behind. The new arrivals looked at the bruiser in the corner who acknowledged them with a nod.

The men walked to Morisi's table. They exchanged greetings and the slender man seated himself across from the Frenchman. He fit Morisi's description of Ali Hassab, though McCarter didn't have a clue as to the other man's identity.

The two men spoke, their voices drowned out by background chatter and other noises. McCarter aimed his phone at the two men and stared at their image in its screen. Both shot furtive glances his way and he knew things were about to blow apart. He snapped a picture of the men. He hit a couple of buttons and sent the image to the other team members so they could identify Hassab if he bolted.

Another couple of minutes passed. Impatience began to gnaw at McCarter. His tea grew cold, and the big thug in the corner stared at him with sphinxlike intensity. Morisi was supposed to lead his contact outside where Phoenix Force could grab him. But, McCarter realized, the treacherous bastard seemed to be dragging things out.

Suddenly the Briton heard footsteps to his right. He whirled and saw the big thug racing toward him. Using his thick forearms like baseball bats, the guy knocked aside other patrons and headed straight for McCarter.

The former SAS commando made a play for his Browning. The big bruiser reached him before he could clear leather. He grabbed two handfuls of McCarter's shirt and yanked him from his seat. At the same time, Morisi, Hassab and the third man rocketed up from their seats and bolted in different directions.

McCarter finally freed the gun. But, with a sweep of his hand, the man batted it from his grip. He thrust McCarter against the wall and the breath exploded from the commando's lungs. Fingers reached out and encircled McCarter's throat. A thumb pressed hard against his esophagus, robbing him of his air.

McCarter's foot rocketed out for the bodyguard's groin. But the toe of his boot collided with the hard muscle of the guy's thigh. Starved of oxygen, the Briton's vision began to blur. A croaking noise escaped his lips as he struggled unsuccessfully to grab another breath.

MORISI THREADED his way through the small kitchen.

His contact, Ali Hassab, was just a step behind. Hassab had left his personal bodyguard to handle that damned Brit. Morisi regretted only that he couldn't stay long enough to see the man die.

Morisi arrived at the rear door and reached for the release bar. His collar suddenly jumped into his throat, causing him to gag. An unseen force pulled him backward, spun him and slammed his back against a wall. The cold steel of a handgun pressed against his throat. Hassab, his face a mask of rage, glared at him. The Arab's heavyset associate, Yazid Thubaiti, stood behind his boss.

"Tell me what's going on," Hassab said. "Or you go nowhere."

"It's a setup. I was forced to call you here. Otherwise they were going to kill me."

"Who was going to kill you?"

Morisi gestured with a thumb toward the tearoom. "The man in there. And his friends. I don't know who they work for. British. Americans. I'm not sure. But they want Mace."

"Someone's looking for Mace?"

"Yes, damn it!"

"And you led them here?" The man's voice didn't climb above a whisper, but it took on a hissing quality that telegraphed his anger. "You led them to me? Are you insane? Mace would have killed us both."

Morisi stared into the other man's hard gaze. He opened his mouth to speak, to explain himself. Before he could, a handgun's report drowned out his words and the world went black.

HASSAB STARED at the man on the floor. A pool of blood already forming around him. The gunshot at such close range had nearly decapitated Morisi. The gruesome sight didn't bother the Arab at all. He wished he could kill the bastard a thousand times over to punish him for his betrayal.

Ears still ringing from the pistol shot, Hassab felt something warm and sticky coating his face, neck and shooting hand. With his empty hand, he ran a finger down his cheek, inspected it, saw it glisten with blood. He wiped it on his pants. Panic threatened to overtake him and his mind raced through his options. He turned to Thubaiti and motioned in the direction of the tearoom with his pistol. "Go. We must contact Yahya, tell him someone's coming for him. That they want Jack Mace."

Thubaiti nodded and slipped from the kitchen.

Hassab spun on his heel, burst through the back door and into an alley that ran beside the tearoom.

A short man with heavy shoulders and biceps stood in his path. The guy held a small Uzi in his right hand. The barrel was pointed directly at Hassab's midsection. He froze.

"Drop the weapon," the man said. One look into the man's dark brown eyes, made even more severe-looking by his heavy brows, told Hassab that he'd better comply. He knelt, set his pistol on the ground and came back to standing. He kicked it toward the man without being asked.

Scooping up the pistol, the man shoved it into his waistband.

"So, obviously you speak English," the man said. "That saves us time."

Hassab nodded, but was thinking of Fareeq, the big man inside the restaurant. Sweat broke out along Hassab's hairline and on his back. Where was he? Surely he'd taken care of the man inside by now.

"Did you hear me?" the man asked.

Hassab nodded again. He licked his lips and spoke. "You want to question me, correct? I can't imagine what you want with me. The man you're looking for remains inside."

"Really, and who am I looking for, amigo?"

"Well…"

"And why should I trust the word of a man whose clothes are smeared blood? Someone else's blood for that matter. Turn around, and put your hands against the wall."

"Your friend is in trouble," Hassab said, a desperate quality sneaking into his voice.

"What the hell are you saying?"

"Your friend. He's inside. Another man attacked him."

The man scrutinized him for a stretched second. With the Uzi, he gestured at the wall even as he tilted his head and spoke into an unseen microphone. "Cal! David! Situation report. Now!"

MCCARTER FELT the last bits of struggle drain from his body. Black spots began to swirl in his vision. He knew unconsciousness and ultimately death lay just ahead.

With his last vestiges of strength, he reached around his back. Outstretched fingers that almost seemed disconnected from his senses searched for the Charter Arms Bulldog pistol holstered at the small of his back.

A fingertip brushed against the rubberized grip. The former paratrooper moved to grab the weapon, but his attacker shook him furiously, like a dog with a rag. His flagging senses and the violent shaking caused him to lose track of the weapon.

I'm gone, he thought. I failed.

Through the noise of his panicked thoughts, he heard a rumble, like distant thunder. All at once, the pressure on his throat eased and his body plummeted to the floor. He rolled over on his side and gulped large amounts of air into his oxygen-starved lungs.

He heard two more rumbles. Each sounded successively sharper as he regained his senses. He glanced up and saw Calvin James standing over him protectively. The former Navy SEAL clutched a Glock 20 in both hands and swept it over the room.

McCarter fisted the Bulldog and rolled onto his side

to study the room. He found his attacker and two other men lying dead on the floor. The restaurant otherwise was empty. Reaching down, James grabbed the Briton by the arm and helped him stand.

Movement registered to his right. He spun, the Bull-dog leading the way.

He caught Encizo stepping into the room. The Cuban held up his hands, grinned. "Down boy," he said. "We're all friends here."

McCarter lowered the weapon. His throat hurt like hell. He rubbed it almost unconsciously, not wanting to think about how close he'd come to dying. When he spoke, his voice came out with a tortured rasp. "Where's the little pencil neck who snuck out the back? I'm ready to stick my foot up his arse so far it'll pop out his belly button."

"He's in the kitchen, cooling his heels," Encizo said.

"He give you any trouble?" McCarter asked.

"Not once I cracked him in the head with the Uzi."

"It's a gun, not a baseball bat," McCarter said. He gave the two men a wink. "Good job, lads. Sorry I dropped the ball on this one."

"Shit," James said, "I wouldn't want to have tangled with this circus freak. I mean, not if I was scrawny and ill-trained like you."

McCarter smiled. "Rafe, get me Hassab. I'm feeling damned frustrated, and he's about to bear the brunt of it. What about Morisi?"

Encizo drew the first two fingers of his left hand across his Adam's apple in a slashing motion. "Dirt nap," he said.

"Damn," McCarter said. "I hate it when they get off lucky like that. And the big chap?"

Encizo and James exchanged glances.

"Damn," James said.

"Wonderful," Encizo replied.

"I'll go after him," James said.

McCarter spoke up. "No. We need to grab our new friend and get the hell out of here. I doubt if the local police will be amused with our antics."

CHAPTER EIGHTEEN

Musa Yahya puffed listlessly on his cigarette and said a silent prayer that God would vanquish those who, even now, were burning across the desert to kill him.

He paced the floor and considered what he'd been told. A group of men, at least two of them Americans, were hunting him. From what Thubaiti had told him, they wanted information about Jack Mace and knew he could provide it.

Stubbing out the cigarette, he lit another and dragged on it slowly. The news of an attack had disturbed Yahya, of course. He detested Mace and his boss, Dale Farnsworth, and hardly considered them worth dying for. Just as importantly, he saw no need in losing all he'd worked so hard to build just because he'd provided the slave labor and some of the skilled workers Farnsworth had needed to help transform the former underground nuclear laboratory into a home base for the Americans. Also, using his old contacts in Libya's military and intelligence, he'd recruited another forty mercenaries on Mace's behalf. But most important, he knew where Farnsworth and Mace had set up shop. This, he realized, made him what intelligence and military agents liked to call a "high-value target." The thought prompted him to spit in anger; he was no man's target. Particularly not for Americans who thought they could enter his country, his home and threaten him. So, no, he wasn't willing to fight and die for someone else. But if these commandos came for him, they'd find that they faced a formidable enemy.

A knock sounded at the door. Without thinking, he whirled toward it. His hand dropped to the Colt .45 handgun that lay on his desktop.

"Yes?" he asked.

"It's Khalid."

"Enter."

The door opened and a hulking man came into the room. He wore desert camouflage fatigues, the cuffs and collars frayed at the edges, the colors faded by several shades because of too many years of wear. Like his clothes, his face showed evidence of too many campaigns. The lower half of his face was a mosaic of hair and skin, the bald patches in his beard created by old bullet scars that wouldn't allow for hair growth.

Shutting the door behind him, Khalid set to the floor an M-60 ES, a cut-down version of the machine gun used by U.S. soldiers. Legend had it that Khalid had taken the weapon from a U.S. Navy SEAL, part of a team that'd been dispatched to Sudan to take out an al Qaeda training camp. To listen to the other mercenaries tell it, Khalid had killed the man with his bare hands and taken the weapon from him.

Yahya had no way of verifying the story, of course. Khalid wasn't given to bragging, and chances were just as good that he'd happened across the weapon at one of the arms-trading bazaars in the frontier between Pakistan and Khalid's home of Afghanistan. What Yahya knew was that his personal bodyguard was a stone-cold killer, efficient and remorseless. It'd take a small army to get past him.

Khalid nodded. "Farnsworth is sending us two choppers filled with men. He wants these people stopped here and he's not afraid to give us the men and equipment necessary to make it happen. I've also set up machine gunners outside this building. No one can get inside it without getting shredded alive."

"Go on."

"I will position myself and two other men outside the door. If they do get this far, I will cut them down."

Yahya smiled grimly. He knew that in those cramped quarters, no soldier could get past Khalid. He'd butcher them like cattle, no matter how many came. Still, this was his own life he was gambling with, too precious a currency to risk. He rubbed his beard between his thumb and forefinger while he ruminated over his options.

"How many do we have in the pens?"

Khalid thought for a moment. "Forty-five at least. Maybe more since the last hunter team returned to the compound."

"If things begin to go badly for us, here's what I want you to do."

KNEELING, MCCARTER WITHDREW a rolled-up piece of paper from his pocket, unrolled it and laid it on the ground. He set a stone on it to hold it in place. The sheet held a blown-up satellite image of group of buildings of various sizes and shapes, corralled by a fence. Someone had marked several points on the picture and identified the shapes with the words "stable," "motor pool" or "pens."

Encizo and Hawkins knelt around the picture while James, hands on his knees, bent and studied the sat photo over McCarter's shoulder. Hawkins stood a dozen or so yards away, scanning the area for possible threats.

"This is where our best mate, Musa Yahya, is hanging his hat, lads," the Briton said. "From what Hassab told me, it's a slave camp. I guess some of the human rights organizations marked this place a long time ago. Most of the intelligence we've got on the buildings actually came to us thanks to firsthand testimony from people who'd either escaped the place or had been purchased by the human rights people. So it's pretty good stuff. Not perfect, but I feel at least reasonably confident in it. Otherwise, we'd be shaking down some more people to get better information."

Using his pencil as a pointer, he drew an imaginary circle around a large building fronted by three smaller structures. "The big place is Yahya's house. The three places in front are cinder-block buildings used for storage, bathhouses and the like." He tapped two more structures on the camp's east end. "These are barracks. There's a helipad next to the main house."

He pointed to two more gray squares on the camp's west end.

"These are the slave pens," he said. "From what we've gathered, most of these people don't stay at the camp for more than a few days. Then these bastards take them somewhere to sell them. The handful that stay longer occasionally end up sleeping in slightly better quarters. Those usually are young women. I don't think I have to say more about that, do I?"

James's lips compressed and he shook his head in disgust. "Man, these slaver pigs deserve to die twice."

McCarter nodded his head in agreement. "Unfortunately, we're going to have to settle for once. For the most part. In Yahya's case, even less. We need him to cough up information about the underground bunker in Libya or else we can all go home."

"The Farm couldn't get a better location?" James asked.

McCarter shook his head. "They've nailed it down to within a hundred-mile radius, thanks to some help from a Libyan expatriate who claims to have worked with the program during the 1990s. But they usually only flew him there at night, and did that only infrequently. That makes his information sketchy at best. We have three possible sites, but two are Libyan army outposts."

"Attack the wrong one, and end up with an international incident on our hands," Encizo said.

"Right," McCarter replied. "We need this bastard to tell us where we're going. So let's go see if he's in a chatty mood."

JAMES STOMPED the Hummer's accelerator. It responded with a growl and lunged forward, gathering speed with each passing moment. Scrub brush crunched under the vehicle's tires. It rocked to and fro as James rolled the big vehicle over stones and other obstacles.

Cutting the wheel right, he guided the vehicle onto a dirt road leading to the front gate of the compound ahead of him. Four guards stood outside the gate, each armed with an AK-47. Initially, they watched his approach with open defiance. It quickly melted to concern as they realized the Hummer wasn't stopping.

James couldn't help but grin as he bore down on the hardmen.

According to intel provided by Stony Man Farm,

the compound housed a slave-trading operation. Janjaweed militants kidnapped men, women and children from their homes and sold them into bondage. That made him see red. As far as he was concerned, it was high time to teach this pack of killers a lesson in fear.

When the Hummer roared within a dozen or so yards of the gate, two of the thugs turned tail and darted away. The other two held their ground. One stood directly in the vehicle's path. A second was positioned to James's right, several yards from the hurtling vehicle.

Autofire erupted from the barrels of the guards' assault rifles. The 7.62 mm rounds thwacked against the Hummer's hood, grille and windows, sparking off its armored exterior. At the last instant, the shooter in front of the Hummer hurled himself sideways.

The vehicle missed the man by inches, but it hammered into the security gate with enough unfettered force to rip the barrier from its hinges. The all-terrain tires grabbed hold of the wood, wire mesh and steel rods, mangling them.

James slammed the brakes and cut the wheel hard. The vehicle spun ninety degrees, kicking up roiling clouds of dirt in the process.

The guards were back on the attack. They poured through the gate, their weapons chattering. He grabbed an Uzi from the seat next to him, jammed the stubby muzzle into the gun port and laid down a burst of 9 mm stingers. Two of the gunners fell under the sizzling hail of gunfire. The remaining two men sprinted in different directions. One dived behind a pair of rusted oil drums that stood near the fence; the second ran from James, carving out a zigzag pattern as he sprinted away.

James peppered the oil drums with sweeping bursts

from the Uzi. The hidden shooter keeled over, clutching his bullet-ridden chest. He shuddered once and died.

A quick glance toward the fence told James that the other members of Phoenix Force were racing toward the compound, their guns blazing. Janjaweed soldiers had lined up along the fence, unloading automatic weapons-fire in the direction of his comrades. A couple stood on a catwalk that ran the length of the front fence, firing down on the advancing troops. James was sure more would arrive quickly.

He exited the Hummer and locked it. A menacing reflection in the driver's-side door prompted James to whirl in time to catch one of the enemy gunners coming up from behind. The man's upraised arm dropped and a dagger plunged toward James's neck. Moving with lightning speed, he threw his arm out sideways and knocked the man's forearm off course with a blow from the Uzi. At the same time, the man's other hand jabbed out and landed square against James's chin. It was a solid blow, and his head jerked to the right. He let himself fall back a few inches until his back connected with the Hummer's door. The move gave him a few precious inches of space. Raising his foot, he stomped hard on the arch of the man's foot. The guy cried out. While the man was distracted, James reached out, grabbed him by the hair and yanked his head downward. In the same moment, the Phoenix Force commando raised his knee and drove it into the man's face. The man went limp and fell to the ground, unconscious.

McCarter's voice came through the warrior's earpiece. "If you're done with your title bout there, mate, we could use a steady hand, a little help."

"Couldn't you always?" James said.

Gunfire blazed in James's direction and drummed

against the Hummer's hood, which was behind him. He ducked then skirted around the vehicle's back end and edged along the passenger's side. He caught the shooters approaching the vehicle in a wide arc, their weapons grinding out streams of 7.62 mm ammo. Popping up from behind his cover, James hosed down the ragged line of fighters. The unforgiving barrage cut them down.

The thunder of explosives swelled to James's left, momentarily overpowering the steady rattle of gunfire.

The Phoenix Force commando whirled and saw a pair of blasts ripping through a section of the catwalk. Flames and smoked boiled up from the strike point. The blasts sent a half dozen or so fighters tumbling toward the ground, several of them with their clothes ablaze.

James reloaded his weapon and burst from behind the Hummer. A few of the fallen fighters lay on the ground, apparently stunned. Two more, their weapons clutched in their hands, were trying to stand. Another had rolled onto his stomach and was shooting from a prone position at James's teammates.

The warrior unloaded a swarm of steel-jacketed slugs at his foes. The bullets rent the Janjaweed killers and upped the casualty rate by three.

James's attack caught the attention of the fighters still positioned on the catwalk. The warrior spun on a heel and darted for the Hummer, triggering his weapon and the engine on the run with the remote key fob. A storm of automatic fire chewed into the ground at James's heels.

He climbed inside the vehicle, hit the gas and wheeled the Hummer toward the fence. The aerial position the catwalks provided gave the enemy a decided advantage over Phoenix Force.

For the moment.

As the vehicle gained speed, James guided it toward the vertical posts supporting one end of the catwalk. The big vehicle's reinforced front end bludgeoned the posts. Steel ground against steel, generating an unearthly screech.

Unlike the gate, the hollow steel posts bent and creased, but didn't break. The impact jarred the concrete moorings, too, without actually ripping them from the ground.

The force threw James forward. Though the air bags had been deactivated, the safety harness held him in place and prevented his head from striking the steering wheel. He heard the unmistakable thud of bodies striking the Hummer's roof before they bounced to the ground.

He slammed the vehicle into park and tried to collect himself.

A voice buzzed in his earpiece.

"Cal, you okay in there?" T. J Hawkins asked.

"Yeah," James replied. "Anyone for a chorus of 'It's Raining Men'?"

"Son, you say that again and people are gonna start talking."

WHEN THE SHUDDERING of the catwalks knocked several shooters to the ground, McCarter sprang to his feet and charged for the compound. Manning fell in behind him while Hawkins and Encizo laid down streams of suppressive fire to cover their advance. For this leg of the mission, McCarter was carrying an M-4 fitted with an M-203 grenade launcher, along with his Browning handguns, knives, garrotes and other weapons of war necessary for the raid. Manning carried the same assault rifle/grenade launcher combo, along with a .44-caliber Desert Eagle handgun, which rode in a thigh holster.

A group of hardmen braved the onslaught of gunfire and charged out from behind a cinder-block building, their guns blazing. Without breaking stride, McCarter and Manning cut loose with the M-4s.

The British commando shot from the hip and downed two of the gunners. Simultaneously, Manning hosed down three more of the marching killers with a sustained burst of 5.56 mm tumblers from his M-4. An instant later the Phoenix Force commandos had sprinted through the gate, dropped to one knee and began to churn out streams of suppressive fire, giving Hawkins and Encizo a chance to close in on the compound.

A line of bullets whistled several inches from McCarter's left ear. Moving his head and rifle in unison, the warrior spotted a gunner hunkered down behind the rear end of a black Toyota Land Cruiser. The muzzle of his adversary's Kalashnikov rifle protruded from behind the vehicle, churning out autofire, the barrage closing in quickly on the Phoenix Force commander. His battle-honed reflexes kicked in and prompted him to dive forward to avoid catching a bullet.

The enemy gunner stayed cool and fast under fire. He peppered the ground in front of McCarter with another hail of bullets as he tried to line up a good shot. Small bits of dirt flew into the Briton's eyes, causing him to squint while he lined up a shot with his M-203. An HE round whooshed from the launcher's barrel and struck the Toyota, exploding on contact. Windows exploded and red-orange flames boiled out from the point of impact. A peal of thunder boomed from inside the vehicle. A secondary explosion occurred almost instantly when flames reached the gas tank and ignited its contents.

The accompanying force lifted the vehicle off its wheels and thrust it several feet into the air before it crashed back to earth. Engulfed in flames, the shooter stumbled around, screaming, his weapon abandoned as he tried to beat out the flames with his hands. McCarter loosed a mercy burst into the man's chest, ending his suffering almost immediately. The Phoenix Force leader broke open the M-203 and thumbed another HE round inside.

In the meantime, Manning's combat senses alerted him to impending danger. Turning, he caught one of the Janjaweed fighters advancing toward him. The enemy gunner held an old black man tight against him, a human shield, and pointed a small automatic pistol at Manning. If the Janjaweed hardman's fear-filled eyes were any indicator, he intended to slip through the gate and leave the killzone behind.

Manning leveled his gun at the two men. He caught the old man's gaze and gave him a tight smile, hoping to reassure him. Blacks in the Sudan for so many years had suffered inhuman treatment that Manning was afraid the old man might assume that the commando would shoot right through him to take down the Janjaweed fighter. He wanted the man to know that wasn't the case.

The old man got it. He began kicking furiously at his captor, jabbing him with bony elbows. The Janjaweed gunner thrust the old man away from him. Before he could focus back on Manning, the warrior bracketed him in his sights and pounded his midsection with gunfire.

With his teammates inside the compound, Manning sprinted for the old man who suddenly found himself in the middle of the melee. When he reached the old man, he crouched next to him, held out a hand to help. With the big Canadian's assistance, the old man rose unsteadily. Manning scanned their surroundings for more threats, but found that his comrades were taking the fight to the enemy.

A second Toyota Land Cruiser roared around the corner of a nearby building, its tires kicking up clouds of dust, and hurtled toward Phoenix Force warriors.

Encizo whirled toward it and fired his multiround projectile launcher at the vehicle. A 40 mm round arced at the vehicle and lanced through its windshield. A heartbeat later fire ripped through the speeding vehicle. The burning Toyota veered from its course and collided with James's Hummer, which he'd abandoned minutes before. The collision caused more pieces from the now-empty catwalk to fall upon the two cars even as flames ripped through the Hummer.

A pickup truck barreled into view from behind a cinder-block building. Three fighters stood in the truck bed, firing their weapons at the Stony Man warriors. The Cuban triggered the weapon a second time and sent a round whooshing at the pickup. The projectile pierced the truck's grille and exploded, yet the burning vehicle continued to bear down on Phoenix Force.

Encizo's eyes widened as he watched the vehicle approach. "Shit," he muttered.

"Everybody!" he yelled into his throat mike. "Move!"

Glancing over his shoulder, he saw McCarter and Manning look around in time to see the blazing wreckage rocketing toward them. The men darted in separate directions, giving the truck a wide berth. Encizo turned left, broke into a sprint and darted through a door leading into one of the cinder-block buildings. The truck exploded outside.

Hanging the launcher between his shoulder blades, Encizo took up his M-4 and stepped back outside. He swept his gaze over the battlefield and saw that at least two dozen mercenaries and Janjaweed fighters lay scattered, either in whole or in parts, across it. It had been a short and bloody battle so far, and it was nowhere near finished.

LEGS PUMPING, sweat streaming down his neck and back, Hawkins surged toward the motor pool that lay on the camp's west end. When he reached the edge of the last building, he dropped to one knee and took the LAW rocket from his back and set it on the ground next to him. Studying the motor pool, he saw two more Land Cruisers along with three pickup trucks that he guessed were used for transporting captives. Oil drums were lined in three rows of three to his left.

He telescoped the LAW open and brought it to his shoulder. Bracketing the oil drums in his sights, he triggered the weapon. The round lanced into the oil and exploded, igniting columns of flames that shot a dozen feet or more into the air. Billowy black smoke rose from the burning containers, choking the sky with its toxic mix.

Discarding the empty LAW, he took up his M-4/M-203 combo and fired an HE round into the motor pool. Hellfire tore through two of the Toyotas even as Hawkins reached inside his satchel for another HE round. The second round arced up before dropping into one of the pickup truck beds. The explosion ignited the gas tank, the force lifting the vehicle into the air before gravity reasserted itself. The blast rent steel and melted plastic and rubber into slag.

Hawkins thumbed another HE shell into the M-203

and began to move again. He left behind the burning motor pool and began to make tracks for Yahya's home.

A voice boomed in his earpiece. "T.J.!"

"Go, David."

"Location?"

"I'm near the motor pool. I was heading for the big man's house."

"Scratch that," McCarter said. "I just spoke with Barb. Crew from the AWACS plane says we have two more birds coming our way. Filled with reinforcements most bloody likely."

"Roger that."

"I need you, Rafe and Gary to work your magic with them. Let Cal and I handle this creep holed up in the house."

"Probably for the best," Hawkins said. "Everything I'm touching today blows up."

"The choppers are coming from the west," McCarter said. "Hold your position and I'll send the others to join you."

"Roger."

Minutes later Manning and Encizo, both of whom carried 40 mm multiround launchers on their backs, caught up with Hawkins. Manning carried a pair of RPG-7s. He held out both the fifteen-pound weapons to Hawkins. The younger commando took the weapons, holding each by its front grip, his index finger looped outside the trigger guards. He shot Manning a questioning look.

The big Canadian flashed his friend a grin. "I stole these from their armory," he explained. "Thought they might come in handy."

"Time to cock and roll then," Hawkins said, returning the smile.

JAMES KNELT in the dirt, hidden behind a line of empty oil drums, and studied the hardsite. Yahya's home was hardly palatial. In fact, it was little more than a one-story building that measured perhaps two thousand square feet. Like the compound's other structures, it was constructed of cinder blocks painted beige. It differed from the others primarily in size, but also through such features as window air conditioners and barred windows.

Hardly palatial, sure, but it was better than the slaver deserved.

About twenty yards from James's position, he noted a trio of shooters had barricaded themselves behind sandbags. An HK 21 belt-fed machine gun poised on a tripod was visible over the top of the sandbags. The other two men were scrutinizing their firing zones over the barrels of AK-47s, the barrels of which rested on the sandbags. To the right of the first group of hardmen stood a second knot of gunners, similarly armed and hidden behind sandbags. Let McCarter deal with them, James thought.

The commando licked his lips to moisten them. His clothes and skin, particularly the layer underneath his Kevlar vest, were soaked with perspiration. He keyed his headset. "You ready to move, David?"

"Nearly. Just let me get into position, so I can give them a couple of 40 mm love taps. Then we can storm the house, take it out fast and furious. Just remember—we take Yahya alive. Everyone else on his team is expendable."

"Roger that."

James waited another sixty seconds or so. His senses were hypertuned into his surroundings, listening intently to the sounds of combat emanating from within the compound. Occasionally he glanced over his shoulder to make sure no one approached his six.

"Okay, lad, on a three count, go ahead and lay down some fire on those bastards."

"With pleasure."

James brought the M-4 to his shoulder and waited for McCarter to finish his count. When he did, James popped around from behind his cover and caressed the assault rifle's trigger. The weapon's full-auto assault tore into the group of gunners closest to him.

An instant later the head of one of the AK-47 shooters disappeared in a red mist. Surprise had given James about a one-second advantage. He watched as the machine gunner scanned for the source of the gunfire and began swinging the tripod-mounted weapon in his direction. James triggered the M-4 and dragged it in a figure-eight pattern. The burst of autofire ripped into the machine gunner, knocking him backward.

The third shooter seemed unfazed by the sudden outbreak of gunfire. James saw him lining up a shot in the commando's direction and swung the M-4's muzzle, emptying the weapon in the man's direction. Stray shots pounded into sandbags, shredding them. James's initial burst missed the Janjaweed gunner, but prompted the man to drop out of sight to avoid taking a round. The Phoenix Force commando wheeled behind the oil drums and threw himself to the ground for cover. Bullets drilled into the drums before exploding out the other side, passing within inches of James. He scrambled to find a spare clip for the M-4.

While he reloaded his assault rifle, he heard a hissing sound cut through the air. A moment later a loud boom rang out throughout the compound. Dirt showered down on the commando. James smiled grimly.

McCarter apparently had entered the fray. More hissing heralded a second strike, this one close to James. Two 40 mm HE rounds collided with something, this time closer to James. He peered around his cover and saw plumes of smoke rising from inside the gunner's nest.

"Ready to hit the house?" McCarter asked through the com link.

"Let's go."

GUNFIRE AND EXPLOSIONS crashed outside Yahya's house. He flinched, his breath catching in his throat. These commandos were getting closer to him, much closer than he'd expected. He felt trapped like a cornered animal.

"Khalid!"

The door opened and the big man stuck his head inside the room. He gave Yahya a questioning look.

"Progress report. Give it to me. Now!"

"They've broken through our outer defenses, the security fence and our ground troops. Our men outside are gone, dead. They'll be hitting us soon."

Khalid's tone remained even, as though he were discussing the weather rather than a mortal threat to their lives.

"You are prepared?"

Though he'd tried to keep his voice calm, commanding, to project courage, his words came out sounding brittle, strained. He flushed with embarrassment. He looked at Khalid, hoping to determine whether the bigger man had detected his fear. If it had registered with Khalid, he gave no outward indication. He just stared at Yahya with fathomless eyes that revealed nothing, like a cobra's stare.

"You are prepared?" Yahya asked again, this time putting more force into his words.

"Of course," Khalid replied.

Yahya gestured at the door. "Go then. Go and deal with these bastards."

Khalid turned and left, closing the door behind him.

Yahya moved to his desk. He stared for a moment at the satellite phone that sat on the right corner of his desk. He squelched an impulse to pick it up and call Farnsworth. He wanted to curse the man for bringing this wrath down on his head. Yahya was just a business-man. He knew he'd have no quarrel with these attack-ers under other circumstances.

His fingertips stopped just before they touched the phone. He jerked back his hand as though it'd been scalded. What the hell was he thinking? What if they had the ability to trace the call? What if he successfully survived this assault, destroyed his attackers, only to run afoul of Farnsworth?

He shook his head. He couldn't risk it. Instead, he grabbed the .45-caliber Colt that lay next to the satel-lite phone. He checked the load, paced the floor and waited as the sounds of war grew louder.

THE SOVIET CHOPPERS carrying Farnsworth's thugs ap-peared first as small dots on the horizon. But Hawkins could imagine how they looked. In his mind's eye, he could see the steel gunships casting big shadows that glided along the ground, winding their way between bunches of scrub brush like sharks searching a reef for prey. Rotor wash whipped sand and dirt into large clouds, the cresting waves of earth announcing their im-pending arrival at Yahya's compound.

Hawkins watched the craft approach and estimated

their distance, trying to plan the optimal shot. He and Manning were crouched on either side of an aluminum shed situated outside the compound fence. They'd found a bedsheet and torn it into strips, wrapping the fabric around the lower half of their faces to protect their mouths and noses from the dirt. Old goggles found in a garage hanging from the handlebars of a stash of motorcycles shielded their eyes from the grit and debris.

"I'll call the shot," Manning said.

"Clear," Hawkins replied into his throat microphone.

"We don't get another shot. If these SOBs skate past us, we're likely going to have to fight them on the ground."

"If they land in here," Encizo chimed in, "I'll pound them with the 40-mm warheads. If that doesn't work, I'll have to get creative."

"You always were the creative, sensitive type," Manning said.

"Forget it, and I'll gut you like a mackerel," Encizo replied.

"Stand ready, you clowns," Manning said.

Hawkins saw that the choppers loomed much larger. They began to sink toward the ground. He brought up the weapon, rested its wooden stock on his shoulder and peered through the sight, trying to line up a decent shot on the warship's cockpit. The second RPG-7 lay close at hand, should he need it.

He knew that he and Manning wanted to hit their targets head-on. And, with the RPG round's 3.5-second fuse, timing was crucial to making a kill shot. Manning began the count. When Hawkins heard the demolitions man reach "one," he triggered his weapon.

The round whizzed forward, leaving a white trail of smoke in its wake. It collided with the craft, detonating with a loud boom. A red-orange burst of flames accompanied by searing heat ripped through the craft. Flames exploded throughout the helicopter's interior, immolating its occupants. The fire reached the fuel tanks and a second explosion flashed and roared as the flaming wreckage plummeted to the ground.

Another explosion to Hawkins's right ripped through the sky and he knew Manning's target had been decimated.

CHAPTER NINETEEN

McCarter brought the M-4/M-203 combo to his shoulder, aimed at the front window and fired. The projectile shattered the windowpane and flew inside. A second later the stun round he'd fired exploded with a flash. He and James broke from their cover behind stacked fifty-five-gallon drums and headed for the building.

As James reached the house, he moved to the right side of the front door, resting his hand on the knob. McCarter raised his assault rifle to his shoulder, took a deep breath and gave his teammate a nod.

James twisted the knob and pushed the door inward. McCarter waited a couple of beats, then rocketed through the doorway.

Muzzle-flashes burst forth from an AK-47 held by a lanky Janjaweed fighter, a guttural war cry bursting from his lips. The man seemed to be firing indiscriminately, as though he couldn't quite get his bearings. The Briton assumed that the man had been affected by the flash-stun grenade that they'd fired through the window.

McCarter tapped out a pair of quick bursts that

drilled into the man's chest, transforming it into a blood-soaked ruin and knocking him from his feet. A second man popped out of a hallway situated across the room and to the Phoenix Force leader's left.

Exposing only an arm and part of his face, he let loose with a spray of fire from an Uzi, which he was firing with one hand. McCarter ripped off a pair of quick bursts that hit the wall the man stood behind. The bullets tore through the plasterboard and struck the man dead center in the chest, killing him before he hit the ground.

McCarter came around the corner and leveled the M-4 down the hallway. He immediately spotted a big man, the lower part of his face covered with a patchy beard, standing at the other end. Before the Briton could line up a shot, he saw that the big machine gun the man wielded was aimed his direction, and spun away from the hallway entrance. A volley of bullets tore through the corridor and chewed through the walls. Slugs splintered wooden furniture and shattered window glass.

The shooter stepped from the hallway and began to sweep the M-60 across the room in a horizontal arc. McCarter and James fired in unison at the bearded man. He howled with pain, staggered back a couple of steps, but didn't stop firing the machine gun. The Briton's weapon ran dry, but James continued to direct his assault rifle's lethal fury into the shooter's center mass until the M-60 fell quiet and the gunner sank to the floor.

With McCarter in the lead, the two Phoenix Force warriors moved down the hallway, which was littered with spent shell casings and cigarette butts.

They found only one door closed. Filling his left hand with the Browning, McCarter emptied three rounds into the door, transforming the lock into mangled steel. He drove a booted foot into it and the door swung inward, McCarter rocketing in behind it.

He spotted Yahya poised in a corner. The Janjaweed killer's hand, filled with pistol, arced toward the Briton. Suddenly the Sudanese man stopped in midmotion, his eyes darting between his two opponents.

Apparently, McCarter thought, the guy didn't have the stomach for two-on-one combat.

"Drop it," James commanded.

The gun fell to the floor with a thunk.

McCarter motioned at a rolling chair with the barrel of his M-4. "Plant your arse there, you bastard. It's time for us to have a chat."

Without taking his eyes from the two commandos, Yahya moved to the chair and backed gently into it. He kept his back ramrod-straight, resting his hands, palms open and down, on the tops of his thighs.

McCarter stowed the M-4 but kept the Browning handy. He walked up to the slaver, halted a foot or so away from him and stared.

James stood off to one side, his jaw muscles rippling as he ground his teeth angrily.

"You two are dead men." Yahya spit. "As soon as my people finish with the rest of your team, they'll come for you. If you know what's best, you will get the hell out of here now. Go!"

"Thanks for the warning," McCarter said dryly. "But we went to all this work to see you, I can't bring myself to leave yet. Besides, I'm not too worried about your people. Most of them are outside, bloating and rotting. Maybe you'd like us to take you out there, show you just how much tough guys impress us."

Yahya remained silent.

"You know where we can find Dale Farnsworth," McCarter said.

"I know nothing of the sort," Yahya said. "You've been misinformed."

"Aw, fuck this," James said. He stepped up to Yahya and gave him a backhand across the face that snapped his head right. Yahya brought his hand around, rubbed his palm over his cheek and stared at James.

"Maybe you'd like to ethnic cleanse my ass out of existence?" James said. "Is that what you want, little man? Why don't you drag your ass out of the chair and put me in a pen, like you did all those poor bastards out there."

"You're armed," Yahya replied. "You'd kill me before I stood."

James crossed the room to a table and stopped. He set his Uzi on its top, followed by his side arm and a Colt combat knife. Wheeling, he strode back to Yahya and held out his hands, fingers pointed down, palms exposed.

"Now?"

Yahya swallowed hard and looked at McCarter. He noticed Yahya staring at him and shrugged.

"I'm sitting this one out, mate," the Briton said. "You got your dumb ass into this, and you can get it out. Or not." He nodded at James. "But, frankly, my money's on this lad, especially when he's pissed."

"C'mon, killer," James said. "Get up. Get up so I can knock your ass back down. Maybe chase you across the desert like a damn animal."

Yahya made no move to rise. He stared down at his hands, which now were clasped together, apparently studying his interwoven fingers.

"What do you want?" he asked without looking up.

"Retribution," James said.

The Arab looked up at James and held his gaze for several seconds.

"You mean it," he said.

"Bet your ass. You raped any little girls lately, hero? Killed any unarmed old men?"

"I have information," Yahya said. "I can tell you what you want to know. Perhaps we can strike a deal of some sort. I know how the game is played."

James spit on the floor. He'd dropped his hands to his sides, clenching them into fists.

"No deal," he said, shaking his head. "I'll beat you so hard, you'll be begging to rat out that piece of shit Farnsworth. I'll break bones you didn't know you had. Pulp your internal organs. You read me?"

"Yes," Yahya said.

James heard a tremor in the other man's voice. It was taking every last ounce of self-control he had to restrain himself. He could play the good-cop/bad-cop routine with the best of them. But this time he wasn't playing. Seeing people cooped up in pens, sold like cattle, brutalized by cowards, filled him with a rage that threatened to overcome his professional detachment. If the stakes weren't so high, he thought, he'd kill the son of a bitch right there and make the world a better place.

McCarter interrupted his thoughts. "What can you tell us, little man?"

Yahya turned to look at McCarter, though James occasionally caught him casting a wary eye in his direction.

"I can tell you how to find Farnsworth."

"Where?" McCarter asked.

Yahya gave him the coordinates, which McCarter committed to memory.

"What's his troop strength?"

"Forty," Yahya replied. "Give or take a few. Most of them are mercenaries. Many of them I recruited myself. I can give you a roster of names, if you'd like."

"Then we have a deal. You will not hurt me?"

James felt his body tense, and he wanted to protest. McCarter looked at him, cocked an inquisitive eyebrow. Reluctantly he replied with an affirmative nod.

James turned and gathered his weapons while Yahya pulled up a list on his laptop and printed it out for McCarter. The Briton neatly folded the papers into eighths and stuffed them into his shirt pocket, before ordering Yahya to put the computer into its carrying case so they could confiscate it.

In the meantime, James moved to Yahya's discarded Colt .45, turned it over in his hands, admiring its nickel-plated finish. He took the pistol, slipped it into his belt at the small of his back and turned to face the other two men. He saw McCarter knocking the man's satellite phone to the floor while Yahya protested. The former British commando flipped the guy the bird and stomped on the phone until pieces began to break off.

"You knew we were coming to Khartoum," McCarter said. "How?"

"Farnsworth told me."

"And he knew how?"

Yahya shrugged. "A source within the CIA, I suppose. Perhaps he had people planted at the airport. I do not know. I just took his orders and tried to make it happen. That's what I do for people."

"Yeah," McCarter said, "you're a real mover and shaker."

Yahya gave him a puzzled look. "I do not—"

"Forget it," McCarter said. "It's slang."

"I see." The tone of his voice indicated otherwise.

"This underground bunker," McCarter said. "Does the Libyan government know Farnsworth has moved in?"

"Yes. I was the one who brokered the deal. I used my old intelligence contacts to make it happen."

"They know what he's doing there?"

Yahya shook his head no. "They think he's selling conventional weapons to terrorists and running training camps. He's running the money through so many accounts it's nearly impossible for them to track it. They think he's a freelance soldier from Johannesburg trying to make a living."

"Just a working stiff."

"What?"

"Never mind," McCarter said, shaking his head.

"More slang," Yahya said.

"So they don't know what Farnsworth's doing there?" McCarter pressed.

"No."

"But you do."

"Yes. He's got the scientist and the computer worm. He didn't want to tell the Libyan government. He was afraid—how do you say it?—that they'd want a piece of the action. Or sell his location to the Americans. As it was, they weren't sure it was worth their while to turn him in."

"Understood," McCarter said.

"You know, I can be a good friend to the Americans," he said.

"Who said we're Americans?" McCarter asked.

"Or whomever you are. I know a lot of things. People tell me things in Sudan. I—what is the phrase?—keep my ear to the ground."

"Good way to get your head run over," McCarter said. "Forget it, Yahya. Just count yourself lucky that my friend's not using your head for a soccer ball."

The friendly look drained away from the man's face. "Yes, of course. But you will keep your promise."

"Absolutely," McCarter said. "Though it does pain us to leave you above ground like this."

McCarter moved toward the door. James stood for another minute and stared at Yahya before turning and heading for the door.

When they walked outside, McCarter found several black Sudanese standing in small groups. The other three Phoenix Force commandos stood by. James approached one of the small groups. He reached behind his back and withdrew the seized Colt. "Any of you speak English?"

A woman stepped forward. "I do," she said. "I learned from some Christian missionaries that once lived with us."

"Do any of you know how to use this? It's a Colt .45."

The woman turned and posed the question to her group. Two of the men and one young woman nodded yes.

"The man who captured you, who enslaved you, is in that house. I can have my friends take him out before we leave. Or I can let you do it."

The woman turned and explained this to the others. One of the men walked up to James, stood and held out his hand. James placed the handgun into the man's palm.

"Tell him there still are weapons in the house."

The woman did. Nodding, the man left them and marched toward the house. Others who'd heard the exchange fell in behind him until about a dozen blacks were heading for the house.

YAHYA PULLED the last stack of American dollars from inside his safe and stuffed it into his duffel bag. Next, he pulled out a dozen or so CDs containing duplicates of all the files on his laptop. He'd need all the information they contained, including a list of bank accounts, to get started again.

A bitter taste filled his mouth as he realized he'd have to build everything from the ground up. He'd have to buy new vehicles; build a new house, new barracks and new slave pens; and rebuild his human inventory. He had a warehouse full of RPGs and assault rifles in Khartoum that he could sell for quick cash. He knew the Taliban and the Iraqi insurgents always needed more of those things to continue fighting their holy wars. Besides, now that the Americans had cost him everything, he had no issue selling weapons to that country's enemy. Not that he'd ever shied away from it before. But now he was motivated.

He'd have to leave behind the slaves, the horses and the camels, let them all perish from dehydration or starvation. A brutal end, perhaps, but hardly anything he should concern himself with. No, he had too much to do. He had to rebuild. After that, he'd take out the people who'd done this to him. He'd use every contact he had in Libyan intelligence as well as others, track them down and have them killed.

He was so engrossed in thought that he almost missed the sound of a footstep. He stopped cold and listened, his chest suddenly tightening until it became hard to breathe. Were they coming for him? What the hell could they want? He'd told them everything he knew.

More footsteps were audible from the hallway. He uncoiled from the floor and turned toward the doorway.

He saw a couple of the blacks, the ones his men had captured, standing in the doorway. They moved into the room, followed by more. He opened his mouth to yell at them, order them from his building, his home. He saw one of the men clutching a pistol—his pistol—and he froze. At least one of the other men was carrying a blood-splattered AK-47 that Yahya assumed came from one of his dead hardmen.

He held up a hand. "You can't—"

A white-hot sensation bore into his abdomen and he suddenly found himself gagging on his words. He tasted blood and a choking sensation seized his throat. Fiery shafts pierced his chest and stomach. He stumbled, realizing that he'd been shot only when the weapons' reports registered with him. More bullets punched through his torso, jerking it from side to side. His legs went out from under him and he hit the ground, his body numb to the pain, the shock of multiple bullet wounds. How absurd, he thought, to be shot this many times and not feel it. Everything went dark.

JAMES WATCHED THE GROUP file out from the building. The two men carrying weapons cast them aside and intermingled with the others. A hand clamped down on his shoulder. He turned and saw McCarter. "We've got some folks coming to pick them up," he said. "They're going to take them to refugee camps where they can be safe."

James nodded.

"I know it's not much, Cal, but it's all we can do for them. At least we freed them."

CHAPTER TWENTY

Stony Man Farm, Virginia

How much more time until it all went to hell? Brognola wondered. He watched the cyberteam working hard at their computers, each trying to unearth some critical piece of data that might help them locate Gabriel Fox. At this point, they were hacking into every government database imaginable—CIA, FBI, Pentagon, Homeland Security—searching for the slightest lead.

It had been long, hard and frustrating work. He saw their faces etched with a toxic mix of fatigue and adrenaline, and wondered when one of them might hit the jackpot.

Barbara Price approached Brognola, a pair of manila folders pinned under her arm. She handed the folders to him.

"Read them now?" he asked.

"If not now, soon," she said.

"What's the abridged version?"

"I pulled a couple of markers at the NSA. Looks like Jack Mace has a friend. A very well-heeled friend."

"He got a name?"

"Dale Farnsworth."

Brognola's brow furrowed. "No bells ringing here. Should I know him?"

Price shrugged. "Maybe, maybe not. He is—or was, at least—a banker. He comes from a long line of bankers up in Chicago. They had some legitimate clients, you know the ones who open a passbook savings account for a toaster. But they did most of their work for the more unsavory types."

"Such as?"

"Middle Eastern and African strongmen. Terrorist groups. Russian mobs."

"They laundered money."

Price nodded. "Laundered it, transferred it, hid it. Whatever the customer wanted."

"Customer service is so important," Brognola said.

"Especially when the customer is the CIA."

Brognola straightened a bit. "Say what?"

"Right. Farnsworth was working both sides of the fence, so to speak. He'd launder the money for the bad guys, then give the information to the good guys. His only stipulation was that the government not get too greedy. And by that, he meant not to make it too obvious that he was selling people out."

"In other words, not bust everyone at once."

"Or in some cases at all. Sometimes following the money for months on end helped the CIA gather more intelligence than they ever could get by arresting someone and sweating confessions out of them."

"Makes sense," Brognola admitted. "So what was his angle? He had to be getting something out of it. I mean, the guy wasn't just a Good Samaritan, was he?"

Price shook her head. "His family had been laundering organized crime money since the Prohibition days. It was almost an open secret. People didn't know about the terrorism connections, of course. The locals just averted their eyes and pretended it never happened. During World War II, the OSS actually recruited his father to launder money for suspected Nazi sympathizers. Again, there wasn't anything diabolical about it."

"They just wanted to have a paper trail so they could bust the bad guys," Brognola interjected.

Price nodded. "Exactly. And his father, Alexander Farnsworth, was more than happy to help. From what we've ascertained, he was a real patriot. His son, on the other hand, put up a good act, but had more diabolical intentions."

"He wanted the money," Brognola said.

"And the access. Not just to our politicians, but to those in other countries. And, again, these folks didn't know he was keeping triple books on everything. His shareholders saw what he wanted them to see. The CIA saw what it was supposed to see. And he saw the real books."

The big Fed sipped from his coffee cup. "Hey, this is good coffee. Maybe we should send the Bear out into the field more often. Anyway, so where'd he go from there?"

"He actually wanted to be trained as an agent. The Company wanted his help so they agreed. He spent several months at their training facility. He underwent weapons, hand-to-hand combat and other types of training. According to his file, he actually had a real knack, particularly when it came to killing people."

Brognola rolled his eyes. "Why doesn't that surprise me?"

"It shouldn't. According to his case officer, Farnsworth has at least a dozen confirmed kills to his name. That was one of the reasons the Company eventually dumped him. He was getting too wild for their tastes, particularly after what happened in Washington, D.C., two years ago."

"Which was?"

Using her finger, Price scanned through the report until she found the information she needed. "He established an international bank that was supposed to help fund new business investment in Russia and China when those countries opened their borders to more free trade. But he tried to continue on business as usual, loaning money to bad people like Jack Mace. Old dog, new tricks. All that. Unfortunately for him, someone leaked the information to the press, the Securities and Exchange Commission and a couple of senators. Next thing he knows, there's a big investigation and his board—most of whom were selected by the CIA—end up booting him out and buying up his shares."

Brognola winced. "Ouch. So he's pissed."

Price nodded. "Very much so. According to his psychological profile, he doesn't like to lose. He lost. He's pissed. And he's got money to burn."

"And CIA contacts to boot," Brognola said. He sat up straight and set his empty foam cup on a nearby table. "Any luck tracking the money?"

Price shook her head no. "We're working on it. His accounts are a tangled mess. But my instinct tells me this is our guy, the one who's been underwriting this whole conspiracy."

"Get me some proof, Barb," the big Fed rasped. "And I'll take it to the Man. In the meantime, make sure the guys in the field know this."

CHAPTER TWENTY-ONE

Lyons knew he was being followed.

The guy trailing him had tried to hide it, of course. When Lyons looked back, the man averted his gaze, feigned interest in a shop window or the contents of a newsstand. Occasionally he disappeared altogether, only to resurface a couple of minutes later. Lyons guessed that the man was getting help from spotters. The notion that someone was perched on a rooftop or the upper story of a building, watching him, only added to the Able Team commander's unease.

Lyons was walking through the Old Town section of Prague. His papers identified him as Scott Irons, an agent with the U.S. Justice Department who was in Europe working an arms-smuggling case.

Frankly, he was unsure whether his tail was a Czech official sent to keep tabs on an American agent, or a criminal charged with assassinating a lawman. He and Blancanales, who also was traveling under an assumed identity, had told the state authorities they'd come to the Czech Republic to gather information on several men believed to be providing arms to terrorists and criminals. And he'd made it clear that Quissad, the former Iraqi military man, topped their list of must-see people.

Lyons's strategy was simple. Unleash some thunder and fury in Prague and see what they could shake loose.

The Able Team leader stopped at a newsstand and selected an English-language newspaper. He dropped a few coins into the palm of the vendor's outstretched hand, tucked the paper under his left arm and shot a look at his tail. The man had disappeared again. His purchase complete, Lyons continued down the street, threading his way through the throngs of tourists moving in his direction.

"Looks like I've got a buddy," Lyons said into his throat mike. "Though I don't see him at the moment."

"He'll be back," Blancanales replied. "He slipped inside a flower shop. I think he was going to buy you a dozen roses."

"Aren't I the lucky one? You see anyone else monitoring my movements?"

"Negative." Blancanales had been following his teammate in a rented car. "Could be someone on the roofs or something monitoring you, though."

"Could be," Lyons agreed. "I guess it's time to engage our little friend. You get an ID on him yet?"

"Negative. I got a couple of digital snapshots of him, and sent them to the Farm via e-mail. Haven't heard squat from them yet."

"Well, I can't wait any more. You got my back?"

"Always. Let me know when to drop the hammer."

Lyons acknowledged the traffic. A tight smile formed on his lips. He, Blancanales and Schwarz had a friendship forged in the crucible of combat. They'd shed blood in the same hellgrounds and he had no doubt he could count on Blancanales to be there when things got nasty.

The Stony Man fighter scanned his surroundings. Despite the cold, knots of tourists still stood out in the open. They clustered outside the Gothic architecture of the chapels, shops and houses that comprised Old Town. Even more had gathered outside the Old Town Hall. The building featured two clocks. The first was an astronomical clock designed centuries ago to represent the rotation of the sun and moon when people still believed that Earth was the center of the universe. The second clock stood atop a tower. When the hour struck, a skeleton figure, representing Death, situated to one side of the clock, pulled a rope, two doors opened and statues representing the Apostles moved in a predetermined pattern.

Lyons checked his watch and saw that less than a minute remained before the hour struck. He looked for a place to slip away from the crowd. Like the other Stony Man warriors, Lyons knew he'd rather take a bullet than initiate a cross fire that might result in unnecessary civilian deaths. Additionally, if he could find a decent escape route, a quick dash might force anyone else watching him to come out in the open and give chase.

He turned once more, locked eyes with his pursuer and let his gaze linger.

Shooting the guy an obscene gesture, the commando walked briskly away.

Lyons headed toward a nearby restaurant, but bypassed the front door. He vaulted an iron railing surrounding the outside eating area and wound his way around the empty tables. It was time to see just how serious the guy really was about following him, he decided. Shortly, he came out on another street, this one fronted by the Vltava, a river that passed through Pra-

gue's center. Lyons headed left and strode up the street,
barely paying attention to the shops on either side.

"Ironman?" It was Blancanales. Lyons activated his
throat microphone.

"Go."

"I lost my visual."

"Right. I'm by the river. I decided to play hide and
seek with our little friend."

"Clear. Give me a minute to get through traffic and
I'll be right with you."

Lyons looked behind him, spotted his tail. "No time.
My boy's catching up. Gotta keep moving. I'm heading to our predetermined spot."

"Clear."

Lyons moved quickly up the street, reaching a multi-
story structure surrounded by a tall wooden fence. He
glided along the fence, was well out of the sight of the
street, until he came to a padlocked gate. He fisted the
Beretta 92-F with its attached sound suppressor and
drew down on the gate. Though he preferred the Colt
Python, he'd decided to bring along the Beretta for
stealth reasons. He triggered the weapon twice. The
lock ruptured and the gate flew open.

Slipping inside the barrier, he trod through the court-
yard. He reached the back door, tried the knob and
found it locked. A quick rap against the windowpane
with the pistol butt shattered the glass. He reached in,
unlocked the door and moved inside what proved to be
a kitchen. Lyons raced through the room and into a
large dining room, though it was barren of furniture. He
stepped into a short corridor and found an alcove, the
walls of which were lined with coat hooks. Moving out
of sight, he flattened against a wall, listened.

A board creaked underneath someone's weight.

Moments later a gray shadow fell across floor. It grew larger as the guy approached. Despite the man's best efforts to remain quiet, Lyons heard his slight breathing, the rustle of fabric.

The man crept to the edge of the alcove, then stopped. Molding outlined the door and made the space visible to passersby before they reached it. Lyons tensed, knowing the next second or two would mean the difference between life and death.

All at once, the man came around the corner. His weapon was leveled at shoulder height as he sought a target. Lyons sprang off the wall and grabbed the guy's shooting wrist, immediately taking control of the other man's weapon. He jabbed the Beretta's muzzle under the man's chin.

"Please move," Lyons challenged. "Please."

Fingers loosened and the man let his weapon fall to the floor. Lyons grabbed a handful of his pursuer's shirt and shoved him against the wall. Snarling, the guy tried to drive a knee into Lyons's groin. The Able Team leader sensed the attack. He pivoted at the waist so the man's knee struck his muscled thigh instead of the family jewels.

"Weak, man," Lyons said. "Very weak."

Lyons thought he heard another door close somewhere within the building. Was it Blancanales, or another batch of gunners? Only one way to find out. The warrior spun the other man around and struck him against the back of the skull. The man's knees buckled underneath him and he fell to the ground, unconscious.

The American slipped from the alcove, and as he did, a bulky man armed with an Uzi came into view.

Lyons brought up his weapon and tried to acquire a target. In the same heartbeat, his opponent's Uzi spit a line of flame in his direction.

BLANCANALES GUIDED the Skoda sedan to the curb and brought it to a halt. Reaching across the seat, he grabbed a satchel that contained an MP-5 subgun, spare ammo and a pair of stun grenades. He popped open the door and felt the brisk wind strike his face. Stepping onto the street, he scanned his surroundings, pretending to take in Prague's beautiful architecture while he was actually searching for danger.

A microsecond before he grabbed the car door to close it, he heard the squeal of rubber scraping against the pavement. He turned and saw a dark blue Mercedes round a corner two blocks away. The car hit the straight-away, the growl of its engine gaining in volume as it shot toward the Able Team commando.

Blancanales's combat-trained mind sized up the situation. If he took a step back, shut the door and dived over the hood, he'd be roadkill before his feet left the ground. Better, he decided, to go through the car than over it.

Thrusting himself through the door, he lay across the vehicle's bench seat and bent his legs far enough to bring his feet inside the vehicle. In that same instant, the Mercedes whizzed by, its bumper striking the driver's door, ripping it from its hinges. The impact rocked the sedan, like huge swells buffeting a skiff.

He heard the Mercedes engine grow fainter as it sped away. Grabbing the passenger door's handle, he popped open the door and launched himself out of the car. His hands struck pavement, scraping his palms. From farther up the street, tires again screamed in protest, drawing his attention. The Mercedes rocketed down the street toward him.

Blancanales was on his feet, his hand diving beneath his jacket for the Beretta 93-R holstered there. By the time he cleared leather, the Mercedes screamed to a halt. Doors flew open as four gunners disgorged from the vehicle, their weapons held in plain view.

The Able Team commando could see that several pedestrians had stopped and were watching the situation unfold.

A pair of city police broke away from the crowd gathered across the street. Both were shouting at the gunners from the Mercedes while also grabbing for their side arms. Before either had covered much ground, though, one of the thugs opened up with his SMG. Bullets hammered into one officer's gut, felling him. The same gunner hit the second officer in the legs. Before the officer hit the ground, several bystanders began to scream and run from the scene.

The warrior saw a woman caught up in the stampede trip and fall to the ground. She tried to lift herself up, but apparently had injured herself in the fall. A small boy with sandy-brown hair stood next to her, crying, his small hands grabbing at her arms in a vain attempt to help her.

Rage welled up in Blancanales. His first instinct was to go to the family's aid, remove them to safety. But he knew better. In this case, he was the target. If he moved toward those two, he'd draw fire in their direction, make them even more vulnerable to these killers who were so hell-bent on getting him.

The best thing he could do was to lead the killers away from here, away from the innocents milling around.

With that finished, he'd mete out justice.

He raced down the sidewalk, trying to grab some distance from his car. One of the gunners, a heavyset man with scarlet cheeks, spotted Blancanales. The hardman raised his handgun and fired. The first salvo missed Blancanales by a couple of feet and instead slammed into the brick facade of a building behind the Latino.

When Blancanales found a decent opening between two parked cars, he dropped into a Weaver stance and squeezed off a triburst of 9 mm manglers. The bullets drilled into the shooter's chest, opening red holes in his white dress shirt. A second hardman whirled toward Blancanales and tried to bring his SMG into play. The Beretta sighed as it spit out another triburst. The slugs punched through the Mercedes' tinted windows and drilled holes through its steel exterior.

Blancanales wheeled and sprinted away from the scene, legging it past three storefronts. A sidelong look into the rear windshield showed him the reflection of at least two hardmen chasing him on foot.

An alley opened to his right. Pivoting on his heel, he entered its mouth. Empty beer bottles and discarded papers littered the ground. It stank of stale beer and rotting food. Blancanales stopped to unzip the satchel hanging from his shoulder.

Footsteps slapped against the sidewalk outside the alley. He knew his pursuers would be upon him in a second.

Reaching inside one of the bags, he palmed a flash-stun grenade, flattened himself against a wall and waited. A couple of seconds later, two of the men came into the view at the mouth of the alley. Their guns held high, they started forward. Blancanales activated the bomb and tossed it toward them. It hit the ground with a clank and the two men halted. Before either could make another move, the device let off a bright white flash and a loud boom. Blancanales sprang into action, his Beretta chugging tribursts that punched through flesh, broke bones and slammed both men to the ground. The third shooter came around the corner of one of the buildings at the end of the alley. Before the guy could size up the situation, Blancanales squeezed off another burst that punched through the man's center mass, knocking him to the ground in a boneless heap.

Blancanales heard the cry of sirens and knew the police would be there at any moment. Once they found one of their officers lying dead in the street, they'd be looking to deal out some payback on the men who'd done the killing. They'd also want to lock down the entire area until they got their hands on the shooters.

The commando grabbed the mobile phone clipped to his belt. Opening it, he hit a preset button and waited as the call dialed and passed through a series of cutout numbers. It rang twice before Carmen Delahunt's voice boomed on the line.

"Politician," she said. "As I live and breathe."

"I need you to make a call," the commando said.

"Sure," the fiery redhead replied. "What's the problem?"

In clipped sentences, Blancanales brought her up to date on the gun battle. "I need Barb or Hal to contact the local police, wave the flag and keep them off our backs. They lost an officer a few minutes ago, so they likely won't be in the mood to grant favors. But I've got the shooters here, if they want to come pick them up. Or pick up their remains."

"And you want the police to let you and Carl skate out of there without any problem, right?"

"You're a mind reader, Carmen."

"No, you're just predictable. You're like my kids. You only call when you need something. Anyway, I'll pass it up the chain of command. I've got you located on our GPS. I assume that's where they can find their cop killers."

"Exactly."

"We'll clean things up from here."

"Great," Blancanales said. "I need to go check up on Carl."

LYONS HURLED HIMSELF through the air, diving from the path of the autofire spitting from the Uzi. The SMG unleashed a dozen messengers of death in a heartbeat. In the same moment, Lyons struck the floor. The shooter whirled toward him, the weapon still grinding through its clip. Lyons stroked the Beretta's trigger twice and opened a small hole in the man's forehead. The hardman staggered into a wall, but his finger held down on the Uzi's trigger, unloading it into the hardwood floor inches from Lyons's thigh.

"Son of a bitch," Lyons muttered as he came up into a crouch.

His breath was coming fast and blood thundered in his ears. He recognized that his body was reacting to the stress of combat. He took a moment to consciously slow his breathing as he swept his gaze over the corridor, checking for intruders.

A shadow fell across the doorway leading from the entryway into the corridor. Lyons flattened himself against the wall and leveled the Beretta ahead of him. His muscles tensed in anticipation of conflict. A heartbeat later, Blancanales stepped through the door, his own Beretta at the ready.

Lyons let out a breath, grinning.

"Bang," he said. "You're dead."

Blancanales froze, but cast an eye toward Lyons.

When he saw his partner, he let the gun drop to his side. "I already knew you were here," he said. "I could smell that cheap aftershave."

"That's not mine," Lyons said. He pointed at the corpse laying at his feet. "It's his."

"No wonder you killed him."

"C'mon," Lyons stated. "I've got someone I want you to meet."

LYONS HELD THE GLASS under the faucet of the bathroom sink and filled it to the rim with cold water.

He returned to the living room and tossed the glass's contents into the man's face.

The man, who already was awake, sputtered and closed his eyes while the liquid rolled downward, following the contours of his face. "What the hell, man?"

"Little preview of coming attractions," Lyons said. Placing the glass on a nearby television set, he sat on the foot of the bed, putting himself at eye level with the guy. He fisted the Beretta holstered underneath his jacket and pulled a sound suppressor from his jacket pocket. Threading the two together, he set the weapon on the bed beside him.

"Hope you like cold water," Lyons said. "My friend and I, we figure we'll dump you into the river. After I blow away your knees and elbows. Makes swimming a real treat. Usually, I like to use a .357 revolver, but we're trying to keep all this on the QT. So I'm stuck with this thing." He patted the weapon that lay next to him.

"I voted for electrocution," Blancanales said. "Maybe let you take a bath with a radio. Or a color television. But he's got a real affinity for floaters. Who was I to say no? Though just between us, I don't really think you're going to be floating."

The guy turned his head back toward Lyons and shot him a defiant look.

"I know what you're thinking," Lyons said. "We're playing good cop-bad cop with you. Well, guess the fuck what? We're not. Your boss is up to his neck in raw sewage. We're here to make sure he drowns in it. Him and anyone else on his team. You help us and you live. You fuck with us—and I mean even just a little bit— you're the *Titanic* and I'm the damn iceberg."

"Screw you," the guy said, his lip curling into a sneer.

Lyons's hand snaked out and he delivered a stinging backhand to the man's cheek. The blow cracked like a rifle shot and whipped his head left. An angry scarlet mark appeared on the guy's unshaven face. When he turned back to Lyons, the warrior could see the man's rage and fear. His lips compressed and his jaw muscles rippled. The guy spit some blood onto the floor between himself and Lyons.

"Go to hell!" he shouted.

Lyons shook his head. "Don't bother calling our bluff, princess. There's nothing to call. You tried to kill us. I killed your friends." He nodded at Blancanales. "So did he. Killing you will be no more meaningful to me than taking a piss."

For a minute the guy stared at Lyons, who unflinchingly met his gaze. Lyons guessed that the hardman was scouring his face for some sign of queasiness, a clue that the whole thing was a bluff. It took nearly a minute, but he seemed to realize that his captors were deadly serious. His shoulders sagged. "What do you want to know?"

"Quissad sent you."

"Yeah."

"He always this sloppy?" Lyons asked. "Killing us

would just bring the law down on his neck. He's got to realize that. What the hell's his problem?"

Another pause. When the guy spoke, he did so haltingly, as though selecting his words carefully.

"He's not thinking clearly," he said. "Even on his best day, Quissad's...uptight. Now he's ready to explode. He's got a big deal in the works. He doesn't want it screwed up. You were asking questions. That meant you two had to go."

"Big deal? You mean, as in the computer worm?"

The guy shrugged as best he could with his arms bound. "Maybe. He doesn't tell me that shit."

"You're saying you don't know."

"I'm saying he didn't tell me." The guy stared down at his lap when he spoke.

"Get smart or get swimming," Lyons said.

"Shit! Okay, yes he's been talking about this damn computer thing. A virus or worm or whatever it is. The Mexican is bringing it here."

"You mean Cortez."

The man nodded. "Quissad has some potential buyers flying in this evening to take a look at it. From what I hear, they don't want to meet his price. But I think they're pretty motivated to buy it."

"Who is it?" Blancanales asked.

"All I know is what I've heard."

"Which is?"

"The buyers are some of Quissad's old cronies from Iraq. None of the high-ranking people. Just some mid-level bureaucrats who are mad because they lost their cushy jobs, their nice houses and their nice cars."

Blancanales rounded the chair and stood in front of the guy. He crossed his arms over his chest and stared down at the man. "Just how pissed off are we talking? Pissed off enough to want to strike at America?"

The man nodded yes. "Or Britain. Or both. Once they get it, they can fire it off whenever they want at whomever they want."

"You have names?"

"Yes, I was supposed to pick them up at the airport and take them to a meeting."

"Where?"

"Tariq Khan—"

"Who?"

"One of Quissad's lieutenants."

Blancanales nodded his understanding.

"Anyway," the guy continued, "Khan operates a furniture store and a warehouse in Prague. The cover story is that he owns it. But really Quissad does. I was supposed to drive them there. Quissad hates these guys. He doesn't want to see them. But, if they have the money, he'll deal with them. Or, in this case, let Khan handle them. Khan's a better suck-up than Quissad any day."

"This store, what's the address?" Lyons asked.

The man told them and Lyons memorized it.

"It has a huge warehouse," the man said. "Quissad uses this to store and ship weapons."

"So whom were you picking up at the airport?" Lyons asked. "We need names and other information. Whatever you can give us. Otherwise you're sunk and that's not just a figure of speech."

CHAPTER TWENTY-TWO

"Let me do the talking," Blancanales said.

"You always say that. What? Am I socially inept or something?"

"Hey, look, a full moon," Blancanales said, pointing skyward.

"Nice dodge."

"That's why I'm the Politician," Blancanales said with a grin.

"I figured it was because you spent money like a drunken sailor and screwed anything with a pulse. Look, this is the place. Should I open the door for you?"

Blancanales donned his shades. "Do that. And you might want to toss in a 'sir' or two to help our cover."

"We don't have a cover," Lyons shot back. "That's why everyone here's trying to kill us. Get your own damn door."

"How about a hug then?"

Lyons made an obscene gesture. "Just watch your ass in there. I'll go through the back."

Blancanales approached the entrance, which consisted of two pairs of glass doors. On either side of the entrance stood display windows that highlighted the luxury furnishings the store purported to sell. Blancanales pushed through a pair of glass doors and felt a pleasant rush of warmth greet him as he stepped inside. He swept his gaze over the shop and found a pair of security cameras fixed to the walls and staring down at him.

During his scan, he also noticed a brunette with an olive-colored complexion heading his way. Before she could speak, he said, "Hello."

"Oh, you speak English," she said, smiling. "Are you American? You certainly sound like it."

"American? Yes, I am as a matter of fact."

"What can I help you find?"

"Tariq Khan."

Her smile waned almost imperceptibly. Brown eyes sharpened as she scrutinized him. "Sorry, but Mr. Khan's in a meeting. Can I help you...?"

"No."

"Um, you do have an appointment, don't you? Mr. Khan's an extremely busy man. He doesn't see anyone without an appointment. I'm sure you understand."

Blancanales flashed her his Justice Department ID. He assumed Khan was watching, maybe even listening, from somewhere in the building. The way he figured it, he might as well make the death merchant sweat a little.

"I'm with the Justice Department. United States Justice Department. I want to speak with Mr. Khan about some of his business dealings. Now."

She swallowed hard. "Is he in some sort of trouble?"

"If he was, would you know anything about it?"

She shook her head vigorously. "Absolutely not."

"Then I shouldn't be wasting your time, should I? I want to see Mr. Khan, and I want to see him now."

"Sure, I understand. Unfortunately, well, he's not here."

"You just said…"

She brushed her fingertips along her cheek and chewed on her lower lip. "Well, what I meant to say is that he's at an offsite meeting. I forgot. But, yes, that's definitely where he is. Could you elaborate on what sort of business dealings you want to discuss? Is this something I can help you with?"

"You send someone to kill us today?" Blancanales asked, his tone even.

The woman's eyes widened and her hand flew to her chest as though to keep her heart from leaping out from it.

"Certainly not!"

"Well, your boss did. I wanted to speak with him about that. He hurt my feelings."

The woman gave him a look of incomprehension.

"That's right," Blancanales said, nodding. "Killed. As in organs-rotting, body-crawling-with-maggots dead."

"You—you must be mistaken," she said.

Blancanales's gut told him the woman's shock was genuine. He stepped into her space, moved his face closer to hers. She tried to back away, but collided with a hutch and found herself trapped between it and Blancanales.

"Ma'am," he said, "I'm giving you the benefit of the doubt. Go home. Please. If you're protecting this man, it's going to come back to bite you. He's not worth the jeopardy that you're putting yourself in. Trust me. Who else is here?"

"Another saleswoman and a janitor. Mr. Khan and his group."

"Group?"

"Some friends arrived just a little while ago. And he has some associates that accompany him everywhere. He's a wealthy man and—"

Blancanales motioned for silence. "Got the picture. How many friends?"

The woman bit her lip. "Four. Two older men, two younger ones."

"How many 'associates'?"

"Six."

Blancanales looked to his right and saw a woman, her blond hair cut in a pageboy style, straightening cushions on a cranberry-colored couch. She watched the exchange from the corner of her eye. He looked back at the lady in front of him.

"Grab her. Get the janitor. I want all three of you to grab your stuff and disappear. Just dump your cell phones on the floor and go. Now."

In less than three minutes, she and the others had left the building. Blancanales locked the door behind them. Drawing his twin Berettas, he wheeled around and strode toward the rear of the store, ready for a face-to-face meeting with Khan.

LYONS EDGED along the store's exterior wall. He held the sound-suppressed Beretta in front of him at shoulder level.

As he neared the corner, he heard voices and smelled cigarette smoke. He flattened himself against the wall, peered around the corner. Two men, both olive-complected with jet-black hair, stood with their backs to him. Halogen spotlights fixed to the warehouse shone down on the men, illuminating them. One man, his hair trimmed closely to his scalp, was positioned at the front of a midnight-blue BMW sedan. His foot rested on the bumper. The second man—nattily dressed—smoked as if he were on fire, and rocked back and forth on his heels. He was saying something in rapid-fire Arabic that, save for a couple of swearwords, Lyons couldn't recognize.

The Able Team leader pivoted around the corner with his weapon raised. His foot accidentally struck a discarded beer bottle, which sent it spinning across the asphalt. The guards wheeled toward him, grabbing for their weapons.

The nervous guy darted left and produced a small submachine gun from under his coat. Lyons's sound-suppressed Beretta sighed twice, the subsonic slugs hammering the man's breastbone and sending him hurtling into a pair of garbage cans. Buzz Cut fired three shots from a crouching position.

The bullets whined within a few inches of Lyons's left ear. Holding his ground, the Stony Man commando fired the Beretta, the handgun chugging out a trio of rippers that struck Buzz Cut in the chest. A line of red dots appeared on his chest and he dropped to the ground.

Lyons trotted over to Buzz Cut and knelt beside him. Rolling the guy onto his back, he searched through the hardman's pockets. Using the BMW's keys, he stuffed the bigger man into the luxury vehicle's trunk and placed the smaller man across the bench seat in the vehicle's rear.

The Beretta held at the ready, Lyons edged toward the back door and opened it with a key card he found in the second gunner's pockets. He stepped inside and shut the door behind him. Holstering the Beretta, he reached under his knee-length leather coat and unlimbered the SPAS-12 shotgun from its rig.

Activating the headset, he asked Blancanales, "How are we looking?"

"They've got a great deal on sofas."

"You're a laugh riot. You know that?"

"Easy, big man. I sent folks home for the night. It's just us, Khan and their customers."

"And a bunch of gunners with a hard-on to kill us."

"Details. Details."

CHAPTER TWENTY-THREE

"Damn it all!" Khan said. "We've been breached."

Seated at his desk, he watched the deadly incursion on a pair of security monitors as the situation unfolded. Nausea gripped his insides when he watched the blond man sneak through the rear door and into the warehouse. The other monitor depicted a second gun-wielding intruder advancing through the showroom toward the elevators leading to the offices.

Khan felt the eyes of his security team bore into him as things went to hell. He knew they wanted him to make a decision. His mind raced through the options but, with his own life on the line, he found it difficult to pick one. After a few uncomfortable seconds, he looked up at the security chief. The hired killer, a former Fedayeen Saddam soldier, stood about six feet tall and kept his potato-shaped head shaved. Khan saw a sneer ghost the man's lips. In a brief, humiliating moment, he realized that his face had betrayed the terror that he felt about this incursion.

"Split up and stop them," Khan snapped. "I want three of you in front, three in back."

"What about you?" the security chief asked. "Who stays behind to protect you?"

"What about me? I can take care of myself. Besides, these bastards never will get close enough to harm me, will they?"

He gave the man a pointed look that caused the sneer to evaporate. Khan realized that, like his other guards, this man considered him weak, barely worthy of their services. But the guards were terrified of Quissad, who viewed failure as a capital offense.

"Of course they won't," the man said. "Everything will be fine. They'll never make it to the stairs or the elevator. I will see to it personally."

"Send the others away. I have another task for you."

The group of hardmen exited the room. When the door closed, Khan jerked a thumb over his shoulder at the wall that separated his office from the conference room.

"I want Libbi and the others killed," he said.

"Killed?"

"Yes. Here, now. I want them dead."

"But Mr. Quissad—"

"Is the one who requested this. Get on it."

Nodding, the man turned and left the room. Khan reached across his desk and grabbed his mobile phone. He dialed up Quissad and pressed the phone to his ear.

"Hello?" Quissad said.

"We're being hit."

"It's the Americans."

"Yes."

"I figured as much."

"You figured as much? You figured it how?"

Quissad chuckled on the other end, apparently amused at Khan's reaction. "Our driver disappeared. He

was part of a team I sent to take down the Americans.
None of them returned. However, all their bodies except
for his were recovered. I had to assume he was captured.
My sources within the police have since confirmed it.
I guess the Americans turned him."

"You didn't tell me."

"Regardless, you should have been prepared."

Before Khan could reply, he heard a machine gun
rattle in the next room and he flinched. The onslaught
continued for about three seconds, accompanied by the
sounds of men shouting and bullets pounding into walls
and ricocheting off furniture. The gunfire stopped as
suddenly as it began.

"What the hell was that?" Quissad asked.

"Libbi and his people. They're gone."

"You got the money?"

"They transferred it an hour or so ago."

"Excellent. Now, what about the Americans? You
sent security after them."

"Yes, yes. Of course I did."

"Are they up to the challenge? These men obviously
are good. I'm not sure what drives them, but they aren't
easily killed."

"Neither am I," Khan said, trying force bravado into
his voice. "I'll deal with them."

Quissad laughed. "I doubt that."

The words stung Khan's pride like a scorpion strike.
He ground his teeth and stayed silent.

"Go condition red," Quissad said.

"That could create some inventory problems," Khan
replied.

"We'll absorb the loss easily. Trust me. Anyway, it's
my fucking inventory. Shut up and do it. I'll send a
chopper for you. Just follow the protocol."

The line went dead. Angry, Khan heaved it across the room where it struck a wall and shattered into several pieces.

"Bastard," he muttered.

He uncoiled from his chair, walked to the wall behind him. Grabbing a Renoir copy by its frame, he jerked it from its moorings and tossed it aside. A safe was built into the wall behind the picture. In a matter of moments, he had the safe open. From down below, he heard stuttering gunfire and the occasional booming of a larger weapon.

He reached inside and retrieved stacks of American dollars held together by rubber bands. He tossed them into a valise. Next, he removed a stack of CDs that contained detailed records for both the legitimate and illegitimate businesses in which he was involved and dropped them in next to the money.

Below him the gunfire continued to intensify. Any minute, he guessed, the police would be coming to investigate the noises.

Finally he extracted a pair of cylindrical objects from the safe and gingerly set them on the desk.

He looked at the pair of thermite grenades and thought of the items stored in the warehouse. At least one thousand assault rifles were slated for shipment to Chechnyan rebels. Six centrifuges used for uranium processing had already been bought and paid for by North Korea. Now none of these items would get to their intended recipients.

He shrugged it off. After all, as that prick Quissad had informed him, it wasn't his inventory. It wasn't his problem. And, if setting off these thermite grenades killed the men downstairs, it was worth the loss.

A BLAST OF AUTOFIRE cut through the air just inches above Cal Lyons's head. He dropped into a crouch and raised the Franchi shotgun defensively. He saw Quissad's men, all of them armed to the teeth, positioned on the stairs. Two of the gunners raked the area around Lyons with automatic gunfire. The storm of suppressive fire allowed a third man to dart for the ground floor.

His shotgun banged out a barrage of sound and fury that vaporized the lead gunner's pelvis and abdomen. The hardman was dead before he hit the floor. Lyons swept the muzzle a few degrees right and blasted a second man with the shotgun.

A fourth man, stocky and lumpy-headed, sprinted down the stairs. His submachine gun churned through the contents of its magazine. Once again Lyons found himself faced with withering sheets of gunfire. When slugs began to tug at his overcoat, the warrior instinctively went to ground. He took cover behind a palette loaded with large-size cardboard boxes. Constant streams of autofire speared through the boxes. The rounds brought with them shards of glass and wood as they exited the containers.

Blancanales came in loud through his earpiece. "Ironman! Give me a sitrep."

"Alive," the commando said. He reloaded the Franchi while he spoke. "There were three. I took it down to one, but another guy joined the fray. Stick with the mission. I've got this."

"My ass."

"Seriously. You get Khan. We can't let those Iraqis buy Cold Earth."

"But… Damn, looks like I've got worries of my own. 'Bye."

"What've you got, Politician?"

"Shooters. I can handle it."

His face a mask of rage, Lyons shot to his feet, ready

to spill some blood. The Franchi led the charge and boomed three more times. He caught the stairwell shooter as the guy was reloading his SMG. Two of the shots nailed the man in his midsection and eviscerated him.

Bullets sizzled past Lyons's face. He whipped around and spotted a fourth man firing from behind a stack of boxes. The warrior lined up a shot and started to fire. A cold realization hit him and caused him to hesitate. He was about to shoot at boxes that may or may not contain munitions.

A pallet loaded with mattresses offered cover and he took it. He reached under his long coat and grabbed a knife sheathed on his hip. The shooter stepped into view again and swept his SMG in a blistering arc that shredded the mattresses that protected Lyons.

Lyons flicked the knife at the shooter. It sailed end over end before burying itself in the man's thigh. The guy's eyes bulged and he stumbled forward, clawing at the knife while he continued to fire his machine pistol.

Resting on his left side, Lyons drew down on the man at an angle and triggered the shotgun twice. The one-two punch nearly cut the man in two. The man crumpled to the floor as Lyons rose from cover.

He started for the showroom at a dead run, ready to mow down anyone crazy enough to stand in his way. He snapped and snarled at his comrades, sure, but they were his friends. Brothers in blood. If any harm had come to Blancanales, Lyons knew he'd waste anyone and everyone involved.

Motion to his left caught his attention. He twisted at the waist and brought up the shotgun. He spied someone at the top of the stairs. He started to raise the shotgun, ready to cut the bastard down, when something stopped him.

The sound of metal clanging against metal.

A pair of cylindrical objects bounding down the steps.

He was moving even before his mind fully processed what he saw.

Grenades!

As soon as the grenades left his hands, Khan sprinted for his office and locked the door. His desk was shoved to the side. A ladder stood in the middle of the room, the top of it extending through the ceiling. He knew he'd have only a few seconds before all hell broke loose.

He grabbed his valise and climbed up the ladder. When he reached the square opening that led onto the roof, he shoved the bag through it first and then followed it up. The cold winds bit through the fabric of his dress shirt and slacks, tousled his black hair. His eyes searched the horizon for the chopper en route to pick him up. When he saw nothing, a cold thrill of fear raced down his spine. What if Quissad lied? What if the treacherous bastard decided to not send a chopper? Decided to leave him to die?

The beating of chopper blades emanated faintly from behind him, still distant. He thought of the grenades ticking down to zero downstairs and his fear swelled until he though it might burst through his skin like a tangible force. He waved furiously with both hands at the chopper as if to hasten its arrival.

The craft buzzed over the tops of buildings until it reached his. It circled overhead like a black bird of prey. The rotor wash whipped his coattails around him, and he squinted against the sudden maelstrom that enveloped him.

After it completed one revolution around the building, the craft halted and a harness attached to a rope dropped to him. He wrapped himself in it and, within minutes, the crew pulled him aboard, helped him out of his harness and led him to a seat. Once seated, he set the valise on the floor in front of him and squeezed it between his knees.

The chopper's engine whined louder as the pilot coaxed more power from it. The craft climbed skyward, quickly distancing itself from the impending explosion.

Khan risked one last look through his window.

Over the chopper's noise, he heard the guttural rumble of an explosion build to a hasty crescendo below him. The warehouse's exterior shook and the rumble of a single explosion quickly swelled into peals of thunder. Columns of boiling red-orange flames ripped through the roof and blasted skyward. Although the chopper had put some distance between itself and ground zero, shock waves from the blast still buffeted the craft. It wobbled as the pilot rode out the onslaught.

Khan leaned back in his seat. In his mind, he did something he almost never did. He gave a prayer of thanks for his escape. And for the Americans' demise.

A MINUTE EARLIER Blancanales found himself on the bull's-eye. Three gunners had burst into the room, their SMGs spitting fire. A fusillade of gunfire shattered the windows of a nearby curio cabinet and filled the air with glass shards. Blancanales leaped sideways to avoid the bits of razor-sharp shrapnel. He hit the ground behind a couch and rose to his feet almost immediately, triggering the Berettas. The weapons spit twin streams of fire. Parabellum slugs shredded wood, glass and upholstery and pinned Quissad's shooters behind makeshift shields fashioned from couches, chairs, dressers and trunks. One of the gunners broke from cover. Blancanales drew a bead on the man, fired and drilled him with a triburst. A second thug, this one armed with a double-barreled shotgun, popped up from cover. Blancanales emptied the second Beretta's magazine into the man and felled him.

With no time to reload, he stuffed the empty Beretta into his waistband. Switching the remaining Beretta to single-shot, he kept the pressure on the final shooter, pinning the guy behind a heavy oak bar.

The Beretta clicked dry. He dropped behind the couch, reloaded both guns and came back up in time to nearly get his hair parted by a sustained burst from a submachine gun.

Blazing sheets of autofire slashed through the room and shredded Blancanales's cover, bullets also piercing the large display windows at his six. The sustained gunfire forced the Stony Man commando to the ground. He crawled to the end of the couch and waited for the gunfire to subside. When the room fell momentarily silent, he sprang up and scanned for a target.

He could see only the top of the shooter's head poking up from behind furniture. Before Blancanales could attempt to line up a decent shot, Lyons burst through a pair of double doors leading into the showroom.

His sudden appearance startled the thug, who whipped toward him. The SPAS roared twice. The twin blasts disintegrated the man's head and neck and filled the air with a red mist.

Lyons raced for the front doors.

"Go, go, go!" he shouted.

Blancanales uncoiled from the floor. He wheeled toward the windows, jumped onto the display platforms, covered his face with his sleeves and launched himself through the glass. Lyons followed him a heartbeat later. A trail of glinting glass followed both men as they hit the ground.

Blancanales heard a guttural noise swell up from inside the building. Before he could react, Lyons grabbed him by the arm and yanked hard. "Go."

The men broke into a run. An instant later the remaining windows exploded, bits of glass whizzing through the air. From a reflection in a window in front of him, Blancanales saw boiling clouds of fire sweeping through the building at his back, spilling onto the streets.

The warriors raced for a line of buildings across the street. They brought up their pistols and unloaded them into the windowpanes in front of them. The glass disintegrated under the concentrated onslaught. The men heaved themselves through the window, hit the floor and rolled.

Blancanales collided with something solid and couldn't move any farther. He covered his head and rode out the explosion. A thunderclap pealed from across the street, accompanied by several smaller ones. The room suddenly brightened, its every feature exposed by the novalike blast of light from across the street. Bits of brick torn loose from the furniture store's exterior and other debris pelted their cover.

As the last reverberations from the explosions died away, Blancanales came up first in a kneeling position, then rose to his full height. Lyons stood and brushed the dirt from his overcoat and pant legs.

Blancanales stared at the fire across the street, the orange glow dancing over him, highlighting his grim features.

"You know what I'm thinking?" he asked.

"No."

"I think this is the part where we fake our deaths and go home."

"What?"

"Hey, c'mon, it's not like they killed Gadgets. They just hurt him."

"If we turned around and went home, he'd never let us live it down. He'd rib us forever. I couldn't stand it."

Blancanales nodded slowly. "That is a fate worse than death. Okay, let's take out these bastards."

CHAPTER TWENTY-FOUR

Fox tapped a few more keys on his laptop keyboard and completed his task. He turned to the man standing behind him and said, "I'm finished. Tell your boss."

Farnsworth's toady, a scrawny man with straw-colored hair, grinned. "Yeah, I'll tell him. He'll be ecstatic. You may have just worked yourself out of a job."

The guard patted his submachine gun to underscore his point.

"I should be so lucky," Fox replied. He shot the guy an obscene gesture, and the guy laughed.

The programmer turned back to the computer screen and rubbed his eyes, gritty and swollen from lack of sleep. The two technicians who'd watched him write code from their own terminals stood, stretched and began to move around the room. One of them, a rangy-built man with red hair and a ruddy complexion, lit up a cigarette. He caught Fox looking at him and offered him the pack. "You want one?"

"Dying for one," Fox said. "But first I want to hit the can. You got the card?"

The guy nodded. He reached inside his pocket, withdrew a security card and tossed it onto Fox's desk. "Knock yourself out. And remember, it only opens the washroom. You can't use it to go anywhere else."

Fox scowled. "Like I got somewhere else to go." He started to stand, but stopped. "Shit," he muttered.

"What?"

"Forgot something." He plopped into his seat and hit a couple more keys on his laptop, which had been hooked into Farnsworth's network.

"What the hell you doing? We're supposed to monitor everything you do with the computers," Smoker said.

Fox shrugged. "Chill, man, I'm already done. Go look at your screen if you don't believe me."

He held his breath while the guy scrutinized him for several seconds and, finally, shook his head. "Ah, to hell with it. No damage you can do at this point."

"Precisely," Fox said. You just keep believing that, moron.

A minute later Fox stood in the bathroom. He turned on the faucet, let the water run. In the meantime, he scanned the room for cabinets that might contain cleaning supplies. He came up empty. Not even a mop handle that he could use as a weapon. He ripped a paper towel from a dispenser, wadded the paper and tossed it into the trashcan.

He returned to the computer room. Smoker held out the cigarette pack, a lighter tucked inside the plastic wrapping. Fox took it. He turned the cigarette pack over, dumped a smoke into his palm, slipped it between his lips and lit it. He returned the pack with a grateful nod.

The second programmer, a guy with a generous middle, leaned against a wall. Pale blue eyes followed Fox's every move. His palm rested menacingly on the butt of the stun gun clipped to his belt.

Fox held the man's stare for a minute, sneered. He turned and dragged off his cigarette. He felt the man's eyes bore into his back. Smoker sat at one of the computer stations, his eyes locked on the PC's monitor. Fox studied the screen and saw the code for Cold Earth displayed on it. Eyes riveted to the screen, Smoker tapped the mouse with his right index finger and scrolled through the file.

"This is incredible," he said, shaking his head.

"Incredible pain in the ass, you mean," Fox stated. "Thing's cost me everything. Including my wife."

"Easy come, easy go," said the heavyset man behind him. Sarcasm was evident in his voice.

"I guess," Fox said. "Especially when all the women in your life have a staple through their navel."

He turned and headed for the coffeemaker. The path took him within inches of the heavyset programmer. Fox could feel barely contained rage radiate from the man. You get it first, he thought. Just on principle.

He brushed past the heavyset man, but avoided his stare. When he reached the coffeemaker, he grabbed the half-full pot from the burner. "Hey, Orca," he called over his shoulder, "where's the cream?"

Heavy footfalls thudded behind him. "What the hell'd you call me?"

A palm struck Fox in the middle of his back. The force of the blow propelled his body into the counter.

"Hey, dumbass, ease up," Smoker called.

"Screw you. I'm giving this SOB the Taser," the bigger man said.

Fox risked a quick glance over his shoulder and saw the man, his face tight with rage, grabbing for the stun gun holstered on his belt.

Smoker protested again. "Hey, I'm serious. Back away from him. Farnsworth will have your…"

Fox whirled. His right fist, still clutching the coffee-pot, arced in a roundhouse strike. The pot hit the man's face and exploded into dozens of glass fragments. A dozen cuts opened on the man's face and scalding hot liquid saturated his skin and eyes. He screamed and covered his face with his hands. Fox drove his foot into the man's groin until his shin struck the guy's pelvis. The impact caused his leg to go numb.

The man sobbed and his body sagged. Fox dropped on top of him and grabbed the stun gun from its holster.

"What the hell?" Smoker yelled.

Fox pulled the weapon free, twisted at the waist and triggered it. The wires snaked through the air until the contact points buried themselves in Smoker's chest. Fifty thousand volts poured into him and caused him to jerk in place. A second later he dropped to his knees and then pitched forward onto his face. Fox turned back toward the other man and drove a fist into his nose. He felt cartilage splinter under the impact. Felt his knuckles turn warm and sticky with blood.

His fist rocketed down twice more and both times struck the man's left eye. The bones forming his eye socket collapsed under the impact. The man struck out weakly with his right fist. His body charged with rage and adrenaline, Fox slapped the punch away. Fox grabbed a handful of the man's hair and bounced his skull off the floor a half dozen times until the man's eyes closed and his body went limp.

Fox shot to his feet and crossed the room. By this time, Smoker had rolled onto his back. He lay there and groaned. Fox dropped the sole of his foot on the man's throat and drove down the sole with the force of his weight, crushing the man's windpipe.

He returned to the laptop, punched a few more keys and smiled grimly.

The secure door leading into the room slid open. The straw-haired guard stepped inside. He quickly assessed the carnage and trained his SMG's muzzle on Fox.

"Stop!" the guard shouted.

Fox ignored the warning and surged toward the guard. The guy grinned and Fox realized he was going to die.

Before the guard could fire, Mace surged forward and drove a shoulder into the guard. The collision knocked the man from his feet and prevented him from firing his weapon. Fox was aware of Mace's arm arcing down toward him, his hand filled with a collapsible baton. The weapon struck him in the temple and a white light exploded behind his eyes. He felt as though his skull had just caved in. He took another step or two before his knees buckled and he crashed to the floor. As Mace and Farnsworth gathered around him and looked down upon him, he slipped into blackness.

CHAPTER TWENTY-FIVE

Ahmed Quissad found the young woman fascinating. She had olive skin, lighter than his own, but smooth and beautiful. Sleek black hair hung well past her shoulders and had the sheen of sunlight reflecting off the Tigris River. Her sea-green eyes were sharp and intelligent, but Quissad also thought he detected a hint of vulnerability in them. The latter quality might drive a lesser man to want to protect the woman. Quissad, however, simply saw it as an invitation to exploit her. He ran an appreciative gaze over her curves, which were highlighted by the red minidress she wore.

The bartender approached her and set a drink on the bar in front of her. She began to open her purse, but Quissad slid up next to her, close enough that her bare arm rubbed against his own. He set a gentle hand on top of her purse, trapping her hand inside.

"We won't look at your money," he said.

She turned, smiled. "Thank you," she said. "But that's really not necessary."

"Please accept my offer. I would consider anything less an insult."

Withdrawing her hand, she shut her purse and smiled. "Well, I wouldn't want to insult anyone."

"Of course not."

She raised her drink, tipped it slightly, as though toasting him. "Thank you, Mr...."

He moved his lips close to her ear, so he wouldn't have to shout to be heard over the blaring dance music. "Mr. Kusa," he said, breathing deep of her perfume. "Omar Kusa. I own this place."

He saw interest flicker in her eyes. He knew women craved powerful men. The way he saw it, they all wanted to be taken care of, like children. Even those who fancied themselves independent needed to be relieved of all responsibility, otherwise they crumbled under the weight of the world. He believed that they lost their way, like a stray dog.

"It's wonderful," she said, casting a glance around.

"I'm glad you like it," he said. "It's just one of my many holdings in Prague."

"Really?" she asked.

"Yes. You are surprised?"

"Only that you'd buy me a drink." She cast her eyes down demurely.

He waved dismissively. "Consider it a gift of appreciation," he said. "For a good customer. I've seen you here before."

"Oh, you've noticed."

"Of course. I miss little. What brings you here?"

"I'm an American. I'm here on business for a couple of days. I'm staying nearby. I get bored at night." She gave him a meaningful look.

"You're lovely. I want to learn more about you. Did you know that we have a second club upstairs? Something a little quieter. I'd like you to see it."

She opened her mouth to reply, but her gaze drifted from his and focused on some point over his shoulder. Curious, Quissad turned and saw a brown-skinned man in a black-leather duster approaching. Cortez. He turned back to the woman and set his hand on hers.

"A business associate. I must talk with him. You'll wait for me, of course."

She licked her lips, nodded. "Of course."

"Excellent."

TURNING ON HIS HEEL, Quissad found himself face-to-face with Cortez. The other man's eyes were red-rimmed and his hair tousled. He regarded Quissad with soulless eyes that would have projected menace to a coward. Quissad mentally brushed it off. He'd killed a pair of U.S. Special Forces soldiers in Iraq when that damnable country had invaded his homeland. Neither had been easy prey. Rather each had been formidable and their conquest, as he saw it, was a testament to his own skills as a warrior.

"We must talk," the man said. He looked past Quissad at the green-eyed beauty, gave her a smile and let his eyes travel over her. He then turned back to the Iraqi. "Talk alone, I mean. I have news."

"Of course," Quissad said.

NADIA RABIN'S EYES followed the Iraqi and the other man as they moved away from her and eventually melted into the crowd. She set her drink on the counter. Threading her way between the gyrating, sweat-soaked bodies populating the dance floor, she kept her distance from the two men.

They stopped at an elevator door, waited for it to open. Rabin, a Mossad agent working undercover, dipped a hand inside her purse and extracted a cellular telephone. Clicking it open, she aimed it at the men and captured their images digitally. She checked the results and, satisfied, sent the images via e-mail, closed the phone and slipped it back into her purse. While in her purse, her fingertips brushed the cold steel of the SIG-Sauer P-230 chambered in .380. She'd entered the country unarmed, but a contact in Prague had supplied her with the weapon and other equipment after she'd departed the airport.

She returned to the bar, happy to find her seat still unoccupied. Climbing back onto the stool, she crossed her legs and signaled the bartender for a fresh drink. While she waited, she pondered how best to perform her mission. The goal itself was simple: she'd been sent to assassinate Quissad. Weapons he'd sold to Palestinian terrorists had been used to launch attacks against Israel, and Tel Aviv wanted him eliminated.

The bartender brought her drink. She swirled the vodka in her glass, plastered a smile on her face and watched the bar patrons dance. Bringing the drink to her lips, she took a sip and let it roll down her throat into her stomach where it created a pleasant warmth.

She felt eyes upon her. She turned to see a pair of Arab-looking men in what looked like expensive suits staring at her. When they saw her look, one man averted his gaze while an older one, his head shaved, his face marked with a well-trimmed mustache and beard, smiled at her and raised his drink. She scowled at him and turned back around. Her heart hammered in her chest and her mouth turned dry.

She guessed the men worked for Quissad, but that didn't necessarily explain why they were monitoring her. Was it to shoo away other suitors? Or did the Iraqi suspect her of something? She'd come here several nights in a row, hoping to attract his attention. But had she drawn the wrong kind of attention? If so, the huntress knew she quickly could become the prey. She shuddered, but not at the possibility of dying. She knew Quissad was a vicious animal, a man who'd specialized in the rape and torture of women while he'd been part of Saddam's regime. And like a vicious animal, there really was only one way to dispense of him—quickly and finally. She didn't want to consider failure, especially if it meant ending up at his mercy. She'd prefer a quick death to falling prey to his perverse nature.

Besides that, she also knew that her failure would allow him to continue plying his deadly trade. Countless innocent Israelis—men, women and children—stood to suffer violent, fiery deaths because of the murderous tools he peddled. She wanted so badly for him to face justice, a final sort of justice, that she almost couldn't fathom failure.

At times, she wondered about her chosen profession. She wasn't a heartless killer. But this time, knowing the stakes, knowing the man she'd been asked to exterminate, she felt a tingle of anticipation at the prospect of slaying him. She had no illusions that her actions would end all violence in her embattled country. But she could make a difference, perhaps save a few lives.

In the meantime, though, she knew she had to romance the devil, play the passive, demure woman that a human predator like him would find irresistible. She'd seen how he'd looked at her, like a butcher inspecting a side of beef. She checked her watch and saw that it'd be at least another thirty minutes before her rendezvous with him. She drained the vodka and smoked a cigarette to pass some time. Afterward, she reapplied the lipstick with the help of her compact mirror. With a glance, she saw that the two men who'd been staring at her were gone.

She heard a rumble sound from somewhere outside the building, possibly even underneath it. It briefly overtook the din of throbbing bass and overdriven guitars. A tremor passed through the building, causing glasses to bounce off the edge of tables and fall to the ground where they shattered. Although the music continued, people stopped dancing and gave one another panicked or questioning looks. The lights came up and patrons began to move toward the front doors, choking the exits.

Rabin slid from the bar stool and got out of the panicked patrons' way. Almost immediately something about the explosion struck her as suspicious. Although it'd gotten people's attention and ignited a frenzy, it didn't seem to have done much more than that. She'd been to the scene of more than one car bombing in her time and had witnessed the destruction wrought by expertly used explosives.

There seemed to be none of that here. Black smoke had begun to waft up through the air ducts. Fire alarms wailed. Emergency lights flicked on and doused the room in white light. Overhead sprinklers came to life, showering everyone, including her, with cold water. She didn't see any signs of real structural damage—floors rupturing, mortar dust falling, glass shards whizzing through the air.

She pushed her way through the sea of people rushing toward the door. Opening her purse, she slipped her hand inside and fisted the SIG-Sauer. She kept it inside her handbag so as not to attract attention to herself. As she broke free from the crowd, she saw a man standing at the foot of the stairs. He had a wide back that seemed to stretch his jacket to the breaking point. Water had matted his blond hair against his head. Another man lay crumpled at his feet, his head twisted at an odd angle.

What the hell was going on here? she wondered. Who was this man? Considering Quissad's notoriety in the underworld, the stranger could be anyone from an Interpol agent to a competing criminal looking to eliminate some competition. Regardless, she couldn't let him derail her mission. Drawing her pistol, she held it flat against the top of a trim thigh and advanced toward him.

As she closed in, she vowed that if she got even the slightest hint of interference, she'd send him out on a slab.

USING HIS THUMB and forefinger, Cortez held the disk between its edges. When it caught light from the overhead lights, he angled it until it glinted. Just like gold, he thought. He held a fortune in his hands and it felt damn good. If they sold this—no, *when* they sold it— he was out of the trash work. No more alleyway hits on thugs or opposition politicians for a few spare pesos. No more straddling the line between law officer and criminal so he could make ends meet. He'd walk away with enough money to live out the rest of his natural-born days lying on a beach in the Cayman Islands, getting drunk and laid with hedonistic regularity. Yeah, as soon as this thing went down, life would be one big celebration. First, though, he had to bust his partner's balls, give the guy a wake-up call before he sank them both.

"Who's the woman?" he asked.

Quissad, who sat across the table from him, wrapped the fingers of his right hand around the glass of whiskey.

He paused and stared over his glass at the other man. "Just that. A woman. Nothing to concern yourself with."

"Consider me concerned," Cortez said. "We haven't come this far to have you screw it up over a piece of tail. Understand? Did you have this bitch checked out?"

Quissad's eyes narrowed and his fingertips paled as his grip on the glass hardened. "Of course I checked her out," he said. "Do you think I'm an idiot? That I don't understand the stakes here? I had her checked out long before I ever introduced myself. I didn't survive thirty-plus years in Iraq by being stupid and careless."

"Last I checked you weren't in Iraq, amigo. Don't look at me like that. You know where I'm going with this. We're not in some stinking dictatorship where you and your pals control everything. This country is crawling with spies and cops of all stripes. If any of them have gotten wind of what we're up to, then we need to stay one step ahead of them. Tighten the circle."

Quissad returned the drink to the table, its contents untouched. "Really? Please educate me as to how that works."

"That means don't go thinking with your dick! Do that and you're begging to get caught. For all you know, the woman's here to get information, to shut us down."

Cortez clenched and unclenched his fist while he watched the Iraqi seethe. Quissad pressed the fingertips of his left hand to his lips as though restraining his words. With his right hand, he swirled his glass over the tabletop in small circles. He seemed to be mulling the Mexican's words, which Cortez considered a good thing.

He set aside his glass, laced his fingers together and leaned forward on the table. He smiled and gave Cortez a small nod.

"Of course, you raise a good point, my friend," he said. "You've single-handedly kept this operation seamless and I appreciate it." Cortez started to protest, but Quissad silenced him with a gesture. "Speaking of security, I wanted to let you know that Tony Drake, your friend in Mexico? The CIA man? He's been captured. Even as we speak, he's in official custody—how do you say?—spilling his guts."

Though he made a conscious effort to keep his expression stony, Cortez suddenly found it difficult to breathe, as though his ribs were being squeezed in a vise. His throat tightened and he coughed to loosen it. He studied Quissad's face, trying to determine whether the man was bullshitting him. A cold feeling oozed over his insides as he realized that Quissad wasn't.

"Shit."

"Excellent choice of words."

"When?"

"Within hours after you left the country. Apparently someone shot up his restaurant and took out some of his people."

Anger caused his fists to tighten and his face to grow taut. "What the hell happened? Did the Mexican government nab him? If so, I've got connections. If I drop a word or two, that fucker's one dead gringo."

Quissad shook his head. His face featured a smug grin. "Not the Mexicans. The Americans. It was the DEA that lifted him out of the country, as a matter of fact. At least that's what *my* people in the Mexican government say. Don't look so surprised. I have sources in your country, too. And I pay a hell of a lot better than you."

"Where'd the Americans take him?"

"No one knows. He just disappeared."

"Then he's getting grilled. Is anyone following me?"

Quissad shrugged. "You tell me."

"Cut the shit, you bastard. This is serious."

"Of course it is. And, to answer your question, yes, someone has been here asking about you. And me. Not all that surprising, considering that you shot a federal agent, kidnapped someone and fled the country. Did you think they'd reach the border and wait for the proper paperwork to go through?"

"Screw you. You got names for these agents? Or anything else that might help me find them? We need to plug this leak as soon as possible."

"I already took care of it. There are many honest men and women in the police department, but there are a few who live beyond their means. They're always more than happy to take my money in exchange for some information. In this case, they've been most co-operative."

"And?"

"Two men, American agents, Justice Department, are here in Prague. I've already sent someone to deal with them before things proceed further."

"I'm impressed," Cortez said. And he was, as much as the admission pained him.

"When it comes to the type of money we're looking at, I can be very resourceful," the former Iraqi soldier said. "Oh, and the woman? She's Mossad. That one took a little more digging. Her fake identity—she claimed she was American—went fairly deep. But I finally got the necessary information. I have many friends in the Palestinian territories. A couple of them were willing to offer up the information."

"She know about this?" Cortez asked, holding the disk up.

"Who knows? Maybe. Maybe not. I have quite a reputation in Israel. That more than likely is what prompted her to come here. I keep selling the Palestinians the bombs and rockets that kill her people."

Before Cortez could respond, the door opened and a muscular young Arab dressed in black jeans and a black windbreaker, a white T-shirt and tennis shoes entered. He had the thick shoulders and arms one usually associated with steroid use. His face was a mask of barely contained rage. Cortez noticed that the left breast of the man's jacket was slicked with some shiny substance. He stopped several feet from Quissad, clasped his hands behind his back and focused his eyes on the ceiling, apparently waiting for the other man to acknowledge him.

Quissad turned slowly toward him. "You have something to say?"

Nodding, the man approached Quissad. Casting a suspicious glance at Cortez, the man bent to whisper in his boss's ear. Quissad held up a hand to stop him. "Please, Farid. I have no secrets from my partner," the Iraqi said. "Whatever needs said can be said for him, too."

Cortez thought his new business partner was full of shit. But he was curious as to what the nervous thug needed to share, so he acknowledged Quissad's feigned graciousness with an equally insincere smile.

"The Americans," the man said. "We weren't able to subdue them. They got away from us."

"I see," Quissad said quietly. "And it cost us how many people?"

"A dozen. Maybe more. The final tally isn't in yet."

Quissad rose from his chair and walked to the one-way glass window staring out onto the club. "So an attempt to capture two people cost us at least a dozen others. Do I understand this correctly?"

His face stoic, the man said, "Yes, sir."

"Really? A dozen former soldiers and mercenaries couldn't bury two men. I find that just astounding. They must really have been something for that to have happened."

Drowning as the man was, he brightened at what seemed to be the extension of a lifeline to him by his boss. "They were fiery, capable fighters," he said. "I've seen few as good as that."

Quissad turned to the man. "You sound almost like you admire them."

"No, no, sir," the man said. "I'm just making a statement of fact. These men were tough. They were unusually good soldiers."

"The fedayeen were unusually good soldiers."

"Yes, sir. The best."

"You were Fedayeen Saddam."

The man straightened a bit and his face hardened. "In my heart, sir, I still am."

Quissad exploded with withering laughter. "In your heart, perhaps. But not in your spine. Your spine has softened to jelly. You bring shame to your former country and your former leaders."

"With all due respect—"

"Shut up!" Quissad yelled. "Shut your mouth. You have no respect to offer me! Do you hear what I'm saying? You want to speak to me, speak as a soldier. You have to prove yourself. Show me you still have the pride of your nationality, your heritage coursing through your veins."

"Sir?"

Quissad nodded toward Cortez. "Shoot him. Kill him."

A confused expression washed over the man's features. "Kill him? But he's your guest."

"Shoot him!"

The big Iraqi made a play for his weapon. Cortez swore and upended the table with a kick. It struck the man's pistol hand and knocked the weapon's muzzle toward the ceiling. The weapon discharged with a loud roar. Cortez was already reaching for his own pistol. Before he could finish the action, though, another handgun cracked behind him. Even as his fingers closed around his handgun's grip, a single red dot appeared on the man's chest, in between his pectorals. The Iraqi soldier stiffened and withered to the floor.

Cortez whipped around toward Quissad, his weapon tracking in on the Iraqi. Before he could line up a clear shot, though, he saw the black hole of Quissad's pistol muzzle trained on his forehead. Smoke curled from the barrel. Cortez froze and the two men faced each other for a stretched second.

His breath hung in his throat. Blood and echoes from the shot roared in his ears. He ran through the numbers, but knew any last-ditch play would leave him dead.

Suddenly, Quissad's lips split into a grin. Then he laughed and let the gun's muzzle drop. Maybe the laughter should have relieved Cortez. It didn't. Rather he felt overcome with rage, humiliation and confusion.

"What the hell's the deal?" he yelled. "You loco or something? Quit your damn laughing and answer my question."

Quissad looked at the other man, shook his head as though he pitied him.

"It was a lesson," the Iraqi said. "For both of you.

Two lessons, actually. Farid failed me, put me at risk. I couldn't allow that and just let him walk away. In Iraq, we had severe consequences for mistakes. That made us strong. Then, when I gave him an order, a chance to redeem himself, he balked. Two mistakes. Both fatal. With me, there is no other kind of mistake."

CHAPTER TWENTY-SIX

Johnny Stark climbed the stairs leading to the third floor. He took a moment to get his bearings and headed for apartment 3-C. Once there, he pulled a folding knife from his overcoat pocket, unlocked the blade and went to work on the door. He occasionally glanced over his shoulder to check his surroundings. A few minutes later, the latch gave and the door swung inward. He stepped to one side, so he wouldn't be silhouetted when it came open.

Stark held his breath for a moment, waiting to see what would happen. This was, after all, the apartment of Gabriel Fox, the CIA geek. Stark and his crew already had done their best to shut down any silent alarms that might have been planted by the Agency. But that didn't mean it hadn't left behind a human alarm or two, ready to nab Fox or his captors, should they come.

Reaching around the doorjamb, he grazed his fingertips along the wall until he found a light switch. He started to flick it up, but stopped himself. The last thing he needed was to turn on some lights and alert anyone at street level that an intruder had entered the apartment.

He stepped inside and shut the door behind him. He set his bag on the floor, reached inside, withdrew a set of night-vision goggles and fitted them on his head. He activated the goggles and the room came into focus, bathed in various shades of eerie green.

Taking a hand radio from his jacket, he put it to his lips and whispered, "I'm in."

Standing erect, he locked the door and secured it with the chain.

He'd come looking for a hot property and the last thing he needed was some clown coming in behind him, unannounced, looking for the same thing. He fisted the .38 Colt Detective Special and quickly searched the apartment for people. The more important search could wait a few minutes, he decided.

Once he was satisfied that the place was clean, he began a more thorough survey of the apartment. He found himself surprised at the modest furniture, a couple of pieces with the arms worn threadbare from years of repeated use. From what he knew of Fox, it made sense. The guy had spent his youth being shifted between foster homes and government orphanages and prisons. He probably was reluctant to set down roots. A few feminine touches—curtains, family pictures, wall hangings—could be found throughout. But otherwise the place looked more like a prison cell than a home.

"Some stinking genius," Stark muttered. "Guy lives like a pauper."

Stark knew, without a doubt, that if he had this guy's brains, he'd be making the big bucks, living high on the hog. He'd work for the highest bidder, not for a bunch of chump bureaucrats tossing out peanuts. He'd be a big damn deal. If he had the brains, which he knew damn well he didn't.

He shook his head, disgusted with Fox's lack of imagination and self-interest. Keeping the gun handy, he wound his way through the apartment, sidestepping furniture and a few discarded books and CDs.

He moved to the guy's desk and found it bare. Regardless, he searched through the drawers, just so he could say he had. When you worked for Farnsworth, you covered the bases because to do otherwise was sheer suicide.

The guys from Langley more than likely had removed anything of value. Or at least he was sure they thought so. From what Farnsworth's Agency mole had passed along, the place had been gone over with a fine-tooth comb. Any searches of the most obvious places was perfunctory, insurance against missing something important. Insurance against fatal punishment meted out by Farnsworth.

After a search of the living room and the kitchen—looking at the underside of drawers and furniture, reaching into the grimy pockets underneath cushions—he checked out the two smaller bedrooms, but walked away empty-handed. He moved into the master bedroom and swept his gaze over the interior. A large, framed photograph stood on a dresser. It was a woman, pretty, with a sweet, generous smile. Stark'd seen the same face in several other photos and assumed it was Fox's old lady, the one Mace had snuffed.

Judging by the number of pictures hanging in the place, Stark guessed she'd been Fox's real prize in life, rather than furniture or fast cars. What a damn chump. Diamonds were forever, people weren't worth a shit. The faster a person realized that, the faster he took what he wanted and had a hell of a good time.

The bed covers were still in disarray. A drawer hung

open and a sweatshirt sleeve snaked to the floor, curved and lay flat against the carpet. Like the rest of the apartment, the room smelled of cigarette smoke and some floral potpourri.

Stark knelt next to the closet and slid open the door tentatively. Reaching inside, he used his hand like a croupier's rake to pull out a bunch of women's shoes until he'd cleared most of the floor. He crawled his upper torso inside, felt a few pieces of clothing brush against the skin of his bald skull. Laying the .38 on the floor within easy reach, he again produced the knife, clicked it open and jammed the blade into the space between the wall and a strip of molding that ran the length of the bottom of the closet. When the tapered end stopped slipping in easily, he applied more pressure to break it away from the wall. With a hard pull, he pried the baseboard from the wall until it came loose. Setting the knife and the baseboard aside, he reached into a rectangular hole in the wall and felt around until his fingers touched something inside.

He pulled the hidden item from inside the space. When he saw the laptop wrapped in plastic and clear packing tape, he smiled. He popped open his briefcase, slid the machine inside, replaced the baseboard and the shoes, then closed the closet.

A minute or so later he stepped into the hallway and shut the apartment door behind him. He knew Farnsworth would be pleased, which meant good things for Stark, particularly a large payday.

A sandy-haired man, slender and dressed in a navy-blue suit, approached Stark. The man's left hand came up and he showed Stark an ID of some sort. "Sir, I'd like to ask—" the man began.

Stark already had the revolver in his hand. The gun

erupted twice. Bullets drilled through the man's starched white shirt. Crimson geysers of blood spurted from the man's chest as he stumbled backward. Even as the man folded to the ground, a second man exploded from the stairwell. The muzzle of his auto-loading pistol was tracking in on Stark. The thief emptied the revolver into the man. Bullets punched through the guy, sending him stumbling into the wall.

Holstering the empty Colt, Stark grabbed a pistol from the nearer dead guy, shoved it into his overcoat pocket and kept walking.

CHAPTER TWENTY-SEVEN

Russia

The truck turned off from the snowy access road and rolled toward the guard shack. When the driver braked, the wheels squealed thanks to the snow and moisture caked to the brake pads. Vladimir Serov sat motionless behind the wheel, waiting as the young guards argued over who'd brave the bitter cold to check his identification.

The smaller of the two soldiers—Serov guessed the man stood about five feet, six inches—stepped from the guardhouse and approached the vehicle. The man carried his assault rifle, canted across his chest at a forty-five-degree angle. His breath hung in the air in white wisps as it froze in the punishing temperatures of the Russian winter.

Serov rolled down the driver's-side window. He held out his identification card. The man scowled, snatched it from his hand and gave it a cursory glance.

"You are early," the soldier said.

"I have paperwork from last night. I must complete it before my next shift."

"Or perhaps you are hiding out from your wife. Maybe she even threw you out again. How many times would that make it this year?"

Serov forced a smile and a hollow laugh. "You know me too well, my friend. I must come here, where there are armed guards, to keep the old crone off my back."

The man shared another laugh. The guard returned Serov's identification. Serov gave him a grateful wave and guided the truck through the gates. Parking his truck in his designated spot, he gathered his belongings, exited the vehicle and headed for the imposing structure ahead of him. Fear fluttered in his gut as he passed through a second checkpoint. He'd worked at the nuclear facility for more than a decade. He knew virtually every guard and scientist on the premises. But whenever he pulled a job for Farnsworth, an intoxicating mixture of fear and excitement overcame him. Would this be the night when it all fell apart? Would he find guards or government agents waiting for him at his locker, ready to arrest him, throw him into a gulag somewhere?

If he was perfectly honest with himself, he'd admit that these little seizures of terror were the only thing that made his life worth living. He hated his job, pushing the same buttons each night at a nuclear power plant, until he could do it in his sleep. He hated his wife, his small apartment stuffed with two generations of her family. Hated his damned gray existence. Stealing secrets for Farnsworth and the CIA were his bright spots, the all too rare moments when he felt as though blood still coursed through his veins. The money the Americans forked over for these occasional jobs was nice, of course. But he considered the excitement the true payment.

The next line of guards waved him through. He bantered with them, setting their minds at ease, as he did night after night.

Stepping into the control building, he lighted a cigarette. He made a conscious effort to not shake his head disgustedly at the men gathered outside the building. Most were like him, second- or third-generation soldiers. Underpaid, when they were paid at all. Like his father before him, Serov had been a Soviet soldier before the old regime crumbled. Being a soldier and a government employee afforded him access to the very commodity that made him so in demand as an espionage agent.

Farnsworth had recruited him nearly a decade earlier, when the American worked as the CIA's station chief in Moscow. It had taken little prodding for the American to turn Serov against his homeland. Promises of American dollars filtered into black accounts had provided ample motivation for a bored and struggling man such as himself to turn against his government. And, to his credit, Farnsworth had always made sure the checks grew proportionately with the amount of access Serov gained to Russia's nuclear weapons and energy programs.

After Farnsworth returned to the states to retire, a new station chief had taken over and the work soon dried up. The man was much more concerned with terrorists stealing nuclear-weapons components than he was with other secrets. With increasing frequency, Serov had been considering taking his information elsewhere, or even fleeing the country so he could spend some of the money he'd earned over the years.

Then came the call from Farnsworth.

The American needed one final job performed. It was

relatively easy, and the payoff was huge compared to past payments. Serov had taken the money—half up front, half upon completion of the task—no questions asked.

When he reached the final checkpoint, the guard administered the retinal scans and voice-recognition tests. When he passed those tests, the guard punched in a series of buttons on the console. A massive steel door came open with a hiss. Serov nodded at the guard and passed through.

As the door closed behind him, the Russian made his way through the tunnel that led into the reactor's control room.

A handful of men and women—civilian and military personnel—populated the room. Most were seated at their workstations, monitoring the brightly colored digital gauges that tracked heat, pressure and other aspects of the reactor.

The shift supervisor, a dour man with a deeply lined face, rose from his chair and came to Serov.

"You are here," André Voloshan said.

"Yes," Serov said. "Obviously."

"That is good," Voloshan said. "Pavel has called in sick. He has a stomach illness of some kind and had to be hospitalized."

Serov wasn't surprised. The two men had met for drinks the previous night. He'd spiked the other man's drink with lye. "Of course he's sick. He eats and drinks like an animal."

"Regardless, you will take his seat and finish his shift."

Serov nodded. "Of course." He made his way to Pavel's workstation and powered up the computer. He waited several seconds while it came to full power. In the meantime he shed his coat and hat, draped them over the back of his seat, and exchanged greetings with his co-workers. As the others returned to work, he dipped a hand inside his coat pocket and palmed a CD that Farnsworth's surrogate had handed him last night.

The young woman, an auburn-haired beauty with sea-green eyes, had been evasive about the contents of the disk. That worried Serov only a little. After all, odds were that Farnsworth never would do anything to betray Serov. Not because he was a man of honor, but rather because he wouldn't want to lose a good source or risk Serov fingering him as a CIA handler.

He downloaded the file and followed the other steps outlined by the young woman the previous night. Once he completed the tasks, he ejected the disk, returned it to his coat and threw himself into his work.

A half hour later he got to his feet, ready to reward himself with a cigarette. Scanning the room, he found his supervisor engaged in a conversation with a pretty blonde who only recently had joined their team. Apparently she was either too young or too naive to see the lecherous bastard for what he was. Whatever. None of it was his problem. And it'd be even less of a problem when he left work tonight, drove to Moscow and caught a flight under an assumed name to the Cayman Islands. At that point, everyone could just go fuck themselves.

Serov caught his supervisor's eye. He waved his cigarette pack at the man. "Smoke break." The man waved him on and resumed his conversation with the young lady.

Serov had taken a few steps when it happened.

Red lights came to life overhead. Sirens rang out warning tones, heralding a problem of some sort. What the hell?

Stuffing his cigarettes back into his shirt pocket, he returned to his seat. He assumed the whole thing was a drill of some sort. A feigned meltdown or terrorist attack, something to test their response time. He ground his teeth to hold his irritation in check. More bureaucratic nonsense.

He scanned his monitor. A warning flashed on it.

Core heating. Meltdown in progress.

Serov felt terror well up from deep inside. It traveled the length of his throat, constricting it, like an icy hand clasped around his windpipe.

His training kicked in and his fingers began dancing over the keyboard. He tried to initiate the appropriate emergency sequences. The computer didn't respond.

Judging by the terrified looks of his co-workers, their sometimes frenzied attempts to get their computers to respond, he wasn't the only experiencing the locked system.

What the hell had Farnsworth given him to download?

From the corner of his eye, Serov spotted his supervisor approaching. His heart hammered hard in his chest and he felt a compulsion to run. Did they know what had happened? Had someone noticed him loading the rogue file onto the system?

"The cooling system has shut down," his supervisor said. "The fuel rods are overheating. We need to reset the system or we'll have a meltdown on our hands. All our backup systems are gone, too."

With his index finger, Serov repeatedly punched the keyboard's space bar, like a child pedaling a single note on a toy computer. "My computer doesn't work."

Fury passed over the other man's features. "None of them work, idiot," he yelled. "That's the problem. If we can't get the cooling system restarted, then all we can do is sit here and watch as the core grows hotter."

"If there's nothing we can do, we should leave," Serov stated weakly.

"Idiot, you know the protocol. We must stay here and keep working. We have to keep trying to shut down the system."

Serov licked his lips, even as the choking sensation threatened to overtake him.

"Besides," his supervisor said, "even if we wanted to go, we couldn't. The doors lock automatically to keep us here. So hold your damn station."

The supervisor walked away, shaking his head.

Serov sat at his desk, numb. He watched the Warning sign pulse on his screen, knowing it was counting down his final seconds on Earth. Damn Farnsworth! Wherever the bastard was, Serov prayed he got his.

CHAPTER TWENTY-EIGHT

Hal Brognola, his cigar clenched between his teeth, paced the Computer Room and waited for some word from the field. He plucked the cigar from his mouth, studied it and decided that it looked how his nerves felt—frayed.

The men of Phoenix Force were burning their way through the Sudanese hellgrounds. They were making progress, no doubt, but the big Fed wondered whether they were moving fast enough. The sooner they nailed Farnsworth and, hopefully rescued Fox, the safer everyone would be. The same went for Able Team—or at least the two-thirds still on the job. Brognola hadn't heard from them yet. But, judging by the news reports of two multiple-casualty shootings in Prague, he guessed Lyons and Blancanales were turning over rocks, seeing what they could find there. The cyberteam was gathering and sharing information as fast as it could, while tracking the various soldiers in the field with GPS units and satellite feeds.

All Brognola could do was stand by, shouting the occasional order or requesting an update. He felt helpless, and he didn't like it.

A telephone trilled and Carmen Delahunt snatched

the receiver from its cradle and put it to her ear. Brognola watched expectantly, hoping for a sitrep from one of the teams. He wanted something to show that the scales had tipped in America's favor.

"Yeah, we got one of those around here. Hang on."

She put the caller on hold and set the receiver in the cradle. "Hal, you've got a call."

"Who is it?" he asked.

"The Man."

"Jeez, Carmen, could you show the guy a little respect?"

She shrugged and turned back to her computer monitor. "United States president, bank president. All the same to me. I've got work to do."

Brognola shook his head. As he took the call, he dipped his hand into his right front pants' pocket and withdrew a half-eaten roll of antacids. He pushed his thumbnail through the foil wrapper and began to cut one loose from the roll. With his other hand, he pressed the button for the President's line. "Yes, sir?"

"Who was that woman?" the President boomed.

"Forget it, sir. It doesn't matter."

"But…" After a couple of tense seconds, the Man sighed. "You're right. It doesn't matter. I'm just tense. Damn it, Hal. Sometimes I swear you're the only bureaucrat who doesn't check his backbone at the door when he clocks in. Have you watched the television lately?"

"No. I have a feeling I might want to, though."

"I think so."

Brognola wheeled toward a bank of televisions carrying broadcasts from a variety of cable and satellite television channels, both foreign and domestic. On CNN, he spotted the Breaking News logo plastered on the screen next to the face of a pretty blond anchor. In the upper right hand-corner, he saw a graphic depicting the outline of a nuclear tower with the words "Meltdown!" emblazoned along the bottom in bright red letters. An icy sensation of fear raced down his spine. Were they already too late? Had the teams failed?

"Shit," he said.

"It's in Russia," the Man said. "So far their government's mum about all but the sketchiest details. But, according to some communications intercepted by our Moscow embassy, the place already is starting to leak radiation. The Russians have people on the ground, trying to clean up the mess. We've offered our help, of course. And we're hoping they'll accept it."

"I take it a computer malfunction caused this?"

"Yes, at least from what we've gathered so far. Unless you believe in coincidences, I think we both know what this means."

"Cold Earth's in play."

"Right."

"Did we have any warning? Have we heard anything from Farnsworth?"

The President informed Brognola of a video message the government received hours earlier that outlined the extortion demands. "I just saw the video a few minutes ago," he said. "I'll have the National Director of Intelligence send you a copy immediately. I've ordered him to disburse the message to my cabinet, the NSC and some others who need to be in the loop. He wanted my clearance first before he did anything."

"What's the upshot of his message?"

"He promised a demonstration. Apparently this was it. Damn it, if we'd have known he was going to do this, we'd have warned the Russians."

"Of course," Brognola said.

"What do you make of it? These extortion demands and the possibility of terrorist involvement?"

"Extortion as a motive makes sense. But I'm not convinced that we're dealing with terrorists, no matter how convincing the tape. Sure it's a possibility. Most terrorists would love to finance their jihad against us with our own money. But, hell, why not just attack us with Cold Earth? These groups really want to kill Americans and destroy our country. So, if these guys are terrorists, why don't they just pull the trigger? Why resort to extortion? Plus, frankly, our field intelligence is pointing more and more toward this Dale Farnsworth. That greedy bastard would love nothing better than to earn some easy cash, even if it means selling out his country. We both know that."

"The National Director of Intelligence sees it differently."

The burn in Brognola's stomach intensified. He placed a hand over his belly and rubbed it soothingly. "Good for the NDI."

To his surprise, the President laughed. "Hey, Hal, I'm just passing along the information and making a request. Just consider what he's saying."

"Which is?"

"He thinks this Gabriel Fox was colluding with the guys who kidnapped him. It's not out of the realm of possibility. That young man came to us with a spotty record. It's conceivable that he's part of this whole conspiracy."

"I'll give it due consideration, sir," Brognola said.

"In other words, you don't buy it," the President replied.

"We've scoured his record. He's been clean since he was eighteen years old. We found no signs of involvement with any terrorist organizations. His wife was murdered during a previous kidnap attempt. With all due respect, sir, it just doesn't play."

"You've pulled our chestnuts out of the fire too many times for me to second-guess your competence. But motive remains a secondary issue here, anyway. I just want you to find the bastards—whoever they are—and kill them."

"Right."

Price entered the room. Brognola caught her eye and motioned for her to join him. Just as she started toward him, the President continued to speak.

"Look, Hal. The guy gave us four hours to make a decision. And, truth be told, I'm not sure which way to go on this. Our policy of not negotiating with terrorists is something I back wholeheartedly. But can we risk it this time? I mean, it's one thing to tell some killers with a couple of hostages to go to hell. I'm not cavalier about that, either. But this is a whole other situation when we're talking about wholesale destruction both in our country and around the world."

"Yes, sir."

"I guess what I'm saying is this—I'll make the best decision I can. I'll stand by my decision regardless of what others say about it. You know that."

"Yes, sir. But you'd rather not have to make the decision."

"Look, here's the deal, Hal. Your guys have two hours to knock these bastards down a peg or two. If it doesn't happen by then, well, I'll have to revert to Plan B."

"Which is?"

"Scorched earth. We reduce the facility to a crater. I don't want to make that order. At least not until your men and the hostage get clear. But, damn it, if it comes to that…"

"Understood, sir. Let's hope it doesn't get to that point."

The President terminated the call.

The big Fed brought Price up to speed on the video demanding extortion money.

"Brief everyone," Brognola ordered. "The clock's ticking on this one. We need to bring it to a close. Contact the field teams and tell them that we have less than two hours—not even 120 minutes—to go before this whole thing disintegrates."

Price swallowed hard but nodded and set about her work.

AARON KURTZMAN FLIPPED through the browser screens displayed on his laptop and frantically hunted for useful intelligence on Farnsworth or the Libyan bunker.

He was seated in an AWACS aircraft tasked with providing radar and other support to Phoenix Force. During the past hour, Kurtzman had hacked into several high-security databases, including ones maintained by the Pentagon, the CIA and the National Security Agency. He'd unearthed nothing beyond what the cyberteam already had turned up, and it disheartened him.

He knew that with each passing moment, Phoenix Force's chances of finding Fox, killing Fox's captors and averting a global disaster dimmed considerably. And, while the others went into battle, he couldn't help but feel useless. His inability to nail down good information on the computer only heightened the feeling.

A clicking noise alerted him to the arrival of an e-mail. Probably Barb or one of the others with an update of some sort, he thought.

He brought up his e-mail window and saw a message highlighted in bold at the top of the list. He read the sender's name and a smile played over his lips.

Gabriel Fox.

Kurtzman opened the message and read it. A scowl tugged at the corners of his mouth as he did. He read it a second time, shivered.

AK,
Cold Earth back in operation. Guy named Dale Farnsworth, guy named Jack Mace wanted it. To hell with me! It's going out! Soon! Would be catastrophic! GF

Working the keyboard, he forwarded the message to Price and the other Stony Man operatives. Then he began searching through his hard drive for a file. When he found it, he clicked the reply button on Fox's e-mail, attached the file and sent it.

"Please, please let this work," he muttered under his breath.

FARNSWORTH AND MACE stood over the young programmer, who lay on the floor, unconscious. Farnsworth stared at the fallen man and seethed. His breath was audible to those around him.

"How far along was he on Cold Earth?" he called over his shoulder.

"Finished," a technician said.

"Good."

The technician strode over to Fox's laptop, which remained hooked into the network, and studied its screen. "Looks like he got an e-mail," the guy said.

The two men turned toward the guy. "What?" Farnsworth asked.

Before he could respond, Mace bulled past him. The arms dealer shoved the technician out of the way and studied the screen's contents. Sliding his finger over the laptop's built-in mouse, he opened the message.

"Sir!" the technician said.

Mace's head snapped toward the other man. He jabbed a finger in the man's direction. "Shut the hell up!"

Farnsworth shot toward his partner. He stepped between Mace and the technician, grabbed the laptop and yanked it from the table until the network cable pulled free. He thrust the laptop across the room. It slammed into a wall and shattered into several pieces.

"Damn it, Jack," he shouted. "Are you an idiot?"

Mace leaned down, his face an inch or so from Farnsworth's. "Shut up, or I'll bury you, you bastard."

"Just remember who's fronting the damn money for this little adventure."

The two men stared at each other for several seconds. Mace finally looked away and made a dismissive gesture at the other man. "Ah, to hell with it. You're right. I lost my damn head."

"Was there an attachment on that e-mail?" Farnsworth asked.

"No!" Mace said. "You think I'm a damn idiot?"

The technician started to open his mouth. Mace glared at him and he fell silent.

"All right," Farnsworth said. "Everyone get going. Let's do a systems scan and make sure we weren't breached."

The technician shot Mace another glance, which the gunrunner met and held. The guy looked away, sat at a workstation and began the systems check.

"At least we have Cold Earth," Farnsworth said.

Mace nodded.

"I'm going to my office. You coming along?"

"In a minute."

Farnsworth shrugged and left. Mace walked up to the technician, who was working furiously at his computer.

"Why did you lie to him?" the guy said. "There *was* an attachment. It's possible we were breached. He needs to know!"

"No, he doesn't," Mace said. "We've come too far for that. Within a couple of hours, we'll have the United States throwing money at us. And I plan to get my fair share. That means Farnsworth doesn't need to know. Within a couple of hours, it won't matter anyway."

"But—"

"But nothing."

He clamped his catcher's-mitt-size hands around the guy's head and gave it a violent twist.

CHAPTER TWENTY-NINE

David McCarter guided the Desert Patrol Vehicle up an incline in the sand. He grinned as the engine roared and the vehicle lurched forward. When he wasn't running black ops, the Briton liked to drive racecars. He promised himself that after this mission he'd grab a little rest and recreation, and hit the deserts of California or Nevada and really put one of these babies through its paces. If he completed the mission. No sense getting cocky, he reminded himself.

Gary Manning was seated next to him. The big Canadian stared at a laptop screen. As the buggy crested the dune and began its descent, he elbowed McCarter. "Stop here," he said.

As McCarter complied, the other two dune buggies descended into the valley and came to a rest beside them.

The commandos, their equipment and the buggies had been dropped from the C-130 several miles back. It had then returned to Chad, taking Aaron Kurtzman with it.

"Let's go through this one last time, lads," McCarter

said. "Our friend Hassab laid it out for me this way. Farnsworth has taken up residence in an empty underground bunker about five hundred yards northwest of here. He also told me that the bunker was actually part of Libya's nuclear program. Since it's all hearts and roses with Libya these days, they aren't using it. Of course, that didn't stop someone within the Libyan government from selling the property to Farnsworth.

"Anyway, the top level doesn't look like a hell of a lot. A motor pool and a few average-size buildings. Gary and Rafe, since you two chaps like to blow things up, you're our entry team. The rest of us will raise a ruckus elsewhere to buy you some time."

Manning shot the Briton a thumbs-up. "Raise a little hell, eh?"

"Always."

MANNING AND ENCIZO were stretched out on a dune that overlooked the compound.

The big Canadian scanned the grounds with his binoculars, double-checking targets and gauging manpower levels. The fence looked to be standard material, a twelve-foot, chain-link barrier topped with razor wire. A motor pool sat on the compound's northeast section. Manning counted twenty guards and other personnel milling around the grounds, which also featured three flat-roofed buildings. A guard tower stood at the north and south corners of the compound.

Manning let the binoculars hang by the neck strap. Encizo turned to look at him.

"What do you think, amigo?" Encizo asked.

"Couple of things," he said. "I have to think this dump gets its Internet access via satellite, like we do when we have one in the field. If we take those out, we probably can stop these SOBs from actually spreading this digital devil."

"Makes sense."

"But first we need to get there. Unfortunately it's open field around the entire perimeter. Our best hope is to circle around, approach from the motor pool side. We can use the vehicles for cover. Plus, we'll be approaching from the north guard tower's rear."

"It's better than nothing," Encizo said. "But not by much."

"Hey, if you wanted easy work, you should have stayed in the insurance business."

"Very funny. Let's go."

They scrambled down the dune and trekked in a circular pattern around the camp's perimeter. The sun beat down on the men. Heat gathered underneath their body armor, and sweat trickled down their faces, gathering underneath their Kevlar.

The dune's incline began to lessen. Soon they'd find themselves without the cover it provided.

Encizo dropped into a crouch and keyed his com link. "We're in position. We're going in."

"Just keep it quiet," McCarter warned.

"Roger that."

Encizo scrambled up a hill. Along the way he unlimbered his Barrett sniper rifle. When he reached the top of a small incline, he dropped into position, ready to cover Manning's back as he approached the compound.

About forty yards separated Manning from the fence. He unslung his M-4 assault rifle and crawled along the sand, working his way toward the guard tower. When he reached the road leading into the camp, he rolled down an incline and moved through a culvert, thankful to be out of sight, albeit briefly.

He exited the drainpipe, but continued to follow the ditch as long as he could.

When it began to bend away from the camp, he took to higher ground. Just then a guard rounded the corner of the tower's catwalk. Manning froze and waited for a sign that the guard had spotted him. The man made a grab for his side arm and opened his mouth to yell.

Before he could, Manning brought up the M-4, which was fixed with a sound suppressor, drew a bead on the guy and squeezed off a quick burst that chewed open the man's chest. The guy wheeled around with the impact, staggered toward the railing and pitched head-first over the side of the tower.

Manning sprinted for the corpse. When he reached it, he grabbed the man by his shirt collar and dragged him to the fence.

As he closed in on the compound, he relied on the parked trucks and Jeeps, along with a small garage, to provide cover. He made it to the fence without further incident. Unpacking a folding shovel from his belt, he quickly began digging his way under the fence until he carved a hole big enough for him to fit through.

He slid a satchel of explosives and his assault rifle under the barrier first. He fisted the sound-suppressed Beretta 93-R and held it as he crawled underneath the fence and into the compound.

Manning came up in a crouch and sprinted for the closest pickup truck. He knelt next to the vehicle, reached inside his satchel and took out a square of C-4 explosive fixed with a detonator. Reaching underneath the vehicle's rear bumper, he attached the C-4 to it. He moved on to the next truck and repeated the process. By the time he'd finished with the fourth vehicle, he heard mayhem break out elsewhere in the compound. Autofire rattled from the direction of the main gate, accompanied by a few small explosions.

"Is that our people?" he asked Encizo.

"None other," the Cuban replied. "David's trying subtlety."

"That'll be the day."

Manning strode over to one of the SUVs and fixed a brick of C-4 inside the right rear wheel well. He heard the pounding of footsteps and orders being traded back and forth. Chancing a look around the rear of the vehicle, he spotted a ragged line of hardmen heading his way.

"Not yet, damn it," he muttered.

He holstered the Beretta and fisted the M-4, holding it at hip level. Stepping around from behind the truck, he triggered the weapon and began hosing down Farnsworth's foot soldiers with a barrage of 5.56 mm tumblers. Two of the men went down immediately as slugs ripped through their bodies. A third guy darted left to evade the barrage. Before he took a step, though, his head broke apart in a crimson haze even as the report of a large-bore rifle echoed through the compound.

Manning gave silent thanks to Encizo and turned his attention to the fourth and final shooter. The guy threw himself to the ground and began to fire from a prone position. A fusillade of autofire slammed into the truck behind Manning and drove him into ground.

Another rifle shot boomed.

"It's safe to come out now, amigo," Encizo said through the com link. "I made the bad people go away."

"Yeah, you say that now. You're up on the hill and I'm down on the ground."

"Let me get you a tissue."

"What can you see up there, eagle eye?"

"Looks like David and the others are raising hell in the front end. That should buy us a little time."

"Until someone notices all these dead guards. Just give me a few minutes. Then we're golden."

"I'll meet you down there."

Manning signed off and began threading his way between the parked trucks. He gave the interior of the garage a quick look, but found no threats. He moved to a pair of gas pumps and fixed bricks of C-4 to them.

He saw a figure approaching the camp, recognized immediately as Encizo. The man had traded out his Barrett for an M-4. Encizo shrugged. "I got bored," he said. "I can't just sit by and watch you hog all the fun, you bastard."

CHAPTER THIRTY

McCarter held the wheel steady and mashed the Desert Patrol Vehicle's accelerator to the floor. The vehicle responded with a roar and rocketed in the direction of Farnsworth's compound. A sidelong glance told him that James was keeping pace in his own DPV. Sand pelted the lenses of McCarter's tinted goggles, and the stench of engine exhaust soaked through the mask protecting the lower half of his face.

Libya, faced with knowledge that Armageddon very well could originate from within its borders, had opened one of its air force bases to the Americans. A wise choice for a country trying to make nice with the Western world, McCarter thought. And he was sure the White House would thank them for their hospitality—right after a squadron of American F-18 fighter jets poised at the airbase pounded the undeclared nuclear facility into a smoking hole.

In the meantime, American crews at the Libyan base were flying Predator drones over Farnsworth's base. The unmanned aerial vehicles were shooting digital photos of the facility that then could be shared with the AWACS plane that carried Kurtzman.

Hawkins sat behind him in the DPV's gunner position, his hands gripping the .50-caliber M-2's handle, situated atop the vehicle's roll cage. He swept his eyes over the horizon and searched for potential targets.

The compound grew larger as they closed in. McCarter aimed the DPV toward the main gates and gunned the engine. Seconds later, a line of hardmen exploded through the gates, their assault rifles zeroed in on the Phoenix Force warriors. Muzzle-flashes blinked at the warriors as Farnsworth's people deluged them with sheets of autofire. Bullets struck the DPV's hood and roll cage, ricocheted and whined through the air.

"T.J., that gun isn't just for show," McCarter said into his throat mike.

"That's what I tell the ladies," Hawkins replied.

Autofire erupted from the M-2's barrel and Hawkins dragged the weapon in a wide arc. The air grew thick with streams of large-caliber manglers hunting for flesh. The unforgiving bursts of gunfire scythed Farnsworth's gunners.

A second hail of gunfire angled downward from the DPVs. Hawkins pinpointed the muzzle-flashes originating from a guard tower. The shooters were unleashing their wrath upon the second vehicle, the one carrying James, who had no gunner accompanying him.

Hawkins again cut loose with the M-2. The heavy machine gun chugged out a withering line of tracking fire that was closing in on the tower. Before Hawkins could nail them, the gunners dropped out of sight. The M-2's barrage chewed through one of the posts supporting the tower's roof, but otherwise did little damage. Nothing mortal, anyway. Hawkins reversed course and manipulated the machine gun in a semicircle. This time he pounded the tower walls with relentless fire.

Before the former Army Ranger could take another pass at the tower, one of the shooters popped up. A quick cloud of smoke burst from beneath the rifle and something was arcing toward the vehicle.

"Incoming!" McCarter said as he cut the wheel left.

"Got it," James replied. He drove his vehicle the opposite direction.

A high-explosive round struck the ground and detonated. Fire and smoke shot skyward, but missed the DPVs.

"Gate, T.J.," McCarter bellowed.

The DPV was less than twenty-five yards from the gate and closing fast. A gunner knelt inside the compound fence, a rocket-propelled grenade poised on his shoulder. He worked to draw a bead on the approaching vehicles. Hawkins spotted the man and directed the M-2's thunder in the man's direction. Bullets lanced through the fence, sparked off metal and kicked up geysers of sand. A salvo of lead speared into the man and felled him. As the dead gunner pitched backward, he fired the RPG in a death reflex. The round shot skyward, curved and struck the ground behind the speeding commandos.

A smile ghosted McCarter's lips as he arrowed toward the closed gates. "Hang on to your lunch," he said. "It's time to show you some real driving."

"Shit," Hawkins said.

McCarter demanded more from the DPV's 200-horsepower engine, coaxing more speed from it. The buggy struck the gate and the impact snapped its locking mechanism. The vehicle shot into the compound. James's DPV followed a heartbeat later.

The Briton stomped the brake and cranked the wheel into a hard left, which threw the car into a 180-degree turn. The warriors suddenly found themselves facing the opposite direction. Two shooters converged on the cars from different directions their assault rifles cranking out searing lines of gunfire.

Hawkins's M-2 flamed to life and he scythed a shooter coming at him from the right. The soldier began to swing the weapon around to get a shot at the second gunner, but before he could, McCarter gunned the engine and the vehicle lurched forward, the front end aimed at the second shooter.

The man dropped his weapon, turned and ran into a cinder-block building.

McCarter slammed on the brakes, parked the vehicle and cut the ignition. Climbing out of the driver's seat, he peeled away his goggles, headgear and helmet. He fisted his M-4 assault rifle with an M-203 grenade launcher.

"Time to go hunting, lads," he said.

Hawkins unbuckled his restraints, removed his protective headgear and dropped to the ground. He fisted the M-60 light machine gun from the back of the vehicle and fell in beside his commander.

McCarter advanced on the building. He plucked a flash-bang grenade from his combat webbing, pulled the pin and tossed the grenade into the structure. An intense white light flared inside the doorway and a crack pierced the air.

His assault rifle poised at shoulder level, the Phoenix Force commander surged through the doorway. Inside, he found the shooter who moments earlier had tried to kill him. Hands cupped over his ears, the man staggered around, his senses apparently overloaded.

The guy's assault rifle lay on the ground where he had dropped it during the explosion.

McCarter strode toward the man, his assault rifle falling free on its strap. He grabbed the man by his web gear and thrust him against the wall with a powerful shove. The guy's chest collided with the wall. The impact caused the breath to whoosh from his lungs. The Briton pressed his advantage and planted a pair of punches into the other man's kidneys.

The hardman dropped to his knees. McCarter planted a boot in the middle of the man's back and forced him to the ground. He then dropped on top of him, gathered his wrists together and bound them with plastic handcuffs.

While the shooter tried to recover from the blows, McCarter rolled him onto his back and searched his pockets. He found a security card, which he stowed in his shirt pocket. The guy stared up at him. McCarter detected a sharpness in the man's eyes that indicated he was regaining his wits. Good.

McCarter drew his Browning and jammed the muzzle under the man's chin.

"No bargains, no bickering, you bastard," McCarter said through clenched teeth. "Answer me straight or your head explodes. What's your troop strength?"

"Thirty," the man rasped.

"All soldiers?"

The guy nodded. "There's a couple dozen computer operators. But most of those folks won't raise a gun against you. They're in it for the payday."

McCarter scrutinized the man's face for signs of deception. Satisfied, he nodded. "The lad, the computer programmer, where the hell is he?"

"Sublevel two," the man said.

"How many levels are in operation?"

"Two."

"Our intel said four." Lyons prodded the man's chin with the gun muzzle.

"Two. It's two," said the man, his upper lip beaded with sweat. "I swear. The Libyans put in the skeleton for four floors—walls, floors, wiring—but they only finished the first two. We don't need more than that."

"Can I get in with your card? The one I just took from you?"

"Yeah. It'll take you anywhere. Except Farnsworth's quarters. That's protected with biometrics—thumbprint scan, retinal scan, the works."

"Where's the access elevator?"

"Building next door," the guy said, motioning with his head. "That card you took will open it."

McCarter pulled away the Browning Hi-Power. The guy's eyes registered fear, but he didn't say anything. "You've been a good sport," McCarter said. "So I won't be sending you to the great beyond. No need to thank me."

The commando raised the weapon, let it fall. Cold steel hit the man's skull and he went unconscious. A shadow fell across the door behind McCarter. He turned to see James in the doorway. The former SEAL held a Franchi Joint Services Combat Shotgun in his hands.

"You going to tuck him in, or can we go tear this place up?" James asked.

"Just trying to win hearts and minds."

James grinned. "Sometimes it's easier to kill them."

FROM INSIDE THE COMPUTER room, Farnsworth watched the battle unfold in real time on video monitors. Occasionally the muffled blast from a shoulder-fired missile was audible even through the thick encasement of earth, concrete and steel. As he watched the battle rage, his mind raced through his options. He'd spent months planning for this. He'd gathered money, contacts, fighters. He couldn't let it all fall apart, particularly because of the actions of five commandos. Five damned good fighters, no doubt. But, still, it was five of them. And they quickly were laying waste to his plans.

Like hell.

He unclipped the two-way radio on his belt and brought it to his mouth. "Mace, are you there?"

"Go."

"Front and center."

"Sure."

While he waited, Farnsworth marched to the gun cabinet. He'd played banker for a lot of years, but he never truly forgot his paramilitary training. His role as hunter, killer, always came first. Years of sitting on his duff in an office, laundering money for others, hadn't changed that.

Retrieving the key from his pants' pocket, he opened the locker, studied its contents for a moment before he selected his armament. He looped a dual-holster gunbelt around his waist, grabbed a pair of .357 Magnum Desert Eagles and stowed them in the holsters. Next he took down an FN P-90 and charged it with a 50-round box magazine. He shoved extra magazines for the weapons into his pockets and a satchel that he could carry over his shoulder.

The door opened behind him. He turned to see Mace entering the room.

"Well, look at you," Mace said. "You've decided to play soldier."

"No playing about it," Farnsworth snapped. "In case

you didn't notice, these SOBs are cutting through our people like a scythe through wheat. I'm not going to sit here, thumb planted in my ass, and let them do it. Not when I'm this damn close."

Mace nodded. "We got another problem," he said. "Fox tricked us. His laptop—the one he had us fetch— apparently he sent out an electronic message to someone. Our guys are trying to track it, see where it went. But they haven't had any luck. Whoever it was must have one hell of a secure setup because we can't track this thing to save our fannies. Our guys keep hitting cutouts of all sorts."

Farnsworth's fists clenched so hard, the knuckles cracked. "Keep looking. Do I have to do everything around here, damn it?"

"Relax," Mace replied. "We will. More important, what do we do about the Americans? We have to assume these are their people. We can't let them hit us without punishing them a little bit."

Farnsworth nodded. "Contact them. Make it simple. They have fifteen fucking minutes to abort this mission. And tell them we're jacking the price to $5 billion."

Mace grinned. "Now you're talking."

"First, get something more than a side arm," Farnsworth said. "Our troops should take them out before they ever get to the elevator. If not, we're going to defend this damn place until we've bled every last damn drop of blood we can."

CHAPTER THIRTY-ONE

His M-60 at his hip, Hawkins trod over the battlefield in search of more enemy gunners. Sweat rolled from his forehead into his eyes. The salt-laden liquid stung the sensitive tissue beneath his eyelids and caused him to squint. When he forced his eyes to reopen, he spotted a pair of hardmen sprinting from behind a small building twenty yards or so ahead and next to a landing strip Hawkins had been charged with securing.

Both men opened fire on Hawkins. His M-60 churned out a storm of 7.62 mm NATO rounds fed from over his shoulder into the high-powered weapon. He dispatched both men with a single sweep of the belt-fed machine gun.

He advanced another dozen or so yards before he found himself under attack again. Gunners hunkered down at either end of a truck unloaded assault rifles at him. He squeezed the M-60's trigger and blistered the truck. Sizzling lines of gunfire ripped through one of Hawkins's opponents. Faced with the withering M-60 fire, the others went to ground. Bullet holes punched through the side of the truck's cab and bed. Slugs shredded the tires and caused the vehicle to drop to the ground.

Hawkins saw something arc in the air and plummet toward him. The Phoenix Force commando recognized the orb as a grenade. He knew he could never run fast enough to avoid its deadly attack. He had no cover nearby to dive behind.

Almost as a reflex, he raised the M-60 and swung it at the deadly bomb. The barrel connected with the device and sent it flying sideways. Hawkins lunged in the opposite direction and covered his head with his hands. The ensuing blast showered him with sand and dirt, but left him otherwise unscathed.

Before he could react, a pair of objects launched skyward from behind him and hit the truck like a fiery hammer. The ear-splitting explosion tore through the air and ripped through the truck and the men using it for cover. Flames leaped from the fire-ravaged wreckage and heat caused the air above the truck to shimmer.

Hawkins rolled over, saw James standing over him, a multiround projectile launcher still smoking.

"Son, that's what I call shooting," Hawkins said, grinning.

James gave him a tight smile and a thumbs-up.

"Airfield secure," James said into his throat mike. Hawkins came to his feet and retrieved the M-60. Both men caught up with McCarter, who stood outside the largest of the three outbuildings. Encizo and Manning were coming forward from the motor pool.

"You wire the motor pool?" McCarter asked.

Manning nodded. "It's ready to go."

McCarter explained what the captured thug had told him. "In a perfect world, we'd just go straight to the bottom floor, grab Fox and fight our way. Unfortunately, we can't do that here. Instead, I need Rafe and Gary to clear the first floor. The rest of us will clear the second floor and stop these bastards from shipping out the Cold Earth worm. If we haven't found Fox at that point, then we look for him."

"Any plans on how to do that?" Hawkins asked.

"Haven't got that far, mate. Still waiting on inspiration to strike."

"How much more time do we have before these guys hit us with the worm?"

McCarter looked at his watch, scowled and shook his head. "Roughly in fifty minutes by the original time frame. But I think we can assume that's shot to hell now that we've burned out Farnsworth. Everything could go to hell at any minute."

MANNING EDGED along the wall, his weapon held at hip level and ready, his eyes sweeping the corridor for threats. He tried to ignore the nervous tickle in his stomach and focus on the mission. It wasn't happening. Accessing the elevator had been surprisingly easy. The four guards at ground level had fallen with relative ease and he and Encizo had been able to access sublevel one without incident. Still, his combat senses continued to fill him with unease. He could feel death close at hand.

"Rafe," he whispered into his throat mike.

"Go."

"I've still got nothing. You?"

"Nada, my friend. As best as I can tell…" The Cuban left the sentence unfinished.

Manning felt his stomach plummet. He waited another heartbeat and said, "Rafe."

Silence.

"Rafe?"

Nothing. Perhaps his friend had encountered a situation that required a stealthy approach. But what if someone had gotten the drop on Encizo? The big Canadian turned and retraced his steps toward the elevator, his legs pumping hard as they hurtled him toward his friend's position.

He followed the curve of the corridor, knowing it soon would spill into a common area that included the elevator. Before he completed his next footfall, a pair of gunners came into view, each man brandishing an SMG. Manning fired the M-4 from his waist. The weapon unleashed a relentless barrage of tumblers that cut down the gunner to the Phoenix Force commando's left. The second gunner threw himself out of the line of fire, his shoulder pounding into a nearby wall. As he dropped, the man's weapon flamed. The poorly aimed burst sizzled the air as it passed within inches of Manning's temple.

The warrior's M-4 rattled out another wave of destruction, blood spurting from the legion of chest wounds. His body went limp and the weapon fell to the floor.

A quick scan of his back revealed no threats. Manning picked up the pace. A strange whirring noise registered with him. Initially, he thought it might be ringing from exposure to gunfire in a cramped space. When the end of the corridor came into view, though, he knew it was something else.

A steel blast door, probably lead-lined and meant to control radiation leaks, was descending rapidly from the ceiling. It would isolate him from his fellow warriors. He considered sprinting for it, and trying to slide underneath, like a baseball player stealing home plate. He dismissed the idea almost immediately. Instinctively, he knew he'd never make it. More likely, he'd end up caught between the unyielding barrier and the floor. It could cost his limb or worse.

He halted and uttered a curse of frustration. A rattle reached his ears and he wheeled around. A hardman, a rangy guy decked out in civilian clothing, moved into view and spotted Manning in the same instant. Jagged tongues of orange flame leaped from the man's assault rifle. Bullets whizzed past Manning, sparked off the steel barrier and ricocheted throughout the close quarters. Manning drew a bead on the guy and fired. A burst of slugs lanced into the guy's eye socket and knocked him off his feet.

BEFORE ENCIZO COULD finish his sentence, a human cannonball hammered into his midsection.

The Cuban caught the vague impression of a big man sheathed in hard muscle. The man's shoulder thudded against Encizo's chest, the blow costing the commando his footing. As he struck a wall, a hand closed around his face, fingertips digging into his temples. Reflexively, Encizo brought up his hands and pummeled the man's wrist, breaking his grip.

As they squared off, Encizo took an opportunity to size up his opponent. The ruddy-faced man probably stood six feet tall, about four inches taller than Encizo. He had the overdeveloped muscles of someone who ingested steroids and he easily outweighed the commando by eighty pounds. From what Encizo had observed, the guy was all strength and no finesse. He, on the other hand, was quick and agile, even though his body hurt like hell. It was a difference he hoped to exploit.

He stared at the guy and let a dismissive smile played over his lips. The thug roared and surged forward, hands poised to grab Encizo, who sidestepped the attack and let the man hurtle past him. The Phoenix Force fighter laced his fingers into a double fist and used it to bludgeon the guy in the back. The hardman collided with the wall, launched himself from it and rocketed back at Encizo.

The warrior held his ground and let the man close in. At the last instant, his hand snaked out and he buried a knife-hand strike into his opponent's throat, the man's windpipe collapsing under his fingertips. Moved by momentum, the man continued to hurtle forward until he collided with Encizo. The combatants landed in a heap. Encizo shoved his gurgling assailant off of him.

He closed in on the air-starved man, who struck out at him weakly. Two more strikes to the throat left the man with a crushed trachea, dead.

Encizo ran a physical inventory. He found plenty of sore spots—his ribs, in particular—but nothing broken. He gathered his lost assault rifle and his knife, and resumed his search of the facility.

He followed the corridor until it stopped curving, then swept his gaze over the straightaway that lay in front of him. He judged it to stretch at least seventy-five yards, with doors lining both sides. Before he took another step, he realized his throat mike had been knocked loose and hung from its cord, nearly touching the floor.

Scooping it up with his left hand, he clipped it back into place. "Gary? Gary? You out there?"

Before he could get an answer, he heard the clicking of door latches. Two shooters popped around doorjambs and rattled off steady streams of gunfire.

Encizo dived forward and brought up his assault rifle. Twin lines of gunfire scythed the air above him as he triggered the M-203 grenade launcher fixed under his weapon's barrel. The frag round cleaved through the air and struck the floor a few feet in front of the gunners. The bomb detonated, razor-sharp shrapnel slicing into them.

Moving ahead, the little Cuban searched three rooms but found all of them empty. In the fourth, he found a desk topped with a PC. He crossed the room to the desk, dropped to his knees and searched the back of the tower for the network cable. When he found it, he yanked it free, set it aside and pulled his laptop from his backpack. After his computer had powered up, the commando plugged the network cable into it. Using his headset, he checked in with Kurtzman, who confirmed that they were able to reenter the computer network.

"Now it's time for me to work some magic," Kurtzman said.

In the meantime, Encizo hurried into the corridor and quickly rifled the pockets of the shooters, stealing both men's keycards. They looked identical, but he figured he could pass on the extras to other members of the team, if necessary.

THE ELEVATOR DOORS parted.

McCarter, wielding his MP-5 with one hand, held the door open with the other and nodded at Hawkins. The former Army Ranger knelt next to the door frame, holding a black-finished aluminum tube with a mirror fixed to one end. He slipped the mirror slightly into the hallway and angled it until he could see the corridor's far-left end. Three armed fighters stood at the ready. Using hand signals, he communicated the information to McCarter. He found four more in the opposite direction.

The corridors stretched a few dozen yards in either direction, ending at a perpendicular corridor that stretched another one hundred yards or so in the opposite direction, essentially forming an O with rooms on either side. According to their outdated intelligence on the facility, the middle section of this floor had been a laboratory for the nuclear program. Such an area lent itself to serving as a nerve center for the facility. McCarter was betting that it remained so today.

He motioned for James and Hawkins to take the right flank, while he took the left. The Briton held up a flash-stun grenade pantomimed a throw and held up three fingers. The other men nodded their understanding and took up their positions. Counting down on his fingers, he reached three and the commandos tossed the grenades, which thundered on detonation. The Stony Man team rounded the corner in a crouch, guns held at the ready.

McCarter found himself facing three gunners, all stunned. He cut loose with his M-4, scything down Farnsworth's troopers, the sustained onslaught of slugs forcing the gunners into a jerky death dance. Easing off the trigger, the Briton ejected the clip, reloaded and trotted forward, on the lookout for more opposition.

CHAPTER THIRTY-TWO

Blancanales trudged through the brackish waters flowing through the catacombs of Prague's sewer system.

The space had the earthen smell of moss or some other vegetation that had grown in the moist, dark passage. From up ahead, he heard the trickle of water as it emptied from the surface into the tunnel. A pair of night-vision goggles helped him navigate the slimy labyrinth, casting his surroundings in various shades of green.

The Able Team warrior was dressed head-to-toe in black. Black combat cosmetics were smeared across his cheeks, and a black watch cap covered his hair. He toted an MP-5 outfitted with a sound suppressor, while his twin Beretta 93-Rs rode in thigh holsters. A nylon satchel slung over his shoulder held rounds for his M-79 and SPAS 12. He planned to hand the shotgun over to Lyons once they met up at the club.

"How much farther?" Blancanales whispered into his throat mike.

"Another five hundred yards," Carmen Delahunt replied. "Not getting antsy, are you?"

"You kidding? It's gorgeous down here. Reminds me—"

"Pol! Shush, quick."

"Damn, what?"

"IR scan is picking up warm bodies coming your way from a tunnel one hundred yards or so away. It runs perpendicular to yours."

"Lovely. Numbers?"

"Six. Two teams of three, actually."

"Any chance of it being the good guys?"

"Negative. We've stayed in touch with the locals. Asked them to alert us regarding any ops. They assured us there'd be none. President to president, I mean. And we've also been monitoring the local police bands, just in case they had their fingers crossed."

"Maybe they decided to renege after Khan leveled a city block."

"You do make an impression."

"It's my easy way with people. Any sitrep from Ironman?"

"All's quiet."

"Clear. Gotta go."

"Watch yourself."

Blancanales brought up the MP-5, sweeping it over the area ahead of him. He continued through the water, moving slowly, silently. His heart rate accelerated and he felt his palms moisten on the SMG he carried as he neared the newcomers.

The first team came into view, walking in a triangle formation. The Able Team warrior crouched in the water, waited. Unlike him, his adversaries were using flashlights. White spots roamed the walls as they moved forward.

Blancanales planned to keep it simple—take out as many as possible. Any survivors got grilled for whatever intelligence they could offer regarding the club.

Save for the occasional sloshing of water, the approaching headforce stayed quiet.

He flicked the MP-5's selector switch into single-shot mode. He'd left the laser sight off, not wanting its red eye to betray his position. Bringing the SMG to his shoulder, he sighted down on the man walking point and squeezed off a shot. The man cried out and dropped his weapon as he clutched his chest and pitched forward. Even as the man's body splashed into the water, Blancanales was moving to the opposite side of the tunnel. The other gunners immediately cut loose with their weapons. Bullets sprayed through the tunnel, chipping away at the walls and slapping against the water. Blancanales switched the MP-5 to full-auto and swept the weapon in a horizontal line that cut down both gunners.

When the last men fell, Blancanales continued to press ahead.

"Carmen," he whispered, "you have any location on my buddies?"

"Fifty yards or less away," she said. "There's a bend in the tunnel up ahead. They're coming at you from that direction."

"Right."

Grimly, Blancanales pushed ahead.

He wasn't sure what the remaining thugs would do. He knew they'd try to take him down, but whether they'd bring the fight to him or wait for him to come to them remained to be seen.

He covered perhaps another twenty yards when he

got his answer. A hellstorm of fire stabbed out of the darkness. He dived forward and found himself submerged for a moment. The cold water bit into his exposed skin and seemed to almost immediately sap his body of any warmth. When he got back onto his knees, more autofire screamed overhead, preventing him from getting to his feet.

Blancanales fisted the M-79 and squeezed the trigger. An incendiary round rocketed forth and burst with a searing white flash. Quickly releasing the straps holding the NVGs to his head, he opened his eyes to the carnage that lay ahead. Flames engulfed both hardmen. One had undertaken a mindless charge toward Blancanales. The second man had dropped into the water and was trying to smother the flames. Blancanales pulled the Beretta from its holster, drew down on the runner and fired his weapon. The triburst speared into the two-legged torch's head, ending his sprint. The warrior dispatched the other shooter with mercy rounds, too. The confined space smelled of gunfire and burning flesh. He felt the contents of his stomach rising to the top of his throat. He fought the nausea and kept moving forward.

Blancanales reloaded the M-79, but then traded it out for his second Beretta. He also fitted the NVGs back onto his head as light again became meager.

Before he reached the bend in the tunnel, he slowed and strained his ears. He heard nothing that indicated anyone was near.

"Carmen?"

"Go."

"What's the IR scan showing?"

"Besides you, there's two hot spots behind you. I'm guessing about twenty yards."

Blancanales knew that was the burning remains of

the two hardmen he'd just put down. "That's the barbecue I'm bringing home. What about up ahead?"

"Zilch."

"Think our last guy went back to the surface world?"

"Maybe."

"That's reassuring."

"Damn it, Pol, I'm a cyberspecialist. Not Nostradamus."

"You're a laugh riot. I'm going in."

BLANCANALES SCRAMBLED up the ladder and through the circular opening leading into the club. He found himself inside a small room. A naked bulb suspended from the ceiling provided the only light. The door hung ajar. A pair of legs tipped with black combat boots poked through the door and into the room.

The Beretta poised in front of him, he crossed the room and knelt next to the prone figure. Grabbing an ankle, he dragged the body into the room with him. Rolling the man on his back, Blancanales saw two neat holes in the man's chest, likely caused by bullets. The guy was unconscious, his face and hands waxen. From what Blancanales could surmise, the guy had taken two rounds to the chest, neither fatal, and had tried to make it back here to report to Quissad. But his body had given up before he could get any farther. Even as the Able Team commando stripped away the gunner's weapons, a last death rattle escaped the man's lips.

Blancanales shut the hatch leading into the sewers, sealed it with a turn of the latch. Exiting the small chamber, he found himself inside a larger room filled with wire racks holding dozens of bottles of wine. Knowing Quissad's appetite for the good life, he guessed the bottles were part of his private stash. He glanced at the ceiling and spotted a smoke detector. Reaching inside his satchel, he took out a brick of C-4 explosives, stuck in a detonator and pushed the plastique under one of the racks.

Moving to the door, he pressed his ear against it, listened hard, but heard nothing. He stepped into the hallway and found it empty. A service elevator stood at the far end, the car missing. He scowled. Time to improvise.

Slipping a hand inside his pants' pocket, he triggered the remote detonator. A loud boom sounded from inside the makeshift wine cellar. The door bowed, cracked and blew outward, its remains slamming into the door opposite it. Boiling flames, tinged black by smoke, lashed through the doorway. Alarms suddenly cut through the silence and were audible throughout the building.

Blancanales grinned. Mission accomplished.

LYONS STEPPED UP to the bar and signaled the bartender, a young redhead dressed in a tight T-shirt and hip-hugger jeans. When she came, he ordered a beer. He didn't plan on drinking it; he also didn't want to make himself conspicuous by walking around empty-handed. He paid the woman and melted into the crowd.

Among the patrons, he saw several men dressed in red T-shirts festooned with the club's logo and blue jeans. None of them looked to be bussing tables, so he decided they were the security. From what he could tell, none of this group was packing, though he didn't dismiss the possibility of a gun hidden in an ankle holster.

This wasn't a soft target, though. He'd spotted several men drifting through the place wearing shades and casting intimidating glances at anyone unlucky enough to catch their interest. From what Lyons's trained eye could discern, most of these guys were packing hardware underneath their sport coats and windbreakers.

Coming through the front door had been a calculated risk, Lyons knew. Cortez had seen both Able Team warriors up close and personal, and likely could pick them out of a crowd. Likewise, Lyons had every reason to believe that Quissad had gathered physical descriptions of the two men who'd spent the past several hours trashing his operations.

A part of Lyons hoped they'd bring it on. He was tired and angry, ready to hand out retribution. The rational part of him knew he had to wait. He didn't mind jabbing a thumb in their eyes by walking around Quissad's place. But he had no intention of instigating a fight in the middle of a crowd of innocents. Once they cleared people out, though, all bets were off.

Several yards away from him, the crowd began to part and crush backward. Bringing the beer to his lips, letting just a slight bit trace a cold trail down his throat, he stared over the can and watched what was unfolding. Surrounded a battalion of heavies, Quissad waded through the crowd and cut a line for the bar. Lyons shook his head in disgust as the man made his way through the club, as though he were royalty.

Setting his beer on an empty table, the Able Team leader bulled his way through the crowd and headed for the bar. When he got there, he ordered another beer and watched the Iraqi strike up a conversation with a woman. He took his second beer and walked away, but kept the man in his sights. When Cortez stepped into the picture, Lyons felt his blood begin to boil. He kept his distance, though, and continued to scrutinize the two men as they spoke for a few minutes and ultimately headed off together for the club's second floor.

Lyons hung back as his targets disappeared upstairs. He could tell the gunners were nervous, what with their boss out in the open and someone obviously gunning for him. Though he'd love to take out both men in a blaze of glory right now, he knew he couldn't. There were too many people around to try anything. He'd wait for Blancanales to stir things up before he made his move.

In the meantime, he circled the bar, trying to get a good look at the woman who'd been talking to Quissad. She slid around ninety degrees on the bar stool and Lyons caught a brief impression of shapely legs. An instant later she was off the stool and moving through the crowd, apparently following Quissad at a distance. Curious, Lyons cut diagonally through the gathered partiers and fell in behind her.

He watched with interest as she produced a cell phone from her bag, aimed it at Quissad and then put the phone away. Why the hell would she do that? he wondered. He considered approaching her and posing the question. However, he guessed that getting within spitting distance of Quissad's conquest for the night likely would attract unwanted attention from the Iraqi gunrunner's muscle.

There'd be more than enough of that coming in the next few minutes, anyway, Lyons knew.

The woman disappeared into a bathroom, then exited a few minutes later. Returning to the bar, she ordered another drink. Scowling, Lyons pondered the situation. She was spying, that much he'd lay money on. The identity of her employer was the real variable that confounded him.

Before he could give it another thought, something thundered beneath the building. Whether dancing or talking, people stopped and shot questioning looks at one another. When fire alarms began to blare and overhead lights flipped on, most of the patrons got the message. Herds of them began gathering their things and heading for the door.

Lyons shot up the stairs, his hand slipping under his jacket for his Colt Python revolver.

LYONS SPEARED HIS WAY through the oncoming pack of panicked patrons pushing their way down the stairs. Though he gripped his Colt Python, he kept it underneath his jacket and out of sight. The last thing he needed was for some innocent person to see the weapon, scream and draw attention to him. Or decide to play hero and confront him. Not that he wouldn't come out on top, of course. He just didn't need the distraction.

He stepped onto the second floor and immediately found himself confronted by a giant. The man wore his snow-white hair in a ponytail and stood in front of Lyons, his arms crossed over his chest. A laminated card pinned to his thick torso identified him as a security guard.

"Where the hell you going, shit for brains?" The guy had to yell to be heard over the screaming fire alarms.

Lyons looked the guy up and down once. He wore jeans and a T-shirt. If he was hiding a piece, Lyons couldn't see it. He gave the guy a vacuous grin and shrugged. He let his spin and shoulders collapse a little, making him seem smaller, less threatening. The guy put a finger in Lyons face. "You hear me? Turn the hell—"

Lyons's left hand looped around in a thunderous roundhouse. When his knuckles collided with the guy's jaw, Ponytail's head jerked to one side as though it were hitched to a speeding truck. Before the guy could react to the first blow, Lyons jabbed him twice more in the softness of his protruding belly. Instinctively, the guy bent slightly at the waist, wrapped his arms around his belly and stepped back. His other hand moving with blinding speed, Lyons brought out the Colt Python and smacked it against the man's temple. His opponents knees went rubbery and he fell to the ground in a bone-less heap.

Leaving the unconscious man behind, Lyons moved past a coat-check closet and what appeared to be an empty banquet room. Two more hardmen stepped into view. One wore an expensive Italian suit and shiny black wingtips that put Lyons own Hawaiian shirt and leather jacket to shame—if he'd actually cared about such stuff.

The second guy—clad in a tweed sports jacket, jeans and sneakers—looked like a low-rent college professor.

Both men spotted Lyons at the same time. The Suit apparently caught a glimpse of the Colt, too, because he immediately lunged to one side and clawed for hard-ware hidden under his jacket. The Professor got the hint and went for his gun, too.

Dropping into a Weaver's stance, Lyons yelled, "Po-lice! Freeze."

Though it was a lie, Lyons figured identifying him-self as a police officer would help him determine whether the two men were armed security guards or part of Quissad's personal entourage of murderers. Sneer-ing, the Suit was bringing his handgun to bear on Lyons. The Able Team commander's Python thundered once and the top of the man's head disappeared in a crimson spray. Even as the corpse slammed to the floor, Lyons spun toward the second man. He caught the guy just as his fingers encircled the grip of a holstered handgun.

"Freeze!" Lyons barked.

The man stopped his play and raised his hands. Lyons got into the guy's space, grabbed him by the shoulder and whirled him around. He shoved the guy against a wall, kicked his legs apart and gave him a quick pat down. The search yielded a switchblade.

"English," Lyons said. "You speak English?"

The guy nodded.

"Where's Quissad?"

Without batting an eye, the guy gestured to his left with his head. "In his office, three doors down. But you need a key card to get in."

Lyons slipped his hand, palm open and facing up, over the guy's shoulder. "Give it up. Slowly."

The hardguy did and Lyons shoved it into his pocket.

Before he had a chance to ask another question, his combat senses wailed for his attention. Whipping his head left, he spied two more gunners heading his way. Both carried Fabrique National subguns. The man nearer to Lyons apparently had drawn the short straw and intended to get up close and personal with the intruder. The second shooter remained several yards back, crouched against the wall, the SMG's barrel tracking in on Lyons.

The Able Team leader guessed they wanted to take him alive.

Good luck.

His hand encircled his prisoner's left bicep. He jerked the guy from the wall, thrust the shocked man between the shooters and himself. In the same instant Lyons squeezed off two shots from the Colt Python. A bullet drilled through the sternum of the man who'd been approaching Lyons. As the man crumbled into a dead heap, the crouched shooter broke loose with a stinging burst from his SMG. Lyons shoved his unwilling helper forward and let him take the half dozen or so bullets intended for Lyons. The guy jerked in place as though lashed by a million electric shocks.

Lyons adopted a weaver's stance and squeezed the Colt's trigger twice. Peals of thunder boomed throughout the hallway as the shooter caught a double whammy in the chin and mouth.

The Able Team warrior popped the Python's cylinder, emptied the spent brass onto the floor and recharged the weapon with a speed-loader. Filling his other hand with a Beretta, Lyons charged forth. An image of his friend, Gadgets Schwarz, lying in a hospital bed, tubes running out of him, flashed through the warrior's mind. He hoped to find Quissad inside, plant one through the bastard's forehead and end his weapons smuggling days forever.

But he really wanted Cortez. Even if they found the computer disks, if the man continued to draw breath, Lyons would consider the mission a failure. And he hadn't come this far to fail.

He hoped.

STARING AT THE COLOR security monitor, Quissad watched the deadly American racing toward his office, presumably moving in for the kill.

A twinge of fear thrilled through him, but died an instant later. He didn't care how many people the man burned through before finally reaching him. Quissad still knew he'd walk away from this unscathed. He scanned the room and saw ten of his best gunners lining up throughout the room, weapons charged, ready to a man to heap punishment on this arrogant bastard. Another carload of hardmen was speeding across town right now to cover his back. And, if it came to a showdown, the former Iraqi soldier knew he'd handled this SOB just as he had so many others. Just because he was the boss now didn't mean he didn't know how to get his hands dirty.

Shrugging off his jacket, he folded it and placed it over the back of a couch. He checked the weapons he carried, a pair of 10 mm Colt Delta Elites, one in a shoulder rig, the second on his hip in a fast-draw holster.

Cortez, his eyes bloodshot and puffy, marched up to him.

"It's definitely him," he said. "The guy from Colorado, I mean."

Quissad nodded. "Thanks for leading him here," he said dryly.

"Shove it. I didn't mean for this to happen."

"And yet you succeeded brilliantly," the Iraqi said.

The Mexican tapped the barrel of his Ithaca pump shotgun against his boot, as though he were considering something. Quissad knew where the man's mind was wandering.

"Don't think about it," he said. "You might get me, but my people will drop you—as the American's say— like a bad habit. I've got money to pay them. You don't."

Cortez gave him a cold smile. "No worries. Right now, you're worth more to me alive than dead. But just remember, I've got your fucking number, amigo." He nodded over his shoulder. "These dim bastards might think you're about to make your last stand here. But we both know better, don't we? Why take a bullet when you can make money, right?"

"Your point?"

"When you decide to run, you take me with you. Otherwise, I'll shoot you in the damn back."

"Done."

THE CRACKLE OF GUNFIRE reached Rabin's ears as she moved onto the second floor, intending to head to Quissad's office. Fear stabbed through her gut, but she paid it little heed. Someone was trying to bag Quissad, the man she'd come to kill, and she wasn't about to surrender her prize so easily. She'd vowed to take him out, for her country's sake. And she also needed to stop his auction and rain down death on Israel's enemies. If she were to make all that happen, she couldn't very well cave in to fear.

Ahead she could see the big blond man from downstairs. One man already lay on the floor, apparently dead. A second man was trying to line up a shot on the big guy. But his gun thundered again and bullets drilled into Quissad's thug. He crumpled to the ground in a heap.

Rabin hugged the walls and crept toward the action. Her palm felt moist against the textured grip of her handgun, but her breath came steadily and easily. Her eyes narrowed as she scanned the corridor up ahead, trying to size up the situation. The hulking man charged toward Quissad's office. He moved with a speed and grace that seemed impossible for a man of his size.

Rabin fell in behind him, albeit at a more cautious pace. The hallway stank of gunsmoke and a whitish haze made it difficult to see ahead. She watched as he stopped outside Quissad's door, studied it for a moment.

She came up behind him, her pistol poised in front of her in a two-handed grip. When she got within twenty feet or so, she yelled, "Stop!"

He whirled toward her, his handgun coming around, too. When he saw that she had an easy shot at him, he froze. He made no move to surrender his weapon.

"Step away from there," she said.

He shook his head. "Forget it, lady. I've come too far to do that."

"I'll shoot."

The man's eyes locked on her own, but she didn't flinch.

"I can tell you'll shoot," he said. "You one of Quissad's people?"

"Go to hell. Put down your gun. I swear I'll kill you."

He gestured with his head at Quissad's door. "If you're one of his people, you'd be better off to do it."

"Damn it. I'm not."

She kept him bracketed in her sights, stared at him for a stretched second. Her mind, her training screamed for her to shoot the man. Regardless of his identity, his intentions, he stood between her and her mission. That made him a liability, one to be eliminated. But she'd never been a practitioner of scorched-earth tradecraft. She'd always been able to pull off assassinations without creating collateral damage, and she wanted it to stay that way.

Something about the man gave her pause. It was possible that they were working at cross purposes, but maybe not.

"I'm an American," he said, interrupting her thoughts. "I'm here for Quissad. I'm not leaving without him. If you're a local cop or something, I'd suggest you get out of here. This is way bigger than you or me, and I have no choice but to keep going ahead."

"I'm here for him, too."

The man grimaced. "Well, we can't flip a damn coin for him. If you want him, you're going to have to shoot me in the—"

He stopped speaking and his eyes flicked over her shoulder.

"Hey!" he yelled.

Before she could react, she felt a searing pain lance through her shoulder, her kidneys. An unseen force propelled her forward. She heard the popping of a handgun, but it sounded far away, unreal. Had the American shot her? A glance told her that he was just bringing up his gun. He charged toward her, one arm out to catch her.

She sank to her knees. He knelt next to her and she was vaguely aware of his arm encircling her waist. Her shoulder pressed into him, his body the only thing supporting her. Something cracked. Several times. Gunshots. He said something in her ear, but with consciousness dissolving, the words sounded slow, distant, unintelligible. To her surprise, the burning points of pain seemed to fade, along with noise. She closed her eyes and blackness overcame her.

THE SHOOTER DIDN'T WAIT for the woman to die before he made a play for Lyons. The guy whipped toward the Able Team leader and the Israeli woman. Lyons's Beretta coughed out a triburst of manglers that drilled into the guy's throat. The thug grabbed at the wounds, falling backward.

Two more gunners were silhouetted just behind the man. Lyons drew a bead on the thug to his right and fired, a burst hammering the man's abdomen, taking him out of play. A weapon's report echoed through the hall. Slugs whistled between Lyons's arm and his ribs and pierced his jacket.

Lyons loosed two more 3-round bursts, the first group slamming into his opponent's nose and effectively vaporizing his head. The second burst flew wild.

The former L.A. cop reloaded as he moved. He knelt next to the woman and saw three neat holes lined up diagonally along her back. He rolled her onto her stomach and found the exiting bullets had torn gaping exit wounds on the front of her body.

He stood and forced his attention back to getting into Quissad's office. A dead bolt clicked back loudly behind him and Lyons spun. Several of Quissad's hardmen had emptied into the hallway, gun muzzles tracking him.

Lyons fisted the Python from beneath his jacket and made a do-or-die play.

QUISSAD LET HIS PEOPLE pour into the hallway. He wanted them to form a human wall between him and the American. As he strode for the door, a cacophony of small-arms fire roared in the corridor outside his office. Quissad filled his hands with the Delta Elites. He burst through the door and aimed both weapons, ready to lay down cover fire of his own. But the invader was invisible behind the line of his gunners.

With his escape covered, Quissad made a run for the stairwell door. A quick look over his shoulder told him that Cortez followed only a couple of steps behind. When he reached the door, he pressed down on the release bar and raced onward.

If he could get to the parking garage below, he'd slip into his BMW and, hopefully, escape. That'd buy him time to get out of the city and, eventually, the country—with the Cold Earth worm still in his possession. Once he gained a little breathing room, he could figure out his next move.

Taking two steps at a time, he raced down the first flight of stairs. When he reached the landing, he felt someone grab him by his shirt collar and stop him. He whipped around. The sudden motion ripped his collar free of Cortez's grip. The Mexican's arm was raised up over his head. Apparently, Quissad realized, his face betrayed his surprise because a smile ghosted Cortez's lips as his arm arced downward.

Something struck the Iraqi's temple and white light exploded behind his eyes. He dropped one of his pistols and staggered back until he collided with a wall. His head spun and his eyes lost their focus. He felt the coolness of the bricks press through the thin fabric of his dress shirt. A dark blur plunged toward him. Cortez! He started to raise his remaining pistol. Something crashed once more against his skull and he lost consciousness.

WHEN THE IRAQI CRUMPLED to the floor, Cortez drove a booted foot into his ribs. Once. Twice. He felt fragile bones give against his steel-toed boots, and a wide smile played over his lips. It all felt so good, he couldn't help but kick the bastard one last time.

As he stood over his partner, he stared at him and shook his head in pity.

"Sorry, my friend," Cortez said. "It's survival of the fittest. And you're not fit to breathe the same air as me. So I'll sacrifice you to our pursuers. In the meantime, I must leave."

Cortez knelt next to the fallen man and searched Quissad's pockets until he found the keys. Should he take the man's weapons and leave him unarmed? The thought of the Iraqi injured and unarmed facing off against the two Americans pleased Cortez. But he decided against it. In the unlikely event that they made it through the wall of hardmen upstairs, Cortez wanted Quissad armed, if only so he could attempt a last stand and delay them.

During his search, Cortez also found the minidisk. He weighed it in his palm for a moment and considered his next move. If he took it with him, there was a chance—perhaps a small chance—that he could sell it. But if they'd identified him, they knew all his aliases, all his underworld contacts. There was an equally good chance that, by the time he was able to stop running, the disk would be useless, either too hot to touch or already outmoded. But if he no longer had it, their interest in him might wane.

He tossed the disk onto the floor next to Quissad and scrambled down the stairs.

CHAPTER THIRTY-THREE

David McCarter dropped into a crouch and grabbed an HE grenade from his gear. Arming it, he tossed it over-hand. As it flew, he dived to the ground, counting the seconds and praying he didn't catch a stray round.

The doomsday numbers fell to zero. The grenade let loose with fire and thunder. McCarter rose from the floor and surged toward the wall of flame and smoke ahead.

Slowly, he moved into the killzone and found four of Farnsworth's thugs on the floor. The injuries three had suffered were obviously fatal. A fourth man was balled up on the floor, flesh and fabric shredded or burned by the explosion. The Briton placed a mercy round into the man's head and continued on.

FARNSWORTH WATCHED the battle unfold on the security monitors.

A warrior himself, he had to respect these bastards tearing apart his stronghold. But he couldn't let their blitz continue unabated. He hadn't come this far to die. Or to walk away without something to show for his efforts.

He turned to Mace who watched the proceedings with a stony expression. If the wholesale slaughter of his men bothered the man, he didn't let it show.

"How many have we lost?" Farnsworth asked.

"At least a couple dozen," Mace said. "Probably more. Casualty counts continue to come in, but I'd be a damn fool to vouch for their accuracy. We've got too much going on to get a good count. We've got people pinned down where we can't get to them. These SOBs have cut a bloody swath through my people."

"Send more."

"Not sure I have many more to send."

"Do it," Farnsworth barked. "And make sure to send our little package, too."

Mace whipped his head toward Farnsworth and stared at him for several seconds. "What? Are you out of your damn mind?"

Farnsworth felt his face turn red with anger. "Which part of the command didn't you understand?"

"But, if we stick them now, we won't get the money."

Farsnworth replied, "Get a grip. If they were going to pay the money, we wouldn't be overrun with commandos right now, would we?"

Mace's lips tightened into a bloodless line and his jaw muscles rippled. Farnsworth met the other man's steely gaze with one of his own and waited for the bastard to remember his place.

"Damn it," Mace protested, "we can't pack it in now. We've put too much into this to give up."

Farnsworth snorted. "Who said anything about packing it in? I'm not going to lose. I may not get my money, but I'm going to let these bastards in Washington think they put one over on me again. I'm going to start a series of nuclear meltdowns that will hobble the United States for the next damn millennium. I'll teach these bastards a lesson. And, by God, I will *enjoy* it. When this is all over, they'll know better than to screw with Dale Farnsworth. They'll know who won and who lost. And if you don't have the stones to call out the order, I'll do it myself."

Farnsworth let the seconds tick down while Mace stared at him. "Go to hell. I'll handle it."

Mace spun on a heel and marched from the control room. Farnsworth watched after him for a moment and a smile formed on his lips while he did. Idiot, he thought. When it came to scoring a hefty ransom, the game was over. At this point it was time to make it out with his skin intact.

And if he got to hand down a little payback on the United States, maybe world capitals like Moscow, Beijing or Tel Aviv in the process? So much the better.

MACE STORMED into the bunker's control room. A sandy-haired man, an Australian mercenary, was seated at a console that controlled security cameras and sensors, handled all internal and external communications and other security features such as elevators and doors. He turned away from his work and gave Mace an expectant look.

"Drop the damn doors," he said. "If they get any closer to the hub, I'll rip off your skull and lob it at them."

The gunner swallowed hard and nodded his agreement. His fingers flew over the console as he worked.

In the meantime, Mace glanced the security monitors and watched the commandos cut through more of his men with relative ease. Some of the best mercenaries in the world, he thought, and they're getting their heads handed to them. Who are these people?

The security man pointed at the third monitor to the right. It depicted a slender, fox-faced man making his way through one of the corridors leading to the main hub where they were located. "This one here," he said, tapping his nail against the screen. "He just took out four of our guys with a grenade. I dispatched four more people to his position."

Mace checked the load on his Heckler & Koch UMP. "I'm going, too. In the meantime, start punching some buttons. We're going Code Alpha."

"Shit," the man replied. He pecked repeatedly at a single key and stared at his screen.

"Yeah, shit. It's time to unleash a nuclear holocaust or two. Do it."

"No," the guy snapped. "I mean, shit, the network just went down, every last bit of it."

Mace whipped his head toward the other man. "What? What the hell do you mean, it's down? We need to send out that damn worm, and we need to do it now."

The guy raked his hand through his hair and stared at the computer for a moment. He attacked the keyboard again. Several keystrokes later, he jerked his hands away from the keyboard in frustration and banged a fist on his desk.

"Damn it, it's not working. It's like we got hit with a virus. But how?"

Mace remembered the attached file he'd opened earlier and a thrill of fear raced through him. He'd done this. Now he had to fix it.

MCCARTER GOT A BAD FEELING in his gut as he wound his way along the corridor. Using his stolen key card, he'd checked three doors and came up with nothing. That he'd found no sign yet of Fox was bad news, he thought. If he recalled the floor plan provided by the Farm correctly, he'd soon reach what had been a primary research lab for the defunct nuclear project.

The corridor straightened, then jogged right. Reaching a corner, he peered around it and saw a handful of Farnsworth's gunners positioned behind sandbags. He pulled back, let his weapon fall slack on its strap, and palmed an M-451 stun grenade from his satchel.

Activating the grenade, he came around the corner and tossed it, watching as it landed behind the sandbag barricade. A second later the bomb detonated. Peals of thunder shook the corridor. Sparks sizzled the air and burned through skin and fabric. Multiple flashes exploded.

While the mercenaries found themselves stricken by sound and fury, McCarter surged toward their position. One soldier stood, his palms pressed against his eyes. A second man slapped at a spot where multiple sparks had seared his flesh.

McCarter's M-4 churned out a merciless maelstrom of lead as he raked the weapon over the stunned fighters. The hail of bullets cut them down in a single pass. Bullets shredded the sandbags and their contents spilled to the floor. Rounds pierced lights built into the walls or ricocheted into overhead lights and ignited showers of sparks.

The Phoenix Force leader surged toward the gunners' position even as he rammed a fresh clip into his assault rifle. He found all three hardmen sprawled about, their fatigues tattered and soaked with blood. Beyond the sandbag barricade lay a single steel door. He vaulted over the trashed sandbags and headed for it.

A swipe of the key card granted him entry. He looked inside and his lip curled into a snarl. Another damned corridor. The bleedin' place was overflowing with the damn things, he thought. He traded out the M-4 for the twin Browning Hi-Powers he carried on his hips. The corridor stretched little more than five yards before he came upon a second door.

He tried unsuccessfully to open the door with his key card. It didn't respond.

"Bloody lovely," he muttered.

Time to frisk the corpses, he thought. Surely one of them had an access card.

McCarter turned—and froze.

A bulky silhouette stood in the door. He couldn't make out the man's face, but the shape of a weapon pointed in his direction was unmistakable.

"Drop the damn guns," the man demanded.

"Bloody lovely." McCarter spit.

CHAPTER THIRTY-FOUR

Blancanales stepped into the main bar area on the club's ground floor. Scanning the room for danger, he found none. At least nothing obvious. He wound his way between the overturned chairs and tables that covered the floor. Wisps of gun smoke hung in the air. Sirens continued to blare, but couldn't drown out the gunfire crackling from the second floor.

Reaching the stairwell, he surged up the steps, taking them two at a time. He held the MP-5 ahead of him, muscles and nerves tensed to react as he waded into another gun battle.

When he reached the top, he dropped into a crouch and spotted Lyons. The Able Team leader had dropped to one knee and was firing two handguns in unison at a wall of killers. Blancanales saw the big man gut one of Quissad's people with a well-placed burst from his Beretta. Other shooters unloaded their weapons in Lyons' direction, bullets tearing through his sports jacket and chewing into the floor in front of him.

Blancanales knew his old friend was putting up one

hell of a fight. He also knew the guy's luck was probably a heartbeat away from running out.

Too many killers, too few bullets.

He cut loose with the MP-5, the sustained volley knocking three shooters off their feet immediately. Another sweep took down a couple more of Quissad's killers.

Lyons's head whipped toward his teammate. The skin of his face was ruddy and his eyes reflected his rage, like a cornered grizzly bear. When he identified his benefactor as Blancanales, he shot him a wink.

Blancanales set the shotgun on the floor and kicked it toward Lyons, then turned back to his deadly work. He caught one guy trying to draw a bead on him with a pair of micro-Uzis. Blancanales whipped around the MP-5 and burned through the rest of the clip. The fusillade of fire stitched the guy from left crotch to right shoulder, cutting a diagonal line of red holes across his torso. The Able Team commando crouched at the knees, ejected the SMG's magazine and grabbed another from his combat webbing. Something whistled past his ear. He hurled himself sideways and rolled. In the meantime, he reloaded the SMG. When he looked up, he saw a big goateed man tracking his movements with a handgun.

Before he could line up a shot, an ear-piercing boom rent the air. Part of Goatee's midsection disintegrated and he collapsed. A microsecond later, a hard guy to Blancanales's left caught a shotgun blast in the shoulder that severed his arm and wheeled him around in the process. He glanced left and saw Lyons lining up another shot with the shotgun. The next blast ripped into the man's torso and took his life before he hit the ground.

Blancanales raked the MP-5 from right to left in a figure eight and took out three more gunners.

A blur of movement registered in the corner of Blancanales's eye. He pivoted to the right and brought up his SMG. He spotted Khan, eyes bugged out, sweat-soaked shirt matted to his body, darting into the corridor. The guy clasped in a pistol in each hand and was leveling them at the Able Team warriors. Moving in unison, Blancanales and Lyons drew down on him and fired. A combination of bullets and buckshot rent the man's flesh, punching him to the floor, dead.

"That had to hurt," Blancanales muttered.

He reached inside his satchel, grabbed a bandolier filled with shotgun shells and tossed it to Lyons. The Able Team leader reloaded the shotgun and scanned for more attackers. Blancanales swept his gaze over the dead, hoping to find Quissad and Cortez among them.

"If you're looking for our friends, they aren't here," Lyons said. He gestured down the hallway with his head. "C'mon, I know where to find them."

LYONS CUT a diagonal path across the hall. Large chunks of plasterboard had been torn loose from the walls, ceiling tiles shredded and disbursed over the floor during the gunfight. Dead thugs lay sprawled on the floor.

Blancanales came up from behind. "Who's the woman?" he asked.

"She came to take out Quissad. What she got was a bullet. One meant for me. As if I wasn't pissed off enough already, they had to go and do that. Now I'm really going to burn those SOBs to the ground."

When he reached an exit door, he peered through the small rectangular window looking in on the stairwell. The landing was empty. No big surprise there, he didn't expect Quissad or Cortez to wait around for a final showdown. He guessed both had already fled the building.

Holding the shotgun by its pistol grip, he pointed the muzzle skyward and hit the release bar on the door. His big frame filling the doorway, he swept the Franchi over the area. The weapon was steadied for one-handed shooting by a stock that fit over the wrist. Lyons peered over the railing, but the stretch of stairs visible to him looked clear.

Moving silently and swiftly, he descended the first flight of stairs, then the second and reached the first-floor landing. He noticed a dark patch of something on the floor, glistened because of the overhead lights. He pointed it out to Blancanales, who acknowledged it with a nod.

Before Lyons could take another step, he heard something else, a metallic squeaking noise from somewhere below them. The shotgun held in front of him, he started for the basement.

QUISSAD FELT THE TEMPO of his heart increase, heard blood roar in his ears as he tried to open the exit door, but found it locked. That son of a bitch! he thought. He's left me here to take the fall. Left me here to die.

He gave the door's release bar one last push, but it still refused to give.

Quissad heard the door above open. He wheeled and grabbed for his Delta Elite handguns. The gun dealer waited several seconds for some indication of what was coming. He forced his breathing to slow as a wave of fear threatened to overtake him. Pointing the twin Deltas up the stairs, he saw shadows shifting on the wall of the landing above him.

Part of him wanted to call out. Surely that damned
American hadn't plowed through all those guards, he
thought. It wasn't possible. But what if he had? If the
man who'd set off the explosion in the basement had
made it upstairs, it was possible the two commandos
had made it through the wall of killers he'd left behind.

Forget it, he thought. He was going to take them
down. Once they came into view, he was going to unload both Deltas into them before they could spot him.
If it turned out that he killed his own people, so be it.
Once he got back on his feet, maybe he'd send their
families a check. Maybe. In the meantime, he wanted
to get out with his own skin intact, which meant it was
time for scorched-earth tactics.

He heard a light scrape, like a shoe sole scuffing
against the floor. Quissad couldn't see anyone, but he
knew that was to be expected. They likely were hugging
the opposite wall, trying to circle around as widely as
possible to keep him from spotting them prematurely.

He moved right, flattened against the wall. The Deltas remained locked at a forty-five-degree angle, ready
to deal death on whoever blundered into his sights.

LYONS HIT THE LANDING, but stayed close to the wall,
trying to keep himself out of the line of sight of whoever stood at the bottom of the stairs.

Blancanales arrived a step or two behind his teammate. He turned, aimed his MP-5 skyward and scanned
their six for potential attackers. When he pivoted back
toward Lyons, the former L.A. cop pointed toward the
final flight of stairs and tapped his chest with the tip of
his thumb.

Blancanales nodded.

Lyons held up a thumb and two fingers, indicating a

three count, and received another nod. He curled them in rapid succession, counting down to the deadly play.

When he hit three, he surged toward the stairwell, the shotgun held at shoulder height. As he reached the precipice, flashes exploded from below. Bullets sizzled past him. In a heartbeat, he saw Quissad, his enraged features illuminated by the muzzle-flashes.

The shotgun thundered three times in rapid succession. The buckshot tore into the Iraqi's chest, ripping flesh like dozens of ravenous piranhas. Force from the multiple blasts punched him backward until he collided with the door behind him. Echoes from the shooting subsided as Quissad's corpse slowly slid to the floor.

NEARLY TWO HOURS LATER Lyons stood outside the club, a foam cup of hot coffee clutched in his hands. Fire trucks, ambulances and police cars were parked outside the building, red and blue lights whipping across its facade.

Footsteps sounded to his left. Turning his head, he saw Blancanales approaching.

When the police had stormed the building, the two commandos had surrendered themselves and their weapons. The inspector they'd met upon arriving in Prague immediately had washed his hands of the pair, and had referred all questions to his superiors, as well as Hal Brognola. The police had cleared them about twenty minutes earlier. Blancanales had spent the last several minutes probing for information about Cortez.

"What's the word?" Lyons asked.

"He's gone," Blancanales replied, shaking his head. "He just disappeared."

"On foot or by car?"

"Car. At least, that's the theory. The forensics guys

searched Quissad's body but found no keys. His BMW's missing. The police said they're looking for the car even as we speak."

Lyons nodded. "I guess that means we turn the town upside down and start hunting Cortez."

Blancanales shook his head. "Not immediately, amigo."

"Why the hell not?"

"I talked to Hal a few minutes ago. For the moment, he says the hell with Cortez. He's more worried about a well-heeled group of vengeful Baathists trying to buy weapons than he is Cortez. Plus, Hal considers him less of an immediate danger, since he doesn't appear to have the disk in his possession."

"We've got to nail this SOB for what he did to Gadgets, right? If we don't move now, we lose him."

"Hal's going to ask the locals to issue an all-points bulletin on the guy. They'll monitor the borders, the airports, all the usual entry and exit points. If anyone finds Cortez, they'll be asked to arrest and extradite him to the United States. Or, if we're lucky, they'll contain him so that we can pick him up ourselves."

"World's a big place," Lyons said. "Could be years before we locate him. Besides, we don't have extradition treaties with everyone."

"Hal swears that there's a good chance of tracking this guy down. Cortez has black accounts in the Cayman Islands and Switzerland. Hal asked Treasury to hunt them down and track them. To help expedite matters, the Man is going to make a personal appeal to those governments to cooperate. In the meantime, the Mexican government has coughed up his known aliases, along with any credit card or bank accounts held under those names. The guy's got to eat. He's got to put a roof over his head. It's only a matter of time before he messes up."

Lyons drained his coffee cup and tossed it into a nearby trashcan. He heaved a heavy sigh. "I've got half a mind to tell Hal to stuff it. Who needs all this bureaucratic nonsense?"

"See you in the unemployment line."

"Damn it—"

"Seriously, Hal's doing what he can. After all the carnage we caused tonight, we're not exactly welcome here. And with the big-picture threat defused, at least on our side, Hal's getting pressure from the locals to get us the hell out of Dodge. He doesn't like it any better than we do. But it beats the hell out of kicking us out of the country, arresting us or putting us into—" Blancanales gestured quote marks "—protective custody. So Hal thinks we ought to get while the getting's good."

Lyons felt an urge to kick the trashcan, but ignored it. "Damn bureaucrats. All right, let's go. Hal sound pissed?"

"Yeah."

"Great. At least something good came out of this. Maybe I ought to put some ketchup on my ass before he chews it off."

"Colorful, Carl. Very colorful."

CHAPTER THIRTY-FIVE

Bending slowly at the knees, David McCarter set the Browning on the ground floor and stood back, his hands raised. He kept his eyes locked on the gun-wielding thug next to him the whole time.

The man with H&K submachine gun gave him a wide smile, lips peeling back to reveal nicotine-stained teeth. The gun muzzle remained locked on the Briton's chest.

"Least you're pleased with yourself," McCarter snapped.

"A Brit? We'll, I'll be damned. I figured it was the Americans coming in to bust up our little party. But it's the goddamn Brits."

McCarter remained silent. After a couple of stretched seconds, the guy jabbed the H&K's muzzle under the commando's chin and pushed up, forcing McCarter to tilt his head uncomfortably.

"Give me some answers now. Before I splatter your frigging head all over this room. And believe me, I'd like nothing better."

"Then I'll save you the anticipation," McCarter said. "I'm not saying shit. So pull the trigger."

A groan arose from the floor. McCarter turned his head right and saw Fox's head moving slightly, the fingers of his right hand curling. Great, McCarter thought, I'm within spitting distance of this guy and I may still not get him out of here.

"Well, I'll be damned," the guy said. "Looks like our pet geek's waking up. I don't suppose you SOBs came all this way, spilled all this blood, to rescue that little piece of shit, did you?"

"Have no idea who he is," McCarter lied. "If you want anything more than name, rank and serial number, you can go to hell."

"You got some brass ones on you. I'll give you that."

The man stepped back, raised the UMP with one hand, pointed it to McCarter's temple. The Briton felt his heart hammer in his chest, heard blood roar in his ears. His mind raced for a solution, a way out of this deadly situation, but he came up blank.

Suddenly everything blurred.

He saw the gunner's head whip right, his lip curling into a snarl. The gun's muzzle strayed from McCarter's temple. The man was moving it to target someone else.

"Down," someone yelled from behind.

McCarter dropped into a crouch. A sudden blast of gunfire exploded above him, muzzle-flashes creating a strobelike effect on the walls, a torrent of brass shell casings falling to the floor. His hand stabbed out for the Browning. Fingers encircling the weapon's grip, he hefted the weapon.

Something warm and wet splattered onto the side of his face, making him wince. Before he could move, the gunfire stopped. The man's jerking legs stilled, buckled, and he struck the floor in a boneless heap, his head tilting toward McCarter. His eyes were locked open, blood trickling from the corner of his parted lips.

The Briton turned to see Hawkins standing over the body, holding his M-60, barrel smoking. When he spotted McCarter, his face screwed up in mock disgust.

"Damn, son," Hawkins said, "that's not your color."

"Southern charm my arse," McCarter huffed. Coming to his full height, he pulled his shirttail to his face and wiped it off. He advanced to Fox and knelt next to him, eyeing him for open wounds. Seeing none, he grabbed him by the shoulder and rolled him onto his back.

McCarter shook his head. The guy's face and neck were a mess of purplish bruises, red welts, scrapes and deep gashes. He scanned him for gunshot or stab wounds, but found nothing. Peeling back Fox's T-shirt, he found his mushroom-white torso also covered in bruises and welts.

"Bastards did a number on him," McCarter said. "He could have internal injuries. But he needs to be examined before we'll know for sure."

McCarter activated his com link. When Price answered, he relayed the news about the rescue. "That's excellent," she said. "We'll send a Black Hawk in to bring you folks out."

"Great," McCarter replied. "We'll take our young friend topside."

"What about Farnsworth?" Price asked.

"Still among the living dead. We're trying to change that."

MOVING WITH WRAITHLIKE silence, Farnsworth ascended the stairs leading to the first floor, his eyes darting around wildly, scanning his surroundings for threats.

· Sweat slicked his forehead and the area between his shoulder blades. His breaths came fast and shallow.

Sneaking out from the second level had been easy enough. Though he had heard gunfire near his quarters, he'd seen no one in the corridor when he'd made his way to the stairwell. The way he figured it, that meant the dead were piling up elsewhere, which suited him fine. He didn't mind blood spilling, as long as it wasn't his own.

Reaching the first level, he slipped through the door and advanced down the hallway toward the elevator leading to the ground level. When he came within a few yards of the doors, he hit the button and waited for the car to arrive. An uncomfortable sensation, the feeling of impending danger, prompted him to whirl around.

A fierce-looking man with dark blond hair exited a nearby hallway. His gun flew up, muzzle trying to home in on Farnsworth.

The former CIA man triggered his Fabrique Natonale P-90. Streams of fire lashed out at the unidentified commando, driving him to ground. A heartbeat later, the elevator door slid open behind Farnsworth and he lunged inside. While he waited for the door to close, he heard loud footfalls slap against the floor.

What if they got hold of the doors, stopped them from closing? From what he could tell, all his people had been slaughtered, except perhaps Mace, who'd dropped out of sight. But at least one commando—and more likely several—continued to stalk him. He wasn't afraid to fight one-on-one, he told himself. But engaging the enemy here was a suicide play. He was too damn smart for that.

Aiming the P-90 at the space between the doors, he caressed the trigger. A torrent of autofire hurtled forth, hopefully driving back his pursuers.

He quit firing moments before the doors closed and leaned back against the wall. He filled his lungs with large pulls of the air laden with gun smoke and mopped the sweat from his forehead with his shirtsleeve.

The elevator came to a stop. The doors parted and Farnsworth darted from the car into the small building that housed the elevator. He cut a path straight toward the door, knocking aside folding chairs and a card table topped with an overstuffed ashtray and half-empty soda cans left behind by the guards.

He rocketed outside, his eyes squinting hard against the sudden overload of natural light. But he still broke into a run, legs pumping, chewing through the seventy-five yards that separated him from the motor pool.

Within seconds, a vehicle lay just within reach, maybe a dozen or so yards away.

Someone from behind him yelled, "Stop!"

Don't stop, his mind screamed. Go, go, go! He hurtled into the space between the lines of trucks and sport utility vehicles, grateful for the cover they provided. He reached a truck—a monster with a V-8 engine and spare fuel tanks—opened the door and climbed inside. He grabbed the sun visor, flipped it down and a pair of keys fell into his lap.

Stabbing the key into the ignition, he glanced out the window and saw a pair of armed men sprinting toward him. The engine turned over and he grinned. Just keep coming, he thought, I'll be happy to run you bastards over. Leave you here, injured, prey to tomorrow's unrelenting sun and stifling heat.

"Welcome to hell, gentlemen," he shouted. He slipped the truck into drive, let his foot off the brake and waited for it to lurch forward.

MANNING STOPPED running, reached into his pocket and withdrew a detonator. He thumbed the first toggle into position, followed by two more.

Thunderclaps crashed in rapid succession. Red-orange explosions mushroomed skyward. Truck and SUV carcasses, tons of mangled steel, interiors ablaze, were catapulted into the air where they flipped and fell back to the earth. Columns of black-tinged hellfire writhed as they choked the skies with black, oily smoke.

Manning watched raging flames consume the vehicles and the garages. Encizo raced up next to him.

"That…" Manning began.

"Had to hurt," Encizo replied. "Yeah."

CHAPTER THIRTY-SIX

Milan, Italy

Kamal Ramadan hammered the table with his fist. The impact caused dishes to jump and silverware to rattle. But it also got the attention of the other members of the Seven who ringed the table. They stopped their inane bickering and turned toward him.

"We will not lose our heads," he said. "I don't care what's happened during the past twenty-four hours. We have a goal and we will not let anyone deter us from that goal."

Nasser Hakim gave him a hard stare. "We already are deterred. They've frozen all our assets. They killed two of our members in Prague. One more this morning in Berlin." He made a sweeping gesture that encompassed the four of them. "We're all that's left of the movement. Some of the men know our money's gone. They're talking about leaving."

Ramadan leaned his forearms on the table and stared at Hakim. "If they say they're leaving, have them killed. Or, better yet, do it yourself."

Hakim's mouth tightened into an angry line, but he nodded his agreement. The other two men nodded, as well. Ramadan smiled and leaned back in his chair. "Remember, we're not alone," he said, wagging his right index finger. "There are other countries more than willing to back us. If the Americans freeze our accounts, we'll get more. It's that simple." His voice gained volume. "We will not be beaten. Not this time. We must know this in our hearts, as Iraqis, that one day we'll restore Baathist rule to our homeland. Our friends—the other members of the Seven—won't have died in vain."

More nods, this time delivered with enthusiasm, told Ramadan that he'd calmed any doubts that may have existed. He took another sip of coffee and returned the cup to its saucer. The men began talking among themselves.

A knock at the door caused a silence to fall over the room once again.

"Come in," he said.

The door opened and he saw one of his guards standing there. The man opened his mouth to speak, but before he could utter a word, part of his stomach burst out in a spray of blood and flesh. He pitched face-forward and the Iraqi saw a vision of hell. A big man stood in the door. He was dressed head-to-toe in black. Combat cosmetics were smeared over his cheeks, forehead and nose. He held a silenced machine gun in both hands. A second man, similarly attired, stood right behind him.

The Iraqi opened his mouth, but died with a scream still trapped in his throat.

EPILOGUE

Gabriel Fox lay in the hospital bed, tubes running into his nose and out of his arms. The steady beep of a heart-monitoring machine and the subdued murmur of his television were the only sounds in the room. Copies of the *New York Times,* the *Washington Post* and *The Wall Street Journal* lay on his bedside table, next to a sweating plastic pitcher of ice water. He didn't bother to open any of the newspapers. All he cared about was what he'd been through during the past couple of weeks. He knew he'd find nothing about that in the papers.

Or, more to the point, he'd find nothing of substance. A news brief in the *Times* had claimed that Dale Farnsworth, an international banker, had perished when his plane went down over the Atlantic Ocean.

The story claimed correctly that no body had been recovered. But it failed to mention, probably because the reporter didn't know, that the man's body had been vaporized in Africa days before. There'd been no story regarding Jack Mace's death, of course. Sure, the guy damn near had turned the world into a glowing, radioactive sinkhole. But as far as most people were concerned, he was just a mercenary, and certainly not worthy of an obituary—or anyone's grief.

So, for all intents and purposes, it was over. In some ways that suited Fox just fine. He was in no mood to relive the events of the past couple of weeks. That included his wife's death, though he knew he'd never truly be free of that burden. It may lessen with time, but it wouldn't go away.

A noise from the hallway grabbed his attention. He heard Kurtzman's voice as the guy spoke with the guards. Fox allowed himself a grin.

Seconds later the door opened and Kurtzman wheeled inside. The door closed behind him.

Kurtzman guided his chair up next to the bed and tossed several computer magazines onto the bed. "Read those," he said. "You might learn something. Study hard enough and you'll be like me someday."

"A dream come true," Fox replied, grinning.

"Many try, but few succeed. How's the patient doing today?"

"Breathing."

"According to the doctor, you're doing better than that. For a guy with four broken ribs, a cracked pelvis, a broken collarbone, internal bleeding and a couple of bruised organs."

"Glad you guys rescued me before I got hurt. Did I mention that I hate the bastards who did this to me?"

"I know some guys," Kurtzman said. "They can make the bad people go away for you."

"So I noticed when your guys wheeled me out to the chopper. Until I blacked out again. From what I saw, your guys really play for keeps."

"They have to."

"I'm not complaining. Just making an observation." Fox shifted a little, trying to get more comfortable. Countless needles of pain stabbed through him as broken bones and bruised flesh protested against the movement. An expletive exploded loudly from his mouth. "Man, that hurts."

"My friends did leave a couple of the computer guys vertical. They brought them back to the States and turned them over to the Justice Department for interrogation. One of the guys said you put up a hell of a fight. He said that they needed Tasers to take you down."

"Mess with the best, die like the rest. Amazing how hard you can fight when you're not afraid to get hurt."

"Or die," Kurtzman said.

Fox felt his face flush. "Yeah."

"You still feel that way? You ready to check out if you get the right opportunity?"

"You volunteering?"

Kurtzman threw back his head and laughed. "Hardly. I just want to know."

Fox considered the question for a moment. "Nah," he said. "I'm not exactly in love with life right now. Still, I want to keep going. I figure that if I lived through the last couple of weeks, I wasn't meant to check out yet. And Maria wouldn't have wanted me to do that, either. She was pretty tough. If the roles had been reversed, she wouldn't have given up, so I guess I owe it to her to not do that, either."

Kurtzman nodded. "Makes sense to me."

"Speaking of dying, what happened to your buddy? The guy who took a bullet in Colorado? He doing okay?"

Kurtzman smiled. "Yeah, he's fine. I guess he's decided to do a little traveling."

Cayman Islands

HE COULD GET USED to living this way.

Cortez smiled at the thought. He stood on the balcony of his apartment, drink in hand, staring down at pretty women passing by on the street below. It had been two weeks since the firefight in Libya. After he'd escaped the country, leaving Quissad to take a bullet, he'd arrived in Spain, fake passport in hand.

He'd stolen enough money from his former boss, Mendoza, to put himself up in style here in the Caymans. And he had a friend who had a friend who likely could help him tap into both Mendoza's and Quissad's black accounts. If he played things right, he'd likely end up rich enough to never have to work again.

It certainly wasn't what he'd hoped for, but he'd make the best of things.

From inside the apartment, he heard the door slam. His smile widened and he moved back inside his luxuriously appointed home.

The past week or so had been a blur for him. After the unpleasantness in Africa, he'd decided he needed a nice break. He'd spent several thousand dollars living it up in the city. Local escort services had been only too happy to provide him with all the flesh he could stand. And he'd yet to reach his threshold.

Tonight he'd requested a redhead and he could hardly wait to see who they'd sent him.

A warm sensation spread through his loins as he headed for the front door. When he reached it, he scowled.

The door was closed, but he saw no one.

Perhaps she'd already headed for the bedroom. A consummate professional. He liked that in his whores.

A quick check of the bedroom yielded nothing. Uneasiness gripped him when he returned to the main room but found it empty.

"Hello?" he said. At the same time, he lifted his shirttails and grabbed the .44 Charter Arms holstered at the small of his back. "Who's there?"

He heard the sound of glass breaking, a sharp sound that caused his breath to catch. In the matter of an instant, his self-disgust at his reaction morphed into rage against whoever was playing this stupid game. If it was a whore, he promised himself he'd teach the little bitch a lesson. If he felt generous, he'd hit her in the gut, but leave her face—one of her professional tools intact. If not, well, she wouldn't be the first woman to feel his knuckles strike the soft skin of her cheek.

Sucking in a big breath, he puffed out his chest and started for the patio. With each step, his rage deepened, caused him to hurtle forth like a heat-seeking missile locked on to a fighter jet's exhaust.

A man stepped from inside the kitchen, a gun in his hand, and Cortez recognized him as the federal agent from Colorado. The one he'd shot from the balcony and left for dead.

"I sent your girlfriend packing," Gadgets Schwarz said. "I told her we had a little unfinished business to clear up."

Cortez nodded slowly while he sized the other man up. "That we do."

"This time," the man said, "you'd better finish me off."

"Gladly."

Lightning fast, Cortez brought up his pistol, his finger tightening on the trigger.

But Schwarz's Beretta was already in play. He squeezed off a triburst. The swarm of bullets drilled as one into the soft cartilage of Cortez's nose, tunneled through brain and bone.

The hardman's knees turned rubbery and he folded to the floor, dead.

Schwarz holstered his weapon. "That's how you shoot to kill, you dumb bastard," he said.

JAMES AXLER

DEATH LANDS

Shatter Zone

In this raw, brutal world ruled by the strongest and the most vicious, an unseen player is manipulating Ryan and his band, luring him across an unseen battle line drawn in the dust outside Tucson, Arizona. Here a local barony becomes the staging ground for a battle unlike any other, against a foe whose ties to preDark society present a new and incalculable threat to a fragile world. Ryan Cawdor is the only man living who stands between this adversary's glory…and the prize he seeks.

Available September 2006 wherever you buy books.

THE
DESTROYER

DRAGON BONES

Living forever totally rocks...

The strange-looking animal touted to be a real live dinosaur was a bona fide apatosaurus. Unfortunately, the dino has been stolen, flash frozen, locked away in secret, awaiting its personal contribution to creating a formula for immortality. Suddenly everybody is a believer in the longevity offered by the poor dead animal and CURE has a crisis on its hands. Smith orders Remo to find the thing and incinerate it before fountain-of-youth seekers rampage the world. But Remo's got bigger problems. Chiun is acting a little off, a little tired—and single-mindedly determined to enjoy a restorative cup of immortality tea brewed with dragon bones....

Dragon Bones is the last installment of The Destroyer published by Gold Eagle Books.

Available October 2006 wherever you buy books.